The Greer and The Silver Skull

TWO CLASSIC ADVENTURES OF

by Walter B. Gibson
writing as Maxwell Grant

plus **Prelude to Terror**
a thriller from Radio's Golden Age

with new historical essays by
Ed Hulse and Will Murray

SANCTUM BOOKS

Copyright © 1938, 1939 by Street & Smith Publications, Inc. Copyright © renewed 1965, 1966 by The Condé Nast Publications, Inc. All rights reserved.

The Shadow Volume 55 copyright © 2011 by Sanctum Books.

The Shadow copyright © 2011 Advance Magazine Publishers Inc. d/b/a Condé Nast. "The Shadow," "The Shadow face design" and the phrase "Who knows what evil lurks in the hearts of men?" are registered trademarks of Advance Magazine Publishers Inc. d/b/a Condé Nast. The phrases "The Shadow Knows" and "The weed of crime bears bitter fruit" are trademarks owned by Advance Magazine Publishers Inc. d/b/a Condé Nast.

"Interlude" copyright © 2011 by Will Murray.

"From Pulp Page to Silver Screen: The Serial That Almost Got It Right" copyright © 2011 by Ed Hulse.

This Sanctum Books edition is an unabridged republication of the text and illustrations of two stories from *The Shadow Magazine,* as originally published by Street & Smith Publications, Inc., N.Y.: *The Green Hoods* from the August 15, 1938 issue and *Silver Skull* from the January 1, 1939 issue. "Prelude to Terror" was broadcast January 29, 1939 on *The Shadow* radio series. These stories are works of their time. Consequently, the text is reprinted intact in its original historical form, including occasional out-of-date ethnic and cultural stereotyping. Typographical errors have been tacitly corrected in this edition.

International Standard Book Number:
978-1-60877-065-6

First printing: November 2011

Series editor/publisher: Anthony Tollin
anthonytollin@shadowsanctum.com

Consulting editor: Will Murray

Copy editor: Joseph Wrzos

Cover and photo restoration: Michael Piper

The editors gratefully appreciate the contributions of Nicolette A. Dobrowlski of the Special Collections Research Center, Syracuse University Library for assistance with Street and Smith radio scripts, and Matthew Schoonover in the preparation of this volume.

Published by Sanctum Books
P.O. Box 761474, San Antonio, TX 78245-1474

Visit The Shadow at www.shadowsanctum.com.

Volume 55

The entire contents of this book are protected by copyright, and must not be reprinted without the publisher's permission.

CONTENTS

Two Complete Novels From The Shadow's Private Annals As told to Maxwell Grant

Thrilling Tales and Features

THE GREEN HOODS by Walter B. Gibson
(writing as "Maxwell Grant") 4

INTERLUDE by Will Murray 57

THE SILVER SKULL by Walter B. Gibson
(writing as "Maxwell Grant") 60

FROM PULP PAGE TO SILVER SCREEN: THE SERIAL THAT ALMOST GOT IT RIGHT by Ed Hulse 111

PRELUDE TO TERROR 116

Cover art by George Rozen
Interior illustrations by Edd Cartier

Death and corruption break out in a crime-fighting organization, and only The Shadow can put his finger on the member who sold out!

The Green Hoods
by Maxwell Grant

A Complete Book-length Novel from the Private Annals of The Shadow.

CHAPTER I
THE MESSAGE IN GREEN

MANHATTAN'S lights formed a galaxy of glitter as Kent Allard, famous aviator, viewed them from his hotel window. Often, early of an evening, he sat there, his blue eyes fixed upon the sparkling brilliance that represented New York.

Tonight, as on other nights, Allard's thin, hawk-like face was inscrutable. He was as impassive as an Aztec god of stone surveying a vast realm below its pedestal.

There were men who regarded Allard as the equivalent of an Aztec god. They were the two Indians who were his trusted servants. Members of the lost Xinca tribe, they had come with Allard

from Guatemala, after he had lived there, presumably, for ten years, following a plane wreck. Here, in the isolation of this magnificent hotel suite, they were ready at his instant bidding.

As like as a pair of twins, the short-built Indians stood stony-faced. They knew the meaning of their master's fixed gaze.

Kent Allard was The Shadow!

Scourge of the underworld. The Shadow chose night as his domain. Cloaked in blackness, he moved everywhere—anywhere—to strike down evildoers who plotted crime. Crooks knew him as a being whose burning eyes shone from beneath the brim of a slouch hat; whose gloved fists gripped a pair of massive automatics.

Many had met The Shadow, often to their own disaster. None had ever pierced the mystery that shrouded his real identity. Tonight, however, mystery confronted The Shadow himself.

Keen eyes turned from the window, to an envelope that stretched between long-fingered hands. That envelope was addressed to Kent Allard. He had opened it previously; again, he drew forth the contents.

A disk of green jade slid to Allard's palm. The object was thin, the size of a half dollar. The only mark upon it was the number 13, carved in the center of one side.

With the disk was a message; it had been typed through carbon paper. The color of the print was green. It read:

> To one interested in matters of crime, we offer opportunity to become a link in an extending chain. As a member of the Green Hoods, you can accomplish much of value. We meet beneath the Landham Theater, at 8:30 tonight; none admitted later than 9 o'clock. The enclosed amulet will identify you by number. Wear the hood and robe that you find in your locker.

The note was unsigned; beneath it, in underscored letters, was typed:

> *Tonight's survey is vitally important. Come.*

This was The Shadow's first knowledge of an organization that called itself the Green Hoods. One that apparently numbered twelve members, since his amulet—the green-jade disk—bore the number 13. The message, though, did not specify whether the Green Hoods met for good or evil.

Allard was considering a deeper significance to the message.

It might be a mere hoax, sent to him as a prank. Contrasted with that trivial possibility was the chance that the message carried an insidious design. It might mean that some shrewd criminal had guessed The Shadow's real identity, and was using this as bait to trap him.

Those extreme possibilities seemed unlikely; there were points against each theory. The Shadow saw a middle answer; its soundness increased, the more he considered it.

The message was neither hoax nor snare. The Green Hoods, through some individual member, had picked Kent Allard as a candidate for their organization without suspecting that he was The Shadow.

Upon Allard's thin lips appeared the faintest of smiles. He remembered something that had occurred last night; an incident that could be the forerunner to this message, which had arrived only an hour ago.

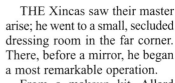

THE Xincas saw their master arise; he went to a small, secluded dressing room in the far corner. There, before a mirror, he began a most remarkable operation.

From a makeup kit, Allard produced substances with which he remolded the contour of his face. A puttyish application reduced the sharpness of his nose. Pressing upward from the chin, fingers widened cheeks and pressed in wax that changed features in their new position.

Touches of temporary dye not only changed the color of eyebrows, but altered their apparent shape. Deft dabs, here and there, completed the transformation.

Though the new visage still had a hawkish effect, it could not be recognized as Allard's. In place of a natural gauntness, it had a masklike appearance; yet, withal, it was natural. The Shadow had done more than merely drop the guise of Kent Allard. He had adopted another actual identity.

The Shadow had become the image of Lamont Cranston, a well-known New York millionaire, whose identity he used, at times.

When their master arose from the mirror, the Xincas were waiting. They did not even observe the new face that The Shadow wore. All that mattered to them was a rare jewel, a girasol, that shone from The Shadow's finger. That iridescent fire opal was the symbol that its wearer was their master.

One servant held a black cloak, the other a slouch hat. The Shadow donned those garments. With his left thumb, he turned the ring so that the fire opal was inward. With his right hand, he pocketed the green-jade amulet that was tonight's token.

One of the Xincas had opened the door to the hallway; he was motioning that the way was clear. The Shadow slid black gloves upon his hands; mere seconds later, he had blended with the darkness of a fire tower.

A taxicab was waiting in an obscure spot beside the hotel. The Shadow boarded it silently, invisibly. A whispered order to the driver and the cab was on its way.

The taxi halted one block from the exclusive Cobalt Club, where Cranston was a member. Leaving the black garments in a drawerlike space beneath the rear seat, The Shadow alighted. With the strolling gait of Cranston, he continued to the club on foot.

Sight of a big official car brought a slight smile to his lips. The Shadow knew that he would find the man he wanted in the club.

That man was Ralph Weston, New York's police commissioner. Cranston met him in the club foyer; as they shook hands, the millionaire expressed regret that he had not been there on the previous evening.

"YOU missed something, Cranston," declared Weston. "Kent Allard was here—you know, the chap who lived among the Xinca Indians—and he gave an excellent informal talk regarding their tribal customs."

"Odd that it interested you, Commissioner," remarked The Shadow, in a leisurely tone that went with Cranston's guise. "I supposed that you concentrated solely upon the study of crime."

"That was just it!" Weston was brisk, in his enthusiasm. "I asked Allard some questions regarding crime among primitive races. His answers were concise, but thorough."

"They interested others than yourself?"

Weston nodded. He declaimed at length upon a chat that he had resumed with other persons, after Allard's departure. One man, Weston remembered, had hoped to meet Allard again. The commissioner had given him Allard's address.

"I don't suppose that Allard will mind it if he calls," remarked Weston. "Maybe you know the fellow, Cranston. He's an earnest sort; his name is Robert Leng."

The Shadow remembered the man, but did not tell that to Weston. Instead, he shook his head negatively. Weston described Leng as a quiet, bespectacled man of middle age, who was something of an expert on photography. He had made a study of black light; its aid to photography in darkness.

"Leng was around here this evening," mentioned Weston. "I could have pointed him out to you, a short while ago. I think that I saw him leave, just about half past eight."

The foyer clock showed twenty minutes of nine. Commissioner Weston was disappointed when his friend Cranston suddenly remembered another engagement, and decided that he must be on his way.

Once outside the club, Cranston's leisurely style ended. A big limousine was parked across the street; it was Cranston's, and the doorman would have whistled for it, had he seen the millionaire. But the supposed Cranston was away before the doorman spied him.

The Shadow calculated that ten minutes would bring him to the Landham Theater. He figured that after he was back in the cab, with the driver hitting a good speed. Lost time had been worthwhile. The Shadow had linked past with future. He had strengthened his theory, regarding the message that invited him to join the Green Hoods.

With it, The Shadow knew the probable identity of one member: Robert Leng.

THE Landham was an old, disused playhouse; its location was on an obscure side street. To reclaim the minutes that he had lost, The Shadow donned his black garb during the ride. He was set, with one hand on the door handle, when the cab rolled to a stop near the theater.

This cab was The Shadow's own. Moe Shrevnitz, its driver, was following orders in perfect style. He didn't stop in front of the empty theater; he pulled into a deserted hackstand just beyond it, so that any chance observer would suppose that he had a vacant cab and was looking for a fare.

That move produced a sudden surprise—one that caught Moe off guard. Before the cabby could signal the news to The Shadow, a new passenger bobbed into view.

She came from a sheltered corner of the theater— a girl whose face showed beauty, despite its troubled paleness. Her dress was dark; so was the cape that she wore. That was why Moe did not see her, until her hand was on the handle of the very door that The Shadow was about to open.

Staring, Moe saw dark-brown eyes beneath a wave of even darker hair. He spied serious lips below a well-formed nose; heard them speak quickly, firmly, as the girl gave an address. She didn't wait to ask if the cab was empty.

Moe had only time to cross his fingers, in hope that the girl wouldn't spot the cab's occupant. Moe's good luck wish was unnecessary. By the time the girl was opening the door on the curbside of the cab, the opposite door was easing shut.

The Shadow had made one of his speedy departures. Low, beside the step on the street side of the cab, he came up beside the driver's seat. Moe heard The Shadow's whisper, telling him that The Shadow had caught the address also. Following that, came the terse order:

"Report later!"

The cab whipped away. The Shadow sidestepped into the space that it had left. A quick glide across the sidewalk brought him to the shelter that the girl had left. There, The Shadow lingered briefly in darkness, watching the cab as it wheeled around a corner.

Even before he reached the meeting room of the Green Hoods, The Shadow had met with a mysterious event. The sudden appearance of the brunette, plus her quick departure, showed some connection with the unknown organization that had chosen The Shadow as its thirteenth member.

That episode might mean coming danger. It keyed The Shadow to the adventure that lay ahead. A low laugh whispered in the darkness; it predicted that The Shadow intended measures that would counteract any coming menace.

Rarely did The Shadow's methods fail. Tonight, he was moving into an uncharted zone, but he was fully equipped for the foray. That, ordinarily, would be enough for whatever might befall. Tonight, it was not sufficient.

The meeting of the Green Hoods was to provide The Shadow with a surprise far more startling than the sudden appearance of the mysterious girl who had traveled away in The Shadow's own cab.

As for the girl herself, she was to play a vital part in one of the strangest campaigns that The Shadow had ever waged against crime.

CHAPTER II
DEATH IN THE LIGHT

IT was pitch-black in the alleyway beside the old theater; the space was silent and deserted. That was as it should be, since the Green Hoods presumably came here singly.

A new member, picking his way for the first time, would probably be expected to use a flashlight. If the game was on the up and up, old members would give him right of way, if they saw the gleam.

The Shadow wasn't chancing that the game was on the level. He used a flashlight, but handled it so expertly that its glitter was entirely concealed. Keeping close to the wall, he held the tiny electric torch in the folds of his cloak. When he flicked the light, it was muffled; its glowing bulb almost touched the wall beside him.

With swift probe, The Shadow found a battered doorway that looked like an old stage entrance. He eased through, used the light along the floor, to discover a spiral stairway that led downward. Once at the bottom of those steps, The Shadow needed his light no longer.

A dull glow greeted him. He was in a windowless basement room that had several passages leading from it. In each passage, The Shadow could see the outlines of squatty lockers. He noted that one row began with the number 1; another with 7; while the number 13 was painted dimly on the first locker in a third passage.

The Shadow reached the gloom beyond the locker. Reaching back, he tried the locker door. It swung open; inside was hanging a green robe, with a cowl-like hood that folded back from it.

So far, The Shadow was positive that he had been unobserved. He had several minutes more before the deadline of nine o'clock, when members, old or new, would no longer be admitted to the conclave of the Green Hoods.

The Shadow had a prompt use for those minutes. He wanted to learn the location of the meeting room; if possible, peer into it, before he would be forced to don the green of Member 13.

There had been nothing in the message regarding the exact location of the meeting room. The Shadow assumed that his own passage would lead there. He followed the gloomy path between stone walls, came to a turn where the light from the entry ended.

Ahead, The Shadow saw a crack of light that indicated a doorway. Guided by it, he reached the inner end of the passage. The door had no knob; it gave a slight sideways yield to The Shadow's touch. He recognized it as a sliding panel, and acted accordingly.

Imperceptibly, The Shadow inched the barrier to one side, so that he could peer beyond. One eye to the space, he became an unseen observer to the very meeting that he had been invited to attend.

THE Green Hoods were in conference, ranged about a circular table that stood in the exact center of a square-walled room.

Except for height, they were all alike; they resembled a group of night riders, clad in green. Drawn hoods came below their chins. Almond-shaped eye-slits and narrow mouth spaces gave no glimpse of the faces that lay behind them.

A single table lamp lighted the scene; it was impossible, therefore, for The Shadow to ascertain if twelve members had already assembled.

One Green Hood stood near the lamp, his costumed form clearly visible, like those of the few nearest him; but those farther around the circular table were clustered irregularly, with some members in the background.

From what he could see of the nearer walls, The Shadow judged that there were several paneled entrances, which allowed the members various avenues of arrival.

THE GREEN HOODS 9

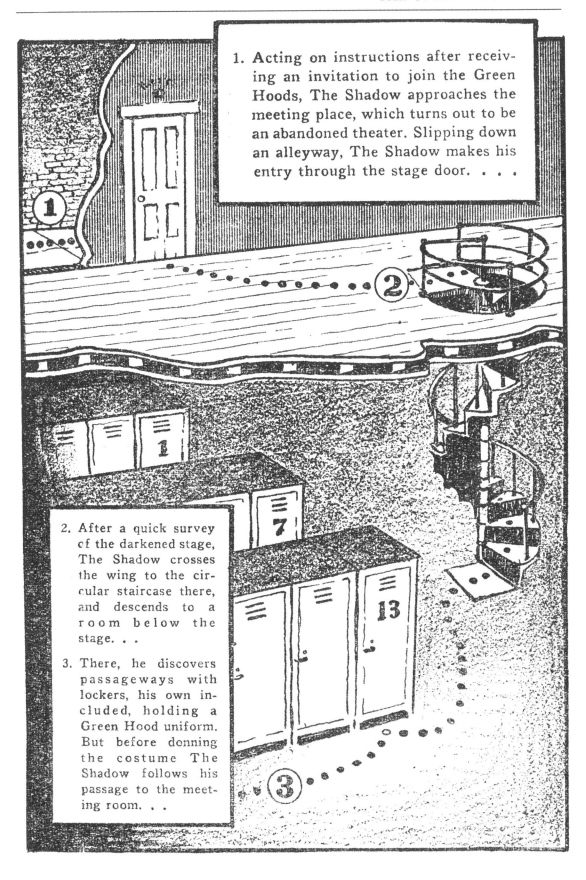

Looking upward, The Shadow noted the ceiling. Though dim, it appeared solid. It had a chandelier with six frosted bulbs. Evidently those lights were not used, because they would throw too much glow upon the meeting.

The member near the lamp had raised his right hand; it was clad in a loose-fitting glove that formed an extension of the robe's sleeve. The others remained silent as the man with the raised hand voiced in a forced, sepulchral tone:

"Member 1 has word!"

Down to the table level descended the raised hand. Its fist opened to show a jade amulet, visible in the lamp glow because its hue was a lighter shade than the dark-green glove that held it.

A few of the Green Hoods craned forward to observe the amulet's identifying number, but the others took the procedure as a mere formality. They seemed more interested in hearing what Member 1 had to say.

The Shadow, too, was intrigued. He decided that he would play the part of an unseen spectator, rather than appear as Member 13.

"I have spoken often of my experiments," stated Member 1, his voice a low roll from his throat. "At our last meeting, I declared that I had completed them; that the Truth Inducer was no longer an idea, but an established fact."

"I promised then to bring the chemical formulas to this meeting, together with the plans for the required mechanism. I have brought them, from my own private laboratory, for distribution among you."

Thrusting a hand beneath the robe, Member 1 put away the jade amulet. He drew a long roll of paper from the robe; as he placed it on the table, the roll separated into single sheets. Member 1 began to sort them on the table, while his eager companions watched.

Evidently, all knew the theory of the Truth Inducer and had been expecting its detailed formulas and plans. The Shadow saw some of the Green Hoods stretch out their hands, while others turned to buzz among themselves.

Drawing his hood tight with one hand, to keep his voice muffled, Member 1 rumbled for the others to be patient. He had the manner of an instructor addressing a group of pupils. Extended hands withdrew. There was a shift of Green Hoods in the background.

Then, the stroke came.

THE man who delivered it had chosen the most timely instant. He was a Green Hood somewhere in the far background, unnoticed by the others, obscured from The Shadow.

There was audible proof of the sudden action he performed. It was the click of a light switch at the far wall.

That sound was useless as a warning. The result it produced was instantaneous.

Every light in the ceiling chandelier delivered a blinding glare. All six were flashbulbs, their frosting a mere surface to cover the material that they contained. For a split-second, the room was filled with a brilliance that had the burn of lightning. Eyes did not have to face it directly to be totally dazzled.

There were hoarse cries from the Green Hoods; a wild shuffle as they staggered blindly for the wall panels. The Shadow could hear those shrieks and shuffles, but the scene itself was gone from his view.

Like the Green Hoods in the meeting room, their prospective Member 13 had taken the effect of that terrific flash.

Instinctively, The Shadow wheeled back along the passage. Despite its darkness, he was gripped by the sensation of vivid light, that formed a tormenting sheet when he thrust his cloaked arm across his eyes.

In those moments, The Shadow was as helpless as the Green Hoods themselves; but, despite his predicament, he was realizing that he possessed an advantage that others did not have. Streaks of light tortured him whether he opened or closed his eyes; but those after-effects were oddly one-sided.

They seemed like shafts that barbed toward the left side of his face, and they gave The Shadow the clue to his own condition.

The Shadow had been peering through the narrow space beside the panel with his left eye only. His right eye, against the wall edge, had been shut almost tight. There was darkness blurring in among the stabs of light. His right eye had not taken the fierce dazzle.

Clamping his left hand over the eye on that side, The Shadow still suffered from the after-impressions; but his right eye sensed darkness more definitely. He couldn't see the crack of the panel, but that was because it showed too dimly.

Groping toward the meeting room, The Shadow guided himself by the sounds of groaning voices, that were punctuated with excited gasps.

An obstruction halted The Shadow's advance. It was the panel; he had blundered against it. Probing quickly with his fingers, he found the open space, pressed his right eye against it. From his cloak, his right hand drew an automatic.

The Shadow opened his right eye.

SEVERAL seconds had passed. It took a few more before The Shadow's eye could focus itself to the scene. First, there was the shifting blur of many green-clad figures—some flaying, others offering helping hands, while a few were huddled near the walls.

In their plight, members seemed varied in opinion. Some regarded all as foemen; others accepted them as friends. The rest were too concerned with their own plight to care about their companions.

The blur cleared as two Green Hoods shifted away from The Shadow's panel, to sag separately, as they groped along the wall.

Directly ahead, The Shadow saw the table clearly. The rolled papers were gone, but a man remained there. He was Member 1; his position was too close to the table lamp for him to be anyone else.

Like the others, Member 1 had taken the full effect of the flashing bulbs; but that, alone, did not account for all that had happened to him.

Where others had retained their hoods, his was gone. In its place, The Shadow saw a large face, with ruddy beard; above it, thick, shaggy hair that matched the whiskers. There was a stare in the eyes of the bearded man. Those eyes were glassy; they bulged from their sockets, straight toward the ceiling.

The stare, its direction—neither could have been caused by the burst of light. The Shadow's gazing eye looked lower, toward the green-robed body that was hunched, breast upward, half across the table.

There was a glitter that showed from the center of a darkish splotch, where red blood dyed the green cloth of the robe. A few moments later, The Shadow identified the sparkling object.

It was the jewel-studded handle of a long, thin-bladed knife that had been thrust straight to the heart of the green-robed man who called himself Member 1.

The leader of the Green Hoods had paid the penalty for his overzeal, in offering his newly invented Truth Inducer to his fellow members. All had been willing to share the knowledge regarding that device, except a single member.

That lone person, a traitor in the midst of the group, wanted it for himself. He had snatched the entire set of formulas and plans; to preserve them for his sole use, he had disposed of the person who created them.

The vivid blast of light had served as cover for a murder. One victim of the blinding flare had been singled out for death. The kill had been accomplished in the midst of a group helpless to prevent the doom that the victim, himself, had been unable to escape.

Not only had the Green Hoods failed to spot the murderer or his deed. The nefarious stroke had been driven home before the light-blinded eye of The Shadow!

CHAPTER III
MEMBER 13

GROPING men in green had reached panels along the wall, though none had arrived at The Shadow's passage. It was plain that once they gained outlet, the Green Hoods would stampede. If any waited longer, they would eventually join the rush, once they saw the murdered form of Member 1.

His eye attracted by the motion along the walls, The Shadow saw panels sliding under pressing hands. It struck him instantly that those were the first exits to open. With that thought came a more important conclusion.

The murderer, himself a member of the Green Hoods, was still in the square-walled meeting room!

Whatever the motives of the Green Hoods, death had been dealt among them through an act of treachery. The killer was a criminal who deserved full vengeance. The Shadow's task was to single out the murderer from the rest of the green-hooded band.

The killer had certainly avoided the dazzle of the lights. He had placed the bulbs beforehand; had pressed the light switch to produce the flash. He had needed only to keep his eyes tight shut. Proof that he had done so was apparent from the quick skill with which he had dealt the knife thrust.

Quickly, The Shadow looked for a Green Hood who was showing no signs of temporary blindness. Such a man would be the murderer. Oddly, no such member appeared among the rest.

A crafty game was being played by the killer. Not knowing of The Shadow's presence, the murderer was calmly biding his time, letting others grope their way ahead of him. He was playing it safe, in case any of the other Green Hoods happened to catch a fleeting glimpse of him.

Within a half minute, the assassin would be gone, along with a blundering throng. There was only one way in which The Shadow could force the issue; that was to make the killer reveal himself. It could be done, and The Shadow knew the system.

With his left hand, The Shadow slid back the panel, sprang into the squarish room. As he came, he loomed his automatic for the largest cluster of Green Hoods. From The Shadow's lips came a shivering laugh that brooked of accusation.

It was a challenge to the murderer. The chilling tone seemed to carry the announcement that The Shadow had picked the man he wanted.

Member 13 had joined the meeting of the Green Hoods. Only one man—the killer—could see him; but the others heard the sinister mirth. They took it as the menace that they all expected.

The result was a double effect.

ONE Green Hood whipped about from a far panel; he yanked an old-fashioned pistol into view. The others forgot the exit; they sidled along the walls, crouching, with hands shielding their eyes, trying vainly to spy the intruder who had issued the laugh.

The Shadow had not only found the murderous member of the green-clad band; he had cleared a path for battle with that killer.

In turn, the Green Hood recognized The Shadow as an outside menace, more formidable than any of the usual members present. He was versed in ways of crime, that killer, for he promptly identified The Shadow as the being who was dreaded by all the underworld. That was why the Green Hood handled his gun with whippet speed, hoping to beat The Shadow to the shot.

That effort failed. The Shadow's automatic thundered its echoes through the cramped space of the meeting room while the murderer was still trying to tug the trigger of his ancient shooting iron.

As always, when there was room for it, The Shadow faded as he fired. His fisted gun was like the fulcrum of a lever: constant in its aim, while his tall shape shifted. That measure was seemingly unnecessary on this occasion, for The Shadow's shot, directed for the killer's gun arm, was far in advance of the Green Hood's action.

Oddly, the green-clad murderer did not falter. Instead, he blasted bullets toward The Shadow. Those fading tactics were useful after all. Slugs were whining past The Shadow's ears, while he stabbed shots in return.

Not one of four bullets clipped the murderer.

The Shadow's accuracy had left him, even at this close range. The reason was the aftermath of that blinding light. Though his right eye had its usual vision, The Shadow had lost proper sense of distance and perspective from the strain that his left optic had suffered.

Green Hoods, flattened on the floor, their heads buried, ostrich-fashion, in their arms, were clear of the barrage. That didn't help The Shadow. If this crossfire kept up, he—not the murderer—would be the one to fall.

So far, The Shadow's shifting tactics, plus the belated aim of the killer, were the saving factors. Once The Shadow reached the side wall, that would be ended. The Green Hood was waiting, half through his open panel, ready to drop The Shadow when the latter was forced to reverse his course.

The Shadow took a sudden, desperate measure.

Ending his fade, he lunged straight for the lingering killer; driving in, he aimed as he came. With amazing, lengthy strides, he cut down the distance. His finger was ready on its gun trigger, to begin a new duel at such close range that the shot could not fail.

The Green Hood had a momentary opportunity to insert a sure shot of his own. He took it; but it didn't have the certainty that he expected. The Shadow's sudden movement had brought a spontaneous backward spring from the killer. He was recoiling as he fired. His gun was pointed a trifle high; the quick snap he gave the trigger jolted it still higher.

Two shots rang out together.

The Shadow's bullet zimmed the edge of the half-shut panel, was deflected away from the green figure just beyond. The slug from the old-fashioned revolving pistol took a slice from the slouch hat brim just above The Shadow's ear.

NEITHER shot had sufficed. The murderer was in flight. The Shadow was whipping aside the panel, to take up the pursuit.

The chase led through a twisty, stone-walled burrow. The cellar of the old theater was more honeycombed than The Shadow had originally supposed. At every turn, the killer was just far enough ahead to be out of range. At last, he clattered up a spiral stairway on the far side of the building.

That was his one chance to drop flight and take up battle. The murderer didn't take it. When The Shadow reached the head of the staircase, a door was swinging shut to mark the Green Hood's departure into the outside air.

His hand on the staircase rail, The Shadow was ready for a long lunge, to cover the distance to the door. A slight motion halted him. He dropped back, letting his body slide down the steps. The door swung open; the glare of flashlights spotted The Shadow. With the beams came shouts; new guns began to rip.

The Green Hood had kept a gun crew waiting outside. He had given them the order to finish The Shadow.

If the thugs had withheld their inrush, they might have bagged The Shadow. Overzeal defeated them. He was sliding away, downward, when their revolvers barked.

Before they could drop their aim, The Shadow was below the level of the top step. His hand withdrew a fresh automatic. Jutting upward, that gun talked from the very floor.

Rowdies withered. Flashlights shattered, were flung aside. As sprawling figures writhed grotesquely toward The Shadow, others of the gun crew dived out through the door. Mockery followed them. The Shadow's taunting laugh promised another welcoming barrage if they returned.

All that came back were the sounds of a hurried scurrying through an alleyway.

It was too late to follow the killer. The gun crew had at least blocked off The Shadow from his trail.

The Shadow made another choice; one that he had dropped only because there had been a chance for pursuit.

Swinging down the spiral staircase, he followed a passage back to the meeting room.

On the way, he passed stumbling members of the Green Hoods, but he avoided them in the gloom. When he reached the meeting room, he saw a few others, the last who were leaving by different exits.

They were regaining their vision; The Shadow could tell that by the improvement of his own left eye. They were welcome to leave if they wanted. The Shadow had other business.

He stopped beside the outsprawled body of Member 1.

THE SHADOW had never seen that bearded face before tonight. He wanted to know the dead man's identity. Guns cloaked, The Shadow opened the front of the victim's blood-dyed robe. He saw a dark suit underneath. An inside pocket bulged with a large wallet.

In the wallet, The Shadow found identification cards, one with the dead man's photograph. The man's name was Smedley Breer; a card gave him the title of professor. That was a link; The Shadow had heard of Professor Breer.

Recognized as an inventor, Breer had attained only spotty success, because he seldom carried ideas to their completion. He had gained a fortune, however, through the development of a tear gas that was very effective, but milder in its after-results than those gases commonly used. Breer had retired after that; little had been heard regarding him since.

There were scrawled papers in the wallet, obviously in Breer's own writing. They were of little importance; but there was one loose sheet that fell to the table. The Shadow opened it. The folded paper was a telephone memorandum with the name of the Hotel Triton printed at its head.

It was stamped with today's date. It was a memo addressed to Professor Smedley Breer. Its terse message read:

Call HYacinth 6-9234 at 8:30 p.m. sharp.

From the folded slip fell a tiny bit of red paper. The Shadow examined it. The paper was a cigar band, of a sort that he had never seen before. Instead of a name, it bore a monogram, composed of the initials "TMS."

On the back of the cigar band was a scrawling, but finely marked, notation in Breer's own handwriting. It evidently referred to the cigar band, for the words stated:

Must investigate this.

Folding the cigar band in the telephone memo, The Shadow took those two items as his only trophies. Once he had put them away, he began to place all other objects into the professor's wallet, to stow the latter in Breer's pocket.

The one pause came when The Shadow held the card that bore Breer's photograph. There was one item on that card that The Shadow required; that was the address where the professor lived.

The Shadow noted it; silently, swiftly, he returned the wallet to the dead man's pocket and took the nearest exit that led from the deserted room.

To a man, the Green Hoods had vanished when The Shadow reached the alleyway by which he had first entered.

If sounds of gunfire had attracted the police, they were coming to the opposite side of the building, where The Shadow had dispersed the thugs. The alleyway on that other side led to a different street.

This thoroughfare was silent. The Shadow could see the tail-lights of Moe's cab twinkling from the obscure parking space. The cabby had returned from his trip, to await The Shadow.

That fact brought a whispered laugh from hidden lips. The mirth was significant, for it linked with something that The Shadow had just learned.

The address named on the card in Breer's wallet was the very one that the mysterious brunette had given when she had departed as a passenger in The Shadow's cab!

CHAPTER IV
MURDERER'S GOAL

PROFESSOR BREER's residence was an old-fashioned house in a row of melancholy houses that lined an almost-forgotten side street. As The Shadow viewed it from the cab window, he found the house to be the very sort that he expected.

It was brick, but faced with a shabby brownstone front. The basement was just below the street level, fronted by a rusted iron fence. The place looked as forgotten as the street itself; an excellent location for an inventor to conduct experiments in seclusion.

The Shadow ordered Moe to circle the block. From the rear street, the cloaked observer was given a chance view that suited him. Between two rear buildings, he saw the back and side of Breer's second floor. Its windows were heavily shuttered.

That marked the location of the laboratory where the professor kept the device called the Truth Inducer.

The cab was nearing the front again. It slackened at The Shadow's command. Away from the fringe of a street lamp, a black shape alighted, blended itself with the darkness near the picket fence.

The glare of flashlights spotted The Shadow. With the beams came shouts; guns began to rip.

An iron gate moved in ghostlike fashion. Its rusted hinges failed to groan under the expert pressure. Passing through, The Shadow reached a doorway to the basement, almost beneath the high brownstone steps that led up to the main door of the house.

Under The Shadow's persuasion, the lower door yielded. Soon, a flashlight was blinking its way through the dingy rooms of the empty basement. From there, The Shadow followed a steep flight of steps up to the first floor. He picked the lock of another door, made his way into a narrow hall.

One noteworthy feature of Breer's home was its total darkness. In a sense, that was odd; for Moe had brought a passenger here, not long before. The cabby had reported that the girl had turned on lights after entering the house.

There was the possibility that the girl had gone out again; but it was also likely that she had retired, even though the hour was fairly early. In the latter event, she would not yet be asleep. Should she be as worried as when The Shadow had previously seen her, she would be in the right mood to hear any noise made by a prowler.

The Shadow preserved a total silence as he moved about the first floor. He passed through a small dining room, furnished in antique style; after that, he entered a stuffy parlor with furniture that dated back to the nineteenth century.

The dining room had windows at the back; the parlor, at the front. The side walls of both rooms banked against the house next door. When he reached the hallway again, The Shadow observed side windows. They indicated a small courtyard on that side of the house.

There were stairs to the second floor. The Shadow ascended them, keeping his flashlight blinking close to the carpeted steps. On the second floor, he found doorways along the hall. All were closed; so was the door of the rear room at the end.

Reaching that objective, The Shadow expected to find the door locked. Instead, it opened almost at his touch.

THE SHADOW entered a paneled room reminiscent of the meeting place where he had watched the Green Hoods.

Correctly, The Shadow concluded that Professor Breer, as Member 1, had designed the meeting room of the Green Hoods. He had arranged the paneled walls in the same fashion as this room in his own house. It followed that this room, like the meeting place, had a secret opening in the wall.

Glimmering his flashlight toward the wall on the courtyard side, The Shadow saw a single, shuttered window.

From outside, he had observed two windows in that same wall; two more at the rear. This room, equipped like an office, was only half a room. The rest of it lay behind the back panel. In all probability, the space beyond was Breer's private laboratory.

Carefully, The Shadow began to probe the panels, searching for the secret opening. The center one was solid. Breer, crafty in method, had evidently placed the sliding door near a corner of the back wall.

The Shadow moved to the left. His fingers, tapping with nearly soundless thuds, could sense the hollow effect of the panel. This was where the opening lay.

To find the catch was the next step. The Shadow was moving his gloved fingers upward, when he became conscious of a slight puff of air. It seemed to come along the wall; but that was a mere caprice of the breeze. The last glimmer of the flashlight showed the rear wall solid, the side window tightly shuttered.

The air current could have come from one place only. Someone had opened the very door by which The Shadow had entered from the hall.

Instantly, The Shadow thought of Breer's murderer.

There was a chance that the killer had recognized the bearded dead man, after pulling away Breer's green hood. That had seemed plausible, but somewhat remote. Certainly, The Shadow had given the assassin no time to look for Breer's identification cards.

In any event, The Shadow had made a speedy trip to these premises and should have arrived first, if this happened to be the killer's destination. Therefore, the silent swing of the door, noticeable only by the wave of air, was indication that the murderer could have recognized Breer and come here also.

Had the new entrant caught the last blink of The Shadow's light? That was a question that needed a prompt answer not by words, but by a move.

Stealthily, The Shadow shifted away from his corner. Neatly avoiding a table and two chairs that he remembered, he regained the front wall, beside the door. There was a light switch on the other side; a reach across it, The Shadow could flood the little office with a glow.

The door, The Shadow noted, was closed. If the other person had actually entered, he had shifted away with a stealth that rivaled The Shadow's own. Perhaps the lurker had also picked the light switch as an objective.

To check on that, The Shadow started an inward circuit. He intended to pass close beside a desk against the blank wall of the room, then approach the light switch from the reverse direction. Brief seconds were all that The Shadow required for that neat move.

The needed time was denied him.

Half finished with his maneuver, The Shadow was facing in the door's direction when lights suddenly filled the room. He was caught in the open, bathed in the glow of three floor lamps. The nearest was beside the desk, almost at The Shadow's elbow.

No *click* of the switch; no person at the door itself. Before The Shadow could spot the person who had tricked him, a firm contralto voice ordered him to raise his hands.

The voice came from behind the desk. The Shadow hesitated only momentarily, then let his half-drawn .45 slip back beneath his cloak. He turned toward the desk, raising his hands to his shoulders. He was face to face with the brunette who had boarded the cab outside the Landham Theater.

THE girl was dressed as The Shadow had first seen her, except for the cape. The collar of her dress was low, her neck showed smooth, with the whiteness of ivory. Her face, too, had that pallor; but, gradually, color returned.

The steadiness of the girl's brown eyes, the firmness of her lips, proved that she was confident that she controlled the situation. She had reason for that surety. In her steady hand the girl held a .32 revolver, its muzzle aimed squarely for The Shadow's heart.

Her gaze unflinching, the girl moved from behind the desk, never changing her line of aim. She placed herself between The Shadow and the outer door. Then, in modulated tone:

"You are The Shadow?"

The Shadow gave no reply. The girl could see his burning eyes; she took their gaze as an admission of his identity.

"Professor Breer has spoken of you," declared the girl. "I do not believe that he regards you as an enemy. It is best, however, that I hold you here until he returns. I am his secretary; my name is Evelyn Rayle."

The girl did not know of Breer's murder. Mentally, The Shadow debated whether it would be wise to inform her of that event. While he was considering the possible consequences of such a statement, the girl added:

"While we wait, you can tell me of your purpose here."

Again, The Shadow maintained silence. There was a sparkle of anger in Evelyn's eyes.

"At least," snapped the girl, "you can inform me how you entered; what you have done while you have been here!"

The Shadow's eyes roved the room. He saw how Evelyn had so suddenly produced the lights. The girl had plugged in a floor socket beside the desk; its triple connection went to all three lamps. The Shadow's gaze came back to Evelyn. The girl's hand was tightening on its gun.

Evelyn was tense again; therefore, dangerous.

"I shall answer your question," spoke The Shadow in a deep tone, a pitch above a whisper. "I entered the front door of the basement. I came directly here. I have been in this room"—his eyes went to a clock on Breer's desk—"precisely four minutes.

"In that time"—The Shadow's tone carried a trace of ironic mirth—"I have done no more than acquaint myself with these surroundings. As to my purpose here—"

The Shadow paused. He was about to tell Evelyn that he was a friend; if necessary, he was willing to throw back his hat and cloak collar, to reveal himself in his pretended guise of Cranston. But the flash of Evelyn's eyes ended that. So did the thrust that she gave the revolver. Urged by sudden antagonism, the girl wanted that weapon closer to The Shadow's heart.

"You have lied!" Evelyn's tone was cold, biting. "That proves that you are an enemy. Something has happened to Professor Breer, and you are responsible!

"You have not deceived me. I heard you enter— fully ten minutes ago—and you came by the back door, instead of the basement. You have been in this room longer than you stated. You may have learned much more than you are supposed to know.

"Unless you tell everything, I shall take prompt action. What that may be, circumstances will tell. I am loyal to Professor Breer. I hold you responsible for his safety!"

EVELYN'S words were dramatic; they carried a real menace. The girl meant what she said; but to The Shadow, her final words were almost a blank. An earlier statement of hers had swung his thoughts to another channel.

Evelyn Rayle had heard someone enter this house ten minutes ago, by the back door. That meant that another intruder had preceded The Shadow.

Someone not stealthy enough to have reached here unheard, as The Shadow had. But a person crafty enough to have solved the secret of the hidden paneling, particularly because he, like The Shadow, had also been at the meeting of the Green Hoods.

That intruder was Breer's murderer. He had recognized the dead professor. He had made a speedy trip here, rapid enough to reach the goal before The Shadow. The murderer's own lack of stealth should have placed him in a predicament, since Evelyn had overheard him. Instead, it had been a stroke of luck for the killer.

The girl was threatening her real ally, The

Shadow. Meanwhile, her actual enemy—Breer's murderer—was beyond the rear wall, in sole possession of the dead professor's laboratory.

A murderer had reached his goal. The Shadow, here to trap that killer, was powerless to move!

CHAPTER V
BALKED BATTLE

TRUTH couldn't help The Shadow's dilemma. The facts that he had already admitted had produced his present predicament. If he told Evelyn that another intruder had entered before him, the girl would not believe it. If he retraced the story, he would strike a snag the moment that he mentioned Breer's death.

If The Shadow related episodes from the beginning, Evelyn might listen. She would doubt the coincidences, however, as he came to them. The fact that he had been chosen as Member 13; that he had looked into the meeting unobserved, was like a build-up to some fantastic tale.

That narrative, too, would lead to the account of Breer's death. The same obstacle was present.

Whatever The Shadow said, no matter how sincerely he stated his own case, precious minutes would be lost. At any moment, the murderer might come from that inner room. Opening the panel, he would see the glow of the office. From the laboratory, he could deliver new death, to both The Shadow and Evelyn.

It was that prospect that forced The Shadow's course.

He could stall Evelyn; but the upshot would be another duel with the Green Hood who had murdered Breer. When that test came, The Shadow would have to whip out an automatic, to shoot for the opened panel.

If Evelyn knew of the Green Hoods—and The Shadow believed that she did—the girl would be doubly convinced that The Shadow was her enemy, for she would take the green-clad murderer as a friend.

The Shadow would have two sharpshooters to contend against, not one. Moreover, he wouldn't fire shots at Evelyn, even if he could have the chance. The girl's ignorance of the true conditions did not make her an enemy.

It was better to make a gunless thrust; to deal with Evelyn, even at risk of his own life. After all, the chances would be less against The Shadow.

Still, they were bad.

This plight was the sort that had taxed The Shadow most severely in the past. He preferred to face a horde of crooks, to one person who was governed by erroneous belief of a righteous cause. Nerve, stamina, inspiration—all went with justice.

The Shadow knew that well, for it was what he represented.

Crooks could quail, as the green-hooded murderer had tonight, under sudden pressure from a just fighter. Evelyn Rayle would not falter in a pinch. She thought herself right, The Shadow wrong.

No ordinary ruse could distract Evelyn's attention. Boldly, the Shadow decided on something that might help in part.

THE SHADOW spoke; his tone had changed entirely. It was the calm, deliberate speech of Cranston.

"Probably you recognize my voice"—The Shadow's gaze eased as he talked—"for you have heard it over the telephone, when I talked with Professor Breer."

Evelyn showed interest. As Breer's secretary, she had actually spoken to persons who had financed the professor's past inventions. She had never heard Cranston's tone before, but its mildness made her think she might have.

"You may even have seen me"—The Shadow was hazarding much on the next statement—"on the evening when I dined with Professor Breer. I think that you were leaving, just when I arrived outside the Hotel Triton."

There was a slight fade of the suspicion in Evelyn's eyes. The Shadow's surmise was correct; Professor Breer had dined often at the Triton. The Shadow had based that assumption on the memorandum that he had taken from Breer's body.

Evelyn was peering closely, trying to see the features beneath the hat brim. With an easy upward motion of his hands, The Shadow forced the slouch hat back, let his cloak collar drop. Evelyn saw Cranston's features; their calmness impressed her, even though she did not recognize the masklike face.

It was the moment for a speedy move.

The Shadow tilted his head toward the lamp beside the desk, that Evelyn might see his face more clearly. His hands were easing downward lazily. His shoulders edged away, drawing his body almost from the path of Evelyn's gun.

Then, before the girl's finger could snap the gun trigger. The Shadow gave a lunge for the desk itself. His left hand hit the edge, just as Evelyn fired. That first bullet was inches wide of The Shadow's right shoulder.

There was another shot coming. Evelyn took a quick step, half backward, half sideward, to reach a new position. She jabbed her revolver straight toward the desk. The gun tongued again, but The Shadow wasn't where it aimed.

He had taken a rebound from the desk—a long, low, sprawly move, below the level of Evelyn's quick fire. His lunge wasn't for the outer door; it was toward the rear wall. Evelyn saw his streaky, flinging dive; she whirled, to shoot again.

There was more to that fading lunge than Evelyn expected. Turning his sprawl into a slide, The Shadow hooked the girl's ankles with one projecting foot. That speedy leg swing flipped her from the floor, just as she was giving the trigger its third pull. The shot went high; the bullet embedded itself in the rear wall, almost at the ceiling.

Three quick shots in as many seconds. One second more, The Shadow was snatching the revolver from Evelyn's loosened fist. He was whipping out an automatic with his other hand; not to hold Evelyn at bay, but to meet an adversary whom he expected at an instant's notice.

Evelyn's shots were an alarm that the murderer beyond the secret panel must have surely heard.

THE SHADOW had not forgotten the girl. He didn't want her in the fray. To prevent the chance that she would enter, or get mixed in, the coming battle, The Shadow took a long spring clear across the office. He shouldered the wall beyond the corner where he had tapped the panel. A dozen feet away from Evelyn, The Shadow swung about.

With his twist, his ears heard the opening slither of the panel. As his gun came around, The Shadow's eyes saw the very man he expected: the green-hooded murderer, on the threshold of Breer's lighted laboratory.

The killer had yanked the panel open before The Shadow had a true aim; but in his turn, the Green Hood was at loss. He had heard the shots; he was looking for their source. He did not see The Shadow until the black-cloaked fighter spied him.

If the Green Hood had depended on any gun— his antique pistol or a modern revolver—he would have lost the duel. The chances were equal at that moment; and The Shadow had previously demonstrated his superior speed. The best that the killer could have done was to wound The Shadow.

It happened that the Green Hood had another sort of weapon; one that could cover a much larger field than The Shadow's automatic. He was holding a light cylinder, which had a lever at the side, a nozzle in the end. He did not have to aim it; his shift away from The Shadow did the trick.

As his left hand gripped the cylinder, the Green Hood snapped the lever with his right. The puff of vapor from the nozzle was a wide-ranged blast that reached The Shadow's face. Pungent fumes filled the room. Under that spray, The Shadow sagged, his gun unfired.

A stagger to the wall; The Shadow rallied. But the effects of the gas made the whole scene nightmarish. He was pumping bullets from his automatic. The Green Hood was ignoring them. The gas had the odor of ether; but it was a different type of anesthetic.

It had The Shadow reeling, groggy. He thought he was aiming at his opponent; but he wasn't. His bullets plowed the ceiling and the floor, but not the wall.

The Green Hood was snatching up a bulging valise. Evelyn recognized that bag, as she did the spray gun. She knew from the robed man's manner that he was not Professor Breer. Evelyn gave an agonized shriek: a recognition of her error.

The Shadow understood it, despite his staggery condition. With a side sweep, he flung Evelyn's revolver across the room.

That toss was meant for the girl; but The Shadow's throw was as bad as his aim. The gun hit beyond the desk; Evelyn had to scramble after it. By the time she had the weapon, the Green Hood was out through the hall, carrying the vaporizing cylinder and the valise.

Evelyn followed. The Shadow reeled after her. He didn't reach the top of the stairs until the girl had hurried to the bottom, firing after the Green Hood as she ran. From above, the whole scene whirling before his eyes, The Shadow saw Evelyn aim point-blank. She pulled the trigger, but the revolver was empty.

IN from the rear hall sprang a trio of thugs. They had guns; they were aiming to kill. Only The Shadow's action prevented it.

He jabbed his last shots down the stairs; the bullets went into the steps, but they made the crooks look upward. Seeing The Shadow, the gunmen opened fire.

Amid the whirl, The Shadow saw the Green Hood turn the cylindrical spray toward Evelyn. There was a puff of vapor; the girl collapsed. The murderer gathered her up, to drag her away helpless.

The Shadow was staggering back along the upper hall. He had been lucky to escape the hasty shots that the thugs had sent in his direction. He was shoving away his emptied automatic, striving to produce a fresh weapon that he couldn't seem to find.

He was hoping, through sheer nerve, to overcome the persistent grogginess that had seized him. He found the gun, tried to steady himself in the hallway.

The mobsters were at the head of the stairs. The Shadow shifted; his shoulder struck the door of a room that must have been Evelyn's. The door was ajar; it gave as The Shadow reeled. The cloaked battler pitched across the floor, to land beside an opened window.

Whether he had regained a temporary grip upon himself, or merely had good luck with his aim, The Shadow at least found the direction of the doorway when thugs arrived there. His wangling finger sent jerky shots.

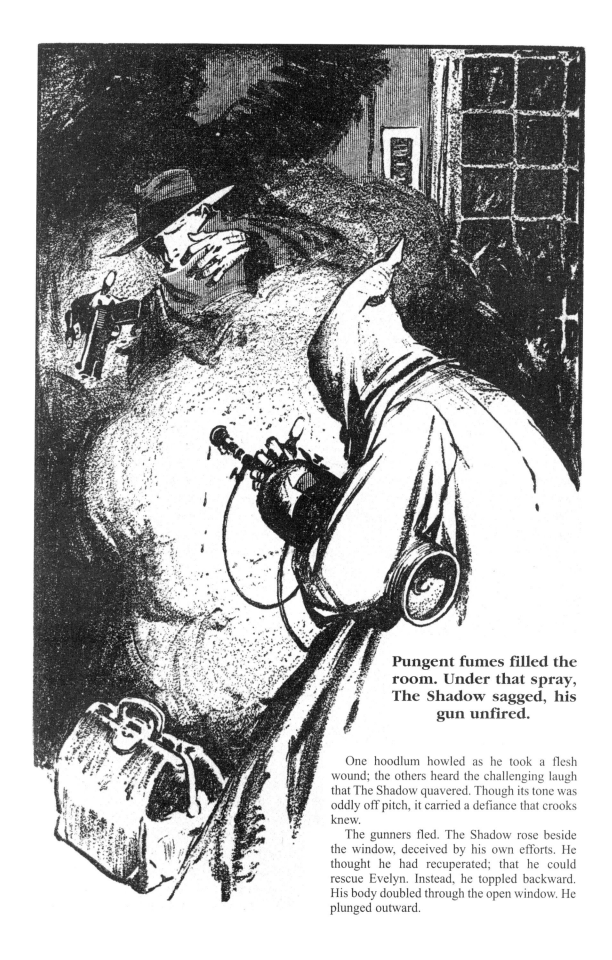

Pungent fumes filled the room. Under that spray, The Shadow sagged, his gun unfired.

One hoodlum howled as he took a flesh wound; the others heard the challenging laugh that The Shadow quavered. Though its tone was oddly off pitch, it carried a defiance that crooks knew.

The gunners fled. The Shadow rose beside the window, deceived by his own efforts. He thought he had recuperated; that he could rescue Evelyn. Instead, he toppled backward. His body doubled through the open window. He plunged outward.

WITH one hand, The Shadow clawed for a hold. He hooked the top of a ground-floor window frame, tightened his fingers in a maddened clutch that slipped a moment later.

That grab broke The Shadow's fall. He was uninjured when he sprawled onto the stony courtyard. The motionless state that took possession of him was due to the gas treatment that the Green Hood had applied.

Sheer exertion had kept The Shadow on the move; but he had collapsed at last. Thugs had followed the path that the Green Hood had taken through the rear of Breer's house. The professor's murderer was clear, with Evelyn Rayle his prisoner.

Strange silence lulled around the old house. From distant blocks came sirens. Gunfire had been reported; police were heading for the place where The Shadow's battle had been balked. The Shadow did not hear those far-off wails. He was lying in a state of total oblivion.

Police cars were entering the front street when flashlights glimmered suddenly in the stone space where The Shadow lay. Hurriedly, two men gathered up the cloaked fighter, carried him to the rear street where a taxi waited, its lights dimmed.

Moe Shrevnitz was the driver of that cab. He had spotted the approach of the Green Hood's thugs. Moe had put in a quick call to Burbank, the contact man who could reach The Shadow's active agents. Those aides had arrived before the law.

Crime held a temporary triumph; but The Shadow's cause could be renewed. Soon, the cloaked avenger would resume his efforts to pierce the mystery that still enshrouded the affairs of the Green Hoods.

One member of that band—Breer's murderer and Evelyn's captor—would hear from The Shadow later.

CHAPTER VI
NEWS FOR THE SHADOW

IT was noon the next day when The Shadow awakened. With his return to consciousness, he sensed the comfort of quiet surroundings. That was sufficient to lull him into another drowse, that lasted intermittently for nearly two hours.

The sound that roused him finally was the opening of a door. Rising upon one elbow, The Shadow stared, half blankly, at a serious-faced man who had the manner of a physician. It was not until the entrant smiled that The Shadow recognized him.

The man was Doctor Rupert Sayre, who had long been The Shadow's emergency physician. Sayre knew The Shadow as Lamont Cranston; hence, his smile was the one that he usually gave his most important patients. It broke the clouds that still had The Shadow befuddled.

Slowly, The Shadow recognized his surroundings as part of Sayre's suite of offices. With an effort, he traced back to the events that had brought him to the place. Once that chain was begun, last night's episodes stood out with vivid reality.

This was one of the rare occasions when Doctor Sayre could read changes of expression on Cranston's face. He recognized that his patient had fully recovered from his dazed condition, which Sayre had correctly diagnosed as the effects of gas. Raising a window shade, the physician produced some newspapers, with the comment:

"These will interest you, Mr. Cranston."

They did interest The Shadow.

There, in bold type, were facts that concerned the Green Hoods. The society was revealed as a group of amateur criminologists, whose purpose had been to help the law by exchanging new inventions in crime detection among themselves.

Professor Smedley Breer was revealed as founder of the organization. That news had come from members of the Green Hoods. Since last night, the scattered members of the band had been flocking to the law.

As yet, their names had not been made public. That meant little to The Shadow for the present. He was looking for mention of a person who did not belong to the Green Hoods.

He found the name he wanted. An expression of relief registered itself on his usually immobile face.

An early edition of one of the evening newspapers had a last-minute story stating that Evelyn Rayle had been found. Police had been looking for the girl who served as secretary to Professor Breer. She had been discovered at a small hotel, in a dazed condition. So far, she had been unable to make a statement regarding her whereabouts the night before.

Sayre saw a sudden steadiness come over Cranston. A slight smile came to the placid lips. Then, the quiet statement:

"Summon a cab, doctor."

Sayre began a protest. Cranston was obdurate. His insistence finally convinced Sayre that he was well enough to leave. The doctor went to the outside office to call the cab.

As soon as Sayre was gone, The Shadow busied himself before a mirror. He stripped off the Cranston disguise, wiped away all traces of make-up. He was again Kent Allard, when he walked out through the little passage beside Sayre's office.

The physician saw him pass and hurried after him. He was too late to overtake his departing patient. The cab had arrived out front; all that Sayre saw were head and shoulders that he took for Cranston's, when The Shadow stepped aboard the cab.

Less than half an hour later, Kent Allard was conducted into the office of Police Commissioner Weston.

THERE was an expectant smile on Weston's face when he advanced to shake hands. Allard saw the reason immediately. Seated beside the commissioner's desk was a frail, bespectacled man whose face was pale and troubled.

That visitor was Robert Leng, picked by The Shadow as the man who had sent him the invitation to join the Green Hoods.

With Leng was another visitor, a middle-aged man of about average height. He was less nervous than Leng, but that was logical, for he was of stronger mold. Allard observed a square-chinned face, characterized by mild, grayish eyes, and lips that had a weary but friendly smile.

This visitor looked intelligent; he had a natural dignity, that gained added effectiveness from his gray-streaked hair. Commissioner Weston introduced the man as Lionel Atherland.

The name was known to The Shadow. Atherland had gained a reputation as a lecturer on social conditions. He had made a survey of conditions that existed in State penitentiaries. His discourses on that subject were thorough, so far as they went. But Atherland had merely attempted to educate the general public on crime conditions.

The police commissioner came abruptly to the subject that The Shadow expected.

"I've been hoping to hear from you, Allard," said Weston. "Leng tells me that he sent you an invitation to join the Green Hoods as Member 13. Did you receive it?"

"I did." Coolly, Allard drew the paper from his pocket. "This came with it."

He added the jade amulet. Then:

"Unfortunately—or should I say fortunately?—I am seldom in New York at night. Two evenings ago, Commissioner, I was at the Cobalt Club. You may remember that I told you that I had postponed an intended airplane flight—"

"In order to be there!" broke in Weston. "That's so, Allard. So you took the flight last night. That explains why you didn't get the letter until today!"

No smile showed on Allard's thin lips. He had simply let Weston form his own conclusion. Inwardly, The Shadow was pleased, for two reasons. First, that in his guise of Allard he was always mentioning proposed night flights. Second, that his Xinca servants never knew anything about their master's affairs, no matter who questioned them.

Both Leng and Atherland had taken the explanation without question. To keep it established, Allard smoothly changed the subject, by remarking to Weston:

"Tell me about the Green Hoods. The matter intrigues me, Commissioner."

WESTON gave the details. Professor Breer was the organizer. As Member 1, he had invited in a friend to be Member 2. Breer had done that without disclosing his identity; and he had given Member 2 the sole privilege of introducing Member 3. The chain had continued in that fashion.

"We have traced to Member 8," asserted the commissioner, "but there we have struck a snag. Member 8 states that he invited a man named Junius Purling to become Member 9. It is a certainty that Purling became a member; but he has not presented himself. Nor have we been able to locate him."

Allard's eyebrows raised. Weston explained that Purling was the traveling representative of a safe manufacturer. He had been asked to join the Green Hoods because of his knowledge of strongboxes. Not long ago, Purling had moved to a new apartment; but no one seemed to know the address.

"Inspector Cardona is checking on the case," declared Weston, in a confident tone. "I believe that he will have traces of Junius Purling within the next few hours."

Allard's eyes turned toward Leng. He made the move purposely, for Weston's benefit. The commissioner caught what was in his friend's mind.

"Since Leng was Member 12," nodded Weston, "you are wondering how we learned of him after the chain broke at Number 9. The answer is a simple one, Allard. Leng presented himself voluntarily. He told us that he was Member 12, but he didn't know who had invited him into the organization—"

"Until I also presented myself." The interruption came from Lionel Atherland. "I was Member 11."

"You see," said Weston to Allard, "we are tracing backward as well as forward."

An approving nod came from Allard, followed by the question:

"And Member 10?"

"We haven't found Member 10," admitted Weston. "He was the man who sent an invitation to Atherland." Weston reached for a sheet of paper. "Here it is, because Atherland kept it. But he has no idea who sent it."

The invitation was in green carbon, like the one that Leng had later sent to Allard. It had been typed on an old-fashioned machine, for the lettering was blocky and irregular. That, however, was a very slender clue—even for The Shadow.

"We must find Junius Purling," insisted Weston. "Since he is Member 9, he can lead us to Member 10. Those two are vital links: Purling and his unknown friend. Someone in the Green Hoods"—Weston wagged a finger—"played traitor last night. He committed murder with this weapon!"

DRAMATICALLY, Weston brought a jewel-handled knife from his desk drawer, laid it on the woodwork in front of Allard's eyes. For the second time, The Shadow was viewing the gem-studded blade that had been responsible for death.

This time, however, the whole knife was in view. Its long, thin blade showed it to be a stiletto; though the stones in the handle were merely semi-precious gems, the workmanship of the silver setting was excellent.

The Shadow recognized that the knife had value as a curio. He was judging its age, when Weston supplied more information.

"A Borgia stiletto," stated the commissioner. "Probably stolen from some collection. Here is another odd thing, Allard." Weston fished in the desk drawer, to find a bullet that he held in his palm. "Some of these were found in the meeting room. Have you ever seen a bullet like this?"

The Shadow had, but did not say so. He remarked, after thoughtful inspection, that the bullet appeared to be of unusual caliber.

"It should be," affirmed Weston. "It was fired from a Baby Paterson—a revolving pistol, invented nearly one hundred years ago. It is .28 caliber; like this stiletto, a gun of that sort is a curio."

The telephone bell rang just as Weston's statement ended. The commissioner answered the call; when he had finished, he told the visitors:

"It's about that girl, Evelyn Rayle, who worked for Professor Breer. She's out of her coma, but she can't remember anything. I wanted to quiz her as soon as possible, but"—the commissioner shook his head—"the physician thinks she should rest at least three hours longer. Maybe Cardona will have a tracer on Purling by that time. Then we can go up to the girl's hotel and talk to her."

Kent Allard had risen. He remarked quietly that he would leave his green-carbon note with the commissioner. Weston seemed annoyed by Allard's departure.

"I had more to tell you, Allard! About the Truth Inducer invented by Professor Breer! Can't you wait a short while longer?"

"Sorry, Commissioner," replied Allard. "I have an appointment. In a few hours, though, I shall be back at my apartment."

"Very well. Call me after you return there."

IN a taxicab, Kent Allard performed a move that would have intrigued Commissioner Weston, as well as Robert Leng and Lionel Atherland. From a pocket, he brought the cigar band with its initials "TMS"; also the telephone memo from the Hotel Triton.

Those clues—The Shadow's own—had some connection with the odd weapons that a murderous Green Hood had used at last night's meeting. The links to the Borgia stiletto and the Baby Paterson pistol were factors that The Shadow intended to learn.

He also wanted facts concerning Professor Smedley Breer and the dead inventor's Truth Inducer. But, like the facts of last night's murder, The Shadow intended to obtain them firsthand.

That was why he had left Weston's office. Allard's appointment was one that he had arranged on a moment's notice. He intended to keep it—not as himself, but as The Shadow.

Within the next few hours, The Shadow would visit Evelyn Rayle. There, in guise of black, he could restore the girl's latent memory of last night's events. Like The Shadow, Evelyn had suffered from the potent gas. The Shadow's own experience showed that one link with the past would produce full recollections.

The Shadow, himself, was the link that would make Evelyn remember last night's events, along with others that had occurred before.

CHAPTER VII
DEATH'S TRAIL

THE gloom of the hotel room lulled Evelyn Rayle. Propped in a big chair, she gazed idly

A Baby Paterson revolving pistol

toward the shaded window. From past the edges of the window blind came odd flickers that had taken her a long while to understand.

Dimly, Evelyn realized that daylight had faded; that the changing light must be due to an electric sign somewhere outside the hotel. Her eyes were not to blame for the changing light. She could see a glow from a hallway transom, and it remained constant.

Outside the hallway door was the perpetual beat of footsteps, that ceased only when the patroller paused to listen. The pacing didn't bother Evelyn. She realized that she was being guarded. But why, she could not understand.

Time was drifting pleasantly. The past, like the future, seemed very faraway, and blank.

The window shade stirred. Evelyn did not notice it. Her eyelids were almost closed; their long, dark lashes showed in the light from the shut glass transom. There was another eye, though, that was wide open, burning in its gaze.

That eye peered past the edge of the window shade, from outside. It was peering into this room as it had looked into the meeting of the Green Hoods, last night.

The shade rose slowly, smoothly; its crinkle was too slight for Evelyn to hear. Blackness blotted out the flickering of the electric sign. Behind that blackness, a hidden hand lowered the shade.

There was motion in the room; it stopped beside a telephone in the corner. A shape gradually arose, came into the transom light.

In the glow was shown cloaked shoulders, a slouch hat above them. There was a glimmer that reflected the glint of eyes. A gloved hand stretched forward, rested upon Evelyn's arm.

A weary sigh escaped the girl. She moved her lips, then opened her eyes. In a moment, she was staring wide.

Before her stood a being of the past, a personage whose mere presence brought back a deluge of thoughts. From one focal point—her previous meeting with The Shadow—Evelyn received two chains of recollections.

Her impressions were running back to earlier events, before The Shadow had arrived at Breer's old house. They were jumping on beyond that time, to her experiences after the lone Green Hood had bobbed from Breer's laboratory to take her prisoner.

"Professor Breer is dead," spoke The Shadow, in a solemn whisper. "His death must be avenged!"

Evelyn nodded. This time, she knew The Shadow as a friend.

"State all that you know," resumed The Shadow, "regarding Breer, his Truth Inducer; the Green Hoods—"

THERE was something almost hypnotic in The Shadow's gaze. Evelyn kept her own eyes fixed on his. Her lips formed statements that were brief, but explicit.

"Professor Breer organized the Green Hoods," she told The Shadow. "Its purpose was good. He trusted all the members; but revealed no names to me, not even that of Member 2. He did not tell me the total number of the members.

"The same with the Truth Inducer. He told me its purpose and what it could do. But he gave no formulas, no plans. Those were to be divulged to the Green Hoods, once the apparatus worked. It did work finally, when he tested it with me."

Evelyn was reaching far into the past. She paused to connect her story. The Shadow's whisper ordered her to describe the tests that Professor Breer had performed. Soon afterward, Evelyn was giving full account.

The girl had scarcely spoken a dozen words before The Shadow understood the momentous importance of the Truth Inducer; why a superman of crime had murdered Breer to obtain sole control of it.

As Evelyn described it, Breer had taken her into the laboratory. There, with the vaporizing spray, he had filled the room lightly with an etherlike gas. That done, he had placed a small portable machine between himself and Evelyn. He had attached a clamp to Evelyn's wrist, another to his own.

All during the test, Breer had kept close watch upon a dial at the top of the machine.

"He asked me questions," stated Evelyn, "and I replied. The gas made me willing to talk—as I am at present—for it was mild. Professor Breer governed his questions by the hand on the dial. When it steadied, I seemed to answer his questions without effort; and my replies were always truthful."

In that brief account, Evelyn divulged the value of the Truth Inducer. As practical as many of the so-called "lie detector" devices, it had an advantage that they all lacked. The results from an apparatus like the Truth Inducer were the sort that could stand the test of a court trial.

A questioner—witnesses as well—could inhale the same gas as the person tested. Owned by the law, the Truth Inducer could be a threat that would shake the world of crime!

Instead, Breer's invention had been acquired by a master crook. With it, the supercriminal could protect those who served him. He could force confessions from crooks who tried to double-cross him.

By seizing rival criminals, he could make them reveal their secrets of intended crimes, or disclose their knowledge of where they had buried the swag from their own crooked jobs.

The Green Hood who had played his hand last night had already demonstrated his strong criminal ability. With the Truth Inducer as his property, that crafty crook had the prospect of creating an organization of his own.

That group would work for evil, instead of good; and its organizer would stand supreme!

THERE was silence while The Shadow considered the insidious developments that the future offered. Evelyn broke the pause. She had remembered more about Professor Breer.

"Last night," the girl low-toned, "I went to a corner near the Landham Theater to watch for Professor Breer. He always insisted that I be there by quarter past eight, on meeting nights, in case he needed to talk to me.

"I was a few minutes late last night. By half past eight, Professor Breer had not arrived. I worried over that; by quarter of nine, I decided that the professor might have met with trouble. I went to the theater itself.

"It was five minutes later when Professor Breer did arrive. He stepped from a cab; as he came through the darkness, I spoke to him. He told me to go back to the house and wait for him, but he gave no explanation for his delay. I took the next cab that I saw."

Evelyn was telling The Shadow much more than she realized. Her own statements proved her absolute truthfulness. The Shadow had the very explanation that Evelyn lacked: the reason for Breer's delay.

The professor had stayed at the Hotel Triton until half past eight in order to call HYacinth 6-9234; after that, it had taken him about twenty minutes to reach the Landham Theater.

Evelyn's statement about taking a cab checked with The Shadow's own observation; her story, too, proved why she had been so alert after she had returned to the house.

The Shadow's next words were a prompting suggestion, rather than a question:

"That gas the Green Hood used last night—"

"Was the professor's special gas," added Evelyn. "He always warned that it would be overpowering, if used in sudden quantity. The Green Hood used the gas to put you out of combat; then, to overpower and capture me."

"And afterward—"

"I must have breathed very little of the vapor"—Evelyn's gaze showed recollection—"because I was half awake when I was carried from a car. I remember the clank of an iron gate, then a passage between two buildings, for there was light showing from above.

"The cement must have been broken, for I heard a stumble and a crunch. After that, my carriers used a flashlight. I saw a concrete wall on one side, brick on the other. Then there was a door; after it, darkness, when I was carried down a flight of stone steps."

Evelyn paused, to picture the next details.

"We went through a dim corridor. There were doors on each side—six altogether, I believe—and some were open. I saw rooms that looked like cells. A door at the end—a square room with no windows—"

Again, the girl's voice halted; she shuddered at memory of some ordeal. Then, in a low pitch that enabled her to steady her tone, Evelyn declared:

"The murderer was there, alone, still wearing his green hood. His men placed me in a chair; he dismissed them. I cannot remember their faces, except as I saw them at the professor's house. The Green Hood seemed to dominate my impressions afterward.

"He attached the wrist clamps; he watched the dial, as he questioned me. He asked me much about Professor Breer. I answered truthfully, though I did not want to do so. I could tell him nothing about the formulas or the apparatus, for those were the professor's own secrets.

"When he had finished, the Green Hood called his men. As I turned about, one of them shoved the vaporizer in my direction. There was another overdose of gas; it came so suddenly that I had no time to escape it. When I awoke, I was here."

FROM Evelyn's story, The Shadow knew that the girl had been more fortunate than she realized. Her ignorance was the reason why the Green Hood had released her. Luckily, too, the Green Hood had not guessed that Evelyn was awake enough to observe the entrance into the underground stronghold.

While Evelyn waited, The Shadow spoke.

"Tell your story to the police," he ordered, "but avoid mention of two details. First, my presence at Breer's house, except as a vague event. You can state that you thought someone was in the little office. You fired your revolver, then turned on the lights. You witnessed a struggle between the Green Hood and someone—"

Evelyn was nodding. She understood.

"As for the Green Hood's stronghold," added The Shadow, "you can describe its interior, from the dim passage onward. Mention open doors; then the square room where the Green Hood awaited you—"

The Shadow interrupted himself. There was a buzz from the corner. It was the telephone bell, that The Shadow had muffled with one of his gloves. The Shadow did not speak as he lifted the receiver. The click was sufficient signal for the man at the other end.

"Hello! Headquarters speaking..." The voice was actually that of Burbank, The Shadow's contact man. "A message for the police commissioner, if he is there... Inspector Cardona has located Junius Purling, Member 9 of the Green Hoods.

"Purling is dead. Murdered in his apartment, C 3, at the Lakeview Apartments. Inspector Cardona is waiting there. The telephone number is..."

The Shadow was hanging up the receiver. He plucked his glove from the telephone bell. Stepping into the transom light, he raised his ungloved left hand. Evelyn saw the strange reflections of The Shadow's girasol.

"Remember my instructions," whispered The Shadow. "You will hear from me again. This token"—he turned his hand so that the fire opal gave a vivid sparkle—"is my symbol of identity."

There was a *swish* into darkness. Evelyn caught a vague crinkle of the window curtain, the slight thud of the closing sash beyond it. The Shadow was gone.

ALONG the ground below, a black shape glided through gloom. As it shifted away, a whispered laugh throbbed from invisible lips. That tone was The Shadow's, but its significance did not concern the talk that he had held with Evelyn.

The Shadow was considering Burbank's call; the mystery that it produced, by bringing a new trail of death. But in the murder of Junius Purling was a rift that promised much. The Shadow had caught final words from Burbank, just before the receiver settled on its hook.

Those words were a statement of Purling's telephone number. It was HYacinth 6-9234, the very number on the hotel memorandum that The Shadow had taken from the pocket of Professor Smedley Breer!

Between the dead members 1 and 9 there lay a definite link; that connection was the murderer who had slain both. This time, the law had been the first to locate death's trail; but The Shadow would soon be on the scene.

With him, the cloaked investigator was carrying an important clue that belonged to himself alone.

CHAPTER VIII
CLUES OF GOLD

WHEN The Shadow arrived at Purling's apartment, he was again Kent Allard. Moreover, he was expected there. Commissioner Weston had called Allard's hotel suite, leaving word for him to come.

Allard was not the only outsider invited. There were five others, all members of the Green Hoods. Weston had decided that such amateur crime investigators might prove useful. Lionel Atherland was one; like others, the lecturer looked awed when he viewed Purling's body.

The dead salesman lay on a blood-dyed carpet in a corner of the apartment living room. A gaping wound showed in his shirtfront. Purling had been shot; the bullet had not quite reached his heart, but he had not long survived the death shot.

That was evident from the ugliness of the wound. The bullet had entered at an angle; deflected by a rib, it had burrowed sideways, producing an effect like a dumdum bullet.

Inspector Joe Cardona was in charge. A stocky-built man, swarthy and pokerfaced, Cardona looked the ace investigator that he was. He had completed his report on the case; he was summing up the details when Allard entered.

"The surgeon's examination places the time of death at eight o'clock last night," stated Cardona. "He doubts that Purling could have lived more than five minutes after the shot was fired. Therefore, the murderer slew Purling, and went to the meeting afterward. There, he murdered Professor Breer."

In placing Purling's murder upon the Green Hood who had killed Breer, Cardona produced an item of evidence. It was an odd-sized cartridge that had been found near Purling's body.

"Caliber .28," declared Cardona. "Identical with ejected cartridges found at the Landham Theater. The killer used the same gun there."

Weston inserted the comment that the weapon might be traced through police permits issued to gun users. Cardona shook his head.

"That Baby Paterson is a curio," declared the inspector. "It belongs in a museum, like the Borgia stiletto. My hunch, Commissioner, is that both came from the same collection."

Weston usually had an aversion to Cardona's hunches. This one, however, had enough logic to satisfy the commissioner. Cardona proceeded with other details.

"Purling evidently guessed something about the murderer," assured the ace. "He tried to write something; but only got as far as one word. That word was 'We'—and he couldn't even scrawl it. He had to print it."

Cardona pointed to a blood-smeared sheet of paper that lay on the table. There, in shaky lines, were the letters *W E*. Just to the right of the letters, Allard observed a sharp dot. Cardona was already explaining it. The inspector plucked up a pencil that lay near the paper.

"The point broke under too much pressure," said Cardona. "Purling never had a chance to start the next word. Maybe he had strength enough to write; but he couldn't take time out to sharpen the pencil, or look for another one."

CAREFULLY, Cardona took hold of a corner of the paper. With his other hand, he pointed to an opened drawer of the table, where the observers saw a medley of odd trinkets, including copper and silver coins of little value.

"Purling may have fished there for a pencil," declared the inspector. "Anyway, he didn't get one. But he found this!"

Cardona whisked away the paper that bore the word "We." Beneath it lay a gold object that looked like a coin, except for its unusual thickness.

"It's a medallion," stated Cardona, lifting the disk. "A French one; the head on it shows Louis Sixteenth. Somehow, this medal has a connection with the murderer. Otherwise, Purling wouldn't have dragged it from the drawer, to hide it under the note."

That golden clue intrigued all present, including The Shadow. But it did not mark the limit of Cardona's discoveries. Stooping above Purling's body, the ace inspector dipped his fingers into the murdered man's breast pocket. From there, Cardona drew forth a gold watch chain.

"There was something on the end of this," announced Joe. "Probably a locket, that's what it would most likely be. Another clue, like the medallion.

"The murderer may have broken it loose and taken it along, only I don't think so. It's more likely that Purling snapped it off and tried to leave it somewhere, because the killer could have taken chain and all.

"My idea is that Purling broke the thing after he'd flopped to the floor and was dying there. But the locket isn't on him, and it isn't in the open drawer. He couldn't have reached up that high to drop it, anyway."

Listeners were thoughtful, particularly Kent Allard. Through The Shadow's brain were flashing other impressions. He was noting the number on Purling's telephone. As Burbank had stated, it was the Hyacinth number that someone had told Professor Breer to call.

Possibly Purling had called the Hotel Triton to leave that message. That was the sort of assumption that Cardona would make, had he known of the call. To The Shadow, however, the answer was that the murderer had called the Triton.

Assuming that were so, how did it fit with the penciled note, the Louis medallion, the chain from which something had been broken?

Those were pieces of a puzzle that could only be fitted after more of the pattern was complete. Most important, so it seemed, would be the finding of the object that belonged on the end of the chain. Cardona was referring to it again; he still used the term "locket" to describe the object.

"If we find the locket," asserted the ace, "we'll know it's the right one. Look at the way this chain was broken. See the slant to it; the little prong pointing up? Nobody could fake that. When we find a locket that fits, we'll have our clue."

ALL that sounded excellent to Commissioner Weston. His brusque manner, however, showed that he was not satisfied. In demanding tone, Weston asked Cardona:

"Where does this lead us, Inspector?"

Cardona showed a grim grin. He had the answer.

"We know that Junius Purling was Member 9 of the Green Hoods," announced Cardona. "That made him the person who proposed Member 10, the only one we haven't heard from. With Purling dead—"

Cardona had no time to finish. Commissioner Weston was snapping a completion of the statement, so excitedly that there was no use for Cardona to continue.

"With Purling dead, there is no lead to Member 10!" ejaculated Weston. "He has hidden his tracks, which makes him the one man that we must find! Member 10 is the murderer among the Green Hoods! By Jove, Cardona! You have struck it!"

Weston's enthusiasm spread like an epidemic. The members of the Green Hoods who were present all joined in congratulating Cardona. One, alone, was less demonstrative than the rest; but that attracted no notice, for he had not been an actual member of the Green Hoods.

That lone figure was Kent Allard.

The Shadow had anticipated Cardona's reply, even before Weston had asked the question. The logic was obvious.

Whoever had murdered Professor Breer had found it necessary to close his trail. To do so, he had to eliminate some link in the chain of Green Hoods. There was another factor, too, that Weston had not mentioned.

With the discovery of Purling's body, every member of the Green Hoods stood accounted for, except that unknown Member 10. The law had already heard from Lionel Atherland and Robert Leng, who were Members 11 and 12.

Joe Cardona's grin had become a pleased one; with good reason. He hadn't been forced to proclaim his present idea a hunch. Commissioner Weston had snapped it outright. There was no smile, however, on the lips of Kent Allard.

To The Shadow, the obvious frequently had a lack of certainty. He was trying to pierce deeper into the cloud that surrounded the purposes of the unknown Member 10.

Weston, meanwhile, was pounding members of the Green Hoods with questions. He wanted to know if any could give a clue to the tenth man's identity. Negative headshakes came as responses. None had known much about Junius Purling; not even Member 8, who had proposed him. One man, however, finally gave an opinion.

It was Lionel Atherland who spoke. "I never

heard of Junius Purling before today," said Atherland, as he pushed his fingers through his gray-streaked hair. "It is apparent, though, that Member 10—introduced by Purling—must have known me."

"That's right," agreed Cardona. "You were Member 11."

"I have wondered often," continued Atherland, "who Member 10 might be. I am still at a loss, in endeavoring to place him."

"Have you checked among your friends?"

"The man might be any one of a great number. I have met many crime students during the course of my lecture tours. Today has produced the only clue. Whoever Member 10 may be, this man"—Atherland indicated Purling's body—"must have known him."

There was a quick snap of Cardona's fingers.

"There's our answer!" affirmed the ace. "I'll have a list of everybody that Purling knew, by this time tomorrow night. I can't get it sooner, Commissioner"—Cardona had noted disapproval from Weston—"because Purling had a lot of out-of-town customers. But in twenty-four hours, I'll have a batch of names for Mr. Atherland to look over."

"And let us hope," added Atherland, "that among these names, I shall find the culprit who was mutually acquainted with Purling and myself."

WESTON was highly pleased with that prospect. When the group filed from the room, the commissioner had forgotten all about the missing "locket" from the end of Purling's watch chain. So had the others, for the moment—with the exception of Kent Allard.

Last of the group to pause by Purling's body, Allard's eyes roved the floor. Under the edge of a large rug, The Shadow saw the faint trace of a bulge. Stepping to the window, he lighted a cigarette in Allard's deliberate style.

Giving a shielded side glance, his keen eyes spied a glimmer of gold from beneath the rug edge.

Making a comment to Commissioner Weston, Allard tossed his extinguished match to the floor. Weston saw the careless action, spoke in reprimanding tone:

"I wouldn't do that, Allard. We must have nothing to clutter up actual clues. Even a match might confuse matters."

"Sorry, Commissioner." Observed by Weston alone, Allard picked up the match. "I think that is all I dropped. There are no ashes on the rug."

As his thumb pressed the rug edge, two of Allard's fingers went deftly beneath. They paused for an instant after Weston turned away. Seen by no one, those fingers brought out the glittering object. A moment later, it was in Allard's vest pocket.

From the feel of the object, The Shadow knew that it could not be a locket. But it was the object that had been broken from Purling's watch chain. The Shadow learned that, as he rode away, alone, in his cab.

The trophy was a coin—a ten-dollar gold piece—that had been made into a watch charm. The tail side of the coin had been scraped; engraved upon it were initials. Oddly, though, they were not Purling's own.

The initials on the gold piece formed a three-letter monogram, composed of the letters "TMS."

That monogram, in turn, was identical with the one that The Shadow had found on the cigar band that he had taken from the wallet of Professor Smedley Breer!

CHAPTER IX
AHEAD OF THE LAW

JOE CARDONA kept his promise of twenty-four-hour service. On the next evening, an envelope was delivered to the apartment of Commissioner Weston. It contained lists of persons with whom Junius Purling had been acquainted.

News of that delivery reached The Shadow not long afterward.

The Shadow was in his sanctum—a black-walled room where blue light glowed upon the surface of a polished table. On the ebony woodwork lay a paper describing certain objects.

Those were the Borgia stiletto; bullets from the Baby Paterson pistol; the paper with the penciled letters *W E*; and the gold medallion that bore the head of King Louis XVI.

These clues belonged to the police. The Shadow had sought more facts concerning them, but, as yet, had gotten no result. Neither, for that matter, had the law.

The Shadow's own clues also lay in view.

One was the phone memo from the Hotel Triton. Careful inquiry had proven that the call there was made at seven-thirty, while Professor Breer had been at dinner. The memo had been sent in to the prospective victim of a green-hooded murderer.

The other clues were the cigar band, with its cryptic monogram "TMS"; and the gold coin that bore the same emblem.

One linked with Breer; the other with Purling. The Shadow had twisted those initials about; he had checked through many of his private crime files, but had not found the name of any man who might be their owner.

There was a report on The Shadow's table from a newspaper reporter named Clyde Burke. Clyde happened to be one of The Shadow's agents. His report gave details of an interview between Joe Cardona and Evelyn Rayle.

The girl had answered the inspector's questions, precisely as The Shadow had ordered. Her story satisfied Cardona. Evelyn had gone back to the old house where Professor Breer had formerly resided. Like others, she was to await the results of the hunt that the law was making for Green Hood Member 10.

Into that sanctum scene came the glow of a tiny bulb upon the wall. It was a signal from Burbank. Picking up earphones, The Shadow received the report of the envelope that Cardona had sent to Weston.

Immediately afterward, The Shadow left his sanctum.

COMMISSIONER RALPH WESTON had a little office in his apartment. He was seated at his desk mulling over Cardona's lists, when a caller was announced. The commissioner was rather surprised to learn that the visitor was Kent Allard. Nevertheless, he ordered that his friend be shown in.

Entering, Allard explained the reason for his chance call. He was planning a sea hop to Bermuda, but would be willing to postpone it, if the commissioner preferred to have him stay in New York.

"You might wait a few days, Allard," suggested Weston. "I think that we are going to trace Member 10. If we do, it would help us to have all persons present—even those who are only remotely connected with the Green Hoods, as you were."

To emphasize his point, Weston showed Allard the lists, with the comment:

"I expect Cardona here within an hour. Lionel Atherland will also arrive here. Perhaps, from this list"—Weston flourished one paper—"we may find the very man we want. One that Atherland knows."

Allard took the list. His eyes scanned it idly, while Weston explained that names upon it were those of persons who had not been located by telephone calls or personal visits. The list had been culled from larger groups of names; cut down to its present size, it enumerated about fifteen persons, with their addresses.

Though Weston didn't guess it, Allard's glance was more than casual. Keen eyes were analyzing every name. Those eyes paused at the very bottom of the list. There, The Shadow read the name and address:

Louis Wenz, 17 A, Marlborough Place.

Returning the list to the commissioner, Allard reached for his hat. Weston exclaimed in surprise:

"You're leaving, Allard? Why, I thought you would like to be here to meet Cardona and Atherland."

"I must make arrangements to postpone the Bermuda flight," returned Allard, dryly. "If I encounter no complications"—he was glancing at his watch—"I shall be back within an hour."

Immediately after leaving Weston's, The Shadow entered his waiting cab. In Allard's tone, he ordered the driver to take him to Marlborough Place.

FROM that list at Weston's, The Shadow had linked a clue.

There was much of mystery surrounding the deaths of Smedley Breer and Junius Purling. Even the weapons used to slay them were bizarre. Quite as curious were the various items that stood as clues; such as the cigar band and the initialed coin.

One clue, however, had given The Shadow food for deductive thought. That was the unfinished note that had been found on Purling's table. In itself, unattached with other leads, that clue presented an oddity.

Given only a few minutes to live, Junius Purling could hardly have begun a detailed message. The word "We" indicated the beginning of a sentence, and that was an illogical effort. Moreover, the pencil point had broken when Purling pressed it against a spot just to the right of the letter E.

From his observation of the clue, The Shadow had reasoned that the letters $W\ E$ might mark the beginning of a longer word, not the complete pronoun that they represented.

The police believed that Purling had been murdered by Member 10 of the Green Hoods, a man whose identity was known to Purling alone.

What, then, would be more likely than an attempt by Purling, in his death throes, to reveal the name that would eventually be wanted?

In the list at Weston's, The Shadow had seen a name that began with the letters $W\ E$; a name so short that, even in the spasms of death, a man might try to inscribe it. That name was Wenz.

As a result, The Shadow was traveling ahead of the law, to investigate the affairs of Louis Wenz, the one man that tangible evidence had produced as a possible Member 10.

MARLBOROUGH PLACE was a restricted residential zone in a secluded district of Manhattan. The Shadow's cab slowed when it reached a side street that fringed a small park.

Directly opposite was an archway, not wide enough for vehicles. Inside was a widespread flagstone courtyard, surrounded by the houses that formed Marlborough Place.

Before the cab could stop, the door was open. A black-clad figure swung clear; a whispered voice ordered the cab ahead. The vehicle had not rolled from sight when The Shadow, fully cloaked, began his glide across the street.

The Shadow passed through the dim archway. Inside the courtyard, he was forced to a circuitous route; for, at intervals, old-fashioned lamps threw their rays upon the flagstones.

On every side, the houses were fashioned like rows; each was two stories high, with its own front door. Above some of those entrances were other lamps that shone. Those caused The Shadow to continue roundabout tactics.

At times, he kept to the shelter of bushes planted near the center of the court. Choosing other opportunities, he edged into the gloom of house fronts.

All the while, he was noting numbers above the doorways. Pausing at the tiny portico of a darkened house, The Shadow saw the number "17 A" painted on a glass transom above the door.

This was Wenz's house, and it looked deserted. The only sign of recent approach lay in the oozy mud just below the front-door bell. Recent rain had caused that stain on the flagstone; a guarded beam from The Shadow's tiny flashlight showed the deep mark of a square-toed shoe, thrice repeated.

That looked like Cardona's trademark. The Shadow could picture the ace inspector stopping here during the afternoon. Probably Cardona had rung the doorbell several times, then gone, after adding Louis Wenz to the list of Purling's questionable acquaintances.

The door of the house was heavy, and apparently strongly bolted, for The Shadow tried it. The Old English windows were also formidable; The Shadow recalled that their strength had been one of the selling points of these houses. The strips that separated the tiny windowpanes were of metal, not wood.

Homes in Marlborough Place were regarded as burglar-proof. That meant that the rear windows would be quite as difficult of attack as the front ones.

A down movement of The Shadow's light showed a cellar grating that looked as though it could be forced. That offered a bad sequel, however, in case there should be a strong door at the top of the cellar stairs. There was one other possible avenue of entry that afforded possibilities. That was the roof.

PICKING an inset portion of the wall, where Wenz's house joined the next, The Shadow began an upward course through darkness. Rough stones gave him a fair hold; but the most helpful feature was his sideways pressure. The nichelike space was cramped; at times, The Shadow actually elbowed his way toward the roof.

Coming across the edge, The Shadow flattened. The city's glow made the roof visible, despite the blocking hulks of skyscrapers that lined the park beyond Marlborough Place.

Creeping forward, The Shadow was low enough to be partly obscured by a small parapet. He was like a streak of living darkness edging in from outer space. No eyes could have been close enough to observe his progress.

From the moment that he had come over the edge, The Shadow had sighted a goal. It was a trapdoor near the rear edge of the roof, in the shelter of another low parapet. It took The Shadow only a few minutes to reach the opening. Once there, he began silent work with a portable jimmy.

There was an oddity about this trapdoor. It opened in the center. To work on it, The Shadow had to flatten squarely upon it.

From its construction, the trap appeared to hinge upward, in two sections; but to operate either half, it would be necessary first to release the center catch.

With twisting pressure, The Shadow wedged the halves of the flat door until they were the fraction of an inch apart. Pausing, he looked along the roofs, noted the bulges of other traps.

None seemed as large as this one. Ordinarily, that would have demanded investigation; tonight, time was too limited to study such differences.

More important, The Shadow decided, was what might be below. He flicked the flashlight through the space beneath him. He saw the gleam of a metal catch; shifting the flashlight, he spied the dim floor of a space that seemed to be a second-story closet. Pocketing the light, The Shadow worked with the jimmy.

The catch clicked loose—so suddenly, that it spurred the warnings that were already flashing to The Shadow's mind.

With a quick whip, The Shadow tried to fling himself clear of the trapdoor; but he couldn't make the safety of the roof. With the release of the catch, hinges screeched their response.

Those hinges operated downward, not upward. The sections of the trap flopped inward with The Shadow's weight. Thanks to his quick sideways flip, The Shadow had a chance for a decent landing on the floor below.

In one instant, The Shadow was gone from the roof; in the next, he had hit the second floor, with the sections of the trap springing shut above his head. In that same instant, the floor splintered like matchwood, sending The Shadow through.

The flooring was a sham; a mere veneer, ready to smash when a man's weight struck it. So was the bottom of the ground-floor closet, when The Shadow hit there. His plunge didn't stop until he reached the cellar, where he took a hard jolt against solid stone.

In taking the trail ahead of the law, The Shadow had come to an unwanted goal. Dropped to an underground pit, he lay slumped and silent in the very spot that enemies had chosen for his finish!

CHAPTER X
FLARE OF DOOM

SHUDDERING echoes followed The Shadow's crash. The shaft through which he had fallen seemed to cough its hollow sigh of satisfaction at delivering a victim to the pit below.

After those short seconds came long minutes of absolute silence, without a stir from the wall where The Shadow lay. At last, whispery murmurs broke the spell.

The Shadow was not alone in Wenz's cellar. Lurking watchers had heard his plunge. Confabbing among themselves, they were delegating one of their number to approach and make certain of the result.

A man crept forward. A flashlight glinted suddenly upon The Shadow's form. It did not show the face beneath the slouch hat; that was buried beneath a cloaked arm that stretched awry across The Shadow's chest. What the light did show, was the face of the man who carried it.

He was an apish thug, whose ugly eyes peered from beneath a cap visor. His leathery lips showed a jeery smile above the collar of a turtleneck sweater. Shifting the flashlight to his left hand, the thug pulled a knife from beneath his sweater.

Ready for a thrust beneath The Shadow's arm, the apish killer shot a look into the darkness over his shoulder. He whispered to his waiting pals:

"It's The Shadow, all right! I'm giving him the shiv, just in case he ain't already croaked!"

Twisting about, the intended killer tilted the flashlight to the position he wanted; poised his blade for the promised stroke. But it wasn't his hand that responded to his next urge. His lips and eyes acted instead.

A grimace accompanied the knifer's bulgy gaze.

The thug was clamped so he could not move. Up from the floor had come a pair of hands, circling to avoid the flashlight's glow. Viselike, they had plucked the assassin's wrists. His fingers, loosening under torturing pressure, were letting both knife and flashlight go.

Through the riveted thug's brain drilled the reality of something that he couldn't understand.

The Shadow was still alive; not only that, he had his strength. The three-story plunge, calculated at least to stun him, had not produced a visible effect upon the black-clad victim!

No wonder the thug couldn't understand it. The trap had been placed by a supercrook who ruled men of crime; a green-hooded murderer who had put henchmen on tonight's job. The thug was gripped by the thought that The Shadow must have some immunity to neck-breaking falls.

That guess was wrong. The master crook was to blame. In designing those thin-wooded floors, the master criminal had expected them to cleave like tissue. They had broken completely, two in a row; but each had absorbed its share of the shock. Those momentary jerks in The Shadow's fall had been lifesavers.

His plunge had actually been three drops; not one. Each was a matter of eight feet, insufficient to cripple The Shadow, particularly since he had instinctively fought to break the successive plunges. Only the last stage of the drop, with its stony finish, had given The Shadow a jar; and he had rallied from that shock.

SO well had The Shadow recuperated that the present odds were in his favor. The thug's knife no longer gave the fellow the edge. His chance to use it ended when it clattered to the floor. A second later, the flashlight took a similar crash. Hitting on its glass end, it was extinguished.

There was a scuffling sound from the wall; gasps, followed by long panting breaths. Those tokens of a brief struggle were heard by the thug's pals near the door of the cellar room.

They were two, those other watchers. One snarled an oath as he pressed the button of his flashlight. The other hit his hand aside, to stop the glow.

"Lay off the glim!" was the hoarse whisper. "What's the sense giving The Shadow something to shoot at? Leave it to me—I'll get him!"

The pair shifted apart in the darkness. There was silence from The Shadow's wall. Then, with a quick skill, the crook who had spoken performed an unusual move.

In the darkness, he brought out a railroad flare. He ripped the cap from it, reversed it and struck it hard against the end of the long tube.

There was a flash of red light; with it, the thug hurled the flare for the wall. He flung it spiked end first, the red blaze trailing after it.

There was wooden boarding against that wall. The spike hit it full force, burrowed deep. Fixed there, it spread its vivid light, showing the floor and the gaping hole in the ceiling above. There, turned half about, trying to rise against the wall, the two crooks saw the figure of The Shadow.

They themselves were beyond the range of the red flare. They didn't bother about their pal; where he was didn't matter. They wanted to get The Shadow before he turned their way.

Two guns spoke in quick staccato. Crooks snarled their glee as the black-cloaked form slipped downward and collapsed.

Three seconds later, they were above the prone shape, the smoke from their revolvers mingling with the cloudy fumes of the red flare. In that crimson light, their faces had the gloat of demons. One whipped away the cloak; it came loose from

The flare spread its vivid light.... There, half turned about, trying to rise against the wall, the two crooks saw the figure of The Shadow.

the shoulders beneath it. The other snatched the slouch hat. An apish face looked up at them with glassy gaze. It was white, that visage, but the red light made it seem as ruddy as theirs. Despite its tinge, they recognized the face. The man that they had loaded with bullets was their pal who had failed so badly with his knife.

THOSE staring mobsters didn't have to be told the details of The Shadow's deceptive move; how he had half choked their comrade, then left him entangled in the cloak, with the slouch hat planted on his head.

The Shadow, himself, made the sinister announcement that proved him alive and active.

His tone was a sibilant laugh from the very door that the mobsters had left. Though cloakless, The Shadow was completely in darkness, while his enemies were trapped in their own red glare!

If that pair had seen The Shadow when his mockery reverberated, they could have preserved their own useless lives. Though they were killers, The Shadow would have preferred to capture them, rather than deliver doom. The crooks would have known what was due, if they had seen The Shadow's drawn automatics. Those big guns had them covered.

Instead of surrender, the pair went berserk. Perhaps the lurid glow inspired them; possibly each took nerve from the other. Whatever the cause, they charged for the doorway, tugging gun triggers as they came.

The door was clamped. The mobsters had fixed it that way. The Shadow had to shift along a stone-walled side of the room, answering with gun jabs of his own. Those tongues from his automatics angled in toward the wide spurts of the attackers' revolvers.

Thugs sprawled, clipped by burning slugs. Wounds couldn't stop that berserk pair. They aimed for the flashes of The Shadow's guns. Only his quick fade back toward the red flare kept him ahead of their fire.

Forced to that extremity, The Shadow had to drive his shots hard home, as the half-sagged killers took final aim in his direction.

There were no more bullets from the revolvers. The would-be killers spread side by side upon the floor, downed by The Shadow's necessary shots.

The flare that still burned from the wall had brought doom to the thugs who had tried to use it for their own advantage.

RECOVERING his bullet-riddled cloak, The Shadow donned it. Planting his slouch hat on his head, he gripped the boarding of the rear wall, pulled himself up to the shattered ceiling.

Once above that level, he found a slight foothold, worked on the door of the ground-floor closet.

It opened. The glow from the flare below gave The Shadow a view of a stairway. Closing the closet door, he moved through absolute darkness. His goal was the second floor; there, he might find the person that he actually wanted: Louis Wenz.

The trap that had caught The Shadow was in Wenz's own home. The Shadow knew that the man who had planted it had guessed wrong as to its merits. That man, hearing shots below, would have supposed The Shadow dead. Therefore, The Shadow held a new advantage by his present stealth.

He reached the second floor. Without using his flashlight, he groped through darkness, listening for any sounds. There were none; rooms were totally empty.

At last, The Shadow arrived at the door of the only room he had not searched. It was at the back of the second floor; the door was closed.

Noiselessly, The Shadow opened that door. Edging through, he closed it behind him. He groped about the room until he came to the rear wall, where he knew that the broken shaft passed beyond the closet door.

There, The Shadow encountered something on the floor. It gave, like a man's body; but it was heavy. The Shadow pressed the button of his flashlight. It failed; the bulb was broken.

Reaching up, The Shadow felt the knob of the closet door; there was a key there also. Inspired by a quick idea, he unlocked the door and opened it.

Up through the shaft came the fading gleam of the ten-minute flare. Its ruddy reflection stretched ghostly across the floor. It revealed the figure of a man in a dressing gown, whose attire marked him as the owner of this house.

Again that glow was a flare of doom. The eerie light showed a peaked face. Drawn lips, goggly eyes were stiffened in death. A knife was projecting from the victim's breast, but it was no Borgia stiletto. Its wavy blade, partly visible, showed it to be another type of weapon—a Malay creese.

A clotted blot told that death had been delivered long before. That splotch looked colorless; for the hue of blood was lost in the crimson light.

The Shadow's whispered laugh was grim, mirthless. It told that his trail of just vengeance was postponed. The Shadow had found Louis Wenz, Member 10 of the Green Hoods, whom the law suspected as a double killer.

But instead of uncovering a murderer, The Shadow had disclosed another victim of the master assassin who still remained unknown!

CHAPTER XI
THE QUARTER HOUR

WHEN the last tinge of red glare faded like a dying sunset, a new light came to Wenz's death room. The Shadow had found a small desk lamp in the corner. Its bulb threw a direct glow upon the body.

From all appearances, Wenz had been dead for some forty-eight hours. That fitted with The Shadow's immediate theory: that Wenz had died like Purling. Instead of merely eliminating Member 9, a murderer had disposed of Member 10 as well.

That was not a surprise to The Shadow. It only showed that the whole case had graduated from the simple to the complex.

Until the present, The Shadow had been willing to accept the simple setup: the theory that one member of the Green Hoods—namely, Wenz—had murdered another—Purling—to cover his tracks when it came to the major stroke of crime. That stroke had been the murder of Professor Smedley Breer, to acquire the old inventor's Truth Inducer.

Scaled to the complex, the game showed the master hand of an evil craftsman who looked far beyond such primitive methods. Someone, conversant with the organization of Green Hoods, had secretly delved into the affairs of that society.

That master crook had eliminated two human links in the chain—Purling and Wenz—blaming the death of one upon the other. That meant that he could be anyone; perhaps an absolute outsider. Obviously, he had some purpose in killing off two of the Green Hoods, in addition to Breer.

What that purpose was might be as difficult to answer as the finding of the actual murderer.

One thing was evident to The Shadow. Neither Purling nor Wenz had been at the meeting of the Green Hoods, two nights ago. The Shadow had not had time to note the actual number present at that meeting. No one could tell if two members had been missing, with one replaced by a nonmember who had attired himself in green; that was, no one but the murderer himself.

Intuitively, The Shadow found himself thinking of the letters in the mysterious monogram. Those initials, "TMS," had bobbed up with the deaths of Breer and Purling.

Would there be a trace of them here, in the room where Wenz lay dead? This was the chance for The Shadow's advance probe before the law arrived. The cellar shots had not been heard outside; but The Shadow could foresee a quest here, after Atherland went over Cardona's list of Purling's friends.

For his present search, The Shadow allotted

fifteen minutes. After that, it would be time to return to Weston's.

ON Wenz's desk was an old-fashioned typewriter. The Shadow studied it, tested some of the keys. The machine was badly out of line; it would be easy to identify any work done on it.

In the desk drawer, The Shadow found some papers that Wenz had typed. They had to do with the subject of handwriting. With them were letterheads that pronounced Wenz to be an expert in graphology. Doubtless, that was the reason why Wenz had been chosen by Purling to join a society of crime detectors.

If handwriting could show peculiarities of temperament, so could typing. The Shadow had often recognized that fact; the pages that Wenz had typed proved it.

Wenz liked embellishments. He used asterisks (***) instead of dashes (—). His old machine had a key with an exclamation point (!) and he had employed it frequently. That was useful with the ancient typewriter. If Wenz had combined an apostrophe (') with a period (.) beneath it, the two would have been out of line.

After his survey of Wenz's typing style, The Shadow continued his search of the desk drawers. He found some sheets of carbon paper, green in color. All were new; but there were some old ones, crumpled in a wastebasket. As The Shadow stooped for them, he observed something else.

Poked above the inner end of a desk drawer was a sheet of thick writing paper, that had almost dropped from sight. The Shadow brought it out. The paper bore a handwritten scrawl:

> Study of handwriting strikes me as useless. The conclusions that you formed in my case were very unsatisfactory, as well as erroneous.
> T. S.

A low laugh came from The Shadow's lips. This looked like the very clue he wanted. It went with the cigar band and the gold coin. Both of those had borne the monogram "TMS." If "T.S.," whoever he was, had a middle name that began with "M," he could be the unknown owner of the monogram.

Assuming that it was T.M.S. he wanted, The Shadow began a search elsewhere in the room. On a mantel above a gas-log fireplace, he saw the end of a blocky wooden box. It was a card index, almost hidden behind a squatty clock.

Opening the box, The Shadow found cards that bore the names of various persons whose handwriting had been analyzed by Wenz.

Under the letter "S," he found Tobias Sherred, whose address was listed as the Middleton Apartments.

On the card was a date of a month ago. Wenz had typed it; there was a check mark after it. That was probably when Wenz had analyzed Sherred's penmanship.

The Shadow replaced the card index where he had found it. He put the "T.S." note back behind the desk drawer. These were clues for Cardona to find.

In the cases of the telephone memo, the cigar band, the monogrammed coin, The Shadow would have left those clues with the bodies of Breer and Purling, had he had time to examine them on those occasions. Because of forced pressure, The Shadow had kept those bits of evidence. This time, it was unnecessary.

Ten minutes of The Shadow's fifteen had passed. He leaned toward the wastebasket. Suddenly, his cloaked figure became immobile. An instant later, his hand plucked swiftly, turned off the desk lamp.

His keen ears had heard a sound: the opening of the door that formed the entrance from the hallway.

Someone had entered the house; perhaps that person had spotted the glow of light beneath the door of this second-floor room. If so, The Shadow could be due for another battle.

TURNING speedily in the darkness, The Shadow looked toward the door itself.

There was a slight beam of light that entered the hallway from a front window of the house. It was sufficient for The Shadow's eyes. In that luminous trickle, he saw that the menace was real.

The door of the room had opened a single inch. An intruder must have heard the *click* of the lamp switch and guessed the lamp's location. The dim light showed the subdued glitter of a revolver muzzle aimed straight for the spot where The Shadow stood!

Death had become a visible threat. The next moments were terrifically tense, but in them, The Shadow performed a rapid analysis of his dangerous situation.

Another man in his position might have come to one disastrous conclusion; namely, that the person in the hall had spied through before the light was extinguished. The natural move, therefore, would be to make a scramble away from the desk.

The Shadow figured otherwise.

If an enemy had spied him, that revolver would already be cutting loose. Therefore, The Shadow knew that he had not been seen. The lamp's *click* was all that had betrayed his position. Having heard it, the intruder was awaiting another sound as further giveaway.

Slow motion, not speed, was The Shadow's lone course to self-preservation.

Gradually, The Shadow eased from his position. His soundless tactics were accomplishing their wanted result of removing him from the danger zone; but they were not enough. He was planning to reach the door, to deal at close quarters with the intruder.

That would not work with this slow progress. The gunner would suspect The Shadow's shift before the goal was reached, if the period of silence persisted too long. That was why The Shadow paused, after circling halfway to the door.

Deftly, he scaled his useless flashlight through the darkness. The lightless torch made a vague thud on the rug, bounded onward to strike the bare floor with a sliding blow. It wound up with a metallic *clink*. The Shadow had slithered it to the proper target: the wastebasket beside the desk.

The sound was deceptive enough to make it seem an accident. The person at the door supposed that there was a human form still close to the desk. Presumably, a shifting foot had bumped the wastebasket.

Looking toward the door, The Shadow saw a forward nudge of the leveled revolver.

He didn't give the intruder time to speak a challenge or open fire. With a long, silent lunge, The Shadow caught the doorknob with one hand. His side twist whipped the door wide. The upward shove of his other fist fastened it upon the intruder's gun wrist.

The revolver dropped as the struggle began. The Shadow was met by the furious efforts of a game, wiry battler. But with it came two tokens that he recognized. First, the feel of the wrist that he gripped; second, the deep gasp from his adversary's lips. Those changed The Shadow's tactics.

Clamping one arm beneath his opponent's chin, he released his wrist hold. Fingers clawed for The Shadow's hand; all that they gripped was the black glove that covered it. The glove peeled away.

The Shadow caught the plucking fingers. He shoved his bared left hand into the light; with his right, he turned the other fighter's chin, so that eyes saw the glow of the girasol, apparent even in that dimness.

There was a choking gasp from grateful lips. The struggle ended. Guiding his opponent across the room, The Shadow turned on the desk lamp. Its light revealed the person who had so nearly trapped The Shadow without knowing who he was.

The intruder from the dark was one who had made the same mistake before. The Shadow's keen eyes were gazing upon the pale face of Evelyn Rayle.

CHAPTER XII
THE CARBON CLUE

THE girl shuddered when she saw Wenz's body. Despite her trust in The Shadow, there was a momentary flicker of doubt upon her face, emphasized by the tightening of her lips. The circumstances looked bad—finding The Shadow the lone occupant of a room where a man lay stabbed by a wavy-bladed creese.

The flicker changed. Evelyn was realizing that her own presence needed explanation. The Shadow, investigating here, could easily assume that she was a murderess, returned to the scene of a crime.

For a moment, Evelyn was shaky. A soft-whispered laugh dispelled her worry. The Shadow had read the emotions on Evelyn's face. He knew that she would have a sound explanation for her arrival.

There was approval in The Shadow's tone. It made Evelyn remember the reason why she had come. From a fold of her dark-brown dress, the girl produced an envelope.

It was addressed to Professor Smedley Breer. Evelyn had opened the envelope and read the note within it. This was The Shadow's turn to do the same.

Like the envelope, the note was typed in green carbon. From the blockiness of the type, The Shadow knew at once that it had been done on Wenz's machine. The style, too, had Wenz's characteristics.

The note was brief, but pointed:

DEAR PROFESSOR:

I am a Member of the Green Hoods *** Number 10 *** and I must give you warning!

I have spoken unwisely, to an outsider that I thought was a friend. He is shrewd *** he has studied all that I have told him *** he has traced back among our Members.

He says that you are the inventor of the Truth Inducer! I believe *** indeed, I am sure *** that he was testing me when he told me.

I dare not come to the meeting tonight. You must also stay away. Beware! You may be betrayed!

LOUIS WENZ

While The Shadow was studying the note, Evelyn spoke in a low contralto.

"It must have been delivered two nights ago," declared the girl. "Instead of mailing it, Wenz put it in the old mailbox that we no longer use. I thought I heard the doorbell ring tonight; but I must have imagined it, for no one was on the steps. But I looked in the mailbox, on the chance that someone had left a message."

"You found this alone?" inquired The Shadow.

"No. There were also some handbills that boys must have left during the past few days. A blotter from a tailoring concern was one. There were three others, all from a grocery store. One was dated today; another, yesterday; the third was from the day before."

EVELYN paused. Her eyes were meditative.

"They stuff that mailbox often," she recalled. "About once a week, I empty it. Often, during the

THE GREEN HOODS

The Shadow caught the doorknob, whipped the door wide. The upward shove of his other fist fastened it upon the intruder's gun wrist.

day, I have noticed boys delivering circulars. Probably one came along tonight with the last of those grocery advertisements."

"You kept those that you found tonight—"

"Yes. They are on the professor's—on the desk that Professor Breer used."

The Shadow made no other comment. Evelyn became anxious.

"I shouldn't have come here," she admitted. "But the message made me realize that Louis Wenz might not be the murderer that the police want. I thought—that if I talked to him—"

There was an understanding whisper from The Shadow. Evelyn watched him reach into the wastebasket, bring out the sheets of discarded carbon paper. The Shadow had not forgotten that his time was limited.

Some of those carbon sheets were little used. One was almost fresh. The Shadow held it to the light, carbon side toward him, so that the marks of the letters would be plain. It proved to be the sheet used in transcribing the message brought by Evelyn. The Shadow read the reversed words.

There was an oddity, though, to that carbon sheet.

The message was double spaced. Between its lines, crowding them, were other words, almost the same as those in the message. Apparently, the note had been started two or three times, then finally completed.

Sentences were sprinkled with dashes and exclamation points. Those punctuation marks, particularly the irregular ones, made it something of a task to trace the final message from the incomplete ones.

The transcription was clear enough, however, to satisfy The Shadow; particularly since it bore indelible proof that it had been done on Wenz's machine.

Folding the carbon sheet, The Shadow placed it beneath his cloak. This was one clue that he intended to keep safe until the law arrived. Any chance visitor might mull among the old carbon papers; but there was little likelihood that the "T.S." note would be discovered at the back of the desk drawer, except after extensive search.

The Shadow returned the message that bore Wenz's typed signature. He placed it in its envelope, as he gave it to Evelyn.

"Go back to the house," ordered The Shadow. "Wait until you receive a telephone call, that you will recognize by its import. You will be told to find this message over again, along with the handbills. Then you will be free to call the police commissioner."

Evelyn nodded. She understood The Shadow's purpose. By that time, the law would be here at Wenz's. Evelyn would be clear of criticism. No one would suspect that she had paid this unwise visit before the law's discovery of Wenz's body.

THE SHADOW had closed the door of the faked closet; hence, Evelyn did not guess how he had entered. She was explaining her own mode of entry. She had come to the back door to avoid observation, and had found it unlocked.

The girl did not grasp the significance of The Shadow's musing laugh. For once, he had been outguessed on a trivial detail by a shrewd master crook. That adversary had correctly pictured the route that The Shadow would follow if he came to Wenz's.

In trying the front door, ignoring the cellar grating by which thugs had entered below, climbing to the roof and tackling the skylight when he found it, The Shadow had done all that the superfoe expected. He had not gone as far as the unlocked back door.

This was but one evidence of the master criminal's craft. The Shadow anticipated more in the future. This whole trail was tinged with strategy. The Shadow had met with it in seeking Louis Wenz. He would find other complications when he met with Tobias Sherred, the man whose middle initial should be "M."

Like the law, The Shadow was up against a supercrook who knew how to cloud the issue. Clues were plenty, but any one of them might be either false or true. To differentiate between those types of evidence would be the greatest problem on this trail of crime.

Evelyn had a flashlight with her. The Shadow used it to guide the girl down the stairs, out through the unlocked back door. Then came a weird experience. Evelyn found herself moving along the street with The Shadow invisible beside her.

If spies of crime had still been about, they would have sworn that Evelyn Rayle had come and gone alone. In fact, when Evelyn had turned the corner, she found that she *was* alone.

There was a cab coming down the avenue; Evelyn recalled that The Shadow had whispered for her to hail it. But by the time the girl had waved her arm, she was conscious of a void beside her. When the cab pulled to the curb, its lights shone directly upon Evelyn.

Stepping to the cab door, she looked along the

sidewalk. There wasn't a sign of a black-clad figure; not even a fleeting trace of gliding blackness. Knowing which way the cab would swing, The Shadow had made his departure in the opposite direction. He had halted Evelyn at a blackened stretch of this avenue, where traffic was light. He had headed across the street when Evelyn waved. From the opposite side, The Shadow watched the girl ride away.

AFTER that, The Shadow continued his own course. He zigzagged across the street, passed the front of Marlborough Place, to blend with the darkened stretches of the park that lay opposite. On the other side of that grassy square, The Shadow entered his own cab, which was waiting at an isolated spot.

More time had gone than The Shadow had intended. During his study of the death room, he had split an hour into four parts. A quarter for the trip from Weston's; another quarter covered his entry into Wenz's house, with the battle in the cellar.

He had allowed a quarter hour for investigation, reserving the fourth quarter for his return to the commissioner's apartment. Evelyn's advent had forced The Shadow to extend the third period by fully five minutes. But the cab was making up for it, by a whirlwind return trip along its former route.

As the taxi wheeled into Weston's block, The Shadow saw a cab pulling away from the entrance to the apartment house. His black garb packed away beneath the seat of his own cab, The Shadow indulged in a whispered laugh that was confined to his own limited surroundings.

Joe Cardona usually came by subway when he visited the police commissioner. Therefore, the departing cab had brought Lionel Atherland. The Shadow would be present to watch the steps by which the law gained its own trail to Louis Wenz.

The Shadow's cab halted in front of the apartment house. From its interior stepped Kent Allard, the faintest of smiles upon his thin, firm lips. In his pocket was one item that he had kept from his black cloak.

That was the folded carbon paper that The Shadow had brought from the room where Louis Wenz lay dead.

CHAPTER XIII
THE LAW'S TURN

LIONEL ATHERLAND had just begun to study Cardona's special list when Kent Allard was ushered into Weston's office. From behind his desk, the commissioner motioned Allard to be seated. That done, Weston again fixed his gaze upon Atherland, who was seated opposite him.

There was another person present. Joe Cardona was at the side of Weston's desk, watching Atherland hopefully. Lighting a cigarette, Kent Allard became the third witness to the procedure; but his manner made him seem a disinterested party.

Atherland shook his head when he had finished the list of specially chosen names. For once, Cardona's poker-face showed disappointment. Atherland looked at other lists—ones that Cardona didn't consider important.

"There are names that I recognize," declared Atherland, slowly, "but they don't seem likely persons. Have you checked on all these people, Inspector?"

"All except the ones on the final list," returned Cardona. "I've checked on them, too, but haven't located them. I didn't go at it heavy, you understand. Just found out that they weren't at home, or in town."

"I understand."

Atherland picked up the final list again. He stroked his squarish chin, while his grayish eyes concentrated on the selected names. Half aloud, he spoke:

"Junius Purling knew all these men. Purling was Member 9. Therefore, one of these could be Member 10, who murdered Purling. Member 10, who brought me into the Green Hoods as Member 11—"

Atherland's musing tone ended. In louder voice, he added:

"Your logic is good, Inspector. Since you haven't located these men, one should be the murderer. Rather, one *might* be the murderer. But I know none of them."

Atherland's eyes had reached the bottom of the list. They stopped there. There was an interval; Atherland looked up suddenly and snapped his fingers.

"That medallion on Purling's desk!" he exclaimed. "It was a Louis medallion, wasn't it?"

A nod from Cardona. Atherland pointed to the list.

"Here's a man whose first name is Louis. Maybe that's what Purling meant!"

Struck by another idea, Atherland picked up the telephone. He put in a call to an agent who had represented him on lecture tours. While Atherland was thus engaged, Cardona studied the name of Louis Wenz.

"The medal could mean Louis," muttered Cardona. "But what about the last name? Purling would have had to write it—"

A light dawned suddenly. Allard's keen eyes noted that Cardona was catching the right clue.

"That's what Purling was trying to write!" expressed the ace inspector. "That 'WE' wasn't a word. It was the start of—"

Cardona was interrupted by Atherland. The square-jawed man was becoming excited over the telephone. He slammed down the receiver.

"Louis Wenz!" exclaimed Atherland. "He's the man! My agent remembered him—a handwriting expert who furnished me with some lecture material. But it came in through my agent. The size of it is that Wenz knew me, but I didn't know him. That's why he would have picked me as a suitable member for the Green Hoods."

THE group set out for Wenz's house. Remembering the locked front door, Cardona suggested that they try the back on this occasion. They found it unlocked.

That pleased the inspector. It gave the law a good reason to enter without a search warrant. An unlocked door of a darkened house in Marlborough Place was sufficient cause for a police officer to claim that he was looking for suspected burglars.

Cardona went upstairs first. His sudden call was one that The Shadow expected. It told that the inspector had discovered the body of Louis Wenz. From that moment, the problem of Wenz's death became a routine homicide case—until Cardona happened to open the closet door.

That produced another startling find. Detectives had already been summoned to handle various details. Cardona sent them down the shaft. When they came up with news of dead thugs below, Cardona was literally swamped with duties.

Commissioner Weston suggested that the others wait on the lower floor. While Lionel Atherland sat smoking a cigar in the downstairs living room, Kent Allard went out for a stroll. That was when he made a telephone call to Evelyn Rayle, using the tone of The Shadow.

Later, Allard was on hand to hear Cardona's summary of crime. In many details, the ace inspector's conclusions fitted with The Shadow's own.

"The surgeon's report shows that death occurred two days ago," stated Cardona. "Wenz was probably murdered about the time that Purling was. Somebody broke into that chain of Green Hoods, and here's the proof of it."

Cardona produced the message that Evelyn had shown to The Shadow. She had phoned Weston's apartment and the call had been transferred here, to Wenz's. Cardona had sent for the typed note.

"It was done on Wenz's typewriter," declared Cardona. "That's plain enough. What's more, Wenz typed it himself. You can tell that by the crazy way he punctuated it—the same as in these articles he wrote on the subject of graphology."

Changing his subject temporarily, Cardona gestured to the opened closet door.

"Wenz may have fixed that trap for his own protection," asserted the inspector, "or else it was put here afterward. Anyway, the murderer used it to snag somebody."

By "somebody," Cardona meant The Shadow, although he didn't say so. Detectives had found the door in the cellar well-jammed, but not locked. It looked as if the fighter who had battled the hoodlums had later made his way out through the cellar grating.

"Those gorillas were killers," added Cardona, "and they got what was coming to them. The only bad angle"—Joe was grim as he mentioned it—"is that the Green Hood has probably got a lot more like them."

In speaking of the Green Hood, Cardona meant the triple murderer. As an organization, the original Green Hoods were defunct. Their garb, formerly the mark of loyalty to the law, had become a badge of evil; the mask of a master murderer.

"HERE are the only clues that count," declared Cardona, pointing to the desk. "First, this knife." He picked up the rugged Malay creese that had been taken from Wenz's body. "It's a curio, like that Borgia stiletto and the Baby Paterson that we haven't found yet.

"Some collector had those weapons once; the same as the King Louis medallion. You were wrong on that, Mr. Atherland." Cardona turned to the lecturer. "At least, I think you were. My hunch is that Purling knew who the murderer really was. He pulled out the Louis medallion to show it belonged to the guy. In trying to write 'Wenz,' he was giving another clue.

"Don't forget, there was a locket—or something of the sort—snagged off the end of Purling's watch chain. So the man we're looking for is a collector, who gave those things to Purling. Somebody who Purling knew, just like Wenz did. I've got an idea that his name is Tobias Sherred."

From his pocket, Cardona brought one of the larger lists of Purling's acquaintances that The Shadow had not scanned. Running his finger down the line of names, Cardona came to the one he wanted.

"Tobias M. Sherred," repeated Cardona, not noting the sparkle that came to Allard's eyes at mention of the initial "M." "Not many people have heard of him; but he's worth a lot of dough. I checked on him, when I listed him today.

"He's gone in for all sorts of hobbies, Sherred has. He drops them, though, so he doesn't rate high in any of them. But Purling knew him, and so did Wenz. Whoever went through the desk drawers here wasn't smart enough to see the note that slipped down in back of the desk drawer."

From the desk, Cardona picked up the scrawl that was signed with the initials "T.S."

"He missed this, too." Cardona lifted the little card index. "It was on the mantel, behind the clock.

It's got Sherred listed in it, with his right address: the Middleton Apartments.

"Suppose we go up and talk to Sherred." Cardona turned to Weston. "Maybe if we ask him what he knows about the Truth Inducer, he'll say that collecting freak inventions is his hobby. And maybe he won't!"

Cardona's sarcasm was significant. It meant that he had labeled Tobias Sherred as a likely murderer whose real hobby was crime. Moreover, he felt that the sooner Sherred was investigated, the better.

Weston concurred with that unspoken opinion. He asked if there were any other clues; when Cardona shook his head, the commissioner decided to start at once for Sherred's apartment.

LIONEL ATHERLAND had a question. He wanted to make sure that his invitation to join the Green Hoods had actually come from Louis Wenz. It had; Cardona proved it by producing the paper in question. Its type was identical with the blocky letters of Wenz's machine.

Kent Allard had a question also, but it was unnecessary to ask it. The Shadow's interest concerned the wastebasket; whether or not Cardona had considered used carbon sheets as items of consequence. It was obvious that the inspector had not.

Those discarded carbons were as good as forgotten. Therefore, The Shadow decided to retain the one that he had reclaimed.

Like Atherland, The Shadow accepted Weston's invitation to go along to Sherred's apartment. The commissioner felt that the visit should not look too much like an official call. He indicated that the presence of two ordinary citizens would counterbalance himself and Cardona.

They waited long enough for Cardona to classify the exhibits; some he intended to carry with him, while others—like Wenz's typewriter—were to go to headquarters. That done, the four set out in the commissioner's official car.

Though Allard's expression was disinterested, he felt a keen relish for the coming expedition. It fitted definitely with The Shadow's plans, this visit to Tobias Sherred.

The clues that pointed to Sherred were definite, though slender and fragmentary. The Shadow was not willing to share Cardona's hunches on the merit of present evidence. He, though, more than Cardona, had reasons to want an interview with Tobias Sherred.

Those reasons were The Shadow's own clues: the cigar band from Breer's wallet; the engraved coin from Purling's watch chain; the initialed note in Wenz's desk, which had eventually been found by Cardona. Thus, The Shadow had three links to Tobias Sherred, in contrast to the one that Cardona had acquired.

Intent though he was, The Shadow would not forget his guise of Kent Allard. His part was to remain placid, his features immobile. Yet all the while, The Shadow would be the keenest of the four observers who were soon to witness Sherred's reactions.

However roundabout the trail might be, it would bring The Shadow closer to the ruthless murderer who had acquired sole use to the insidious title The Green Hood.

CHAPTER XIV
THE HALTED TRAIL

THE Middleton Apartments were old-fashioned, and by no means pretentious. It seemed odd, at first, that a wealthy man like Tobias Sherred would live there; but the reason for his choice of residence was explained when the visitors reached his apartment.

Sherred's establishment took up the entire tenth floor. It was actually eight apartments converted into one. That meant a heavy rental, even at the Middleton.

An elderly servant conducted the party through a succession of long corridors, the floors thick with valuable Oriental rugs. They reached a large reception room as lavishly carpeted as the halls. The walls, too, were hung with expensive rugs; a high-priced collection in themselves.

There, the old servant met a dapper Japanese valet, told him that callers were here to see Mr. Sherred. The Jap left to summon his master.

After a few minutes, ponderous footsteps and a low, rumbly voice announced Sherred's arrival. The man himself stepped in through a doorway. Bulky of build, he surveyed his visitors with sharp gaze. There was antagonism in the glare of eyes that peered from beneath bristly brows, a bluff look on the man's wide, paunchy face.

In booming voice, Sherred demanded to know the reason for the visit. Commissioner Weston countered that by introducing the other visitors.

Some of Sherred's challenge faded when he found that Allard and Atherland were not representatives of the law. He had heard of Allard and said so, while he was shaking hands. At the same time, The Shadow felt the power of Sherred's grip; observed the close scrutiny that the big man gave him.

There was nothing, though, in the impassive attitude of Kent Allard that could have turned Sherred's thoughts to new suspicion. Allard's gaze, though casual, enabled him to form his own impressions of Sherred.

The big-browed man was much shrewder than

his surface showed. The Shadow was convinced that the law would find trouble in pumping much from Tobias Sherred.

It was Joe Cardona who put the reason for the visit, while Sherred was passing a box of cigars.

"We're looking for information about a man named Junius Purling," stated Cardona. "We understand that he was a friend of yours, Mr. Sherred."

"Purling?" Sherred boomed the name, then shook his head. "Never heard of him!"

"He was murdered, two nights ago."

"Murdered?" Big brows bristled. "All the more reason why I probably did not know him. My acquaintances"—Sherred's deep tone was biting—"are not in the habit of getting themselves killed!"

Cardona considered the situation, then remarked as a matter of information:

"Purling represented a safe manufacturer. Our records show that he installed a wall safe here. We know, also, that he paid other visits to this apartment."

SHERRED'S expression changed. It showed a recollection, while his fingers slowly drew the band from his cigar. Others were doing the same with their cigars, and Allard's eyes, almost absent-minded, were noting his own.

That cigar band bore the identical monogram that had been on the band in Breer's wallet.

His eyes changing direction, The Shadow watched as Sherred spoke.

"There was such a man," rumbled Sherred. "But I did not remember his name. Calvin"—this was to the old servant, who stood with the valet, inside the door—"do you remember the man who installed the wall safe here, and later paid visits to see if it was satisfactory?"

"I do, sir."

"Can you recall his name?"

"It was Purling, sir. Junius Purling."

"That settles it." Sherred smiled broadly, gave a shrug as he turned to Cardona. "I did know Junius Purling. I had merely forgotten it."

There was triumph in Cardona's grim expression. He heard Weston's undertone: "Ask him about Wenz"—but Cardona had other ideas first. Joe questioned:

"You collect coins, Mr. Sherred?"

"Yes," rumbled Sherred. "I am a numismatist."

"There are medallions in your collection?"

Sherred shook his head.

"No longer," he replied. "I disposed of them. Ishi"—he turned to the Jap—"unlock the door of the numismatics room. This way, gentlemen."

SOON they were in a room where glass-topped boxes showed lines of rare coins set in a velvet backing. There was a wood-topped table in the corner.

Observed by all, Cardona drew Sherred there. Before the big man's eyes, Cardona produced the Louis medallion and clattered it to the table.

"Did you own one of these, Mr. Sherred?"

Sherred's eyes went rigid. Mechanically, he placed his cigar between his lips, picked up the medallion and examined it.

"I did have such a medallion," he admitted. "But I disposed of it, along with others."

"Is this the one?" quizzed Cardona.

"I could not say," returned Sherred. "Who gave you this medal, Inspector?"

"It was found in Purling's room," informed Cardona. "I understand, Mr. Sherred, that these medals are quite rare. No coin dealer in New York knows where another could be acquired."

For a moment, Sherred's look wasn't pleasant. It changed when he issued a deep-throated laugh.

"Because there is no demand for medallions," he declared. "Bah! I could pick up a dozen of these, through foreign dealers. This never came from my collection!"

"Nor the locket that Purling wore on his watch chain?"

Cardona thought that he had slipped home a startling thrust. He was wrong. Sherred gave an incredulous look, then delivered a guffaw.

"A locket?" His amusement increased. "I never collected such trinkets, Inspector! Look"—he opened the table drawer—"here is the list of my medallions. Learn for yourself what items I once owned."

The Louis medallion was on the list, but there was no mention of a locket. Cardona passed the list to Weston, who showed it to the others. As the commissioner checked each item, The Shadow looked for one he expected, and saw it.

The list of sold items included a monogrammed ten-dollar gold piece.

Noting Sherred, The Shadow speculated on what the man's reaction would have been had Cardona mentioned a gold piece instead of a locket. That opportunity was past; but other developments were due. Cardona was asking Sherred if he knew Louis Wenz.

That started another headshake, which ended abruptly when Sherred rumbled:

"You mean the crank who studied handwriting?"

"That's the man," returned Cardona. "I believe you sent him this note."

With that, Cardona produced the paper that was signed with the initials "T.S."

"I sent it," admitted Sherred. "But I cannot see why it has importance. As I said, Wenz is a crank! If he gave you this—"

"He didn't give it to us."

"I don't quite follow you, Inspector."

"Perhaps you will, Mr. Sherred, when I tell you that we found Wenz murdered—like Purling—and that the two knew each other!"

ANOTHER of Cardona's shots home failed to register as he expected. Sherred took the news of Wenz's death in rather disinterested fashion. With a shrug, he suggested that they go back to the reception room.

"Wait a moment, Mr. Sherred." Cardona was becoming blunt. "I've got another question. Do you collect antique weapons?"

"I do. I have an excellent collection."

"Could we see them?"

"Certainly. Ishi, conduct us to the weapons room."

The Jap started to say something. Sherred rumbled angrily. Obediently, Ishi led the way out through the hall. He unlocked a door, stepped into a room and turned on a light. Sherred, in the hallway, bowed his visitors into the room.

There was a surprise when they entered. There wasn't a sign of any sort of weapon in the room. Instead, the walls were lined with swinging frames displaying mounted sets of postage stamps.

"Why did you bring us here, Ishi?" demanded Sherred, angrily. "This is the philatelic room!"

"One time, sir, it was the room with weapons."

"But they aren't here any longer—"

"Maybe you remember, sir"—Ishi was bowing as he spoke—"but you have sold weapons, long time ago."

Sherred showed bewilderment, then leaned against the doorway and gave a long laugh at his own expense.

"So I did!" he exclaimed. "Three years ago, I parceled away the whole lot. I remember what a time that chap Radcorn had, appraising those curios. He had to make a certified list describing every item, to satisfy the purchasers."

Mention of a list was Cardona's meat. He asked Sherred where it was. Sherred replied that he did not have a copy. He had left that entirely to Radcorn, his secretary at the time.

"Don't ask me what the items were," Sherred told Cardona. "I forget a hobby as soon as I drop it."

"Maybe there's one item you'd remember," insisted Cardona. "That was a Borgia stiletto with a jeweled handle."

"Jewels? I collect them. I have a gem room—"

"We're talking about a stiletto, Mr. Sherred. You don't remember it?"

Sherred shook his head, as if a memory feat would overtax him.

"What about guns?" demanded Cardona. "Did you have a baby Paterson revolving pistol with loading lever? Caliber .28?"

"I had hundreds of guns," retorted Sherred. "All antiques. How could I remember the one you mention?—that is, assuming that it was in my collection."

"Get back to knives, then. I want to know if you owned a Malay creese—"

Sherred interrupted Cardona with a basso objection.

"I've had enough of this folly, Inspector!" boomed the bushy-browed collector. "Get to the point! What is this all about?"

BLUNTLY, Cardona told him. He specified that three murders had been done with the weapons mentioned. When Joe added that the case concerned the Green Hoods, Sherred showed understanding; but even that disappointed Cardona. Sherred promptly claimed that his only knowledge of the organization had been gleaned from recent newspaper accounts.

"You were looking for Member 10, I understand," said Sherred, at last. "From what you tell me, you found him tonight. When you discovered Louis Wenz, you merely landed a dead murderer instead of a live one.

"Since he was the one Green Hood you wanted, it is obvious that he stabbed Breer with the stiletto that you mention. Also that he murdered Purling with the antique pistol. As for Wenz, he was hounded so closely that he obviously committed suicide."

The final remark roused Cardona's sarcasm.

"You've got something, Mr. Sherred," voiced Joe. "That's a swell theory—a man committing suicide by stabbing himself with a Malay creese! Only, you've forgotten something. He'd have needed a helper for that little job. I suppose you'd class the guy that knifed Wenz as an accessory to a suicide."

Cardona's eyes were hardened; they were fixed steadily on Sherred, all the while the inspector spoke. Suppressed rage showed on Sherred's lips, then changed to a bitter smile.

"Come!" snapped Sherred. "I have something to show all of you!"

This time, it was Sherred who led the way, through a new array of corridors. Only Allard recognized where that course would end. His thin lips had the semblance of a smile when Sherred opened a door and gestured the callers through.

They stepped into another corridor. From behind them, Sherred spoke testily, as they turned to face him.

"Solve your own riddles!" jabbed the big-voiced collector. "Should you need to visit me again, Commissioner, or you, Inspector, I would suggest that you telephone and arrange an appointment in advance. You will always find me here. Goodnight!"

A bulky hand slammed the door. The callers heard the clatter of a bolt. Weston looked around; so did Cardona. For the first time, they realized where they were. Tobias Sherred had ushered them out through the side door of his apartment.

Stormily, Cardona started to hammer at the door. He stopped when Weston commented:

"We must wait, Cardona. We shall need more evidence before we can handle Tobias Sherred."

For once, Commissioner Weston had spoken an opinion with which The Shadow agreed. There was still a trail to follow, another clue to find, before either The Shadow or the law could demand a showdown.

CHAPTER XV
THE FOURTH STUDIO

JOE CARDONA did not visit Tobias Sherred the next day, but he did the nearest thing to it. He called Sherred by telephone five times. Commissioner Weston had granted Cardona that permission.

With Sherred lay the reason for the five calls. The irate collector was friendly enough to open conversation every time he heard Cardona's voice; but as soon as he answered a few questions, he became savage and slammed down the receiver.

Cardona had to call up again and again, to resume the quiz where he had dropped it. In this piecemeal fashion, the ace inspector finally gathered all the answers that he wanted. Those went into a report sheet that lay on Cardona's desk. Soon afterward, the full details reached The Shadow.

The data were acquired through Fritz, the headquarters janitor, who always mopped up Cardona's office after five o'clock. On this day, however; the office was mopped twice; once when Cardona was absent, again when he was there.

It wasn't Fritz who did the second job. It was The Shadow. Clad in overalls, shambling about with a dull look on his made-up face, The Shadow produced a perfect impersonation of the real Fritz.

The Shadow was cloaked in black when he arrived in his sanctum later. There, beneath the blue light, he transcribed the questions that Cardona had put to Sherred, with the answers that the wealthy hobbyist had given.

Sherred accounted for his actions on the night of the triple murder. He had gone out at seven o'clock to dine alone at a little restaurant. He remembered the name of the place, which was quite a feat on his part, as it was his habit to dine at many different restaurants.

After dinner, Sherred had gone back to his apartment; he had left there at about quarter of nine, to attend a weekly directors' meeting at a downtown bank. The meeting had been scheduled for nine-thirty. Sherred claimed that be had arrived there early.

Checking on the statements, Cardona had called the restaurant that Sherred named. No one was willing to swear that Sherred had been there that night between the hours of seven and eight.

In his report, Cardona summed it that Sherred could have visited both Wenz and Purling, prior to half past eight on the night that they had died; also, that Sherred could have been at the meeting of the Green Hoods when Breer was murdered.

Since the professor's house was on the way downtown, there would have also been time for Sherred to stop there a while, before continuing to the bank directors' meeting.

Therefore, Sherred could have been the Green Hood who had engaged in murderous crime; a pretender, posing as a member of the organization. Wenz's warning note to Breer had spoken of an insidious outsider, and Sherred fitted that description.

Classing Sherred as the green-hooded murderer was a step; proving him such was another. It was a long skip between those steps; too long a hop for Joe Cardona.

The ace inspector had seen a way to bridge the gap. He had tried to make Sherred cough up a few answers on another subject. Cardona's questions concerned a man who had been mentioned by Sherred; the former secretary, whose name was Radcorn.

Sherred knew nothing about Radcorn; at least, so he said. The fellow's first name was Holton; he had left Sherred's employ for reasons of his own. Cardona, however, would not be satisfied until he found Radcorn. He was already taking steps to locate the fellow.

So was The Shadow.

ON the sanctum table lay reports from searching agents. They gave details regarding several Radcorns. One name particularly interested The Shadow. It was that of Arthur Radcorn.

The man had written several articles on travel. In one of his early efforts—a mere squib, written three years ago—he had used the name Arthur H. Radcorn. If that "H" stood for Holton, he could be the man who might furnish evidence.

The Shadow had already observed the importance of a middle initial, in the case of Tobias M. Sherred.

Tracing Radcorn was a problem in itself; but The Shadow had worked it through Clyde Burke. The newspaper reporter knew many writers.

Through a chain of inquiries, he learned that Radcorn had made trips to Mexico with an artist friend; that Radcorn, when in New York, frequently lived at the artist's studio.

The Shadow had the studio's location. It was on the top floor of an old apartment house in a secluded neighborhood; the fourth in line from the north side of the building. Adjoining the old apartment house was a newer one, two stories higher.

On The Shadow's table lay a plan of the studio building. It presented problems of its own. Reaching the building directly from the street was difficult, for there were empty houses across the way that offered excellent spots of ambush.

The roof was a possible route of entry, despite its narrow ledge. The difficulty there was that a skylight had to be used; once inside, an intruder could be easily trapped. The studios had high ceilings; it would be a long drop through.

Moreover, the roof itself offered places where lurkers could be in wait.

Remembering his previous experiences with thugs who served the Green Hood, The Shadow decided upon deceptive tactics. Not only did he want a chance to search Radcorn's place before the law did; he preferred to have it look as though his quest had failed. That meant a two-person job. Only one of The Shadow's agents was light enough in build, wiry enough in action, to handle his part of the task. That agent was "Hawkeye," who spotted crooks in the underworld.

Tonight, as on other nights, Hawkeye was busy trying to locate the place where the Green Hood had taken Evelyn Rayle to quiz her with the Truth Inducer.

A laugh whispered from The Shadow's lips. He saw a way to keep Hawkeye on the job. He had thought of a substitute, who possessed the needed qualifications, including grit.

The Shadow contacted Burbank, held a brief conversation across the wire that connected with the sanctum. Late reports came in from agents. Those received, The Shadow extinguished the sanctum light. A *swish* betokened his departure.

IN the quiet atmosphere of Breer's old house, Evelyn Rayle was spending a dreary evening. She was still living there, at the law's order, with a plainclothesman on duty outside the house.

Joe Cardona had an idea that the murderous Green Hood might make another trip to Breer's, although no evidence pointed to it. Cardona simply went on the theory that any bet was worthwhile.

Evelyn was reading a magazine. The lamp threw a glow across her shoulder, to form a large circle on the floor. Beyond that, the fringes of the room blended with gloom. The door was no more than a whitish outline.

Unseen by Evelyn, that door moved inward.

There was something eerie in the motion. There was no sound; no token of a living presence. The door itself might have been a pallid ghost, for it swung slowly back to its original position and closed tightly without a *click* of the knob.

A sudden tenseness gripped Evelyn. The girl stared toward the door; she couldn't see it. Gloom seemed to cloud it; then the upper portion of the door frame appeared as a blurred line. The sight was fantastic, especially when more of the door came into view.

It was as if someone had stretched an invisible hand to peel away a curtain of airy blackness!

Dropping the magazine, Evelyn gripped the chair arm. Still staring at the door, she came half to her feet. At that moment, there was a stir close beside her; but Evelyn didn't hear it. She was too intent in her gaze, wondering why she could at last see all the door but no sign of the cause that had obscured it.

A form rose beside the chair. Into the lamplight came a long-fingered hand. It rested upon Evelyn's sleeve, clamped there with a touch that was firm, but not heavy.

From Evelyn's lips came a gasp, as her eyes went downward. A deep sparkle met her stare. She saw a glimmering jewel that shone with purplish hue. From its depths came fiery bursts, that changed the hue to a deep crimson tint.

The Shadow's girasol!

Recognition of that symbol turned Evelyn's gasp into a relieved sigh. The girl's head raised. Her eyes met those of The Shadow. She saw orbs that reflected the light with as strange a burn as that of the fire opal.

Lips spoke. They were hidden by the folds of an upraised cloak collar; but Evelyn knew that tone. Sinister, a terror to men of crime, the voice of The Shadow carried confidence to those who stood for justice.

Each word implanted itself upon Evelyn. Her own eyes sparkled. The Shadow was bringing her an opportunity to aid in finding the Green Hood's trail. If all went well, The Shadow would be ready for his final moves against a master murderer.

Evelyn's nod was eager in its response. She was willing to aid; prepared to obey every command.

THE SHADOW stepped toward the window. Evelyn followed; the sash was open when she reached there, although she had not heard it being raised. The Shadow's hand helped her across the sill. Clad in her dark suit, Evelyn was well-blended with the outside gloom.

A whispered word—The Shadow's gloved hand gripped Evelyn's wrist. She, in turn, took a similar clasp upon The Shadow's arm. Locked tightly, Evelyn let herself swing outward, using her free hand to guide along the house wall.

That trip downward was incredible. It did not stop at the limit of The Shadow's arm reach. He, too, was over the window ledge, letting his own body downward, while his free hand gripped a hold.

Though his method seemed effortless, Evelyn recognized the strength that it represented. By a mere finger clutch, The Shadow was supporting both his own weight and the girl's.

Another low-toned order. Evelyn pressed outward from the wall, released her own grip. That was the signal. The Shadow's gloved fingers relaxed. Easily, Evelyn dropped the remaining distance to the courtyard, landing lightly.

Soon, The Shadow was beside her. He guided the girl to the rear street, where they boarded a parked cab. There was a trip of a dozen blocks; the taxi halted behind an apartment house.

Picking a path with a tiny flashlight, The Shadow took Evelyn through a basement doorway, into a service elevator.

When they reached the top, there was a metal stairway to the roof. The Shadow's light went out before they met the night air. Once on the roof, he warned for silence in a whisper that Evelyn barely heard.

Crouched against a parapet, The Shadow turned Evelyn's chin, so she could gaze to the next roof, two floors below this level. There, raised slightly above a ledge, was a sloped surface that showed a line of skylights; some with a glow, others dark oblongs of glass.

Evelyn's eyes were squarely toward the fourth. It was darkened, but plainly seen in reflected glow from the city. The Shadow had already mentioned what that skylight meant. It was the entrance to the fourth studio; the one that was often occupied by a man named Radcorn.

The search of that studio was to be Evelyn's task. In a whisper almost as low as The Shadow's, the girl repeated her readiness to continue to the goal.

CHAPTER XVI
THE GREEN MENACE

THE first test proved Evelyn's mettle. To reach the lower roof, The Shadow had to let her down from the parapet, as he had done from the window of Breer's house. The value of the rehearsal was evident to Evelyn as soon as she was over the edge. If she hadn't had proof of The Shadow's ability, her nerve might have vanished.

There was an eight-foot gap between the higher building and the one that adjoined it!

The Shadow had cut some of that space, for he was hanging from the cornice, with Evelyn swaying below him. Smooth muscles produced a pendulum motion; with every swing, Evelyn came closer to the other roof.

Seconds seemed interminable; Evelyn wondered if The Shadow's strength could continue. Uncertainly, she began to loose her fingers from the arm above her.

The Shadow's whisper brought her new confidence.

"Wait—until you are sure."

A few more swings, Evelyn gave the signal. The Shadow kept his grip for another swing in the darkness. Timed to perfection, his hand let Evelyn's wrist go free.

The girl felt the outward impetus of that drop. It swung her through the air over the intervening space. It was a six-foot sweep with a safe landing past the edge of the farther roof.

With both hands, The Shadow gave an inward swing that took his body beneath the cornice. A long reverse snap, and he catapulted himself outward and backward.

Evelyn caught a fleeting flash of his descending shape as it precipitated toward her. Half flung about, The Shadow caught the very roof edge as he landed beside the girl.

It was some distance to the skylights. They crossed a flat space, where chimneys loomed like scarecrow sentinels. The Shadow edged Evelyn beneath a string of radio aerials. They went under a squatty water tower supported by three metal legs.

To Evelyn, that hulk seemed a monstrous creature ready to scoop them in its maw.

That fantasy ended. They were on the ledge, crouched low in the darkness. The Shadow worked Evelyn past a lighted skylight. The others were less troublesome; the trip seemed serene when they reached the slanted window that covered the fourth studio.

The Shadow jimmied the glass barrier in silent style. He flicked a flashlight into the space below, saw the dusty floor of the studio. The descent looked safe for Evelyn. Again, The Shadow's strong arm swung the girl into space. But this drop was a simple one.

Evelyn took The Shadow's flashlight with her. Once satisfied that all was clear, she blinked a signal. The skylight lowered above her. Evelyn heard it latch in place.

The girl knew The Shadow's reason for that precaution. Its value was proven, a few minutes later. From his position on the ledge, The Shadow heard the sneaky tread of rubber-soled shoes coming along from the opposite direction. He pulled himself up the sloped roof, flattened there in inconspicuous position.

Halted beside the skylight of Radcorn's studio, the soft-shoed prowler made an inspection of the catch. Satisfied that no one had entered, the guard made a return journey to the other end of the ledge.

Thanks to his plan of accompanying Evelyn, The Shadow had covered the act of entry.

THE watcher on the roof hadn't caught the glimmer of Evelyn's flashlight, for the girl was using it guardedly, as The Shadow had instructed her.

Keeping the light muffled, Evelyn covered the entire studio but found nothing of value. The place looked as though it had been deserted for months.

There was a door at the front. The Shadow had told Evelyn that it led into a little hallway forming an entrance to the studio. Extinguishing the flashlight, Evelyn started to open that door. She made the move cautiously, which was fortunate.

The door was only open a crack when Evelyn caught the blink of another flashlight. She heard the rustle of papers.

Someone was in that entry, apparently engaged in a search of his own!

Evelyn sneaked back to the skylight. As she watched the dull glow above it, she saw a stretch of darkness glide across. That was an intermittent signal promised by The Shadow. A blink of her light, he would open the skylight again.

Louder crinkles from the entry made Evelyn wait. She sensed that the other person's search was finished. It would be better to let him start away, for The Shadow wanted secrecy.

A thud of the outer door told Evelyn that the little hallway was vacated.

Eagerly, the girl headed to the spot. Her flashlight showed that the entry had a tiny closet, with no door. In it, Evelyn spied a fair-sized cardboard box scrawled with the name "Radcorn." It contained an odd assortment of letters and old papers.

Though the search seemed useless. Evelyn made it. The mixed papers weren't many. It wouldn't take long to go through them. As it happened, Evelyn took only half a minute; for she didn't have to complete the search.

Almost immediately, she came upon a manila envelope with the name "Sherred" typed in a corner. Along with a few letters that were within it, Evelyn found a list that bore a notary's seal. The date, the items given, proved this to be the very document she wanted.

Evelyn had found the certified list of Sherred's collection of antique weapons!

Tucking the precious paper in a fold of her dress, Evelyn started back toward the skylight. She was as eager to leave as she had been to come. She didn't know or care why the previous searcher had interrupted his own task; she merely wanted to be gone before he returned.

Evelyn didn't realize a mistake that she had made. In the studio itself, she had been cautious with the flashlight. She had not been so careful in the hallway.

The outer door had a wide crack beneath it; that was something she had noticed, but had not thought about. Evelyn remembered it, five seconds later.

As she blinked for The Shadow, she heard another thump of the outer door. She put away the flashlight, made a quick turn toward the little hallway.

The inner door swung open; a hand pressed a light switch. Lamps came on; they weren't bright, but their glow was sufficient for Evelyn to recognize the foe who had returned.

Framed in the open doorway stood the Green Hood!

SOMEHOW, Evelyn recognized the insidious eyes that peered through the slitted mask. There was enough ugliness in them to identify this intruder as the same murderer who had once captured her. His forced voice grated on her ears, as harshly as it had before.

"Again you have mixed in my affairs"—the Green Hood emphasized those words with a gesture of his gun—"and this time, you will pay the penalty! Try to escape, if you can. It will be no use!

"You came through the skylight." The murderer's comment was a sneer. "Very well, return by it. This time, you will not cross the roof unnoticed. My watchers will hear my signal. Their bullets will riddle you. Unless"—the Green Hood gave a vicious laugh—"unless I should prefer to drop you first!"

Evelyn was staring at the killer's gun. It was the antique pistol that he always carried. Seeing the girl's gaze, the Green Hood forgot the skylight. He drew closer.

"Yes"—his hiss was muffled by the hood over his head—"this gun is best. It means more bullets for the police to study. New mystery, to find you dead in this place—"

This time, it was the Green Hood's mistake that brought an interruption. Just as Evelyn had forgotten the outer door, so did the murderer ignore the skylight. Before his finger could press the trigger of the old revolving pistol, the skylight whipped upward.

In from the darkness, a gloved fist shoved an automatic. Challenging lips uttered a shivery defy that the Green Hood had heard before. He sped a look upward, then made a break for the door, diving as he went. Caught completely off guard, the Green Hood wasn't risking battle with The Shadow.

The space of one short second held the fate of the murderer. In that interval, The Shadow stabbed one shot for the killer's back. By all rights and averages, that should have brought the master crook's doom. Luck, alone, made the Green Hood the exception to the almost certain rule.

Because of Evelyn, The Shadow shifted aim. The girl was too close to the path of fire. That, coupled with the killer's chance side-twist, enabled the Green Hood to reach the safety of the little hallway.

The murderer turned; once he was outside the studio, he hoped for a shot at Evelyn. He took too much time about it. The Shadow was swinging down from the skylight.

Evelyn heard his quick command, caught the outstretched arm. The Green Hood saw the girl hoisted to safety.

Savagely, the murderer fired; but belatedly. Again, The Shadow swung inward as the killer paused. A .45 tongued; but the Green Hood hadn't waited. He was clattering down the stairway of the apartment house.

ON the roof ledge, Evelyn gave quick warning to The Shadow. The men the Green Hood had mentioned were on hand. They fired as they came along the ledge, but their shots were too hasty.

The Shadow swung up to meet the spurts of revolvers. His automatic answered.

One thug took a clipping shot, made a long sprawl over the edge, shrieking as he went.

Another slumped; clawed vainly for a hold. Before anyone could reach him, he took a slow-motion slide over the same roof edge.

The others—four of them—were on the run for distant chimneys. Evelyn saw one flatten like a puppet; another did the same, a moment later. Each mobster's flounder was timed to a spurt from The Shadow's gun.

Even with thugs scattered and fightless, departure by the high roof was no longer wise. The Shadow swung Evelyn down into the studio, then followed.

As they headed for the stairs, the quick-witted girl remembered the list that she had found in Radcorn's papers. She thrust the precious paper into The Shadow's hand.

There was excitement when they reached the street. The Green Hood was on the curb by the next corner, ready to jump into an automobile. He was firing at two policemen who had spotted him. Taking instant aim, The Shadow fired.

The range was too long for such a hurried shot, but the bullet came within an inch of the murderer's ear. He heard it whistle past; he saw The Shadow. Leaping into the car, he fired a wild shot as he went.

That was the Green Hood's last bullet. Madly, he flung his antique pistol at an officer who tried to grab him. The car sped around the corner; a fireplug stopped the bullet that The Shadow fired at the gasoline tank.

Moe's cab wheeled into view. The Shadow's clever cabby was always Johnny-on-the-spot. The Shadow put Evelyn aboard; as the cab spun away, he made his own path through the darkness, picking the space between the two apartment buildings.

Crime had reared up again tonight. Crooks had tried to down The Shadow, to their own disaster. To some degree, however, the Green Hood had gotten results. In addition to his escape, he had spoiled The Shadow's plan to obtain Radcorn's list without revealing his own presence.

That did not disturb The Shadow. He had an alternative: a shift of strategy. A laugh in the dark—a parting strain of shuddering mirth—proved that The Shadow would soon have an answer for the riddle of the Green Hood.

CHAPTER XVII
TWO FROM FIVE

CLIPPINGS and report sheets lay on The Shadow's table. Together, they told all that had happened since the battle in the artist's studio Radcorn sometimes used. Newspaper accounts told how police had sighted the Green Hood; how the murderer had lost the .28-caliber antique pistol. The wanted gun was owned by the law. Ballistic tests proved that it had discharged the bullet that killed Junius Purling.

On a sheet of paper, The Shadow summarized the law's clues in ink of vivid blue:

> Borgia stiletto
> Baby Paterson .28
> Malay creese

To those, he added three more bits of evidence found at Purling's, plus one from Wenz's home:

> Paper with "WE"
> Louis medallion
> Chain with charm missing
> Note signed "T. S."

The writing dried and faded, the way with notations that The Shadow made. But before the ink had finally vanished, The Shadow's own clues lay on the table.

They were five in number. Two were the hotel phone memo from the Triton and the monogrammed cigar band marked with a notation in the handwriting of Professor Breer.

A third was the coin with the same monogram, brought from the room where Purling had died; another, the carbon paper from Wenz's house. The last was Radcorn's certified list of Sherred's weapons collection.

In that list, The Shadow had checked the Borgia stiletto, the Baby Paterson .28, and the wavy-bladed creese.

The Shadow had an afterthought. He added it to the paper on which he had written the law's list of clues:

> Message from Wenz to Breer

That message was actually in The Shadow's own possession in duplicate form, for he had its imprint on the sheet of green carbon paper.

Letting his own clues rest, The Shadow studied data that gave the inside of the newspaper stories. Though the trail led to Tobias Sherred, the law had not yet mentioned that fact. It wasn't wise, for the law didn't have the goods.

Learning of the battle at the studio, Cardona had put in a call to Sherred's home, hoping to find him out. That would have helped Cardona prove that Sherred was the Green Hood. It happened that Cardona had been totally thwarted in that call.

Ishi, the Jap valet, had answered. He had said that Mr. Sherred was tired of talking to the police and would not converse over the phone. Cardona had hot-footed it up to the Middleton Apartments; when Calvin answered the door, the old servant announced that his master had retired.

Joe hadn't insisted on seeing Sherred. By that time, the collector could have arrived home from Radcorn's studio.

Cardona had mentioned these facts to Commissioner Weston, in the presence of Kent Allard. He had also expressed the opinion that the Green Hood had made away with Radcorn's list of Sherred's weapons, assuming that there had been such a list at the studio.

Radcorn, it appeared, was somewhere in Yucatan, getting material for travel articles. There was no way to reach him for purposes of inquiry.

That summary finished, The Shadow turned to an important fact of his own finding. More than twenty-four hours had passed since the studio episode, but in that time, The Shadow's agents had been rewarded after an unceasing search.

They had found the blind alleyway with gate entrance and broken paving. It answered Evelyn's description of the place where the Green Hood had taken her, even to the brick wall on one side and concrete on the other.

The alley lay between the end row of some old houses and the blank wall of a warehouse. It was in a very disreputable district—the sort that the Green Hood would choose for his thugs to visit.

Agents had noted hoodlums skulking thereabouts. Chances were that Breer's Truth Inducer was still housed in the hideout at the end of the alley.

Burbank's signal light glowed. The Shadow answered the contact man's call. The report concerned Evelyn.

She had been constantly guarded by agents of The Shadow, detached from the search duty. She had just finished a trip in Moe's cab. Passing the alley with the metal gate, Evelyn had positively identified it as the right one.

The Shadow's lips phrased a sardonic laugh. Its chilly echoes bespoke future action. The Shadow was ready for a bold move, to crack the case of the Green Hood.

Long fingers plucked the clues that lay on the table. Methodically, they separated the bits of evidence. One by one, The Shadow chose three items: the cigar band, the engraved ten-dollar gold piece, and Radcorn's list of weapons.

The Shadow placed those articles in an envelope. He wrote a note in blue ink, folded it in with the clues. He addressed the envelope to Inspector Joe Cardona.

From the total of five, The Shadow reserved two items for himself; the hotel memo received by Professor Breer; the much-scored carbon paper that had been in Wenz's wastebasket.

It was dawn when The Shadow left his sanctum.

SHORTLY after noon that same day, Inspector Cardona found The Shadow's envelope upon his desk at headquarters. Joe couldn't guess how it arrived there. The one person to whom he would never have attributed the secret delivery was Fritz, the janitor.

In fact, Fritz hadn't actually delivered it. The envelope had been left by the janitor's double, otherwise The Shadow.

Speculation of that angle didn't bother Cardona. He was most concerned with the value of the clues that had popped in from nowhere. Every one was a sure bet.

The cigar band had Sherred's initials; and it had certainly once been in Breer's possession, for the professor's own handwriting proved that.

The coin also bore Sherred's initials, which marked it as a former item in his collection. It linked directly with Purling, for it fitted the broken end of the safe salesman's watch charm.

As for the itemized list of Sherred's weapons collection, Cardona didn't care whether it had come from Radcorn's or not. It was certified by a notary; there would be no trouble proving its authenticity.

Cardona was dubious on one matter only. That was the contents of The Shadow's note. It gave explicit instructions for Joe to follow, in return for the evidence. For a while, the police ace wondered if he dared go through with it. At last, he decided that it was the only course.

Putting the clues in a safe place, Cardona reached for a telephone to call a newspaper office. He was saved that trouble when a wiry, keen-eyed young man strolled into the office. The chance visitor was Clyde Burke, of the *Classic*:

"Hello, Joe!" greeted Clyde. "Anything new on the Green Hood stuff?"

"There is," returned Cardona, "and since you've walked in at the right time, I'll let you make the most of it. Print this in your sheet: We've landed new clues on the case!

"By tomorrow, they'll be public. We'll have the

murderer. What's more—we've got evidence that he doesn't even know about! Play that part big, Burke."

Cardona grinned after Clyde had gone. That story was going to be a jolt for Sherred. It was exactly as The Shadow had ordered it. What was more, Cardona figured that The Shadow had the right dope.

There was one item that Sherred probably didn't know about. That was the cigar band from one of Sherred's own cigars, with Breer's notation on the back. It was a dandy, that clue. It linked Sherred with Breer, as he was with Purling and Wenz.

A FEW hours later, newsboys were shouting the big story. It produced the very result that Cardona expected: a call from Commissioner Weston. Joe didn't answer the telephone; when he heard who was on the wire, he told the detective who answered it to stall a minute.

"Tell him I'm out," ordered Cardona, remembering a suggestion from The Shadow's message. "Say that I'll get to his place at eight o'clock."

The detective relayed that news to Weston. Then, in an undertone, he told Cardona:

"The commish is plenty sore! Wants to know if you left a message for—"

"Tell him this," interposed Cardona, "like you were reading it off a slip of paper. That I've got the clues the *Classic* talks about—I'm out trying to dig up more—I'll be at his place at eight o'clock.

"Say that I want to get hold of all the bunch that were members of the Green Hoods. That I'd like it if he'd call them and have them show up at nine. That maybe they'll help us when they see the clues."

The detective did a good job passing the message along. When he hung up the receiver, he said that Weston sounded a whole lot different. Joe grinned; again, he owed a debt to The Shadow. That sort of stuff, having all the former Green Hoods in for a conference, was the kind that Weston liked.

Clear of headquarters, Cardona found himself in an unusual position. He was keeping out of sight, dodging anyone who might recognize him. He realized he was getting good experience, for he was learning how crooks felt when they were in the same situation.

That wasn't all that Cardona was due to learn. The end of his dodging was to mark the beginning of another sort of experience. There was an indicator that might have given Joe the right idea; but the ace inspector didn't catch it.

The Shadow had ordered Cardona to leave the three items of evidence at headquarters. It didn't occur to Joe that the reason The Shadow wanted them there was because something was to happen to the ace himself.

CARDONA finished dinner at quarter past seven. He decided to walk to the commissioner's apartment, which was about fifteen blocks away.

It was twenty minutes of eight when Cardona strolled past the final corner. There were some touring cars parked at the curb. Cardona didn't notice that anyone was in them, until the occupants popped out.

Inside of ten seconds, Cardona was overpowered by half a dozen thugs, who fairly smothered him with their attack.

Snatched almost from the commissioner's doorstep, the struggling inspector was heaved aboard one of the touring cars. The caravan started; in the middle automobile, huskies had silenced Cardona with adhesive plaster across his face. Battle was useless; they had Joe's wrists and ankles bound.

The cars followed a twisting course. All along the route, the crooks were watching for trailers. Satisfied that they were entirely clear, they pulled into a side street where a warehouse bulked near the end of a long row of houses.

Cardona was carried through a gate, along battered paving. He was taken down stone steps, in through an underground passage past rooms that looked like cells. He was finally planted in a chair set in the center of the end room.

There, a glaring light was thrown on Cardona's face. It made him feel like a prisoner brought into a police line-up. That was bad; but it was worse when the chief of Joe's captors stepped into the light.

Face rigid, Joe Cardona met the gaze of glaring eyes that peered through the eyeholes of a green hood. He recognized the type of robe that covered his captor's shoulders.

Joe Cardona had followed instructions from The Shadow. That deed had brought the police inspector to this plight. The situation was so stunning that the prisoner could hardly grasp it.

Yet the facts were real. Joe Cardona was in the power of the master murderer who masked as the Green Hood!

CHAPTER XVIII
CARDONA TALKS

BOTHERED by the glare of the focused light, Joe Cardona found it difficult to observe the Green Hood closely. There were moments when the robed murderer stepped into the light, but that did not help much.

The green garb was evasive. The lowered hood hid the face, except for its eyes and a slight glimpse of lips through the mouth slit. They weren't enough to provide an adequate description. The best that

Cardona could do was to try to picture how Tobias Sherred would appear, if thus attired.

That gave Joe a jot of satisfaction. He was willing to swear that this figure might be Sherred.

The Green Hood spoke. His voice grated; but it was a forced tone. The tone wasn't as deep as Sherred's usual one, but it could be his. Over the telephone, Cardona had noted that Sherred raised the pitch of his voice when he became excited.

It would be smart business for him to do the same when playing the role of the Green Hood. That was a foregone conclusion on Cardona's part.

"You have talked too much," rasped the murderer. "That is why I have brought you. Since you have talked to the wrong persons"—the Green Hood inserted a sharp chuckle—"I am giving you opportunity to speak to the right one!"

A green-clad arm swept forward; fingers, gloved in a sleeve end, ripped the adhesive plaster from Cardona's lips. A pair of thugs slipped up in back of the prisoner, slashed the ropes that bound him. That done, the pair retired to corners, leaving the Green Hood alone with Cardona.

Curiously, Cardona no longer felt like offering fight. There was a heaviness to the atmosphere of the underground room. It lulled Joe, although he didn't realize it. The truth gas was seeping into the chamber, tingeing the air by degrees.

The Green Hood drew up a chair, seated himself opposite the prisoner. He reached to one side, drew over a small machine that had a dial. He started to attach a rubber tube around Cardona's forearm, like a physician taking a patient's blood pressure.

Cardona was interested. He watched the Green Hood wrap his own arm. It was then that Joe's face lost its contemptuous expression. The ace was up against something that he hadn't expected.

The Green Hood intended to quiz him, using Professor Breer's Truth Inducer!

CARDONA tried to scramble to his feet. The thugs piled from their corners, forced him back into his chair. The mild increase of the gas wasn't bothering them; they had taken previous doses. But the effect was becoming powerful on Cardona.

Monotonously, the Green Hood droned questions. At first, Cardona's lips twitched, holding back replies. Then, spontaneously, he began to answer. The Green Hood was inquiring details regarding the law's investigation.

Every answer that Cardona gave was the truth!

At moments, Joe wavered. Always, the Green Hood had his eyes upon the dial. Whenever it fluctuated, he repeated his question sharply; sometimes he changed its wording. The method worked. Cardona kept on giving the correct answers.

The quizzing murderer was too intent upon the dial to observe anything else. The watchful thugs were completely engrossed with noting Cardona. Their lips were tight, holding back the jeers that they wanted to mouth.

This was great stuff! Joe Cardona, old poker face, blabbing away everything he knew! The Green Hood was a smart guy. Nobody could match him—not even The Shadow!

With side-mouthed words, the thugs expressed those opinions as they drew together in one corner. Their mention of The Shadow was more timely than they knew.

The door of the room had opened a tiny space. An observer stood there—one who had slipped the cordon of thugs, by the simple expedient of being inside the underground lair before the crooks arrived.

A keen eye sparkled at the door edge. The blackened muzzle of an automatic jutted through, as unnoticed as the gloved hand that held it. The Shadow had thrust Cardona into this mess. He was on hand to see that Joe came out of it.

As he watched, The Shadow heard the Green Hood come to the vital questions.

"Today," the murderer rasped to Cardona, "you talked to a reporter—"

"Yeah." Cardona was answering without heavy persuasion. "Burke of the *Classic*."

"And you told him you had new clues?"

"Sure! They came in this noon."

"From whom?"

"From The Shadow. That's what the note said. I've got new evidence, right enough. I put away the things The Shadow sent me."

"How many items?"

"Three."

With a satisfied hiss, the Green Hood paused. He was getting to his climax. Eyes lifting from the dial, the master criminal ordered:

"Name them."

CARDONA hesitated. The dial showed a quiver when the Green Hood eyed it. The robed inquisitor reworded his question, to take the quiz by degrees.

"What was the first clue?"

"A cigar band," admitted Cardona. "It's got the monogram 'T.M.S.' on it. There's writing on the back; and I know who wrote it. Professor Breer. It says: 'Must investigate this'—and that's all."

The Green Hood watched the pointer of the dial steady; then: "The second item—"

"A charm off Purling's watch chain," returned Cardona. "It isn't a locket, like I thought it would be. It's a ten-dollar gold piece. One side's scraped, and it has the same initials as the cigar band."

"And the third—"

"The list I thought you swiped from Radcorn's.

Only, The Shadow must have picked it up, instead. It names all the weapons that we've grabbed. They're from the collection that belonged to—"

This time, desire to speak truth emboldened Cardona. His voice was gruff, his eyes had flash. The Green Hood met Joe's glare; masked lips rasped the question:

"Belonged to whom?"

"To you, Sherred!" Cardona was on his feet, tugging away the wrapping that bound his arm. "You're the murderer I'm out to get!"

The Green Hood was wrenching loose to meet Cardona's spasmodic attack. Henchmen sprang forward, ready to slug the prisoner with their guns. The unnoticed door swung wider; The Shadow was prepared to deliver bullets. The thrust proved unneeded.

Cardona's speed faded. The Green Hood was loose from the Truth Inducer apparatus, shoving Joe back into his chair. The thugs didn't need to swing their guns. The Green Hood's hiss halted them.

"Put him away," sneered the triumphant murderer. "In the second cell on the right. You have one thing in your favor, Inspector"—the tone was biting—"You are harmless! Only your information counts.

"It will never be used against me. What I shall do with you remains to be seen. Perhaps I can use you, once your teeth are drawn. By teeth, I mean those clues. I shall induce you to hand them over.

"Or I may dispose of you. Circumstances alone will tell. In any event, you are helpless. Reconcile yourself to the fact. Later, I shall talk with you again."

A GESTURE of a green-clad arm, and the thugs dragged Cardona to the very door where The Shadow had waited. He was gone, blended with the darkness of an opposite doorway, when the hoodlums shoved Cardona into the cell that the Green Hood had specified.

The murderer came personally to lock the cell door. He listened outside, heard Cardona thrashing about within. There was a clatter, as if Cardona had started a frenzied attack on a grating. Soon, the noise ceased.

Out through the corridor, the Green Hood strode. The Shadow let him pass. The thugs followed; The Shadow heard the command that their chief gave them. They were to watch the alleyway, and make occasional visits to the door of Cardona's cell.

One other point was mentioned. The Shadow understood it from the Green Hood's gesture back toward the innermost room. Other henchmen would be arriving later, to remove the Truth Inducer to another hideout.

Soon, The Shadow was alone in the dim corridor. He glided across, listened outside Cardona's cell. He could hear a muffled stir, inside. It ceased.

Silently, The Shadow began to work on the lock. It was a tough one; but his smooth picks solved it after minutes of effort.

Easing the door inward, The Shadow entered Cardona's cell. He spoke in a warning whisper as he blinked his flashlight.

The cell was empty!

Above, The Shadow saw a wrenched grating. It accounted for the rattles that Cardona had made. The steelwork was strong; Cardona could not have broken it. But the cell had a weakness that Joe had discovered. Mortar had crumpled beneath the whitewash that covered the stones of the window frame.

His strength returning, Cardona had broken the Green Hood's trap. Like the murderer, the police inspector was at large—although Cardona's departure had been somewhat delayed.

The Shadow's rescue was not required.

A laugh sounded, hollow in the confines of the cell. Its tone denoted that the present situation suited The Shadow. Moving back to the cell door, The Shadow closed it from the inside, used his pick to turn the lock.

Brief minutes were all The Shadow waited. He heard shuffling footsteps beyond the door. Thugs were listening outside. The Shadow shook the grating that hung from one edge of the window. The sound satisfied the inspecting mobsters.

Back at the door again, The Shadow heard more sounds. The crew the Green Hood mentioned had arrived. They were taking away the apparatus that formed the Truth Inducer. There was a compressed gas tank with it. The Shadow could hear growls to be careful, as the appliance was lugged along.

SPEEDILY, The Shadow shifted out through the cell window. He found himself in a little air shaft; the window of another cellar was opposite. The Shadow took the same route that Cardona had followed. It brought him to a rear street.

Moving with haste through darkness, The Shadow reached an appointed spot. There, he blinked flashlight signals. A coupé came from the next block. The Shadow jumped in, gave instructions to the man at the wheel—an agent.

The coupé rounded the block. A touring car was pulling away from the entrance to the Green Hood's lair. Another car followed it with a cover-up crew. The coupé took the trail of the crooks who were carrying off the Truth Inducer. In its turn, the coupé was a guide for another automobile, carrying agents of The Shadow.

Ten blocks away, the climax struck.

The car that held the cover-up crew was filled with vigilant thugs. They spotted the trailing coupé and eased to the curb to await it. Nearing their ambush, the light coupé snapped into terrific speed. Its pick-up was more rapid than the mobsters expected.

From the passing coupé came a fierce, challenging laugh; with it, spurts of gunfire from The Shadow's automatics. Crooks dropped low; tried to get a machine gun into play. Before they could release damaging shots, another car came smashing hard upon them.

In a second, the thug-manned car was overturned. Triggermen went bashing to the sidewalk, their machine gun clattering in their midst. Before they could recover from that upset, agents of The Shadow were upon them.

Rising crooks were banged right and left. Groggy, they remained to be picked up by the police. The Shadow's agents boarded their own car, made a swift departure carrying the captured machine gun and a supply of seized revolvers.

Blocks ahead, the car that carried the Truth Inducer was forced to the same mistaken tactics that the cover-up car had used. It pulled to the curb to await the pursuing coupé. The light car swerved, jounced up to the sidewalk. Spinning close to a house wall, it nosed in against the touring car.

The Shadow was on the coupé's running board, one of his big automatics blasting out shots, before the crooks could realize how The Shadow had outguessed them. Some sagged; others dived, took to flight across the street.

When a police car arrived, five minutes later, the coupé was gone. The touring car was empty, save for two slumped mobsters. The Shadow had packed the Truth Inducer apparatus into the back of the coupé.

Three corners away, a weird laugh throbbed from the interior of that coupé. The strange tone came as the car swerved off into a new course. Again, the sardonic mirth of The Shadow predicted new developments.

The Green Hood had staged one climax. Soon, it would be The Shadow's turn to outmatch it with another.

CHAPTER XIX
THE VITAL LINKS

IT was quarter past nine when some cars stopped in front of the Middleton Apartments. The foremost automobile was Commissioner Weston's official car. The commissioner alighted; with him were Lionel Atherland and Robert Leng. Other persons, former members of the Green Hoods, stepped from the next automobiles.

Irritably, Weston glanced about. He saw three men come from the doorway of a store close by. The center figure of the group was Joe Cardona. The inspector was flanked by two headquarters detectives.

"Here we are, Cardona," snapped Weston, testily. "But why did you send word insisting that we leave my apartment and come here?"

"I've been watching for Sherred," returned Cardona. "He's in his apartment, but he got there before I landed here. What I've been on the job for is to see that he doesn't get out."

"Do those mysterious clues of yours concern Sherred?"

"They do, Commissioner. You'll know all about them when we talk to him."

They went up to Sherred's apartment. Weston and Cardona led the way. Atherland was with them, because it seemed well to have him on hand, since Sherred had met him before. The rest of the large group stayed in the background, some coming up in a second elevator.

Cardona asked a question, just as they reached Sherred's door:

"Where is Mr. Allard?"

"You suggested that I summon former members of the Green Hoods," reminded Weston. "Allard was not an actual member."

Cardona remembered the fact. The Shadow's order had been to bring members of the defunct organization; no one else. Weston had interpreted that literally. Something that The Shadow had foreseen, although Cardona didn't realize it.

When Calvin opened the apartment door, Cardona shouldered through. The rest followed, passing the protesting servant. Cardona made straight for Sherred's reception room. He arrived in time to grab Ishi, as the Jap was scudding from the door.

"Where's Sherred?"

Before Ishi could answer Cardona's question, Sherred himself appeared. Gruffly, he boomed outraged words at sight of the wholesale invasion. Cardona gestured to the detectives. They shoved Sherred into the reception room.

"All you've got to do, Sherred," declared Cardona, "is listen to what I've got to say. These witnesses are going to hear it. When we're through, we'll walk out. Only"—Joe shot a wise look at Weston—"I think you'll be going with us!"

THE huge reception room absorbed the large group with ease. Sherred found himself seated at a table, with Cardona opposite. Weston was close by; Atherland was near the commissioner. Others were away from the center of the room.

At the doorway stood the two detectives, watching Calvin and Ishi, who seemed quite bewildered.

At Cardona's order, one of the dicks lugged in a suitcase and placed it beside the table.

"At the last meeting of the Green Hoods," announced Cardona, "Professor Smedley Breer was slain—with this weapon!"

Dramatically, Cardona produced the Borgia stiletto, placed it on the table, where its jeweled handle glittered before Sherred's gaze.

"We traced through the Green Hoods," continued Cardona. "We came to Member 9. He was Junius Purling. We found him dead, killed by a bullet from this gun."

Cardona's hand swept from suitcase to table. The Baby Paterson revolving pistol thumped the woodwork.

"On this paper"—Cardona had the slip with the letters *W* and *E*—"Purling tried to print a name. He left another clue, this Louis medallion. We found a watch chain on Purling. Here it is.

"Those led us to Louis Wenz, Member 10. We were fools enough to think that he had murdered Purling, until we found Wenz dead. In his desk was this note, signed with your initials, Sherred."

Sherred showed his first interest. He glanced at the note, gave a disdainful smile.

"I wrote that note." Sherred shrugged as he spoke. "It does not refer to the Green Hoods. It means nothing!"

"Here is another note," snapped Cardona. "A carbon one, done on Wenz's typewriter. A warning to Professor Breer to beware an outsider. Wenz meant you, Sherred."

Sherred fairly bayed his deep-throated laugh. Weston became impatient.

"Come, Cardona!" insisted the commissioner. "You've got to show us something more."

"Here it comes, Commissioner."

CARDONA flattened a cigar band on the table, pointed to its monogram. He asked Sherred:

"Do you recognize this?"

"Of course!" returned Sherred. "It is one of my own bands."

"And on the back of it"—Cardona turned the band over—"is a notation in Breer's handwriting. How do you account for that, Sherred?"

Sherred shook his head. He wasn't much perturbed.

"It shows a link between you and Breer," asserted Cardona. "And here"—Joe drew a gold piece from his pocket—"is another link, which hooks you up with Purling. This is the charm that fits the end of Purling's watch chain. It has your initials, Sherred."

This time, Sherred showed a look of puzzlement. Cardona expected that. He figured the man would fake surprise.

"And most important of all"—Cardona unfolded a paper—"we have the certified list of your weapons collection. Look at it, Commissioner"—Joe turned to Weston. "It lists the stiletto, the old pistol—and this!"

From the suitcase, Cardona yanked the Malay creese. He clanged the big knife on the table, thundered the accusation:

"The weapon with which Sherred murdered Wenz!"

Sherred was on his feet, storming that all was a lie. Cardona demanded that Sherred account for his actions on this very night. To that, Sherred shouted:

"This is all a frame-up! Look!" He produced a telegram. "This came from Commissioner Weston, telling me to meet him outside the Cobalt Club at eight o'clock. I went there, Commissioner; but you didn't appear."

It was Weston's turn to be stormy. He insisted that he hadn't sent the telegram. Sherred accused Cardona of faking it. Joe retorted that Sherred had probably faked it himself, as an alibi.

"To cover yourself when you bagged me," Cardona told Sherred. "You put the heat on me tonight, Sherred. The Truth Inducer worked, only I knew it was you, tricked up in that green outfit. The cell you shoved me into wasn't strong enough to hold me. You didn't expect to see me here, did you, Sherred?"

The big-browed collector had heard enough. Whatever Sherred's emotions, they drove him beyond his limit of endurance. He saw Cardona reach for handcuffs. With a quick movement, Sherred sprang for the door, shouting for Calvin and Ishi to aid him.

It might have gone bad with Sherred at that moment. The detectives were handling the servants, but the doorway was clear. Sherred was making for it; Cardona, drawing a revolver, had no chance to pursue. Joe's only way to stop Sherred's bolt was gunshot.

Cardona never leveled his revolver. Sherred's dive came to an abrupt stop. A figure had stepped in through the doorway, to halt the big man with a gun muzzle. Sherred sagged back, agape.

He was covered by The Shadow!

COLDLY, The Shadow laughed. His sardonic tone was mirthless. It carried command that even Sherred could not resist.

Slowly, the accused man backed to his chair behind the table. He slumped there, his eyes bulging in The Shadow's direction.

Before the amazed gaze of more than a dozen witnesses, The Shadow stepped to the table where the law's clues lay. It was The Shadow's turn to speak; to provide the vital clues that linked with those already on display.

Chilled silence marked the advent of The Shadow. His purpose here was throbbing through every brain.

The Shadow, alone, could clinch the case against the master murderer, the only man who still was known as a Green Hood.

CHAPTER XX
TRUTH UNINDUCED

THE eyes of The Shadow burned upon Tobias Sherred. Mocking in tone, The Shadow pronounced an order:

"We shall hear your alibis!"

A hard glint came to Sherred's gaze. His paunchy face showed sudden challenge. Abruptly, the big man rumbled:

"All right! I'll give them."

Pointing to the table, Sherred showed a return of nerve as he discounted Cardona's batch of evidence.

"What if these weapons did belong to me?" demanded Sherred. "I disposed of them. Someone else could have used them to frame me. Radcorn's list does not change that likelihood.

"The cigar band? Someone could have picked it up anywhere. At my club—at a restaurant where I dined—and sent it to Professor Breer. From what I've heard of him, Breer was an eccentric character. He would have supposed that the band had some significance.

"Purling printed the letters 'WE'; those show that he knew Wenz, but not me. The Louis medallion; the gold coin with my initials—they may have been mine once; but I had disposed of them, like other things that I no longer wanted.

"The murderer could have planted all those things, to turn the trail to me. Probably he sent that fake telegram tonight. It hadn't occurred to me before."

Sherred paused. His gaze looked pleased—too much so to suit Cardona. Joe rustled a paper in front of Sherred.

"What about this warning that Wenz sent to Breer? It states that an outsider was a menace."

Sherred hesitated. His eyes met The Shadow's. He thought he heard a low whisper. Nerved to the limit, Sherred gained a sudden flash of inspiration. He pounded the table.

"That list didn't get to Breer's before the meeting!" roared Sherred. "You've admitted that yourself, Inspector. What if somebody typed it instead of Wenz?"

"Who, for instance?"

Sherred couldn't answer. The Shadow suddenly supplied the answer. His tone was gibing, as if he wanted to help Sherred's alibi, then wreck it later.

"Someone," spoke The Shadow, with sibilant mockery, "who was a member of the Green Hoods."

"That's it!" Sherred was alive again. "Some member of the Green Hoods organization—"

"We thought that at first," inserted Cardona. "We figured that one member murdered the man who had introduced him, to cover the trail. Purling was dead, so we picked Wenz as the murderer. But Wenz was murdered too—"

CARDONA halted. His eyes had met The Shadow's. Like Sherred, Joe thought he heard a whisper. Though he didn't quite catch the words, Cardona began to ponder.

From his cloak, The Shadow drew two objects. They were the missing clues. One was the telephone memo that Breer had received at the Hotel Triton. The other was the green carbon paper from Wenz's wastebasket.

"For some reason," spoke The Shadow, "the man who murdered Breer deliberately delayed him from reaching the meeting at the usual time of half past eight."

The Shadow's words were addressed to Cardona, but his eyes were upon Sherred. It was the accused man who realized the answer that was already in The Shadow's mind.

"I'll tell you why!" boomed Sherred. "The murderer wanted to pin the goods on me! He knew that I would be here until half past eight, but that I had a directors' meeting at half past nine. I had to be out, away from here, at the time when Breer was slain!"

There was logic in what Sherred said. A crinkle came as The Shadow spread the sheet of green carbon before Cardona's eyes. Holding the paper to the light, Joe saw the letters imprinted upon it.

"Say!" Cardona was suddenly enthused. "I was a dub to miss this one! It's the carbon Wenz used to send the warning to Breer. Wait, though. Why did he type it over, a couple of times?"

"Wenz never used dashes," reminded The Shadow. "His exclamation points were always perfectly typed."

"But there are dashes here, on this carbon! And crooked exclamation points. I've got it!" Joe didn't realize that The Shadow had practically informed him. "Wenz didn't type that message to Breer! The murderer faked it; but had to do it over a couple of times, to make sure it was enough like Wenz's work to fool us!

"What's more, he could have delivered it at any time after the Green Hood meeting. Probably when he went to Breer's to get the Truth Inducer. Or the next night—"

In the midst of that, Sherred inserted a hearty chuckle. Cardona realized what his own words meant.

He was clearing Sherred!

THE SHADOW did the rest. He spoke for all to hear.

"Sherred had no reason to delay Breer's arrival at the meeting," declared The Shadow. "The telephone memo makes it doubtful that Sherred was the murderer.

"The warning, faked on Wenz's typewriter,

clears Sherred absolutely. Its mention of an outsider makes it point to him. It fits with all the other clues; knowing that such links might exist, Sherred would never have typed such a message."

Those words drove home, particularly to Cardona. He caught the inference, that the murderer must have been an insider who knew the ways of the Green Hoods. Cardona faced The Shadow.

"We're back to the original theory," admitted Cardona. "One member of admitted Green Hoods murdered the man ahead of him. But if—"

Joe hesitated. The Shadow supplied the needed words:

"If you had found Wenz dead before you discovered Purling—"

Cardona was on his feet.

"That's it!" he shouted. "Wenz was Member 10. If we'd found him dead, we'd have gone after Member 11. He's the killer—but how he foxed us! He murdered Wenz; then saw that wasn't enough. So—"

"He murdered Purling," spoke The Shadow. "That brought confusion. It led the trail outside the organization of the Green Hoods. That done, he picked a suitable man—Tobias Sherred—to take the blame for the crimes."

From the moment that he began to speak, The Shadow had crossed his automatic over one arm. It was pointed past Cardona, covering someone. Cardona realized suddenly that the gun had a purpose. Joe swung about, just as The Shadow voiced the taunting introduction:

"Meet Member 11!"

THE SHADOW'S .45 was trained on Lionel Atherland. He, Member 11 by his own previous admission, was the murderer that the law wanted. His game was up.

Atherland didn't try to cover it. The insane glare from the murderer's eyes reminded Cardona distinctly of the gaze that he had earlier seen through the front of a green hood, in the cellar square room where the Truth Inducer had been used on Joe.

The Shadow's laugh told more.

Joe Cardona realized that Atherland had planted all the needed clues to Sherred, including the list at Radcorn's studio. Atherland had wanted those clues to reach the law. But he had been troubled when some came by way of The Shadow.

Today, The Shadow's subtle tactics had alarmed Atherland. The Shadow had ordered Cardona to talk of mysterious clues. Knowing that they must have come from The Shadow, since certain evidence was absent, Atherland had wondered if The Shadow held too much.

As the Green Hood, Atherland had bagged Cardona—as The Shadow expected—to find out just what evidence Joe had gained. The Truth Inducer treatment had been a helpful measure.

But The Shadow had kept the two clues that really counted.

That was why Atherland had put Cardona in a cell fixed so that Joe could easily escape. Since the trail still led to Sherred, Atherland wanted Cardona loose.

Once The Shadow revealed the final clues—the real links that didn't fit with the case against Sherred—Atherland was through. Cardona's own experience as the Green Hood's prisoner was added evidence against the actual murderer.

Faced by The Shadow's gun, Atherland stiffened. He tried to mouth words. His fuming utterances were at last coherent.

"You'll never prove it on me!" scoffed Atherland. "You couldn't hook Sherred with good evidence. You can't get me with bad. I'll never talk—"

Atherland broke. He was looking past The Shadow, to the hallway door. There stood Evelyn Rayle; behind her, two of The Shadow's agents, their faces tilted downward as they shoved a square tank through the doorway.

Resting on top of that gas tank was the dialed indicator and other apparatus of Breer's Truth Inducer.

Cardona spied what Atherland saw. The police ace grabbed the murderer's shoulder.

"You're not talking?" jabbed Cardona. "Wait until we hook that dial again, Atherland! This time, *I'll* be asking the questions!"

ATHERLAND'S fist ended Cardona's shout, when it cracked hard against the inspector's jaw. Others grabbed for Atherland; in the melee, The Shadow could not take aim. With savage strength, Atherland kept flinging off attackers.

The murderer grabbed for the Malay creese. The Shadow sped a timely bullet that clanged the wide side of the wavy blade. The weapon went from Atherland's hand. He snatched up the Baby Paterson pistol, aimed between fighters, to shoot at The Shadow.

Although Atherland fired, his aim was useless. The Shadow had sidestepped. However, the shaky shots did some damage. They drilled the side of the gas tank in the doorway. The precious vapor needed for the Truth Inducer began to filter through the room.

That gas wasn't inflammable, so an explosion didn't come to Atherland's aid. Nevertheless, the murderer laughed crazily, as he dropped the antique pistol, now empty of bullets.

Atherland had destroyed Breer's formulas, after memorizing them. He, alone, knew the elements that composed the valuable gas. The Truth Inducer would never again be used.

Moreover, the surge of gas began to benefit Atherland. It was hissing rapidly; it weakened

Atherland's attackers. More accustomed to the vapor's power, Atherland wrested free. He grabbed the last available weapon—the Borgia stiletto.

Men were succumbing to the gas all around Atherland. The Shadow's agents had hurried away with Evelyn, out through the hall, at The Shadow's command. Free, with the narrow-bladed knife in his hand, Atherland wanted another victim. He saw the best of all—The Shadow.

The black-cloaked avenger was sagging in the doorway, his automatic dangling from his fingers. Thinking that the gas had stifled The Shadow, Atherland sprang forward, pulling back his arm to ready a long throw with the stiletto.

Quickly, The Shadow's eyes came over the coat sleeve that muffled his face against the gas. His fist tightened, snapping its gun upward. The big muzzle tongued flame. Atherland jolted as the stiletto left his hand. The jeweled knife sped past The Shadow's head, to clatter against the hallway wall.

The Shadow had faked his sag to bring Atherland's thrust. It was sure protection for the others in the room. But even The Shadow, with the gas seeping all about him, could not take too great a risk with Atherland.

That was why The Shadow's lone shot was aimed straight for the murderer's heart. Atherland was crumpled on the floor by the gas tank by the time his tossed knife, after hitting the hallway wall, bounced to the floor.

Calvin and Ishi had groped to the windows. They yanked them open. Clear air dispelled the gas. Weston, Cardona, Sherred and other witnesses—all saw Atherland's figure on the floor. Beyond, they saw a shape of blackness that wavered, then steadied.

A moment later, The Shadow had faded beyond the hallway door. Emptiness remained where the black-cloaked victor had been, but from that void came a sound that marked the departure of The Shadow.

The tone was a mirthless laugh; a solemn knell that quivered above the dead form of Lionel Atherland.

The Shadow had delivered deserved doom to the triple murderer who had tried to make an innocent man suffer for his crimes.

The reign of the lone Green Hood was ended.

THE END

INTERLUDE by Will Murray

The Shadow on the Silver Screen is the theme for this volume reprinting two exciting mysteries from 1938.

Hollywood rarely did well by the Dark Avenger, but the closest they came to perfection in writer Walter B. Gibson's day was the 1940 serial, *The Shadow,* starring Victor Jory.

Shadow Magazine editor John L. Nanovic first alerted loyal readers to the coming production in the August 15, 1939 issue:

> Here's something that all of our readers will be happy to know. We have just competed negotiations with Columbia Pictures for the production of a new Shadow serial! We gave you a hint of this some time ago, but didn't want to make a definite statement until everything was properly signed, sealed, and delivered—and now it is, so we can tell you about it.
>
> Many of you have seen the previous Shadow pictures, and liked them well. We can give you this promise—that the new Shadow picture will be twenty times better than any of the two previous ones, for Columbia pictures will produce it on a budget that will allow for the best of everything. It will be the leading serial of their year's production, so you can be sure that it will be good.
>
> The picture is already in its first stages of production, with work on the script going ahead nicely. The studio schedule calls for its completion this fall, and release most likely the end of this year, or the first thing next year. As the picture progresses, we will keep you readers informed in this column, and give you more exact dates as they are made definite. We will also give you casting news and information.

The previous productions Nanovic referenced were Grand National's *The Shadow Strikes!* and *International Crime,* both of which starred Rod LaRocque. They were cheap B pictures.

Columbia's *The Shadow* was released in January, 1940. As editor, it was Nanovic's job to liaise with Columbia producers in protecting Street & Smith's interests. This responsibility was not limited to making certain that the authentic Shadow appeared on the Silver Screen, but in selecting appropriate stories to adapt.

Since this was a 15-chapter serial, each installment ending in a cliff-hanger, one single novel would not be enough to adapt. So Columbia ransacked three separate novels, *The Green Hoods, Silver Skull* and *The Lone Tiger,* in order to assemble *The Shadow.* All were from the 1938-39 period. A single radio script, *Prelude to Terror,* supplied an important story element to the frenetic mix.

It's easy to see why these tales were ransacked for the Columbia serial. Chapter serials were usually a violent succession of clashes, death traps and Houdiniesque escapes, and that particular trio of action-packed stories are exactly that.

Although it was based on his work, Gibson's direct involvement with Columbia's chapter play was miniscule. "Victor Jory did a movie serial based on The Shadow," he recalled, "but in those days the movies didn't pay heavily, and the pulp magazines owned all the rights to the stories." In other words, the writer did not participate in the profits.

But that oversight had no impact on Walter's appreciation of the project, which he always considered the top celluloid version of his creation. "I liked the Victor Jory stuff," he admitted. "Of course it was a serial. I saw it in snatches as it came along. But it was very consistent."

By consistent, Gibson meant faithful to his template for the character. After how much The Shadow had been twisted and compressed for radio—and in other media—Walter was always grateful when someone else did the Master Avenger right. Columbia did just that, including Harry Vincent, Commissioner Weston, the Cobalt Club and other pulp details. They can be forgiven for including Margo Lane, then a creature of the airwaves and a total stranger to Maxwell Grant's novels.

Ironically, the two stories we've paired for this volume feature The Shadow in his true identity—a name and face that do not appear in the serial adapted from them! There, as he was on radio, the Master of Darkness was really Lamont Cranston. But of course the actuality ran much deeper, as Gibson often reminded readers:

> He really is a man named Kent Allard who adopted the name of Lamont Cranston simply so that crooks wouldn't know who he was. There was a real Lamont Cranston, a wealthy man who traveled all over the world, and The Shadow saw that he was out of town, or out of the country, whenever The Shadow appeared as Cranston.
>
> Now with the radio stories we did, The Shadow appeared strictly as Lamont Cranston. It was only later that he used that double identity. In fact, he had some other disguises he also used. As you probably know, radio had to be a very well focused form of narration. We were limited to the number of characters. You had listeners who heard them week by week and we just decided to keep him completely in the Lamont Cranston character in those.

Not until 1937, with *The Shadow* radio show starring Orson Welles debuting and the first Rod LaRocque release in the theaters, did Maxwell Grant divulge the Man of Mystery's ultimate secret. Decades later, Gibson recounted the events of *The Shadow Unmasks* in this way:

> So that went along perfectly well for about, oh, six or seven years, and then we suddenly decided, let's give this a new twist. We had The Shadow entering the Cobalt Club as Lamont Cranston, when newsboys rushed up as they did in those days, screaming that there'd been an airplane accident at Wimbledon and some Americas were injured. Fortunately nobody was killed, but the real Lamont Cranston had been in the crash, and there was his picture right on the front page. Just then the Police Commissioner was coming out to say hello to The Shadow as Lamont Cranston, when Cranston suddenly disappeared—just got out very rapidly.
>
> Well, this was the time he had to go down to Mexico and come back as himself, as his real self. It turned out that he was a famous aviator named Kent Allard who had flown off to the Yucatan to visit some Mayan ruins and had never come back. And they had been searching for him for all those years. But actually he landed with an Indian tribe and then come back secretly, because he knew that

nobody in the underworld would find out who he really was if he was supposed to be buried down in Yucatan. So he took off to Yucatan in this story and was immediately found there, and came back and had the pleasure of riding up Broadway in a ticker-tape parade with his friend the commissioner. But his facial image as Allard was quite different from that of Cranston. So from that time on, he had that real identity, but he only used it occasionally. He still played Cranston.

When he related the back story to subsequent generations of Shadow fans, Walter sometimes gave the locale of Allard's crash as Mexico and the Yucatan—as he does here—but the stories never wavered factually from Guatemala, where Allard had reportedly lived among the Xinca Indians as a kind of sky god.

Prior to those events, Allard had been a World War I-era flying ace and master spy code-named the Dark Eagle. Subsequently he found post-war fame as an explorer who flew to exotic locales in his own aircraft. He was inspired by several far-ranging explorers of that era who vanished during headline-making expeditions.

Kent Allard was a prominent figure from 1937 to the beginning of 1939—a year and a half. He joined the Cobalt Club, became friends with Commissioner Ralph Weston, but otherwise showed no evidence of a personal or social life, and certainly collected no supporting characters beyond a pair of Xinca warriors who served as silent bodyguards.

Asked how the rootless and anonymous Shadow supported himself, Gibson once revealed, "Well, curiously, we had that pretty well pegged when he started out as Lamont Cranston, because if he'd been Cranston, why Cranston had a lot of money. That was the purpose of making him a millionaire, so that he would have plenty of funds. But after he turned out not to be Cranston, we were in something of a dilemma there, except that nobody really asked. I think we took it for granted that Allard had dug up Inca treasure or various other things at one time or another. We never did delve deeply into the source of his funds."

The Green Hoods was submitted as "Lords of Crime" in July, 1937 and published a year later in the August 15, 1938 issue of *The Shadow. Silver Skull* came in that same August—just as the other novel was rolling off the unrelenting Street & Smith in-house presses.

As these two exciting exploits demonstrate, Kent Allard is clearly a man of action—a sharp contrast to his other self, indolent clubman Lamont Cranston, who usually served as the cover for The Shadow's secret activities. How he operates is very different from the laid-back Cranston, even though in his worldwide travels beyond the canyons of New York, the actual Cranston is a big-game hunter with a yen for exotic sojourns in Tibet, the Congo and the Amazon.

The Green Hoods proved so popular with readers that Gibson was asked to revisit the theme. *The Lone Tiger* was the result, published in the February 15, 1939 issue. That story inspired the Black Tiger, the criminal mastermind of the 1940 Shadow serial. We'll be reprinting that story in an upcoming volume.

Silver Skull was published in the January 1, 1939 issue. It featured a striking and unusual George Rozen cover, showing an urbane Lamont Cranston magically producing the sinister silhouette of the Dark Avenger with his elegant cigar becoming his weapon of choice, a .45 automatic. It should surprise no one if this cover was inspired by a theatrical poster depicting one of the many famous magicians Walter knew personally. And he knew them all!

For this action volume, we've gone with Rozen's more dynamic *Green Hoods* image. It could have easily gone the other way.

In spite of that emblematic cover, *Silver Skull* is a major Kent Allard adventure. He performs more aerial acrobatics than in any previous exploit, and encounters a new female protagonist who looks like she's being groomed for a regular role. Without giving anything away, this story reads as if Cranston is being phased out in favor of a more dashing Allard, who flies his own combat plane marked by his personal wartime emblem. Yet strikingly, this is the Dark Eagle's swan song for over a year. When he returns, Allard will be but a pale *shadow* of his former self.

So turn the page and begin what appears to be an exciting new direction for The Shadow, but is really the closing of an important chapter in his career, as other media incarnations of the Master Avenger begin to dictate his celebrated future. •

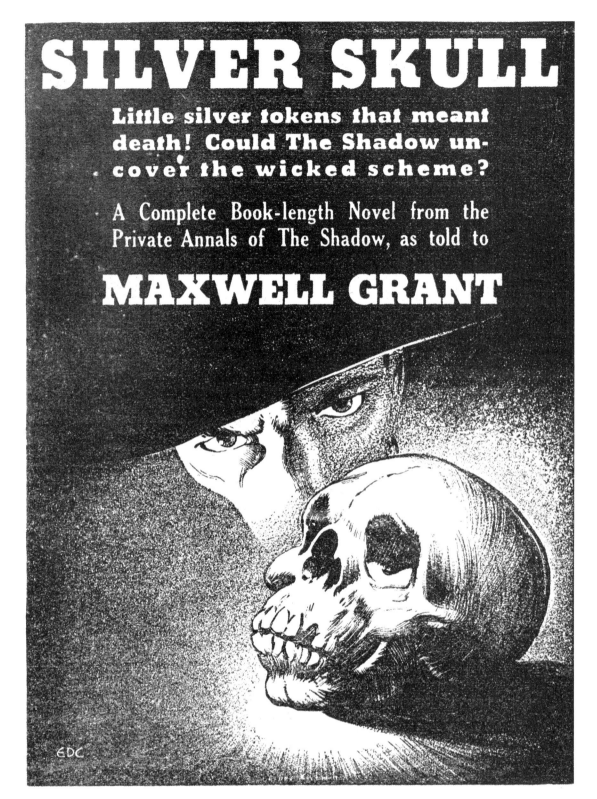

SILVER SKULL

Little silver tokens that meant death! Could The Shadow uncover the wicked scheme?

A Complete Book-length Novel from the Private Annals of The Shadow, as told to

MAXWELL GRANT

CHAPTER I
DOOM'S TOKEN

THERE was something in the night air that Mildred Wilbin did not like. Perhaps it was the fog, a muggy mist not usual during this mild season. But Mildred had driven through such fogs before, when she went to her uncle's home on Long Island.

As she swung her trim canary-hued roadster along the road beside Long Island Sound, Mildred brushed back the stray locks of light-brown hair that had settled toward her eyebrows. With the same sweep, she seemed to take the troubled furrows from her forehead. Her attractive lips lost their solemn droop and favored her with a smile from the rear view mirror.

She was worried about her uncle, that was all; and with very little reason. The fog had suggested a danger, but the menace was too remote to be given further consideration.

Tonight, Mildred's uncle, Herbert Wilbin, was taking a transport plane for Los Angeles. Within the past month, two such ships had crashed among the Rocky Mountains. Therefore, Mildred had logically been worried when her uncle had mentioned that he was going West by air.

Logic of a different sort had ended the girl's qualms. Herbert Wilbin had argued that the planes were flying higher, taking more precautions, because of the recent disasters. That had satisfied Mildred, until this fog had come along. With it, her sense of an existing menace had returned.

But she was reasoning that menace out of mind. This fog was local, confined to Long Island alone. It couldn't bother pilots of a westbound plane. As if in answer to that bit of common sense, the fog began to clear before the roadster's headlights.

Mildred had reached the rise of ground outside her uncle's estate. She turned the car in between two stone gates and drove slowly along the curved drive that led to the mansion.

There was a light beneath the portico that fronted the great stone house. By the glow, Mildred saw a limousine parked there. A gray-haired man—Herbert Wilbin—was standing beside the car, talking to someone within it. Rather than interrupt her uncle's conversation with a parting guest, Mildred cut through a side drive that led to a circle in back of the huge house.

The fog was very slight where Mildred parked, but pitch-blackness settled in the moment that she turned off the roadster's lights. The circular drive was flanked by cedar trees that hid the lower windows of the house. Mildred had to grope past those screening trees, to sight the dim light from the house door that opened onto the rear drive.

She had a key to that door, and while she used it, she felt nervous. She was worried again, not by thought of the fog, but by something that she couldn't explain. There was no breeze in the fog-stilled darkness, yet the cedar trees seemed to whisper.

Mildred's lips were tight, when the door finally unlocked. She felt very grateful for the lights in the rear hall. Grateful even when she saw Fortner, although she didn't like the fellow.

Fortner was her uncle's secretary, a smug, middle-aged man whose hair was prematurely gray.

Perhaps Herbert Wilbin found Fortner indispensable as a secretary; but that, in Mildred's opinion, didn't make up for the man's sneakiness.

For once, she had noticed Fortner before the secretary spied her. He was on his way to Wilbin's study, and it was almost laughable, the sudden jump that Fortner gave when he heard Mildred speak. A moment later, he was stammering—something that Mildred had never known him to do before.

"Why... why, you startled me, Miss Wilbin!" the secretary wheezed. "I thought... well, you said good-bye to your uncle, awhile ago. But... but—"

"But I'm back again," interposed Mildred, with a smile. "I happened to forget my suitcase. It's upstairs in my room. Would you get it for me, Fortner?"

The secretary hesitated; he looked toward the study door, as though duty called him there.

"It's very heavy," added Mildred, "and besides, I left some books in the library. If you bring the suitcase while I'm getting the books, it will save me a lot of time."

Fortner nodded. He glanced toward the front of the house. Noting no signs of Herbert Wilbin's immediate return, Fortner decided to get the suitcase. But he spoke a reminder before he started upstairs.

"Mr. Wilbin has some important letters to dictate," said Fortner. "He can't afford much time, or he will miss his plane. It's a long trip to the airport."

"I've already said good-bye to Uncle Herbert," smiled Mildred. "You won't even have to tell him that I came back."

Quite relieved, Fortner headed for the stairway, while Mildred went into the library. She was picking out the books, when she heard the smooth purr of the departing limousine out front. She glimpsed her uncle when he came in from the portico, but she did not call to him as he went past the library door.

HERBERT WILBIN was smiling as he strolled into the study. He was remembering some quip that he had exchanged with the visitor who had just left. They had chatted previously in the study, for on Wilbin's desk was an ashtray containing cigar stumps, and tall glasses empty except for remaining fragments of ice.

Sitting down at his desk, Wilbin stiffened suddenly, with a slight instinctive recoil. His eyes had encountered a strange object that glimmered dully from the desk: a thing that seemed alive, although it symbolized death.

The object was a silver skull remarkably like an actual death's-head, though it was small enough to have rested within the palm of Wilbin's hand.

Ostensibly, the skull was nothing more than a paper weight, for it rested upon some papers that were on the desk. Nevertheless, Wilbin reached for the skull as though he feared it would burn his fingers.

Laying it gingerly aside, he began to paw through the papers beneath.

A chill gripped Herbert Wilbin; his breath hissed between his gritted teeth. There should have been an envelope among. that bundle; one containing a paper more important than any in the stack.

The envelope was gone, its contents with it.

Hands clamped upon the desk edge, Wilbin eyed the silver skull. This time, his lips hissed words that he spoke as though they were a name:

"Silver Skull!"

The title fitted a certain person, for a reason that Herbert Wilbin knew. A man who should be trustworthy, yet who, by this token on the desk, was otherwise. A flood of thoughts rushed through Wilbin's brain, began to link themselves into connected ideas.

So intent was Wilbin upon his theories that he did not hear the sound of a motor in the rear drive. It was Mildred, departing in her roadster; but Wilbin knew nothing of his niece's brief return.

In the stillness of the study, he was sliding open a desk drawer; his eyes fixed upon the door of the room, he reached for a revolver. Herbert Wilbin was quite sure that he could solve the riddle of the silver skull. Not once did his eyes waver from the door that he so grimly watched.

Soon, the door opened. Into the room stepped Fortner. The smug secretary closed the door behind him and turned toward the desk. The look that he gave was as startled as the one that Mildred had previously witnessed.

Herbert Wilbin spoke in a tone as level as the steady aim of his revolver.

"Tonight, I received a guest," he told Fortner. "A man who presumably knew nothing of my affairs. A man, therefore, who could be left alone in this room, where a most important document was within his reach.

"He found that paper, Fortner, and took it. In its place"—Wilbin gestured with his free hand—"he left this skull! A curious token, because it fits with his identity."

Fortner said nothing. His eyes were gazing at the skull, his lips giving a twitch that tried to express ignorance, but failed.

"As I analyze it, Fortner," added Wilbin, "my visitor—let us call him Silver Skull—could have left this token for one purpose only: to notify someone that his task was done. Since you and I are alone in the house; you are the person for whom the information was meant!"

"NO, no!" Fortner was advancing, shaking his head, raising his hands pitifully. "I know nothing!"

"You know everything," corrected Wilbin. "Halt where you are, Fortner, and tell me what Silver Skull expects to gain. Tell me what you were supposed to do, after you found his token; what measures you were to take to cover the theft of the envelope.

"Unless you speak, Fortner, your plight will be as bad as that of the man who hired you. I shall call the police"—Wilbin's free hand was moving toward the telephone—"and denounce you, too, when I tell them that Silver Skull is—"

Wilbin failed to add the name. He had something else to occupy him. Fortner was leaping for the desk. The man's pretense of innocence was gone; hence, Wilbin did not hesitate.

Coolly, Wilbin aimed point-blank and pressed the gun trigger.

The *click* did nothing to halt Fortner. The gun was empty. Fortner, himself, had seen to that earlier; it explained why he was willing to take a chance. Viciously, he sprang across the desk and locked with Wilbin before the latter could recover from his surprise.

In the tussle that followed, Fortner fought with the frantic instinct of a cornered rat. He managed to twist away from a choking clutch Wilbin got on his neck, and with each spell of freedom, he supplied wild measures to beat off the next attack. At last, luck served the secretary.

Half across the desk, Fortner wriggled free from Wilbin and tried to grab for the swivel chair. He landed in it at an angle and the chair levered backward. Fortner's feet went up into the air, straight toward Wilbin.

Partly through sheer inability to halt his backward plunge, partly through his ability to grasp quick opportunities, Fortner let his left foot fly high in a sideward kick that took Wilbin underneath the chin.

The stroke had more power than Fortner could possibly have put into a punch. Its chance accuracy gave it a knockout force. When Fortner crawled from the chair, he saw Herbert Wilbin lying stunned beside him.

Panting, the secretary went to a window, raised the shade, then the sash. Reaching back to the desk, he picked up the silver skull and showed it at the window. There was a stir from the cedars; hard-looking men came through the open window, and grinned their understanding when they viewed Wilbin's prostrate form.

They took the unconscious victim out through the window. Locking the sash and drawing the shade, Fortner picked up the telephone and ordered a taxicab. He was tidying the room, when the telephone bell rang. Answering it, Fortner heard a chuckle, as his tone was recognized.

The voice at the other end spoke a single word: "Silver—"

"Skull," replied Fortner. Then, in panting tone: "It's done! Everything worked out—"

A drop of the distant receiver cut off any further report. Silver Skull was satisfied with the news. Fortner gave a shrug, then grinned. There was more work for him to do, but it would be easy; *very* easy.

When the taxi arrived at the Wilbin mansion, Fortner was standing beneath the darkened portico, a heavy suitcase resting beside him. When he and his luggage were inside the cab, Fortner gave the brisk order:

"Newark Airport!"

CHAPTER II
LINKS FROM THE PAST

ON the day following the stroke against Herbert Wilbin, rumors of another air tragedy swept suddenly upon the public. A cross-country plane had vanished somewhere in the Rockies, exactly like the two that had been lost before.

Among the passengers listed was Herbert Wilbin, millionaire manufacturer from Long Island.

There was little doubt as to the plane's fate. By this time, the public had learned what to expect when such ships were last reported over the mountains. A few days would bring the discovery of scattered wreckage, in which no person would be found alive.

Until that time, searchers were expressing the usual hopes that they themselves invariably ended.

Midafternoon found two men discussing the missing ship in surroundings quite remote from the Rocky Mountains. The two were in a sumptuous hotel suite in New York City, and though they presented a marked contrast in appearance, both were experienced in the same subject—aviation.

One was Kent Allard, an aviator with a singular career. Years ago, he had had a forced landing in Guatemala, where he had become the white god of a tribe of Xinca Indians. Returned to New York, Allard lived at this hotel, with two faithful Xincas as his servants.

Allard's appearance was as remarkable as his career. His face was hawklike in expression, as solemn and as firm-molded as the features of an Aztec idol. His speech, calm and even-toned, was as lacking in emotion as his countenance. The only expression that might have betrayed his thoughts, came from his keen eyes. But there was something in that gaze that left all viewers baffled.

The other man was Norwood Parridge, a wealthy sportsman whose chief hobby was flying. He was tall, like Allard; but his shoulders had a forward tilt, as though they carried some constant burden. Parridge's face was handsome but haggard, and the lines that creased his forehead had the look of grooves.

"It can't happen again," Parridge was saying, as he paced the floor. Then, bitterly: "That's what I said before, Allard. But it *has* happened!"

Allard's eyes had a sympathetic gaze. Parridge noted it; his shoulders straightened as he stroked a hand through his rumpled dark hair.

"It's not the money in it," he declared. "I'm not worrying about the cash that I've invested in Federated Airways. It's aviation that counts, and that applies to both of us."

"Quite," agreed Allard.

"I'm going to join the search again," asserted Parridge, grimly. "Like I did when they hunted for those other ships. Thanks for your offer to pinch-hit for me, but I've got to go through with it myself.

"Yet, what will it bring? Nothing, except the finding of twisted metal; human bodies charred beyond all recognition. There will be talk of further safety measures, but nothing can come of it. Federated Airways already have every possible safety device upon their planes.

"It's the human element, Allard; the mental hazard that hits every pilot, no matter how experienced he is. That's why these crack-ups always come in cycles. All we can hope is that this particular one is ended."

AFTER Parridge had gone, Kent Allard stood at the window of the spacious living room watching the millionaire's car drive from the hotel. Fixed lips moved; from them came the tone of a whispered laugh. Mirthless, it was a grim echo to the matters that Allard and Parridge had discussed.

Though Norwood Parridge did not know it, his fellow aviator, Kent Allard, had more than an airman's interest in those tragedies among the Rockies. For behind the calm personality of Kent Allard lay a strange identity.

Kent Allard was The Shadow.

Master fighter who battled crime, The Shadow had come face to face with a chain of mystery that carried him into the field of aviation which he, as Allard, knew so well.

To date, The Shadow had accepted these air tragedies as the accidents that they appeared to be; but the third crash, only a few hours old, had produced features that linked with the past.

Stepping to a writing desk, Allard drew typewritten sheets from a drawer and studied them intently.

The first was a report on a man named Carter Gurry, a wealthy Californian who had died in the first crash. Gurry had been planning to place most of his fortune in a motion picture enterprise, when death had intervened. His wealth had gone to a cousin in California, who had promptly set out for Australia.

Next on the list was Roy Breck, a victim in the second crash. Breck, it seemed, had been traveling

West to marry a girl in Arizona. His death had placed his entire fortune, the Breck lumber millions, in the hands of a brother who had already squandered his own inheritance.

Breck's brother, like Gurry's cousin, had promptly faded from the public eye.

Today, close upon the third plane disaster, agents of The Shadow had supplied prompt data regarding a new victim—Herbert Wilbin. There were two possible heirs to Wilbin's wealth: one, a niece, Mildred; the other a nephew, Roger. They were brother and sister.

The two presented an absolute contrast. Mildred's affection for her uncle was marked; and from all reports, Wilbin had cared for his niece. But Roger had shown no regard whatever for his uncle. In fact, Roger Wilbin was at present in South America, for a reason known to The Shadow, although it had not been revealed to the law.

The reason was that Roger had forged his uncle's name to checks totaling some twenty thousand dollars, and Herbert Wilbin had stood the loss.

Nevertheless, The Shadow's report sheets showed that Wilbin's lawyers, believing his death a certainty, had searched among their client's papers and had learned that two thirds of the fortune was to go to the renegade nephew, with only one third to the faithful niece.

As yet, The Shadow had not learned the date of the will in question; but he was sure upon one point—namely, that the will must have been made prior to Roger's crooked work. Likewise, The Shadow was positive that a later will, as yet unfound, must have been extracted from among Wilbin's papers.

Those two points added up to one conclusion: that last night's plane crash had been something other than an accident. Tracing back, the same could properly apply to the previous disasters that had harried Federated Airways.

The Shadow folded the report sheets. His hand was reaching for a telephone, when the bell rang. Answering it in Allard's tone, The Shadow learned that a visitor had arrived to see him. A moment later, the visitor's name was announced across the wire:

"Miss Mildred Wilbin."

THERE was no smile on Allard's lips as he gravely received the caller. Nothing told Mildred that she, of all persons, was the one that Kent Allard had been most anxious to meet at this particular moment. She was conscious, though, of a keen gaze that seemed to sweep her.

In Mildred Wilbin, The Shadow observed a girl of rare charm. Her face had a beauty that strain could not mar.

The girl was not wearing mourning clothes. Until she learned the positive news that the lost plane had crashed, Mildred Wilbin would refuse to believe that her uncle was dead.

Within a few minutes, Mildred was talking of the very subject that she had come to discuss: her uncle. More than that, she was telling Kent Allard why she had chosen to confide in him, although she had never before met him.

"You are a famous aviator," said Mildred, her tone as sincere as her gaze. "More than that, you have undergone hardships. They say that you are wealthy, yet care little for wealth. That is why I believe that you will do what I request, and understand fully why I ask it.

"My uncle may be dead. If he is dead, his death was designed. Therefore you, in the interest of aviation, should investigate the cause."

Allard's nod showed interest. Then:

"What proof can you offer?" he asked. "There must be some reason—"

"There *is* a reason," interposed Mildred. "I have heard from my uncle's lawyers. His will leaves two thirds of his estate to my brother. I assure you, Mr. Allard, that my uncle must have made a later will.

"He intended to leave everything to me. But my feeling in the matter is not selfish. I would give every cent"—her eyes were flashing—"to charity, rather than have the slightest share go to Roger!"

"Then you believe that your uncle's wish—"

"Was precisely the same as mine. There are reasons, Mr. Allard, that I cannot reveal, because my uncle, himself, chose to keep them secret."

It was plain that Mildred was holding back any statement of Roger's forgeries, which proved the sincerity of her story. Sensing that Allard was impressed, the girl pressed her cause with facts that she felt she could properly reveal.

"Fortner could be the man responsible," she declared. "He was my uncle's secretary."

"Tell me about him."

Mildred described the smug secretary, and detailed her impression of Fortner's soft-footed ways. Though Allard listened placidly, his eyes almost shut, Mildred thought she detected a flicker of interest on his part when she mentioned the grayness of Fortner's hair.

"What you have told me may be quite important," decided Allard. "However"—his lips showed the semblance of a smile—"it is a problem for a detective, rather than an aviator. You will pardon my absence for a few minutes, Miss Wilbin?"

Mildred nodded. Allard strolled from the living room; when he returned, a few minutes later, he again displayed his slight smile.

"The matter is in competent hands," he told Mildred, "and I can promise my own cooperation, so far as the aviation angle is concerned.

Meanwhile, I must ask one question. Has anyone followed you since last night?"

Mildred shook her head. She was emphatic on that point. From the window, she pointed out the yellow roadster parked near the hotel. From his own scrutiny, Allard seemed assured that the car was unwatched.

"I have some excellent advice for you," he told Mildred. "You are to take a vacation. Forget everything, until you hear from me. Everything, including your uncle."

"Do you mean"—Mildred's eyes were wide with hope—"that Uncle Herbert may still be alive?"

"Anything may be possible," assured Allard. He was watching a taxicab park across the street from Mildred's car.

"But where am I to go?"

ALLARD gave Mildred the name of a lodge on a Connecticut lake, with instructions how to reach it. He added that she was to use another name while there, so that she could be reached only by persons who were supposed to know that she was at the lodge.

Such precautions, instead of dismaying Mildred, served to intrigue her. She felt sure that the person contacted by Kent Allard must be an investigator of high repute. Confidence gripped her, as she walked with Allard to the door.

"Do not worry about followers," remarked Allard, in parting. "Your trail will be protected."

From his window, Kent Allard watched Mildred leave the hotel. The girl's white attire, with its trimming of brown, made her quite conspicuous as she entered the canary-yellow roadster. The car, too, was easy to observe, as it rolled away through traffic. Those points, as affairs stood, were in Mildred's favor.

A soft laugh came from the lips of Kent Allard. Again, the sibilant tone was the mirth of The Shadow. This time, it carried a note of satisfaction. With Mildred Wilbin safe, available if needed for future information, The Shadow was ready to take up a trail of crime. For he was the investigator whose advice Kent Allard had seemingly sought by telephone.

There were times, however, when chance could mar even The Shadow's plans. In the case of Mildred Wilbin, The Shadow had laughed too soon!

CHAPTER III
SERVERS OF THE SKULL

WHEN Mildred Wilbin drove away from Allard's hotel, a taxi took up her trail. It was the same cab that had parked across the street, and it was driven by one of The Shadow's agents, summoned by that telephone call.

After a dozen blocks, Mildred turned into a side street and made a stop at a jewelry store, where she had left her watch to be repaired. The cab was waiting there when she came out; behind it was a coupé, driven by another of The Shadow's agents.

The coupé took over the trail. Mildred was being watched by Harry Vincent, most capable of The Shadow's aides. With his coupé, it was Harry's task to convoy the girl beyond the limits of Manhattan.

Mildred made another stop, at a drugstore. From his coupé, Harry watched the doorway and satisfied himself that no one had trailed the girl. In fact, at that moment, Mildred Wilbin was entirely safe, forgotten even by the hidden criminal who had plotted against her uncle. There was no way for Harry Vincent to guess the part that chance was about to play.

Making a purchase, Mildred opened her handbag and drew out a change purse. Among the coins, she saw a folded slip of paper and opened it. She recognized the slip as a shopping list that she had used a few days before. About to tear the paper, she saw a notation on the back.

It was a telephone number, Hyacinth 4-9328, and it was written in a meticulous hand that Mildred identified as Fortner's. She remembered instantly that she had found the slip of paper on the telephone table in the hallway of her uncle's home, but not until this moment had she noted the writing on the underside.

Prompted by an immediate impulse, Mildred entered a phone booth in the drugstore. For a moment, she thought of calling Allard first; but she had forgotten the number of his hotel. Dropping a nickel in the paybox, she dialed the Hyacinth number.

A voice answered promptly; a voice that said "Hello!" in a great hurry. Mildred repeated the greeting; the voice evidently expected a woman's call. Across the wire, Mildred heard a smooth-voiced statement:

"John Lenville will be next. All is arranged; but be ready, in case you are needed."

There was something insidious in that smooth tone, that made Mildred's thoughts flash to her uncle's fate. Her fears of crime were not idle; nor was crime ended. She stood at the telephone, too stunned to speak. The voice was repeating the name of John Lenville. Finding her own voice, Mildred asked coolly:

"And after Lenville—will there be others?"

The question was not immediately answered. Mildred found time to scrawl the name of John Lenville on the envelope on which she had written the address of the Connecticut lodge. Then came the voice across the wire, speaking a single word:

"Silver—"

The word meant nothing to Mildred. She supposed that her question had been misunderstood. Calmly as before, she asked if there would be others after Lenville. This time, after a moment of hesitation, the voice replied:

"Yes," it said, briskly. "There will be another. Dr. George Sleed!"

THERE was a click of a receiver. Hanging up, Mildred hurriedly consulted a telephone directory. She couldn't find the name of John Lenville, but she discovered a listing for Dr. George Sleed. His address was in the Eighties, the very direction in which Mildred intended to drive.

Going out to her car, Mildred drove north. Remembering her interview with Kent Allard, she decided that before she called him, it would be best to gather all the information available. That could best be acquired by calling upon Dr. Sleed, a man who, like the unknown John Lenville, was living under some threat.

Reaching Sleed's address, Mildred found it to be a pretentious brownstone house that had been converted into a store and apartments. Leaving her car, she ascended the high steps; in the lobby, she found a bell button that bore the name of Dr. George Sleed, with the listing 2B. She rang the bell; there was a prompt buzz from the automatic door. Mildred entered.

At the top of the stairs, a door had opened; in the waning afternoon light, Mildred saw a uniformed nurse, who greeted her with a slight bow. She inquired Mildred's name; receiving it, the nurse ushered the visitor into a tiny waiting room, then asked:

"Does Dr. Sleed expect you?"

"No," replied Mildred. "But it is very important that I see him."

"Very well, Miss Wilbin. I shall inform him that you are here."

Mildred began wondering what to say to Dr. Sleed, when she met him. Wrapped in thought, she scarcely noticed that the little waiting room was very stuffy. She was roused suddenly by the opening of an inner door. Against the light from an office, she saw a bearded man standing on the threshold.

"Dr. Sleed?" Mildred was rising as she spoke. "I've come to see you because—"

The room was whirling suddenly. Mildred would have fallen, except for Sleed's quickness in catching her arm. He helped her into the office, calling excitedly for Miss Royce. The nurse arrived to find Mildred sagged in a chair, laughing hysterically.

"This patient is very ill, Miss Royce," announced Sleed, reprovingly. "She must be kept quiet. Put her to bed at once!"

Mildred tried to protest, but her voice only choked. The nurse helped her to her feet; instantly, Mildred felt a return of dizziness. She let Miss Royce help her along a hallway, into a white-walled room furnished with a hospital bed and a few chairs. From a chair beside the bed, Mildred watched the nurse close the door, then bring a nightgown from a closet. Placing the garment on the bed, the nurse methodically turned down the covers.

"I'm all right," began Mildred. "Really—"

She gasped, hysterically. She realized that she wasn't all right. Then the nurse was beside her, helping her remove her clothes.

The soft nightie felt very comfortable when it slid over Mildred's shoulders. The bed was comfortable, too. Mildred gave a sigh; nestling her cheek against the deep pillow, she watched Miss Royce gather scattered clothes from the floor and pile the discarded garments neatly on the chair.

"You must rest," advised the nurse, soothingly. "Close your eyes. The dizziness will pass."

MILDRED closed her eyes. Comfortable moments passed until she heard a sharp sound, like the closing of a door; next, a subdued, persistent hiss. Coming upright in bed, Mildred was puzzled by the sight of daylight through clear panes above a frosted window. Her fingers plucking the nightgown, she wondered why she was wearing it instead of her own clothes.

It struck her that she should be in her car driving to Connecticut, instead of in this room. Springing from the bed, she hurried to the window.

Through the clear panes above the frosted ones, Mildred looked out on the front street and saw her yellow roadster parked there. She must get to it.

Going to the room door, Mildred found that the knob would not turn. She pounded for a few moments, then decided that she could save time by getting dressed, while she waited for the nurse. Mildred was slipping the nightgown from her shoulders, when she turned toward the chair beside the bed. A surge of complete hopelessness rendered her immobile.

Her clothes were gone from the chair. Miss Royce had taken them. Mildred's face went pale with despair; a chill seemed to sweep her, as she understood how capably her plight had been planned.

She had walked into a trap the moment that she entered that outer office. Her hysteria had come from laughing gas, piped into the waiting room. She could have been overpowered then and there; but these crooks, Dr. Sleed and the nurse, Miss Royce, would have had a more difficult charge on their hands. They hadn't wanted a chance visitor unconscious in the waiting room, where someone else might arrive.

Instead, they had let Mildred add to her own dilemma. She had become a patient, and had willingly let Miss Royce put her to bed. As she now stood, Mildred hadn't a single possession by which she could identify herself, for her handbag, with all its contents, had gone with her clothes.

Out of a blur of thoughts, Mildred caught the reason why she had thought of laughing gas. The hissing sound, still persistent in this room, had given her the explanation. More gas; but this dose was not of the same variety. Before Mildred could start a frantic dash toward the window, a blackness swept over her.

With a sudden sigh, the girl sank softly to the floor.

In the hallway outside, the bearded man who called himself Dr. George Sleed was watching a dial attached to the wall. The indicator had reached the required point; with a smile that parted his beard, Sleed turned off the gas.

Going back into his office, Sleed picked up Mildred's handbag from the desk. He was interested in the large amount of money that it contained; also in the automobile keys and the licenses that went with them. But he widened his overlarge grin when he found the slip of paper that stated Mildred's destination and the name she was to use in Connecticut.

Sleed rapped on a door, gave the quick admonition: "Hurry, Thelma!"

The door opened. Out stepped the Royce woman, attired as a nurse no longer. From tan-trimmed shoes to brown-ribboned white hat, her clothes were those that had belonged to Mildred Wilbin.

"How do you like me, Doc?" asked Thelma, her voice no longer modulated. "Do I look as classy as the Wilbin dame did, when she walked in here? I ought to, because everything she was wearing fits me perfect!"

"You're about her build," agreed Sleed. "Only, your hair is darker. Tilt that hat a bit."

Thelma obliged. She walked across the room, in excellent imitation of Mildred's style. Sleed beckoned her to the desk.

"More luck," he said. "The Wilbin dame pulled a boner, calling Silver Skull; and another, coming here. This medico racket proved better than I figured it would. But this is the real break. Do you know what the dame has up her sleeve?"

"Nothing!" snorted Thelma. "Nighties don't have sleeves!"

"I mean what she *did* have up her sleeve. She was going to slide out of sight. This is where she was going." Sleed pointed to the address on the slip. "So that's where you start; but shake the trail before you get there."

Thelma Royce nodded her understanding.

"That's settled," said Sleed. "So let's hurry and stow the girl away, so she can be shipped out with the equipment."

ENTERING the little bedroom, Sleed stripped the blankets from the bed and spread them on the floor. Thelma helped him wrap Mildred's nightgowned form in the blankets. The girl looked like a mummified figure, when they placed her in a longish padded box that Sleed had kept here in case a human shipment should be required.

Hurrying downstairs, Thelma strolled out into the gathering dusk. From across the street, Harry Vincent recognized the brown-and-white clothing that she wore and mistook her for Mildred.

Thelma drove away in the roadster. Harry followed. As the ride progressed, he had less and less cause to suspect that an impostor was in the car ahead. He had clocked Mildred's stay in the brownstone house, but the interval had been too slight to provide a clue to the misadventure that she had met.

Reaching a main highway in Connecticut, Thelma Royce glanced into the roadster's mirror, to notice a coupé that dropped her trail. Thelma's laugh was harsh. It told that servers of Silver Skull found their chief delight in adding new victims, like Mildred Wilbin, to those already in the power of an insidious master!

CHAPTER IV
WORD TO THE SHADOW

THE same darkness that marked Thelma's final departure in the attire of Mildred Wilbin, was a useful cover for The Shadow. No longer in his hotel suite, he was garbed in a cloak of black, shrouded by night itself. He was a strange visitor to a place where callers had been coming all day—the Long Island home of Herbert Wilbin.

The callers had been the missing man's attorneys. Like The Shadow, they had been surprised at the terms of Wilbin's will. So they had come to the mansion, bringing assistants with them, to make a thorough search of the premises, hoping to find a later will.

When the black-cloaked figure of The Shadow glided up beside a hedge that flanked the house portico, the lawyers' hunt was almost over. Scarcely a rustle marked The Shadow's course; he paused just beyond the fringe of light that showed beneath the portico.

A final car was waiting out front, a chauffeur at the wheel. Two men stepped from the house; one a lawyer, the other a servant. They were waiting for a third man—obviously, another servant—who was locking up the house.

The lawyer, a man with a troubled face, began to ask some quiet questions.

Darkness encroached from the gloom of the hedge, as though a tree had leaned to stretch its shadow into the sphere of light. That shadow was a living one—The Shadow! He was catching a conversation that he did not want to miss.

All tallied with certain facts that Mildred Wilbin

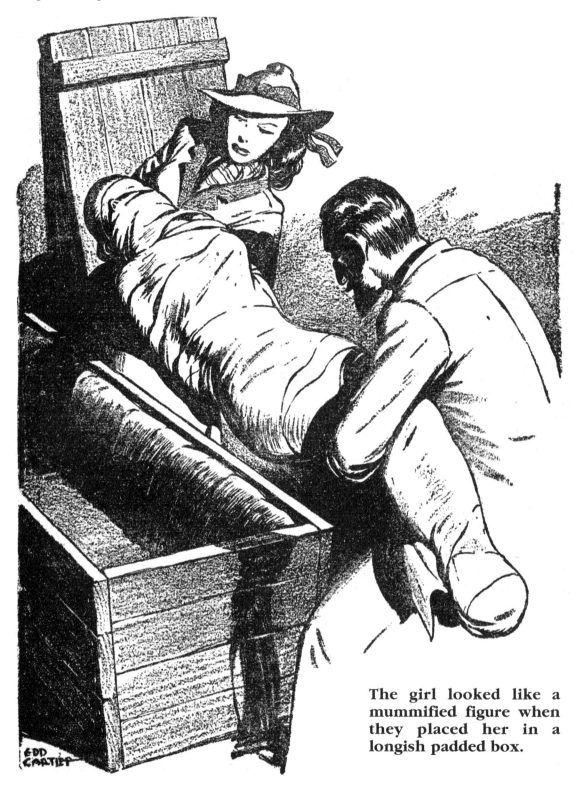

The girl looked like a mummified figure when they placed her in a longish padded box.

had mentioned, plus later details that The Shadow had hoped to learn.

Herbert Wilbin had intended to make a long trip, hence, had decided to close the house. That was why Mildred, like the servants, had departed, leaving only Fortner, the secretary. A trusted man, Fortner, in the servant's estimate.

One fact that the servant mentioned did not seem odd to the lawyer. It concerned Fortner. The secretary, ending his term of employment with Wilbin, had received a sizeable bonus and was going on a long vacation. Just where, the servant did not know, but he recalled that Fortner had talked about taking a cruise, or going somewhere away from all work.

To The Shadow, the news signified that Fortner had found very good reasons to disappear completely.

The light above the portico was suddenly extinguished. The last servant came from the house and in the darkness locked the big front door. The final words that The Shadow heard the lawyer say were indication that there would be no further search.

All of Wilbin's papers had been found in order inside a locked safe; with them, a duplicate copy of a glowing recommendation that he had written for Fortner, to assure the secretary of another job. It didn't seem possible that Herbert Wilbin could have lost or mislaid a new will; not with so competent a man as Fortner in his employ.

The case, as Mildred had suspected, rested squarely upon Fortner; and the very steps that the secretary had used to establish himself were opposite evidence to The Shadow. Particularly, that duplicate recommendation. Perhaps it was actually an original that Fortner had typed with the word "copy," then left in the safe, where it could be found.

But Fortner, no matter how clever he might be, could rate no higher than a tool in schemes of supercrime. He could not have had a hand in arranging the plane crashes that had disposed of Carter Gurry and Roy Breck. The thrust against Herbert Wilbin was but the third episode in a chain of heinous deeds.

ENTERING the locked house was a simple matter to The Shadow. Using a rough stone corner that offered toe holds, he ascended to a second-story roof and soon worked open a window. His flashlight blinked a path that took him downstairs, ending in Wilbin's study.

There, lighting the desk lamp, The Shadow began a survey of some records that he had brought with him.

All pertained to men who answered Fortner's description; not the sort much wanted as crooks, but those who had traveled the borderlines of crime. They were comparatively few, for Mildred's description of Fortner had included a most valuable point: namely, that the man, though comparatively young, had gray hair.

Extinguishing the light, The Shadow began a probe with his tiny flash. He needed enveloping darkness, because he was raising the shades to begin an examination of the windows. As yet, he had not pictured those windows as a place of needed entry, for there was no evidence of any trouble at Wilbin's home.

The Shadow's conjecture was that Fortner might have recently opened and closed one of those windows, merely for ventilation. If so, the pane might show the clue that The Shadow wanted.

It wasn't long before The Shadow's flashlight was glued to the bottom of the window sash, where his free hand was brushing a black powder upon a telltale spot. A fingerprint grew into sight; a low laugh toned from The Shadow's lips. Stepping to the desk, he ran the flashlight along a row of papers that looked like leaves from a rogue's gallery.

Finding the sheet he wanted, he took it to the window and made a close comparison. The print tallied; The Shadow had identified Fortner. Drawing the shade, he returned to the desk and studied the record.

Fortner's real name was James F. Eylan; the middle initial probably represented his alias, although none was listed as habitual with him. He had been the secretary of a fake oil company operating from Texas but had covered himself well enough to be whitewashed by the law.

At that time, as recently, Fortner had merely been a tool. His face, pictured on the sheet, indicated his caliber. Smugness was written all over the features of the youngish gray-haired crook.

Finding Fortner would have to be a future step, even though the trail might begin from here. There was a point, though, that The Shadow emphasized, by writing it in blue ink on the margin of the record:

"Gray hair."

A soft laugh quivered through the room; as it faded, so did the ink that composed The Shadow's written thought. That gray hair was a link—an outlandish link, perhaps between Fortner and his employer, Herbert Wilbin.

If it meant what The Shadow knew that it could mean, strange adventures lay ahead with persons to be sought other than Fortner, or the master crook who had employed the fellow. The Shadow could picture huge crime with a double purpose; the sort that seemed impossible to fail.

But, should it fail, The Shadow would reap a mighty reward; not only in disposing of crooks, but through reclaiming the lives of innocent victims.

The thought offered other moves. The Shadow's

black-gloved hand picked up the telephone, for a call from here would not be amiss, since persons had just left the house. He dialed a number; a quiet voice answered:

"Burbank speaking."

"Report!" ordered The Shadow, in low-toned whisper.

Burbank, the man who contacted all The Shadow's agents for him, was methodical. He reported that the missing plane had just been found, wrecked in the Rockies. All on board had died; their bodies were unrecognizable. Herbert Wilbin, therefore, was officially dead, for he had been checked as a passenger on the ship.

That early discovery of the lost plane would be a blow to Norwood Parridge, for The Shadow knew that the millionaire aviator had hoped to uphold Federated Airways by finding the ship himself. Parridge, however, had left New York only a few hours ago and could not possibly have aided in the search.

Burbank was beginning another report; one that suddenly snapped The Shadow's reverie.

"Report from Vincent," stated the contact man. "Mildred Wilbin did not go directly to Connecticut. She stopped at this address—"

The Shadow was writing down the address as Burbank gave it. He knew, despite the evenness of Burbank's voice, that the statement was preliminary to bad news. The words came.

"I have called Connecticut," announced Burbank. "Mildred Wilbin is not at the lodge, either under her own name or the one she was to use."

"Report received!"

WITH that announcement, The Shadow became a being of speed as well as stealth. He shaded the speed regulations as he whirled toward Manhattan, for every second could be precious.

From Harry's reported position when the agent had dropped the roadster's trail, Mildred should have reached the lodge a half hour ago. Whatever her purpose in stopping in the Eighties; whether or not she had actually left there, as Harry positively believed, the house could hold some answer to her subsequent disappearance.

The brownstone building was dark when The Shadow arrived there. A gliding shape as evanescent as a blackish smoke, he reached the top of the steps and blinked his flashlight on the name plates in the darkened vestibule.

One listing was vacant. It went with the suite that had the number "2B."

With deft jiggles of the loose-hinged front door, The Shadow released the automatic latch. Upstairs, he found the door of 2B unlocked. His probing flash-light showed the arrangement of the rooms to be very much like a doctor's offices, except that all furniture was gone.

Lack of dust was proof that the moving had been very recent. Entering the tiny bedroom, The Shadow closed the door behind him and made a flashlight survey that brought an unusual discovery. There was a light switch, so attached to the wall that it had an open space behind it. The wall was made of thin partition board.

Removing the switch, The Shadow found a two-inch hole, evidently designed to receive a pipe.

Reaching for the doorknob, The Shadow found it would not turn. He was locked in the little room by an automatic door lock, as Mildred had been. The Shadow was anxious to return to the hallway without the long waste of time needed with this tricky sort of lock. He wanted a trail, too, that would lead him to Mildred's abductors.

Suddenly, a solution was promised to both problems. A muffled *click* came from the hallway; with it, The Shadow saw a dim light through the two-inch hole. Someone was coming along the hall unguardedly.

The footsteps halted at the door. Waiting with a drawn automatic, The Shadow was ready for it to open.

Then the footsteps shifted farther—toward the hole that had once contained a gas pipe. The person had decided not to enter the little room. That change of intent could have ended opportunity for anyone but The Shadow. He, however, turned it promptly to a new advantage.

With a quick whip of his gun, The Shadow prodded the muzzle through the wall hole just in time to jab the ribs of the shuffler who was starting past. That jab of steel told the man outside that he had encountered a gun mouth. The Shadow's fierce command, coming sibilant through the improvised loophole, accomplished the rest.

"Stretch!" ordered The Shadow. "Not for the ceiling, but for the door! Open it! You have three seconds—"

One of those seconds produced a gulp from the hapless man outside; the next, a hurried fumble for the doorknob. With the third second came the awaited *click* that brought the door inward.

Through a tiny loophole in a solid wall, The Shadow had gotten the prisoner he wanted, with a strategy so sudden that the man had obeyed every term of capture.

And from that capture, The

Shadow was to gain a trail straight to the crooks who served the master whose title, as yet, The Shadow had never heard: Silver Skull!

CHAPTER V
DEATH RIDES ANEW

IN a stone-walled, windowless room, the man called Dr. Sleed was wiping lather from his cheeks as he stared into a mirror propped on a large box. Sleed paused to grin at a face that he hadn't seen in a long while—his own.

His part as a false medico ended, Sleed had divested himself of the beard that went with it. The move was a useful one, for his appearance had become so different that none of his recent acquaintances would have recognized him.

The beard had given Sleed's face a fullness that it lacked in its present state. His cheeks were actually hollow; their color, too, was conspicuous. Sleed's complexion was almost olive. Most noticeable of all, however, was his chin. It, alone, was sufficient reason for the beard that he had worn.

Zigzagging from the right of his lips down to the left of his neck, was a faint scar that showed a thin white line every time Sleed tilted his head into the light that glowed from above the mirror.

Too old to prevent the growing of a beard, the scar was also faint enough to be hidden by a simple process of makeup. But Sleed, at present, had no equipment for facial improvement except his razor and the soap and brush that went with it. He rubbed the scar with a fingertip, shrugged, and decided to let it remain that way awhile.

A buzzer sounded from beside the wall. Sleed listened, heard a repetition of the sound. He pressed a button; there was the noise of an opening door above. High-heeled shoes clicked from a passage outside. Sleed opened the door of the room to admit Thelma Royce.

The dark-haired woman was still wearing Mildred's clothes—a fact which brought a frown from Sleed.

"Why don't you change that outfit?" he demanded. "Somebody may spot you and link up what's happened!"

Thelma delivered a smile with her over-rouged lips.

"I saw this same ensemble in a Fifth Avenue window," she told Sleed. "The Wilbin dame didn't have any copyright on the idea. What's the matter, Doc—got the jitters? I didn't have, driving out to Connecticut."

"What did you do with the car?"

"I left it at the right place, when I doubled back to town. I told them it was hot; they said they knew how to freeze it."

Sleed was rubbing his chin; his face looked worried. Thelma opened Mildred's bag, took out a powder compact and tossed it to him.

"Dab that scar," she said, "and you'll lose it. I know what's the matter with you. It makes you feel funny, not having your whiskers."

Sleed shook his head.

"It's those truckers," he growled. "They were supposed to bring all of the stuff here in one trip, but they took two. Even then, they sent a guy back to make sure they didn't forget anything. I don't like it!"

"They didn't get wise to anything, did they?"

Sleed shook his head negatively. Thelma, meanwhile, was glancing about the room; she smiled when she noted that a certain box was absent.

"Anyway, you've shipped baby doll," chortled Thelma. "What did you do—label the box 'Handle With Care' and let the mob take it away?"

Sleed nodded.

"Where they took it," he declared, "nobody will find it. I didn't tell them what was in it, though. Headquarters will know, when it gets there."

"And all this junk of yours?"

"It can stay here. We're ducking for a new hideout. Things are going to pop fast. John Lenville is already on his way."

Thelma whistled incredulously.

"You mean," she asked, "that tonight's plane is going to do a dive, so soon after the other one?"

Sleed nodded. It was his turn to show confidence. The designs of Silver Skull seemed to satisfy him. Soothed by his recollections of his insidious chief, Sleed turned to the mirror and began to dab his chin with Mildred's powder puff.

"Better go get the car," he told Thelma. "Have it out back. I'll join you in about ten minutes."

AS the door closed behind Thelma, Sleed smoothed his chin. The scar still showed; angrily, he plastered it with another blot of powder. He was muttering his annoyance because Mildred's clear complexion did not require the dark makeup that was needed for his olive skin, when something, reflected in the mirror, caused his eyes to give a squint.

It was gloomy by the door, as Sleed saw in the glass; but he had gotten a peculiar illusion of melting darkness. No waver of the light could have caused it. Actually, it seemed that some human figure had shifted from Sleed's range of vision.

Sleed spun about, his hand going to his hip. He was greeted with a whispered laugh, weird, chilling, cold as the sight of the gun muzzle leveled straight in his direction. He saw the shape in black; this time, there was no illusion.

The figure was cloaked. Burning eyes gleamed

from beneath the brim of a slouch hat, steady as the .45 that was gripped by the gloved hand below.

Sleed's own hands came up, as his lips gasped a name in one long breath:

Sleed spun about.... He saw the shape in black; this time, there was no illusion.

"The Shadow!"

Slowly; The Shadow moved toward the terrified crook. The silence that followed the whispered taunt chilled Sleed as effectively as the laugh. He knew that The Shadow had recognized him by the scar, which, though hidden, proclaimed its presence by the unspread dabs of powder.

Known as Jigsaw Randley, George Sleed had dabbled in many rackets along with his fake medical game. Murder had been a part of them, and The Shadow knew it. Sleed, in his turn, knew the punishment that The Shadow could mete to killers.

His terror was greater than that of the innocent truck driver who had released The Shadow back at the brownstone house. That fellow had babbled all he knew, told where he had taken the doctor's packing cases, thinking that he had met a ghost. But Sleed, a crook by profession, would have faced a hundred ghosts rather than meet The Shadow.

Sleed tried to plead, but couldn't find the words. Momentarily emboldened, he tried to change his cringe into a sideward sneak among the boxes. The Shadow let him get halfway to the door, then stopped him with a menacing laugh.

Turning, with his own back toward a closet door, The Shadow nipped Sleed's shift with such sudden aim that the crook dropped to his knees, raising his hands to hide sight of the gun muzzle.

"I'll talk!" gulped Sleed. "We took the dame, but she's not hurt! She's safe enough... like—"

His voice ending, Sleed made a violent fling to one side. Before The Shadow's hand could swing, his cloaked form was jarred by a swinging object that carried him half across a packing box. The thing that had thwacked him was the closet door, flung open with a lusty heave.

Pouncing across the threshold of the closet was Thelma Royce, aiming a glittering revolver. The top of the closet had an opening in the shape of a trapdoor. Returning because Sleed had not joined her, Thelma had stopped to listen on the floor above.

She had opened the trap and let herself through, with a skillful silence that had deceived even The Shadow. In her swing of the door, she had again shown nerve. As a marksman, she began to demonstrate that she was the equal of any crook in the service of Silver Skull.

ONLY The Shadow's amazing side twist saved him from the bullets that peppered the packing box, coming in a hot stream from Thelma's gun. His jerky writhe carried him over the box and beyond it, down among other boxes.

Thelma shifted to get a new aim before The Shadow could change position. By her quickness, she retained the odds—or would have, if it hadn't been for Sleed. He thought that Thelma had clipped The Shadow. Bounding forward, swinging a drawn gun, Sleed hoped to supply the finishing touches.

His charge carried him across Thelma's path. His guess was bad as to The Shadow's location. Halting suddenly, Sleed found himself directly between a rising shape in black and his only ally, Thelma.

A gun was swinging straight toward Sleed. Shifting, The Shadow intended to shoot him from the path, then settle scores with Thelma. Sleed flung himself across an oblong box standing on one end, to take a futile gun swing at The Shadow's fading form. The box went over with a crash.

In the split seconds while Sleed was falling with the box, The Shadow changed his tactics. He dropped to pick an opening that would offer shots at Thelma, intending to handle Sleed later. The choice was a smart one, but it didn't allow for the contents of the box that Sleed had overturned.

The box cracked open; a big gas tank struck the floor. The cap of the cylinder bashed loose; with a furious hiss, a deluge of the vapor swept over The Shadow. Sleed, rolling in the opposite direction; Thelma, diving across from the closet door—both escaped before the gas reached them.

They were at the front door, aiming toward The Shadow, who had somehow come to his feet amid a yellowish cloud. They could hear his laugh, strangely maddened. They saw him aim his gun and fire. The shots were wide, as the black figure wavered. Sleed shoved Thelma through the door and slammed it.

Gas trickled beneath the barrier; they could smell it when they reached the stair top. It seemed to carry echoes of The Shadow's insane laugh, that faded while they listened. Sleed drew Thelma out through the front door of the storehouse and locked it with a key.

"We'll double around to the back," he told Thelma. "We can lock the rear door when we get there."

"But what about The Shadow?" Thelma demanded. "We can't give him a chance to stay alive."

"He hasn't a chance!" chuckled Sleed. "I shut the door, didn't I? That settles him. There's twice enough gas in that tank to saturate the room. Which means there's twice enough to kill anybody, even The Shadow!"

The scene in the lighted room below the ground would have added weight to Sleed's argument. There, flat on the floor, his laugh ended, The Shadow lay among billows of the yellow gas still pouring from the broken tank.

Crime still ruled. Death was to ride the air again. Tonight, and in the future—so it seemed—Silver Skull would fear no interference from a being once known as The Shadow!

CHAPTER VI
CRIME'S NEW TRAIL

DAWN was streaking Manhattan's skyline, bringing an end to a night that had been disastrous for The Shadow's cause. Day's approach promised nothing but ill news; for with darkness gone and no word from The Shadow, it was a certainty that the cloaked fighter must have come to grief.

Such was the firm opinion of a man who sat stolidly in front of a switchboard, his back toward the dim light that illuminated a small room. Burbank, The Shadow's untiring contact man, was still on duty, patiently awaiting a call from his chief.

Burbank's figure galvanized suddenly at sight of a light that was now twinkling from the switchboard. His hand inserted a plug into the switchboard; his voice announced automatically:

"Burbank speaking."

The tone across the wire would have been incoherent to any listener other than Burbank. Yet Burbank recognized it as The Shadow's, and from the blurry statements gained facts that he repeated.

"John Lenville"—Burbank spoke the name methodically—"in danger... Passenger... aboard a westbound transport plane... Warning needed—"

The voice of The Shadow kept repeating the warning message.

"Your own number," said Burbank, breaking in. "Needed for return call. Your number... Return call. Your number—"

That drill of words ended The Shadow's repetition. A pause, then a voice, keyed to a last effort, coughed the number that Burbank wanted.

The call was ended, and from the forced tone that issued from The Shadow's throat, Burbank could only conjecture that his chief had subsided into senselessness.

As quickly as he could, Burbank contacted Newark Airport, calmly announced that danger threatened a westbound plane that had left Newark the evening before. The news electrified those who heard it, for Burbank's tone was too businesslike to meet with argument.

The Shadow's message had gone through. Excited voices were promising to warn the planes by radio. Then, as Burbank opened a directory that listed New York phones by their numbers, he contacted Harry Vincent.

Checking from the telephone number, Burbank gave Harry the address from which The Shadow had called. He stated that other agents would cover Harry's search for The Shadow. The moment that Harry's receiver clicked, Burbank began to call other numbers.

DESPITE the dawn, the streets were still gloomy when Harry Vincent reached his destination, twenty minutes later. He saw an old squatly building once used for offices, but which had evidently been turned into a very poor warehouse.

There couldn't be much of value in the place, for the locked doors looked unprotected by any alarm system. Harry, aided by other Shadow agents who were gathering, broke in the rear alley door.

They waited to make sure that the sound had not been heard, and while they tarried, they scented the nauseating odor of a sickly gas. Then, with nostrils muffled in handkerchiefs, the rescue squad invaded the premises that Sleed and Thelma had abandoned.

In a tiny office on the ground floor, they found The Shadow. He was motionless, but his breathing was steady. While the others carried the cloaked victim out to the cab, Harry made a rapid investigation.

He found that The Shadow had crawled up from a cellar room, where the gas was stronger than anywhere else. It was there that he had been overcome; and Harry wondered, at first, how The Shadow could possibly have recuperated while in that cellar chamber.

Then Harry saw the closet door, wide open, with the gaping hole above it. In his hurry, Sleed had forgotten about that outlet. Through it, much of the gas had gone to the floor above, and dissipated. The Shadow's recovery had followed.

He had made that trip to the floor above much sooner than any ordinary person could have managed it; which accounted for his collapse, after he had called Burbank. Harry was sure, however, that The Shadow would rapidly get over his relapse.

SEVERAL hours later, Harry's belief was realized. The Shadow awoke to find himself in a little hospital room, which he promptly recognized, because he had been there before.

Unlike the premises maintained by the faker, Sleed, this was part of a bona fide physician's office. It belonged to Dr. Rupert Sayre, a personal friend of The Shadow.

Sayre knew The Shadow as Lamont Cranston, a wealthy New York clubman and world traveler, for The Shadow usually donned the Cranston makeup whenever he ventured forth in black. Resting in bed, with eyes half closed, The Shadow heard the door open softly. He looked up to see Sayre.

Noting that his patient had recovered, Sayre solemnly produced a newspaper, with the comment:

"This may interest you, Cranston."

The headlines told another harrowing story. Again, a westbound transport plane had crashed in the Western mountains, this time under circumstances that were more tragic than ever.

A mysterious warning had been received regarding

that very plane. Who had sent it, and why, no one knew. The airports had radioed the plane to turn back, but it had already reached the fatal zone.

Radio replies had suddenly ended; nothing more had been heard from the doomed ship.

Searchers expected to locate the wreckage within the next few hours, for they had reports of the plane's last location. Among those already in the vicinity was Norwood Parridge, who had started West the previous afternoon. Mention of Parridge interested The Shadow; but there was another name that seemed more important at the moment.

That was the name of John Lenville. Listed as a passenger on the crashed plane, Lenville was reputed to be the wealthiest of all the victims. He was not a New

The call was ended, and from the forced tone that issued from The Shadow's throat, Burbank could only conjecture that his chief had subsided into senselessness.

Yorker; he came from Chicago, but he had been in Manhattan the day before.

Lenville, it seemed, was a man of many enterprises, who often visited New York on business. His best friend in town was a man named Louis Harreck, who had seen him just before plane time, yesterday evening.

As Cranston, The Shadow could definitely place Harreck. Like Cranston, the chap was a member of the exclusive Cobalt Club.

Doctor Sayre saw Cranston roll shakily from bed, heard him call for his clothes. Though he tried to recommend more rest, Sayre knew it was no use. Lamont Cranston, otherwise The Shadow, was one patient who decreed his own orders.

Within the next hour, Lamont Cranston strolled into the elaborate foyer of the Cobalt Club, with only a slight pallor visible upon his masklike face. It was the luncheon hour; as he expected, he found Louis Harreck in the grill room. Harreck looked very gloomy.

Then he was hearing words of calm-toned sympathy. To his surprise, Harreck learned that Cranston had also known Lenville. He didn't realize that all the details that Cranston supplied came from the newspaper report.

"Poor Lenville," groaned Harreck, for the tenth time. "If he had only missed that plane, as he nearly did!"

Cranston's eyes showed an interest that produced further details.

"Lenville was stopping at the Hotel Gladmere," explained Harreck. "Just why, I don't know, for he had never stayed there before. I suppose he liked to try new places. Anyway, I knew he was in town, and I'd called two dozen hotels to find him.

"They said he was leaving when I finally tried the Gladmere, so I hurried over there. The clerk told me he was in the lobby, but I didn't see him, until the clerk said he'd just spotted him going out the door.

"I headed after him, but Lenville was in his cab pulling away, before I could overtake him. His back was turned, so he didn't have a chance to see me, and I suppose he didn't hear me call. The doorman said he was in a hurry to reach the airport, but I found that out too late to follow."

WITHOUT knowing it, Harreck was revealing a remarkable fact. It was possible that the man he had run after was not John Lenville at all. That hadn't occurred to Harreck; but it did to Cranston.

It fitted with a theory that The Shadow had already considered; and this case might strengthen that very theory to a high degree.

"Have you been to the Gladmere today?" asked Cranston, quietly. "Possibly Lenville left some belongings there, or maybe some messages."

The suggestion appealed to Harreck. He decided to visit the hotel, and invited Cranston to come along.

Everyone proved most obliging at the Gladmere. The manager produced everything that pertained to Lenville, including the card on which the Chicago man had registered. That card particularly interested The Shadow.

It resembled other cards that lay on the manager's desk, bearing the imprint of the Hotel Gladmere. But when The Shadow casually handled the card, he noted a slight thickness that differed from the others.

Harreck identified the signature as that of John Lenville; and Cranston offered no dispute. The signature could be Lenville's, but it was possible that he had been induced to put it on that card in someplace other than the Hotel Gladmere.

It would have been easy, also, for someone to have posed as Lenville, by simply sliding that card on the hotel desk already signed. Subtly, The Shadow used Cranston's casual methods to sound out the clerk who had last seen Lenville

His description tallied with Harreck's, but only roughly. He remembered Lenville as tall, rather nervous of manner, and very choppy in everything he said. A man whose face was rather roundish, but conspicuous chiefly because of the heavy gold-rimmed spectacles that he wore.

By the time they went up to Lenville's room, The Shadow was more than ever convinced that the guest had not been John Lenville. In these crimes, crooks had a clever way of taking persons out of circulation and letting others carry a false trail—as in the case of Mildred Wilbin and Thelma Royce.

The evidence in Lenville's room convinced Harreck that his friend had been there. On a table were some folded memo sheets, printed with the name of one of Lenville's companies. In the wastebasket were two envelopes addressed to Lenville, which had been torn open.

When the group left the hotel room, those objects, again consigned to the wastebasket, were in Cranston's pocket. Also the memo sheets. Oddly, he was the only person who had handled them, and he was wearing gloves. It was after he had left Harreck that The Shadow made use of those finds.

Riding by cab, Lamont Cranston reached a rather dingy neighborhood, where he disappeared in broad daylight. He reappeared in a black-walled room, where only a single light glowed blue upon a corner table. The room was The Shadow's sanctum, somewhere in the heart of New York City and known only to himself. He kept his complete file of records here.

From the envelopes and memo sheets, The Shadow obtained an excellent collection of fingerprints, which appeared to belong to one man. From their general classifications, The Shadow reduced the search to a few hundred file cards, that he placed in a sorting machine.

Automatically, cards were rejected, until only one dropped into a special compartment. That card bore the name and photograph of a crook named Nick Delt, who bore a fair resemblance to John Lenville.

Delt wore no glasses in the photo. By appearing with conspicuous spectacles in a hotel where Lenville had never previously been, the crook had passed as the Chicago man; but only by dodging Lenville's friend Harreck. The missing John Lenville, supposedly a victim in a plane crash, had not gone to the Hotel Gladmere at all.

Like Wilbin's secretary Fortner, Nick Delt had performed a fade-out. His part as a tool was ended. What The Shadow wanted to know was where Lenville had actually disappeared to, before Delt had taken his place. Somewhere in New York Lenville must have met a false friend, just as Mildred Wilbin had encountered the alleged Doctor Sleed.

The clock on the sanctum table showed three p.m. A soft laugh issued from The Shadow's lips. There was still time in which he, as Cranston, could solve the riddle of Lenville's disappearance, by visits to offices where the Chicago man had been.

The bluish light clicked off. Complete stillness came with the ensuing darkness. The Shadow had left that gloom, to begin a hunt by daylight.

CHAPTER VII
WORD TO THE SKULL

DURING the next few hours, The Shadow was covering a route that had taken John Lenville an entire day. During that course, he met bankers, brokers, businessmen, who were pleased to meet a friend of Lenville's. There wasn't a doubt that the real John Lenville had met these men, a day ago.

By dusk, it seemed that The Shadow's trail was due to be a barren one. He stopped at an insurance office, which everyone believed was the last place that Lenville had gone. There, talking with the man who had interviewed Lenville, The Shadow struck a fortunate clue.

"Lenville was going somewhere else," recalled the insurance man. "Come to think of it, I remember where. Did you ever hear of a promoter named Alfred Zurman?"

There was a negative headshake from Lamont Cranston.

"Neither did I," said the insurance man, "but Lenville asked me about him. He said that the fellow had some stock that might prove valuable. Let's look up the name Alfred Zurman."

The name was listed in the telephone book, with the address an old office building far from the beaten track. Riding to that objective, The Shadow felt no doubt that Alfred Zurman could supply facts concerning Lenville. Zurman's place of business had an obscurity similar to the offices of the pretended Dr. Sleed.

Zurman's office was on the third floor, with a light showing through the transom, and it opened into a courtyard. With Cranston's usual calm, The Shadow entered, to find a man rising startled from behind an old desk.

Sallow, sharp of feature, Alfred Zurman looked like a criminal and a very worried one. He wasn't happy to receive a visitor, and began to mutter something about "closing up the office." The Shadow, meanwhile, placidly placed a briefcase on a chair and sat down on the other side of the desk.

Introducing himself as Lamont Cranston, The Shadow brought up the name of John Lenville. Apparently not noticing the twitch that came to Zurman's face, he told the man that he was interested in acquiring any stocks that Lenville had wanted to buy.

"I never met Lenville," objected Zurman, sourly, "so I don't know what stuff he wanted. Come around tomorrow, Mr. Cranston, and maybe we can do business."

To Zurman's relief, his visitor bowed agreeably and went from the office. Listening at the door, Zurman heard footsteps descend the stairway. Finally, he latched the door and started pacing back and forth, eyeing the telephone all the while.

When, at the end of ten minutes, the telephone bell began to ring, it brought a grateful gasp from Zurman's lips as he answered it.

There wasn't any need for Zurman to identify himself; his hoarse voice told who he was. In fact, Zurman was so frantic that he actually began to chide his master, Silver Skull.

"You should have called me earlier," he said. "I've got the jitters, waiting here!... No, nothing bad has happened... No, nobody has been asking after Lenville. Except—"

Zurman's voice broke suddenly. During his hoarse conversation, he hadn't noticed that the door had opened. A skillful hand had settled the latch silently, almost while Zurman had watched. The personage who had entered had advanced to the desk entirely without Zurman's knowledge. But he was manifesting his arrival at this moment, in a fashion that brought a chill to Zurman.

The round muzzle of an automatic was freezing the back of Zurman's neck, while a tone, low-whispered in the fellow's ear, added further emphasis.

A full-fledged crook, Zurman knew the intruder's identity, but he didn't voice it. The whisper was warning him against that deed, and it was in the tone of The Shadow!

ZURMAN might have been a ventriloquist's figure, the way his mouth began to open and shut. When he finally spoke, his words were the ones The Shadow ordered—words that reached Zurman's ear in a sibilant whisper, and seemed to pop from his mouth but in Zurman's own voice.

"Nobody has been asking after Lenville," repeated Zurman. "I was just trying to say that it worries me, staying here, with nothing to do—"

The receiver was leaving Zurman's hand, plucked away by The Shadow. Zurman caught the words that came from it, but The Shadow heard nothing but the slam of the receiver.

Whatever the voice had said, Zurman would know. The Shadow's gun left the crook's neck, to bob suddenly between his eyes. Zurman knew what The Shadow wanted and gulped the information.

"He said I could lam," declared the crook. "That's all he said. Then he must have hung up."

The Shadow did not inquire who had spoken. That could be wangled from Zurman later; for the present, it was sound policy to let the crook think that The Shadow knew all about his master. Reaching his free hand to the desk lamp, The Shadow extinguished it. The room was dark, save for a dull glow from the courtyard.

In that dimness, The Shadow became an invisible shape; but Zurman's face, pale despite its normal sallowness, showed white and terrified. In a sense, The Shadow had increased the criminal's disadvantage; and the effect on Zurman was visible.

"I didn't snatch Lenville," the fellow protested. "It was the others—the ones who came here!"

"State at whose order!"

Totally unwitting, Zurman would have spoken the name that The Shadow wanted, except for a most startling interruption.

So suddenly that it left Zurman breathless, a blinding light glared from across the courtyard, flooding all but the most remote corners of the little office!

Instantaneous though the occurrence was, it failed in its immediate purpose. Before any eye could have benefited by that probing light, The Shadow swept Zurman to a corner and dropped beside him, away from the glow.

To all appearances, the office was empty. There wasn't a living target in sight for any gunners to mow down.

ZURMAN'S quivery voice was grateful. He was suddenly accepting The Shadow as his protector. He thought that Silver Skull had double-crossed him; for Zurman hadn't known that his chief had a headquarters in this very building, that it was from there that the telephone call had come.

Unfortunately, Zurman didn't say the name of his master; nor did The Shadow question him further. Zurman was so cowed that The Shadow could forget him while other business needed attention.

That light, for instance.

Close to the floor, The Shadow reached the window. Below the level of the sill, he poked his automatic straight for the glowing spot of light. Unseen, The Shadow was prepared to shatter the brilliant floodlight—not only as a challenge to its owner, but to produce an added effect upon Zurman.

Before The Shadow could press the gun trigger, the light flickered. It was a small light, not much larger than a motion-picture projection, and the thing that had caused it to flicker was a slide.

His attention centered upon gaining a perfect aim, The Shadow still gazed across the courtyard. It was Zurman who took a look toward the inner wall of the office. There, pictured upon the whitish surface, the crook saw the gigantic outline of a silver skull!

To Zurman, that was a promise from his former master: a pledge that Silver Skull would still stand by him. It was a call for Zurman to rally, with future reward his claim if he did. Granting Silver Skull an insight that could match The Shadow's, Zurman believed that the master crook knew all.

Perhaps Silver Skull did. At least, his stratagem brought results. Cowed no longer, Zurman leaped from his corner, flung himself toward The Shadow. The crook was yanking a revolver as he came. His wild, defiant cry was a shriek that penetrated to the office beyond the courtyard.

The slide dropped from the light. Again, the spotting glare ruled. It showed Zurman driving toward the window, his revolver pointing downward.

The Shadow, warned by Zurman's cry, to protect himself jabbed a shot that clipped Zurman.

Faltering sideward, the crook collapsed half across the windowsill, as The Shadow twisted away.

Even in that move, The Shadow showed keen calculation. The corner that he took was toward the door. He was aiming when the door crashed inward bringing two marksmen into sight. The Shadow met them with gun blasts that jolted one, then the other, out into the hallway.

There were shouts, as other crooks hauled away their overbold comrades. With a stairway near, they were stumbling toward safety when The Shadow arrived. The Shadow ignored them, to seek a corridor to that other office across the courtyard.

There was none. The Shadow encountered an intervening wall. From a window, he saw that the light was gone. His superfoe, whoever he was, had finished the thrust and made a hurried departure. The only possible clue that might remain still rested with Zurman.

Returning to the office, The Shadow saw the criminal make a dying gesture. Zurman had dropped his gun, but he was pulling his fist from his pocket as if trying to draw a weapon. Before The Shadow could

There, pictured upon the whitish surface, the crook saw the gigantic outline of a silver skull.

reach him, Zurman sagged. His fingers loosened, as his hand stretched across the windowsill.

He was dead. The Shadow departed by the stairway route that the gunman had used, to find it totally deserted.

Back in the office, the body of Alfred Zurman lay with downward-tilted face. The crook's sightless eyes were bulging toward the courtyard. There beneath a grating, where it would be unnoticed amid accumulated rubbish, lay an object that The Shadow had failed to see when it fell from Zurman's hand.

That object was a tiny silver skull, a token that Zurman had carried to identify himself as the server of an insidious master, whose title, Silver Skull, was still unknown to The Shadow!

CHAPTER VIII
THE DELAYED CLUE

BY the next afternoon, The Shadow had good cause to regret the too-early death of Alfred Zurman. The facts that the cornered criminal could have supplied were becoming more important that ever, in The Shadow's search for some unknown crime chief.

Every lead of The Shadow's had reached a dead end.

To begin with, there were such men as Wilbin, Lenville, and the other victims who had gone before them. The law had given them up as dead; and their past affairs were practically a blank.

Crooks like Fortner and Delt had vanished as completely as the victims—a fact that helped The Shadow's theory, that some of the supposed dead men might still be alive. But the theory did nothing to create a trail.

There were other tools, lesser ones; but only Zurman had come into the limelight, and he was gone. As for "Dr." Sleed and his slim-figured companion, Thelma Royce, though The Shadow knew that they had captured Mildred Wilbin, he had not learned how she had been lured into the predicament that had resulted in Thelma's acquisition of Mildred's clothes and car.

According to Sleed's interrupted testimony, Mildred was alive and unharmed; but how long she would remain so was another question; which meant that a trail was imperative, even though it might prove costly to The Shadow.

Late in the afternoon, The Shadow, as Cranston, made a stop at the Cobalt Club, intending to look up Harreck, on the flimsy chance that the fellow might recall some odd clue regarding Lenville. Harreck wasn't at the club, but another man was there, waiting especially to see Lamont Cranston.

The visitor was Norwood Parridge, returned from the West. The fact that he was here to see Cranston was in itself unusual, for the two had seldom met. It was only as Kent Allard that The Shadow had met Parridge frequently, and there was no way where the man could have linked the two personalities.

Hence, The Shadow treated Parridge almost as a stranger, scarcely recognizing the wealthy aviator until a club attendant pointed him out. Once they were together, Parridge saw no identifying resemblance between the calm, masklike features of Cranston and the thinner, longer face of Allard.

Parridge talked as one wealthy man to another, treating aviation from the commercial standpoint. He stated that he had hardly reached the West to investigate one plane crash, when he had learned of another. The news had brought him back to New York immediately, to confer with the directors of Federated Airways.

"Last night," explained Parridge, seriously, "I ran into a most unusual coincidence. I learned that one of the victims in the latest crash had intended to invest heavily in Federated Airways. I refer to John Lenville. Did you ever meet the man, Mr. Cranston?"

Remembering his chat with Harreck, The Shadow nodded; then stated quietly that he and Lenville had been acquainted.

"Did he ever speak to you about investments?" persisted Parridge. "Would you have known that he intended to buy half a million dollars' worth of shares in Federated Airways?"

There was a shake of Cranston's head. Parridge looked disappointed, but his eyes had a hopeful gleam, despite his haggard expression.

"We called Chicago," declared Parridge, "and talked half the night. We learned that Lenville had actually spoken of a half million that he intended to invest in Federated Airways, but his associates cannot find a trace of his funds.

"Federated needs money badly. We'll have to fight down the stigma of those horrible tragedies, or go bankrupt. Like the other big stockholders, I'm already in up to the neck. On top of it, one of our own unfortunate crashes produces this mystery of a missing half million dollars."

THOUGH Cranston's features remained immobile, the brain behind them was rapidly at work. Here, at last, was reason why crooks had dealt with John Lenville. Unlike the cases of former victims—Gurry, Breck and Wilbin—there had been no question regarding Lenville's will. His estate, it seemed, had been in thorough order.

The catch lay in Lenville's finances. Why should some master crook connive to get cash after Lenville was dead, when it could be acquired before? It seemed obvious to The Shadow that Lenville must have somehow been parted from five hundred thousand dollars before he was abducted.

As with all the dealings of Silver Skull, the matter

seemed outlandish. Even Parridge had not picked up such a theory, while with the directors of Federated Airways. They were distracted, those men, but not crazed enough to propose the seemingly preposterous.

Parridge, in fact, had a much different and very plausible theory, which he advanced in a tone of confidence.

"We know that Lenville wanted to invest," he asserted, "but for some reason, he had postponed meeting us. We attributed it to the air crashes; but that could not have been the reason, for Lenville, himself, booked passage on one of our ships.

"We can only assume that Lenville did not have the money that he claimed. He may have found it good policy to let his associates think that he kept a special fund of half a million dollars. But most of Lenville's wealth was all on paper.

"This morning, when I stopped at my office, I found a letter that had evidently been delayed, or delivered there while the place was closed. It was from Lenville, written before he left Chicago. It mentions you, Mr. Cranston, and it seems to fit with my opinions."

Parridge produced both the letter and its envelope. The Shadow saw that the postmark was several days old, The letter itself was quite formal, addressed to Norwood Parridge as a director of Federated Airways.

It stated that Lenville was interested in the purchase of Federated securities, but that he would first have to conclude another business deal with Lamont Cranston, a wealthy New Yorker. That failing, he might have to make a trip to the Pacific Coast; but in any event, he would see Parridge within a week.

The situation was curious. Here was a letter from Lenville, claiming the very sort of acquaintance with Cranston that The Shadow, as Cranston, had pretended with Lenville. The letter was signed with Lenville's scrawly signature, and there was no doubt about its authenticity.

There was a chance, however, that Lenville had not written it a few days ago, as the date proclaimed. Remembering the registration card at the Hotel Gladmere, The Shadow could picture Lenville signing this typewritten letter under threat, just as he might have been forced to sign that card.

The letter could be a cover-up, to encourage the theory that Lenville was seeking funds. His half million dollars could logically be regarded as a myth, on doctored evidence such as this. The one brightening fact was that Lenville, though being used, was probably still alive, as The Shadow had hoped.

Parridge didn't seem puzzled that Lenville had mentioned Cranston in the letter, in view of their supposed acquaintance. The Shadow, however, was looking for the reason, knowing that it must have been the idea of a hidden crook, not of Lenville.

The answer was plain. Through Harreck and others, it had become rumored that Lenville and Cranston were friends. Because of Cranston's reputed wealth, his name was the sort that would seem plausible when mentioned in connection with the turnover of a mere half million dollars.

From across the table, Parridge was tapping a paragraph in the letter, while he commented:

"This is the one part that puzzles me. The address where Lenville said he could he reached while in New York. That isn't the address of the Hotel Gladmere."

Parridge was right. It wasn't the Gladmere address. It was a number on a side street, in a forgotten area of Manhattan. It reminded The Shadow very much of the hideouts used by such crooks as Sleed and Zurman.

Perhaps the game was to bring Parridge there, but The Shadow could see that the haggard, darkish man had no intention of visiting the place; for the simple reason that Parridge agreed with the supposition that Lenville was dead. Therefore, he would logically regard the trip as useless.

It might not prove useless to The Shadow. He was more than eager to find a trap like the one that had discommoded Mildred Wilbin. In the indifferent manner of Cranston, he returned the letter to Parridge, with the comment that he would notify him if anything turned up concerning Lenville.

LEAVING the club, The Shadow calculated that he had half an hour before dark settled. Time enough to make crooks think that their snare had bait. Though they might be trying to lure Parridge, because he might know too much about Lenville, they wouldn't be totally disappointed if they saw Cranston as the nibbling fish.

All that The Shadow intended to do was nibble. He was carrying no guns at present, and he simply took the first cab that came along. Stopping at the corner nearest to the address in Lenville's letter, The Shadow strolled along the block until he came to the house in question.

He ascended the house steps and entered an open vestibule, very much like the one at Sleed's. Though the place seemed deserted, there was a button at the side of the vestibule. Whether it connected with some apartment or with a caretaker's room did not matter. The Shadow intended to tingle the bell, wait a few moments and stroll away in the dusk, allowing himself to be noticed as a visitor.

But when The Shadow pressed the single button, the result was quite unexpected. He received perhaps the most jolting surprise of his singular career. That contact changed the innocent-looking vestibule into a quick-acting trap.

The floor slithered inward beneath a locked door, sweeping right out from under The Shadow's feet.

The floor slithered inward beneath a locked door, sweeping right out from under The Shadow's feet.

Almost from midair, The Shadow performed an amazing dive toward the outer steps; but that desperate recovery was blocked by a heavy door that slashed across the opening.

Outwardly, the barrier looked like a house door, but its inner surface was of steel that The Shadow's hands could not clutch. An instant later, he was spinning down into the basement below, and only a series of quick acrobatic twists saved him from serious injury.

Though jarred when he landed, The Shadow was half to his feet when he heard the trap slide in place above his head. The dull *clang* told him that the floor of the vestibule was metal-sheeted on the under side. Once shut, it enclosed The Shadow in a pit of absolute darkness.

No laugh came from The Shadow's lips as a dull glow suddenly appeared, rising painfully from dimness to illuminate the scene about him. Whatever this plight, he intended to retain his pose of Cranston for the present.

His face was calm, his manner a trifle dazed. But despite their listless look, The Shadow's eyes were keenly interested in the increase of the light. For as that glow rose to a ghoulish, greenish gleam, the trap became an inhuman scene.

The Shadow was facing one of the strangest sights that his eyes had ever seen!

CHAPTER IX
THE SKULL SPEAKS

THE room itself was bare-walled, unfurnished; scarcely ominous, except for the fact that the walls were stone, and windowless. True, the place was sealed, and its grimy interior had taken on a deadly green from the indirect illumination high in the corners. But The Shadow had been in worse spots than this.

What made the room insidious was the fact that it was occupied—not by a human master but by a thing which, though seemingly alive, should have been dead!

Set in a niche at the far wall of the room was a life-sized living skull which glared at The Shadow, even with its eyeless sockets. A skull that gritted its teeth to emphasize its unchanging grin.

Green light shimmered from the death's-head, giving it an olive tone that looked like withered flesh. The thing could do more than glare. It spoke, with words that grated from its tight-closed teeth.

"You are welcome here, Shadow!" rasped the skull. "Welcome, even though you have come earlier than I hoped!"

Another listener would have felt full horror at hearing the skull speak. Not so The Shadow. Those words, despite their sepulchral note, merely dispelled the illusion that first had seized him.

No lipless mouth could have supplied the perfect pronunciation that the skull had used. With all its lifelike appearance, the head was no more than a mechanical contrivance wired for sound.

The distant speaker who was using it had no way of seeing what The Shadow did, nor could he hear what the prisoner said. The Shadow demonstrated that to his satisfaction, by strolling close to the skull and addressing it in the cool tone of Cranston.

The thing merely spoke again, as if by prearrangement. Its manipulator, in his ignorance, displayed a false contempt for The Shadow's courage.

"You cringe, Shadow!" jeered the skull. "You wonder how I know your identity; how I learned that you call yourself Lamont Cranston. When you have ceased to tremble, I shall tell you!"

By the time that last sentence came, The Shadow, far from cringing or trembling, was standing close beside the skull, examining its construction. The object glittered when viewed at close range. It was made of silver, and only at a distance did the green light's reflection make it look alive.

"I am Silver Skull!" The tone was boastful. "I am the one that you have sought and failed to find, until I chose. You are but the last of my many victims. Others have lived, but you shall die!"

From those bragging words, The Shadow divined that the master crook had proclaimed the actual title by which he was known to his followers: Silver Skull. Moreover, a quick link with a fact that The Shadow already knew, was proof of who the master killer was.

In an instant, the whole game was swept into sight. It fitted with everything that The Shadow had surmised; and this revelation added all the needed details. But with it came the stark realization that Silver Skull would not have so disclosed his game, unless positive that The Shadow could never escape this trap.

Therefore, escape was doubly imperative.

Through it, The Shadow could not only preserve his own life; he could hunt down Silver Skull. Once away from here, The Shadow could produce that master crook at almost any moment that he chose!

SILVER SKULL was gritting the details that he had promised; how he had learned that Cranston had sought facts concerning Lenville, and had therefore been the man who visited Zurman the night before. That, according to Silver Skull, had proven Lamont Cranston to be The Shadow.

"One thing alone remains," concluded the metallic voice, while The Shadow was rapidly tapping walls to see if any one offered an outlet. "That is the manner of your death. Your doom is already on its way. Listen!"

The Shadow listened. From vague spots high on the walls, came the rapid hiss of gas. Those pipes were too many to reach and plug. Within a very few minutes, this room would be completely filled with the asphyxiating vapor.

"Do not console yourself," came the harsh voice of Silver Skull, "with the thought that you may escape, as you did once before. This room is tightly sealed, and will remain so until the time comes to dispose of your corpse! That will be done automatically."

As proof of that future event, there were sharp crackles from live wires at intervals along the ceiling. The Shadow knew exactly what they signified. Once the room filled with gas, the sparks would ignite it. The Shadow would be blasted into nothingness, along with the masonry of this subterranean snare!

"You have entered by the only way," reminded Silver Skull. "That entrance is closed. You will go out by the only possible exit. A route that will take you from this world!"

The Shadow's fists tightened suddenly. His eyes burned from the fixed features of Cranston as vividly as the sparks that crackled from above.

Why had Silver Skull so carefully emphasized those points?

Because, besides those ways that he had mentioned, there was another; one that would serve both as entrance and exit. A way that Silver Skull had wanted The Shadow to overlook.

Followers of Silver Skull had planted this trap. Their work must have depended upon easy access to the place. Staring at the skull, The Shadow noticed the niche beyond it. It looked like an archway, but it had been camouflaged. It had been originally a doorway, leading to the back of the cellar.

The base of the niche was masonry, but the back of the recess might be wood. Stretching above the metal skull, The Shadow began to pound the plaster. It was woodwork, yes; but stout, and heavily bolted from the other side. Too strong to be demolished with bare hands.

Gunless, The Shadow had no way to blast that barred half door. Nor did he have a single tool that would be useful in the work. He had found the way to escape, but through his own folly in coming unequipped, he was still trapped.

Dropping back from the alcove, The Shadow could smell the strong odor of the gas. He wavered, as he inhaled it. Soon, what strength he had would fail. All the while, those taunts from Silver Skull were maddening him.

Quickly, The Shadow ripped off his coat and tie.

Of a sudden, The Shadow clamped his hands upon the shelf that bore that skull of metal; the projected mask, as it were, of the person who called himself Silver Skull. Gritted teeth were still issuing that laugh. Silver Skull had railed too long.

By forcing his taunts upon The Shadow, the master crook had suddenly awakened his visitor to a solution of the present problem!

CLAMPING both hands to the metal skull, The Shadow ripped it from the shelf. The wires that were used for the remote control, were broken by the yank. Short-circuited, they added sparks to those that crackled from the ceiling. But the mechanical skull no longer transmitted laughter.

It had become nothing but a chunk of metal, and a very heavy one, for its size. A battering ram in miniature, that skull; the very type of tool that The Shadow required. With both hands, The Shadow bashed the skull against the back of the alcove. Woodwork crackled under the stroke.

More blows followed. Powerful ones, that splintered the stout half door. Unmindful of the increasing gas, The Shadow had literally pounded a path to freedom. Hurling the skull to the floor, he doubled himself into the alcove and drove his full weight against the weakened wood.

The barrier split, sending The Shadow headlong into the rear cellar. Rolling over, he came to hands and knees and raised himself, to begin a sprint through the darkness that lay ahead.

The gas, however, was issuing from its many pipes much more rapidly than The Shadow supposed. He had not gone more than a dozen feet before the vapor ignited. There was a terrific tremor through the whole house, as the gas chamber burst with one huge explosive puff.

A sheet of green flame roared through the space that had been The Shadow's outlet, overtook the fugitive as he was sprawled by the blast. For an instant, The Shadow seemed lost in that licking streak; then the flame was gone.

Blinded by the sweep of flame, The Shadow could not see the route ahead. Deafened by the blast, he could not hear the crashing masonry about him. Half paralyzed by the long hurtle that he had taken, he was unable to raise his hands and ward off chunks of stone or falling beams that came in steady rain.

He seemed to be staggering into endless space, black space, soundless space, where things struck against him with jolts that he could not feel. For moments, he seemed to stumble upward; then he took a short downward lurch that flattened him. After that, it was a crawl along the level.

His eyes saw glimmers of light, his ears caught a jargon of sounds. Objects weren't hitting him any longer; but it might be that he simply didn't notice them. For The Shadow's strength was slipping, along with oozes of dampness that he did not recognize as blood.

Gradually, all effort failed him. His crawl ended as his limbs stretched forward to flatten, helpless. His recuperating senses left him. Nearer to death than life, The Shadow could no longer seek to escape the toils of Silver Skull.

With both hands, The Shadow had bashed the skull against the back of the alcove. Woodwork crackled under the stroke.

CHAPTER X
CROOKS FROM THE PAST

THE neighborhood about the old blasted house was filled with stirring clangor. First-comers converged upon the street in front of the ruined house. Fire sirens were wailing, bells clanging, above the crackle of flames that weaved from the broken brick walls.

In the rear street, their faces reddened by the glare, two persons were seated in an old two-door sedan. Their expressions had a demoniac touch, for they were pleased by the event that they had witnessed. Those watchers were George Sleed and Thelma Royce.

"Come on, Doc." Thelma's voice now showed anxiety. "Let's scram! There's no percentage in sticking around. We know the guy must've got the works."

Sleed shook his head. He was straining from the window, trying to make out something on the ground just beyond the range of the ruddy glow. Suddenly, his heavy lips emitted a harsh exclamation:

"Look there!"

Thelma looked. Sleed was pointing to an alleyway that led to this rear street. A flicker from the burning house showed a human shape, prone and limp, upon the paving. Sleed was out of the car an instant later, hauling Thelma with him.

Together, they rolled a man's form into the car, and while Thelma was still pulling the door shut, Sleed started to wheel away.

In the course of fifteen minutes, Sleed parked in a space behind an antiquated apartment house. He and Thelma carried their inert prisoner up an inside fire tower and laid him on a couch in a poorly furnished living room.

"It's Cranston, all right," declared Sleed, after poking through the scorched pockets of the unconscious victim. "The guy that Silver Skull was out to get. I guess I told you why, didn't I?"

"Yeah," returned Thelma. "Because he's supposed to be The Shadow!"

Her tone was somewhat dubious. Sleed noticed it and raised an objection.

"He's The Shadow, all right," declared the fake physician. "Only The Shadow could have gotten out of that warehouse cellar where we left him, and only The Shadow could have squeezed from the tighter jam he was in tonight."

"All right," agreed Thelma. "So what? The guy's croaked, and that's the end of The Shadow. All we've got to do is sink the body somewhere; then you can carry on the phony trail, like Silver Skull told you."

Sleed shook his head. He was eyeing very steadily the prone shape of Cranston.

"He isn't croaked," he decided. "He's pretty bad off from loss of blood, but he's not dead yet—and won't be!"

In professional style, Sleed brought a physician's kit from a corner. Thelma guffawed, when she saw him open the bag and take out instruments and bandages.

"What do you think you are?" she queried. "A doctor?"

"Why not?" returned Sleed, coolly. "I had an office once, didn't I?"

"Yeah, but no patients ever came there!"

"The Wilbin girl did. She took me for a doctor and accepted my advice."

"Sure! But you had to turn her over to me. I get the credit for prying her out of those fancy duds that we needed in our racket."

Sleed scarcely heard what Thelma said. He was busy probing The Shadow's wounds, stanching the flow of blood in expert style. He was humming to himself when he began to apply bandages, in a fashion so rapid that Thelma gaped.

"Say!" Thelma's voice showed admiration. "You *are* a medico, after all!"

"I *was* one," returned Sleed, "until reasons came along that made me quit the profession, just when I'd gotten into it. By the way, Thelma, where is that nurse's outfit of yours?"

"I put it away. You told me to wear a dark outfit tonight."

"I've changed my mind. Get into that nurse's dress, while I call up Silver Skull."

WHILE Thelma was making the change, she could hear Sleed on the telephone. He was giving Silver Skull a firsthand account of the explosion. Sleed made the description impressive.

"If the guy wasn't blown into chunks," Sleed told Silver Skull, "he's nothing but a mash, anyway. Because the roofs, walls, everything, was falling down into that cellar. There's not a chance that he's still alive!"

The Shadow was stirring very feebly as Sleed hung up. Thelma stepped into sight, giving a final pat to her nurse's costume. Sleed gave an approving nod as he noticed her trim, spotless appearance.

"I've figured it out, Doc," said Thelma. "You're a smart guy, and I'm sticking with you! You've got a right to look out for yourself. What Silver Skull won't know, won't hurt him."

Sleed raised his eyebrows, interested. Thelma proceeded with her statement.

"Silver Skull told you to head for the West Coast," she said, "pretending that you're Lamont Cranston. When you get there, you'll pick up ten grand that's waiting for you; then you lose the trail. Good enough.

"Only, Silver Skull don't always bump off these boobs that disappear. He keeps 'em alive, whenever he can use them in his business. So you're going to try that stunt yourself. Why not?

"You've got The Shadow, haven't you? There's plenty of big-shots—counting Silver Skull—who would hate to see The Shadow get back into circulation. You've got a gold mine, Doc—"

She stopped suddenly, staring at the pale face of Cranston. The Shadow's eyes were open; in them, Thelma saw a faint trace of the glitter that she had observed on another occasion. She felt an instinctive fear. Even in his present state, weakened and helpless, The Shadow was a factor to dread.

Sleed saw the reason for Thelma's qualms; but he noted, also, that The Shadow still lacked strength to strike. Coolly, Sleed brought a hypodermic syringe from his medical kit. While he was preparing it, he remarked:

"This will hold The Shadow for a while. It will keep him out of the picture a lot longer than you'll need, Thelma. Because you won't have to look out for him very long."

He punctured the flesh below The Shadow's shoulder, injected the contents of the hypodermic. The Shadow's eyes had already closed; he made no further effort.

"You've got a good bean, Thelma," approved Sleed, "but you don't want to get too far ahead in your ideas. Shaking down a lot of big-shots could become a pretty tough proposition. My own idea is somewhat different."

He stood back, to study The Shadow carefully. He decided that the patient needed another coat, and Sleed had one that would do. Thelma brought it from the closet; The Shadow was limp in their grasp, as they put the fresh coat on him.

Sleed glanced at his watch. He had plenty of time before his plane started for the West. He picked up the telephone and called a taxi.

"I'll wait out front," he told Thelma, "with the doctor's kit. I'll bring the taxi driver up with me, and when he sees a swell-looking nurse like you, he'll figure I'm a real medico, sure enough."

"And he can help us lug The Shadow," nodded Thelma. Then, her eyes suddenly puzzled: "But where are we taking the guy?"

Perhaps it was Sleed's recollection of The Shadow's recent recuperation that caused the crook to become suddenly secretive. At any rate, Sleed did not reply in his usual tone. Instead, he leaned close to Thelma's ear and whispered words that caused her to look puzzled, until he supplied an explanation.

As that came, Thelma's face showed sharpness. She was hearing Sleed's tale of a double-cross that left her breathless; and she listened, with a tightening smile, to the final details that concerned it.

When Sleed had hurried downstairs to await the cab, Thelma took a look around the hideout that they were about to leave, then gazed contemptuously at the doped form of The Shadow.

"You're smart, Shadow," sneered Thelma, "but not as smart as Silver Skull. Maybe Silver Skull can be outsmarted, too, but you won't be around when that happens!"

By which Thelma Royce implied that The Shadow, wherever he might be imprisoned, would find no future chance to deal with Silver Skull.

CHAPTER XI
DEATH IN THE AIR

A HUGE airliner was wending westward, away from the pursuing dawn. Below lay a sleeping world, but the myriad lights of cities had been left far behind. Ahead lay mountains, their summits dim against the starry sky.

The plane was the *Traveler*, speediest skysleeper in the service of Federated Airways, bound on a trip wherein flying conditions had proven ideal. With dawn about to break, the altimeter registering a height much greater than that of the loftiest mountains, this skyliner was showing that some of the Federated ships could fly without mishap.

This was the plane upon which Silver Skull had booked passage for Lamont Cranston, only to turn the ticket over to George Sleed, that the crook might lose the trail.

At the front of the aisle that led between the rows of sleeper berths, a blond stewardess was glumly studying the many unmade beds. Until a month ago, those berths had always been filled with passengers. Then business had dropped off in proportion to the number of accidents that had befallen Federated Airways.

Thought of those accidents was very bitter to Geraldine Murton, the stewardess. The newspapers had sobbed black ink over the deaths of passengers. She wondered what those same newspapers would have to say, if this trip ended in a crack-up, This was one voyage where passengers were distinctly in the minority.

In fact, there was only one passenger on board, as drawn curtains outside a single berth gave proof. It was something of a mystery to Geraldine why even one passenger would ride the *Traveler*. It was common knowledge that Federated simply ran the skyliner to keep up what little company prestige was left.

Forgetting the sleeping passenger—Lamont Cranston was the name he was booked under—Geraldine let her thoughts drift to the past. The smooth flight of the *Traveler* always made her ponder over a problem that was very close to home, particularly as her home was aboard a plane.

Why, with the flight officers that Federated ships carried; with two-way radio that gave them contact with the ground; with a course marked by hundreds of beacons, and a steady signaling radio beam—why could these ships meet with such frequent disaster, even when among the mountaintops?

The crack-up hoodoo didn't hound the planes of other lines. They had courses as difficult as Federated, and their ships were no better equipped. The tendency had been to blame the smashes on the pilots; but on that point, more than any other, Geraldine could offer sound dispute.

She knew these pilots, understood how confident they felt. Far from being nerve-shaken because of the recent crashes, they took the viewpoint that the jinx was ended. Tonight Geraldine, knowing the competency of the men at the controls, had felt safer on the *Traveler* than she could have on any other plane.

Faint dawn was streaking through a window near the rear of the plane. Passing the lone berth that had the drawn curtains, the stewardess reached the rearmost window and glanced downward. Below were peaks of mountains, gray in the darkness of the ground; black patches, that meant clusters of trees nestled in lower gullies.

Then, against a patch of black, Geraldine saw a streak of silver—a winged arrow, driving upward.

It was smaller than the airliner, and speedier. As it zoomed up beneath the tail of the larger ship, Geraldine recognized it as a pursuit plane. She saw a machine gun mounted above its cockpit, and wondered why an army aircraft should be navigating these mountains at dawn.

Then a tiny figure hooded with a silver helmet, was busy with the gun. In the confines of the airliner's air-conditioned cabin, Geraldine could not hear the sound that followed, but she saw the spurts of flame that issued from the machine gun.

As she recognized the horror of what was to come, Geraldine Murton had solved the riddle of past disasters.

That pursuit plane with its demonish silver-hooded pilot, intended to shoot down the giant *Traveler*. It was to be murder in midair, the thrust of a pirate plane against a defenseless skyliner!

Here was to be another tragedy; and from the closeness of the pirate plane, Geraldine realized that she had no more than a few seconds in which to hurry a warning to the pilots.

TURNING to dash along the passage, Geraldine saw a stir of the curtains at the one closed berth. Out from his nest swung the lone passenger, apparently just awake, although he was fully clad except for his coat. He stared at Geraldine as she shouted; she noted the blink of his eyes, the hollowness of his cheeks.

The stewardess didn't have to tell what she had seen. The passenger knew it. Like Geraldine, he could hear a crackle from the pilot's room ahead, see the chunks of metal popping from the passage near the connecting door. The machine-gun hail had already reached the skyliner.

The closeness of his own doom seemed to drive the lone passenger berserk. Flinging his arms wide, he threw himself in Geraldine's path. Though she knew that a warning could no longer aid the pilots, the stewardess was stubborn in her effort to reach the door ahead. In the struggle, the man started to push her toward the plane's stern.

Across the man's shoulders, Geraldine saw the door of the pilot room fling open. One of the flight officers rolled through, a bloody sight. Machine-gun bullets had finished him; and the other, at present handling the controls, was sinking from his seat.

No longer resisting the trapped passenger's drive, Geraldine flung her arm across her eyes.

The skyliner had begun a nose dive toward a mountain ridge. Flame spurting from its sides, the big ship was beyond the sight of the killer plane that had crippled it. A mass of plunging metal, the *Traveler* sheared off the tops of trees that snapped like slender saplings. It struck into rock and soil with a force that broke wings from the fuselage, twisting the whole ship into a distorted ruin.

Flames enveloped the thing that was no longer recognizable as an airplane, except for its uptilted tail. The nose had taken the brunt; the wings, as they shattered, had protected the ship's long stern.

As the flames licked high, a tiny door cracked open. Out pitched the uniformed figure of the stewardess, to land on the ground beside the settling tail.

Then came the passenger, in a grotesque sprawl that carried him beyond the girl. Eyes opening, Geraldine could see the rising figure of the man against the sweep of flame. The thought struck her that he must have realized what was due, the moment that he had seen her excitement.

A killer, like the silver-helmeted murderer in the plane! Probably the man whose life the vengeful attacker had sought, in a duel between crooks.

In that frantic analysis of the lone passenger, Geraldine Murton had summed the very intentions that normally belonged to the crook who styled himself Dr. George Sleed. But in this emergency, the passenger from the plane did not act in the ratlike fashion that Geraldine expected.

Beneath the glare of the flames that were consuming the plane, he stared blankly at the half-stunned stewardess as though wondering who she was. In dazed fashion, he leaned forward, plucked her uniform and dragged her away. Once clear of the furnace-like heat, he hauled the helpless girl half to her feet and steered her toward the nearest cluster of trees.

The metal of the shattered skyliner was white-hot. The withering fuselage curled like a burning match. The tail from which the stewardess and her rescuer had escaped, was twisting downward into the half-melted mass. Soon, it was a coiled lump of ruined metal, that no observer would consider to have been a place of temporary refuge after the crash had come.

Flames faded; but daylight was plain in the sky. From a distance came an increasing hum; a tiny airplane appeared above the ridge. It was the pursuit plane that Geraldine had seen, come to make sure that none aboard the skyliner had survived. After circling twice, the ship departed.

The closeness of his own doom seemed to drive the lone passenger berserk.

Standing close to a tree, Geraldine's rescuer watched the plane head toward the irregular horizon. His expression was dull no longer. Instead, his eyes were keen; in their sharpness, they had observed the insignia painted on the side of the scouting pirate plane.

Those eyes had seen a black triangle centered with a most appropriate symbol, a skull, painted in silver. A token that denoted the identity of the murderer who had added one more airliner to his toll: Silver Skull!

From his hiding spot upon the ground, the lone observer phrased a laugh so sinister that it faded as reluctantly as the dwindling darkness. With that laugh, he proclaimed a most singular fact.

This rescuer who had saved Geraldine, despite her own opposing struggles, was not George Sleed, the crook who had been scheduled to make the trip in place of Lamont Cranston.

The passenger from the skyliner was The Shadow!

CHAPTER XII
THE SHADOW'S PLAN

UNTIL nightfall, The Shadow and the rescued stewardess trekked their way among the mountain slopes, seeking a route back to civilization. They stopped at times, to rest at shady spots where they found mountain pools; and with thirst quenched, they made light of hunger.

During that intermittent hike, Geraldine gained a more accurate impression of Lamont Cranston. At one of their resting places, she told him of an earlier opinion she had formed.

"I thought you were a crook," she said. "The way you looked at me last night, when you were placed on the plane! Your eyes had a horrible stare; your face was distorted!

"This morning, when I encountered you, I saw traces of that same expression. Knowing that murder was in the air, I thought you were a party to it."

A slight smile came to Cranston's thin lips. This was the time to question Geraldine regarding certain matters.

"You say that I was placed aboard the plane," he remarked. "I suppose that the man who brought me there also looked rather a doubtful character."

"He did," recalled Geraldine. "He said he was a doctor, but I mightn't have believed him, except for the nurse he had with him. She appeared to be quite competent."

"He told you his name?"

"Yes—Dr. Sleed. And the nurse was a Miss Royce. But I noticed something odd about Sleed."

"I can tell you what it was. A diagonal scar that ran across his chin."

Geraldine nodded. She remarked that the scar had made her suspicious, because of Sleed's efforts to keep his chin from view. Anyone might have a scar, but only a crook would seek to hide one.

It was then that The Shadow, with Cranston's inimitable calmness, explained how he had fallen into the hands of crooks. An adventuresome individual, so he said, he had delved too deeply into the affairs of a master criminal called Silver Skull.

Last night, he had been doped, which accounted for his condition when he was started on the trip. But his experience represented but a part of the whole story. It was simply an index to the cunning of Silver Skull.

"Certain men of wealth were supposed to die," explained The Shadow, "because, in every case except Lenville's, Silver Skull had seen to it that their money would go to persons for whom it was not intended.

"For that very reason, the victims—Gurry, Breck and Wilbin—did *not* die. The reason"—he was staring at Geraldine's astonished look—"is quite obvious. Silver Skull intends to bleed the heirs who received those fortunes.

"He can do it, quite easily, if he has not already done so. Very easily, because he can prove to them that the real owners of the fortunes are still alive. Remember, he is dealing with renegades, who are not much better than crooks themselves. They will play the game he wants, rather than lose their share."

The dry chuckle with which Cranston ended that comment gave Geraldine another thought. Cranston evidently foresaw that by the time Silver Skull had finished bleeding the weaklings, they would have none of their wrongly inherited wealth. Silver Skull, it seemed, was a master of the double cross.

The Shadow's next statement proved that point.

"To fake the deaths of victims," he resumed, "Silver Skull had them booked as passengers aboard Federated planes. Persons had to go in their places; and in arranging that, Silver Skull was more than ingenious.

"He sent his own crooks as substitutes; the very ones who had helped dupe the victims. For Wilbin, he sent the man's own secretary, Fortner. In place of Lenville, he sent a crook named Delt, who had posed as Lenville for a day.

"They thought that their own trips would be safe; that they would lose the trail and receive a reward, when they reached the Pacific coast. Instead, they died while on their way there."

GERALDINE began to understand Cranston's own case. She listened with added interest, as he detailed it.

"My death was planned as a real one," he stated. "Sleed was to carry the trail. But Sleed was a better calculator than those who had gone before him. He guessed what had happened to others, like Fortner and Delt.

"When I fell into his hands, he saw his opportunity. He simply placed me aboard the plane, where I was supposed to be, and let Silver Skull do the rest. A very grim jest on Sleed's part; one that to all appearances was completed."

As they hiked farther through the mountains, Geraldine began to hear The Shadow's future plans. Since both Silver Skull and Sleed believed that Lamont Cranston was dead, it would be best for him to continue the illusion.

Sleed, of course, would be keeping out of sight, letting Silver Skull believe that it was he—not Cranston—who had been lost in the crack-up.

It would be necessary, too, for Geraldine to disappear. The world could think, along with Silver Skull, that no survivors had left the wrecked *Traveler*. That suggestion so appealed to Geraldine that it brought a firmness to her determined lips.

She would be able to do her part in hunting down the mysterious Silver Skull; in gaining vengeance for her friends—the pilots and others of the personnel—who had died in the series of disasters. She was willing to cooperate in any way that Cranston required.

With dusk at hand, it seemed that their campaign against Silver Skull would have to be delayed at least another day. But Cranston had hopes of an earlier beginning. He hadn't tramped these mountains without purpose.

Often, he told Geraldine, he had been lost in such mountains as the Himalayas, where habitations were far less frequent than in this section of the Rockies. All through the day, he had been gauging their course to gain outlooks over new valleys.

From the knoll where they stood at present, he picked out a feeble curl of smoke rising from among some trees. They promptly took that direction.

It was dark when they stumbled upon a cabin in the forest. The door was open; they found smoking embers in the fireplace that occupied a wall of the single room. There were crackers and canned goods on the shelves; an oil lamp on the table.

While they were eating, Geraldine asked: "Where are the people who own the place?"

"Out searching for us," replied Cranston, promptly. "Or to put it more accurately, for our plane. There is a town near here"—he pointed to an outspread map that he had laid on the table; the map had been in a hip pocket—"and the chaps who live here must have been there some time today."

Thought of the town pleased Geraldine, until she realized that she and Cranston could not come into sight without revealing the very facts that they planned to keep secret. If radio reports had reached the nearby village and searchers were scouring the mountainsides, the future might prove very difficult.

She watched Cranston's finger move along the map, saw his eyes show a gleam. He looked at the pencil flashlight that Geraldine carried and gave a smile.

"Let's rearrange things here," he suggested, "so that there will be no traces of our visit. Then we'll start along. We haven't very far to go."

They used the flashlight to pick their way through the darkness, with Cranston guiding their direction by the north star. At the end of two hours that to Geraldine seemed almost aimless, they came to a steep slope so covered with chunks of stone that it might have been the remnants of an avalanche.

Cranston drew a satisfied breath. He helped Geraldine up the slope; but before they reached the top, he was telling her to stop and remain low.

From somewhere came a vague rumbling that faded, rose again, each time with greater fervor. The sound took on a gaspy tone; from an angle, half a mile away, a giant searchlight split the night. The roar became the thunder of a locomotive.

They were on the side of a railroad embankment that The Shadow had noted from the map. The train was a freight, a long one, pounding its way upgrade.

OUT of sight below the backside, The Shadow and Geraldine almost felt the big Mogul champ by, the glare from the open firebox lighting the roadbed. There was a maddening clatter of passing cars, that dwindled only when flats were rattling past.

A clattery finish signified the caboose. When the self-made fugitives poked their heads over the embankment, they could see its taillights twinkling the rails.

The Shadow hurried Geraldine along the track in the direction taken by the freight. It seemed a fruitless chase, although the going was easy along the comparatively level roadbed. At the end of two miles, however, the reward came. They sighted the caboose standing beyond a curve.

The freight had taken to a siding, and would probably remain there quite a while, since there was no sound of an approaching train along the one-track line. The present task was to avoid any members of the train crew, and The Shadow managed that by picking a course above the track. That could be done, for at this spot the track ran through an open cut.

He and his companion were above the level of the caboose roof when they passed it. A hundred feet ahead, they slid down beside the train and moved farther forward in its shelter. It was when they could hear the panting of the big ten-wheeler up ahead, that The Shadow used the flashlight in guarded fashion, until he found the door of an empty boxcar.

"This is better than the Himalayas," remarked Geraldine, as they rested in the boxcar's gloomy depths. "At least, we've found a way of getting somewhere without walking all the way."

"Exactly!" came Cranston's agreement. "As soon as the other train passes us, we'll start rattling for Denver. It will be difficult to talk then, so we'd better make our plans."

"Regarding Silver Skull?"

"Yes. It is obvious that he must have a base somewhere near the spot where he shot down the *Traveler*. Within a hundred and fifty miles, at most."

Geraldine agreed. She knew the Federated route. All the lost planes had come to grief within a range of a few hundred miles. Previously, however, no one had recognized the significance of that fact.

"Wherever the base is," continued Cranston, "a good airman could locate it without attracting too much notice, if he pretended that he was looking for the *Traveler*."

Again, Geraldine agreed. She was wondering, though, how the right pilot could be found, when Cranston asked:

"Did you ever hear of Kent Allard?"

"Have I?" laughed Geraldine. "Who hasn't! Do you know him, Mr. Cranston?"

"Quite well! I believe that when he hears from me, he will come to Denver immediately. You can join him when he arrives, and give him all the details that he needs."

Geraldine was surprised that Cranston did not expect to aid in the search for Silver Skull. Then came his reminder that Sleed was still at large in New York; that, if located, the fake doctor could probably disgorge much-needed facts. The hunt for Sleed seemed a logical task for Cranston.

Those arrangements had all been made when a passenger train came clattering by on the main track. Its lighted windows had scarcely flashed from view, before there was a jolt along the freight train's length. There were chugs from the Mogul, rapid as the spins of its ten big wheels.

Then the freight was on its way, battering, swaying down the grade, clanking and clattering. But that tumult was music to the tired ears of Geraldine Murton. It meant the end of a long, hard trail, with a promise for the future.

The girl was asleep, her blond head resting comfortably on Cranston's shoulder, while his arm, encircling her snuggled body, protected her from the lurch and swing of the jolting car.

Then the lips of The Shadow phrased their strange, sinister laugh; a tone that was lost amid the roar and rumble of the onrushing train.

That laugh was another promise; the culmination of all that The Shadow had made.

Its mirth predicted ill for Silver Skull!

CHAPTER XIII
THE DESERT LAIR

FROM the tiny cabin of a trim biplane, Geraldine Murton was watching the landscape a mile below, viewing a scene that seemed as monotonous as the droning of the plane's motor.

This was the second day of the search for some trace of Silver Skull, and with that tedious hunt, Geraldine found her thoughts reverting constantly to past events.

She remembered her arrival at Denver; how she had disguised her uniform well enough to register at an obscure hotel. There, Lamont Cranston had left her; but he had handled everything in an amazing style.

How he had managed to keep his identity undisclosed, Geraldine couldn't guess; but she knew that, somehow, he had wired New York and had promptly received funds by telegraph. Clothes had been delivered at Geraldine's room, to replace the stewardess uniform that she wore. Money, too, had arrived there, to defray her expenses.

Then Kent Allard had called. The famous aviator had heard her story; together, they had mapped out their search. Here they were, together in this plane, engaged in that painstaking quest. Quite a contrast to that long hike and train ride with Cranston.

It was interesting to contrast the two, Allard and Cranston. Each man seemed the other's opposite. Looking at Allard as he handled the controls, Geraldine saw a firm thin-featured face, with gaunt lines that might have been hewn from solid stone. He seemed possessed with an energy which he was careful to reserve for tests that were to come later.

Contrarily, Cranston had shown no such indications. His manner had been a leisurely one, but behind that pose had lain tremendous endurance. His face, fuller than Allard's, had masked his expressions as capably as his manner had concealed his strength.

Of the two, Geraldine could not decide which she liked the better. She wished that she could see them together, and thereby make her choice. It never occurred to her that she was asking the impossible.

Of all the skillful tactics adopted by The Shadow, none was more subtle than his method of keeping his two personalities entirely distinct. No one could ever have mistaken Kent Allard for Lamont Cranston, or vice versa.

Geraldine heard Allard speak. His tone was steady, rather than calm; blunt, in contrast to Cranston's half-drawl. He was asking Geraldine to check the airport guide, to identify a town that he saw below.

The girl thumbed through the thick book, found the page that Allard wanted. While the plane was changing course, she glanced idly at other pages, noting the insignia of private aircraft that were interspersed through the information section.

She had noted various emblems on other private ships that they had seen searching for the lost *Traveler*. She remembered the symbol on this plane of Allard's a black hawk against a golden circle.

There were colored plates in the front of the book, that illustrated all such insignia. Geraldine was turning to those pages, when Allard reached over and politely took the book away from her.

"Look below," he said, coolly, "and tell me what you see."

"It looks like desert," declared Geraldine. "Very rough, with no more chance for landing than in the mountains."

Allard nodded agreement.

"It's the last stretch," he declared. "We have flown everywhere else within the estimated range. Simple elimination tells us that the base must be somewhere near."

STARING below, Geraldine felt that Allard was mistaken. The light of the setting sun showed hopeless tracts of cactus-studded soil, where bare rocks poked above the alkali surface. They were miles from the last town, and the book didn't list another landing field anywhere in this vast area.

In fact, the ground was becoming worse as it billowed toward the chunky foothills. Rocks were everywhere, and one cluster in particular seemed a warning landmark, that to any aviator would symbolize the futility of bringing a plane to earth on this terrain.

A gleam had come to Allard's eyes. Geraldine noticed it because she was looking at him, wondering why he was heading straight for that mass of boulders, the last place where a search might logically prove worthwhile. Then, as they neared the spread of rocks, she saw his finger point.

Curiously, those boulders weren't banked as closely as Geraldine had thought. They seemed in tiers, because some were larger than the others, and between lay steps of level ground. Noting one space in particular, Geraldine gave an excited gasp.

The stretch formed a rough oval, its smoothed surface free of the cactus clusters that were so frequent elsewhere. This isolated spot, shunned by passing airmen, had all the makings of a landing field off in the lost reaches of the desert.

The very rocks that most aviators would pass by with a glance were a perfect beacon for anyone who knew this secret airport. Moreover, those boulders could serve as ideal lookout spots for anyone scanning the sky in search of prying planes.

Cannily, Allard was skirting the hidden base, making his visit appear an accidental one. He didn't shy off suddenly, for that would have been a giveaway to observers. Instead, he merely took a natural swing in the direction of the distant mountains, as though they were his objective.

To all intents, he was a searcher for the missing *Traveler*, picking another hunting ground among the mountains. Not having flown across the space amid the rocks, he would not be credited with having noticed it.

During the next quarter hour, Allard kept constant watch upon the dials. Then, as dusk was closing about the biplane, he veered and took a direct course back toward the rock-bound airbase.

Geraldine knew they couldn't land there openly, and she was totally at loss regarding any alternative. Allard, however, had a plan; as he undertook it, Geraldine was gripped by awe and admiration. A few miles short of the hidden airport, Allard was dipping for the desert soil!

There were rocks here, many of them; but there were spaces, too, if Allard could find them. Yet Geraldine almost preferred the rocks. She could foresee devastating results when the wheels hit the rough dust-strewn ground. Vaguely, she remembered that Allard had once landed safely in a jungle, and she could only hope that he would equal that miraculous feat.

The landing came. To Geraldine, it seemed a cross between a perfect three-point and a pancake, if such could be possible. The plane shivered as it plowed the heavy soil, mowing through sagebrush and cactus.

Then Allard was helping Geraldine to the ground, reflected silver against the darkening sky. The amazed breath that Geraldine took caused her to choke from the dust that she inhaled. Allard steered her from the murky cloud around the plane, and they began their march toward the rocks, a few miles away.

They were a stout pair: Allard, in his aviator's costume; Geraldine, her slacks tucked into high boots, helmet and goggles above her jacketed shoulders. Both were armed with automatics that Allard had brought along. The next hour offered them real opportunity, for the full moon had not yet risen in the desert sky.

Allard did not slow their pace until they reached the fringe of rocks. Then, with a low whisper for Geraldine to copy him, he used tactics that he must have learned in the Central American jungles. He became a gliding shape among the rocks; slow, cautious, but so elusive that Geraldine could scarcely follow him.

Fortunately, the tall, slim blonde was built for this sort of work; a fact upon which The Shadow depended. She was almost his own shadow, as they stole among the forbidding boulders, seeking some trace of a human lair. When the test came, however, it was only Allard who was quick enough to meet it.

He stopped with silent suddenness, flung out an arm to hold back Geraldine. The girl stumbled; she failed to repress a startled exclamation. A sharp snarl answered; from between two rocks, a long-limbed human figure flung itself straight for them.

THE guard didn't betray himself by a light. Instead, he swung hard in the darkness, using a rifle as a club. Simultaneously, The Shadow's hand made a cross slash; there was a hard *clang* as the full weight of his automatic met the rifle barrel.

Then came a quick struggle in the darkness, where Geraldine heard thrashing figures that she couldn't see. A flashlight blinked; in its glow, Geraldine saw a rangy man stumbling toward her, his rifle gone, his hands flapping like his wobbly lower jaw.

She heard Allard's voice, a brisk, low-toned command:

"Take him!"

Geraldine thrust an automatic's muzzle against the guard's ribs. He gave a groan and sank against a rock. Holding him at gun point, Geraldine saw beyond the fellow's shoulder and thereby witnessed the next event.

Allard had swung the flashlight about, to disclose a rough flight of steep stone steps beneath a looming boulder. Below, a man was stepping through an iron door, aiming a rifle upward. He had heard the cry from the outside guard and was stepping out to learn the trouble.

The Shadow's bold use of the flashlight proved the best move possible. Blinking into the gleam, the man with the rifle couldn't see the figure behind it. He thought, for a second, that the person with the light must be the other guard turning to summon him.

That second was enough. In it, Geraldine saw Allard take a reckless plunge that matched his daring landing in the desert. It looked like a breakneck dive, down those stone steps, but The Shadow counted on something that would break his fall and found it: the figure of the man below.

Landing full upon the guard, he flattened the fellow, rifle and all. Finger jarred from the trigger, the foeman dropped the rifle and tried to grapple as The Shadow snapped off the flashlight. Again, Geraldine was hearing a thrashing struggle; amid it, gargly efforts toward a shout that was never given.

Getting a throat hold on the guard, The Shadow was using his elbows to ward off the man's gripping hands. Tenaciously, The Shadow's clutching fingers were doing more than hold back the alarm that his foeman tried to shout. They were choking the fellow into final submission, which came with the very suddenness that The Shadow expected.

The figure sank limp beside the rifle. Up the steps came Allard's low voice, telling Geraldine to march her prisoner down. She did so, by the greeting glow of the flashlight. Still groggy, her charge didn't try to make trouble. He could feel the nudge of the automatic that Geraldine kept pressed against his ribs.

While Geraldine covered with gun and flashlight, The Shadow put her prisoner to work helping bind and gag the man who lay senseless. After that, Geraldine found herself assisting Allard in the binding of the first prisoner. She saw Allard open the metal door; beyond, the flashlight showed a vaulted passage that led beneath the rocks.

There was a small room to one side, filled with boxes of canned goods. That was where The Shadow stowed the prisoners, with Geraldine's aid. Then, in the steady manner of Kent Allard, he beckoned for the girl to follow him into the deeper passage.

Guiding their course with cautious blinks of the flashlight, The Shadow was setting out to explore the depths of Silver Skull's desert domain!

CHAPTER XIV
THE SHADOW'S CALL

THE route that the invaders had used was not the only entrance to this lair. The Shadow learned that from two things that he observed as they went deeper; first, the absence of any guards; second, the fact that there were other passages leading upward, obviously to outlets where watchers were on duty.

Though the situation presented opportunities to deal with scattered guards in little groups, it was better to learn more about the lair before beginning that campaign. Therefore, The Shadow and his blond companion kept to the deeper course.

They reached a dimly lighted hollowed room that had been hewn from crevices among deep-buried rocks. The chamber was a large one, totally deserted, and for the first time, The Shadow was interested in a passage that led upward from it. It was a broad, low-ceilinged slope, with track marks among the rocks.

Exploring it, The Shadow and Geraldine came into another chamber, where a mammoth shape was spread like a silent, moody creature from some prehistoric age. The flashlight's puny glitter reflected from the thing's broad wings, to reveal it as an old transport plane.

The room was an underground hangar. In front of the plane was a huge stretch of canvas supported by metal struts. Unquestionably, the outer surface of that canvas was painted to resemble a rocky layer of the desert.

Leading straight to the landing field, the opening would allow the plane's crew to get the ship rapidly into the air. It happened, however, that none of the crew was about. The hangar, like the hollowed-out underground meeting room, was completely deserted.

The big transport was not the ship that Silver Skull had used to sink the *Traveler*; but there was space here for his pursuit plane and a few others, should he require it.

Geraldine saw Allard produce a flat box that he had brought from his own plane. Telling her to keep watch, he stepped into the transport. When he returned, Geraldine asked, hopefully, if he had put the big ship out of commission. Allard shook his head.

"It may prove best," he said, "to let that plane leave. The box that I hid aboard gives out automatic radio impulses. It will be better in the plane, as it will enable us to trace the ship's course with a direction finder, if she leaves."

They returned to the hollow center room. There, Allard found new interest in a single passage that led deeper into the ground. He decided that it deserved inspection before they took other steps. Descending, they left the dim light of the center chamber, only to meet a new glow from below.

Past a turn, The Shadow viewed a narrow corridor, with doors in it that looked like cell openings. A guard was strolling in the opposite direction; finishing his round, he went to a room beyond. The Shadow could hear muffled voices.

"There's a reserve crew here," he told Geraldine, grimly. "But maybe I'll have a chance to look into some of those cells."

Reaching the first cell, The Shadow looked through the bars, to see a girl stretched on a cot staring at the ceiling. She was wearing slacks, like Geraldine's; a flannel shirt that was open at the neck. Above a smooth, white throat, The Shadow could see a determined chin that he remembered; particularly when he noted the distinct brown of the girl's rumpled hair.

The prisoner was Mildred Wilbin!

THE cell door had a bolt, out of reach from inside, but easily manipulated in the corridor. The Shadow slid it silently, but instead of opening the door, he took a quick glance down the corridor, then rejoined Geraldine.

He told the blonde who the prisoner was; then made a steady-toned suggestion that left the choice absolutely to Geraldine.

"Suppose you change places with her," he said. "She may be able to tell me a great deal about Silver Skull. You have a gun and if a pinch comes, you can help. Especially, since they won't expect an attack from your quarter."

Geraldine promptly agreed to the plan. She sidled into the corridor, opened the door of the unlocked cell. The Shadow heard low whispers, as the girls talked; then Mildred came out and bolted the door behind her.

She had scarcely joined The Shadow before the guard returned. In his patrol, he glanced into the cell; but The Shadow and Mildred saw him go his way without suspecting what had occurred.

Having recognized Kent Allard, Mildred was eager to tell of her adventures; but she kept silent, at her rescuer's warning, until they had reached the central cavern. There, she waited again, to let Allard look around the place.

He saw a door, opened it cautiously and found a tiny wireless room, quite deserted. They entered the room and Mildred began her story.

She told how she had found the telephone number on Fortner's slip and had called it; but she had difficulty in describing the vague voice that had mentioned John Lenville, then Dr. Sleed, as coming victims.

Then she explained that she had visited Sleed to warn him, only to find herself feeling very ill. She told how Sleed had turned her over to the nurse, Miss Royce, who had seemed very sympathetic and had promptly helped her to undress for bed.

Very suddenly, as Mildred remembered it, she had been entirely unclothed, waiting for Miss Royce to unfold a nightgown for her. But she hadn't come to her senses until she had been tucked into bed. Then she had roused, too late.

"The room was locked," recounted Mildred, "and I could hear gas entering it. Miss Royce was gone, and she had taken my clothes along. I wonder"— Mildred's frown was a perplexed one—"why she bothered to take them, since I was helpless."

The Shadow explained how Thelma had changed her own attire, so she could pose as Mildred and drive away in the yellow roadster. Mildred's eyes flashed indignation; along with it, The Shadow could see determination. Like Geraldine, Mildred was a girl upon whom he could depend in any clash with crooks.

Meanwhile, other matters needed prompt discussion. First, that ill-chosen telephone call that had been the cause of Mildred's later embarrassment.

"After the voice had named Lenville," quizzed The Shadow, "did it say anything that you didn't quite understand?"

"Yes," returned Mildred. "It said something about 'silver'; but that was all."

"You should have replied 'skull,' to complete the countersign. Since you failed to do so, the voice recognized that you were not Thelma Royce and promptly tricked you."

"Skull?" questioned Mildred. "Silver Skull? It sounds like a name."

"It is a name. Of the crook we must seek. So tell me what happened to you after you were gassed."

Mildred sensed urgency in Allard's tone, and rapidly supplied the details.

"It must have been hours later," she related, "when I found myself lying on a cot, wrapped like a mummy in a lot of blankets. Men were in the room, removing a big square box that was padded on the inside. They carried it out and closed the door.

"I squirmed out of the blankets and rested a short while. All I had on was the nightie that Miss Royce had given me. But these clothes"—she gestured to the flannel shirt and slacks—"were on a chair, so I dressed myself in them.

"I am sure that the place was in the East, because, later, I was put aboard a plane and brought here. It was a night flight and I saw the sunrise. It was behind us."

News that Silver Skull had an Eastern base was important to The Shadow. He asked for its description and Mildred told him what little she could. The place had reminded her of a cabin, a very large one. She was sure that other prisoners were being kept there.

"Perhaps my uncle is still alive," declared the girl. "He and others—like John Lenville."

THE girl saw Allard ponder. The Shadow agreed with Mildred's theory, but he was trying to deduce why she had been brought to the desert base. The only plausible reason was that Silver Skull was on his way here, and intended to quiz the girl.

That offered complications. Under present circumstances, it would be best to forestall Silver Skull. The thugs who guarded this hidden air base were numerous, but of comparatively poor caliber. They could be handled easily, a few at a time.

Some of those crooks would talk. From them, The Shadow could learn the location of the Eastern base and fly there. He would be on his way while Silver Skull was arriving at a scene of chaos, here in the desert.

Then, his gaze upon the wireless set, The Shadow formed a plan that offered better prospects.

He calculated the potential results that would come if he sent out an SOS from here—a call to the law, bringing a score of planes to the hidden landing field.

News of a secret base illegally maintained would bring results without mention of Silver Skull. Soon after sending the call, The Shadow could be on his way, flying the big transport plane upon which the crooks here depended.

They couldn't hear the wireless call go out. The transport would be taking off before they could stop it. As guides and crew members, The Shadow could bring along the two guards who lay helpless; and in addition, he would have Mildred and Geraldine.

Silver Skull, even if he intercepted the message, would not guess that the sender was heading East with informants telling him how to reach the other base. Only one person, in Silver Skull's estimate, would be capable of such strategy: The Shadow.

And Silver Skull believed The Shadow dead!

Mildred, watching Allard, saw his fingers come to life. As if imbued with an impulse of their own, they began to send the message. Three times, The Shadow repeated the message giving the location of the desert base.

Next, he was dismantling the set. Crooks, when they found it, wouldn't be able to flash news to Silver Skull. Their ship gone, they would be stranded here. Surrounded by the desert, they would find it useless to flee. The law could conquer them while The Shadow was soaring to another mission.

With Mildred, The Shadow hurried through the passage by which he and Geraldine had reached the central cavern. The prisoners were lying as The Shadow had left them, in the storeroom near the metal door. Unbinding them, he was explaining exactly what they were to do, when he became conscious of a faint, muffled thrum.

The Shadow told Mildred to go up the steps and report what sounds she heard. Once she had opened the metal door, the thrumming noise became very loud. It was Mildred who saw the rest.

Against the risen moon, a swift plane sped overhead. It dropped an object that burst in midair, emitting a lurid, crimson flare. In that spurt of vivid light, the plane was outlined like a hellish bird.

Upon the plane, Mildred saw the leering symbol of a silver skull, stained scarlet by the glow. She knew the flare to be a warning, meant for the guards that Allard had intended to leave at their various posts.

Silver Skull had been the first to catch The Shadow's call. Close to his own domain, the master crook had come to flash the word, then make for other parts.

No longer did the odds lie with The Shadow. The balance favored the fighters who served Silver Skull!

CHAPTER XV
CRIME'S RALLY

BY the time Mildred was down the steps, blurting the news of Silver Skull's passage overhead, she saw that Allard was already on the move. He had turned the prisoners around, to start them down the passage at the point of a gun.

He motioned toward the little storeroom, telling Mildred to pick up the rifles and bring them along.

Then Allard was on his way, driving the prisoners ahead of him.

The rifles made a heavy, cumbersome load, but Mildred lugged them gamely as she stumbled toward the moving gleam of The Shadow's flashlight. She was hoping that they could still release Geraldine, and get aboard the plane in the underground hangar. That plan, however, was doomed.

Suddenly, the flashlight stopped its forward movement. Catching a blink that seemed like a beckon, Mildred hurried ahead. In the dim glow at the entrance to the central cavern, she found Allard waiting, with the prisoners cowed against a passage wall.

The Shadow put away his flash. Then, with one sweep of his left arm, he gathered the rifles from her. With his right hand, he planked an automatic in Mildred's hand. In clipped words, he told the girl to keep the prisoners covered; to stay here. Strapping one rifle across his back, he started forward with the other.

Mildred suddenly saw the reason for The Shadow's move. Men had already come from the guardroom below, and from the noise they were making, were in the hangar, preparing for a quick flight. They weren't wasting time in raising the reinforced canvas. They were slashing it with axes, when The Shadow, running up the broad passage, ordered them to stop their work.

It was evident that Allard meant business. The startled crooks stopped abruptly, proving that The Shadow needed neither black cloak nor sinister tone to make such foemen yield. There was a mutinous air, however, among those thugs, as they stood with uplifted arms. Instead of cowering, they muttered. The situation needed only some chance change to set it awry.

The break came before The Shadow had time to properly subdue his new prisoners. There was a slashing clatter from a door that flung suddenly open. Two crooks sprang, fuming, from the wireless room, where they had found the wrecked equipment. They ran partially up the hangar passage, saw the figure of Allard clad in aviator's costume and took him to be the sort of foe that they could handle.

Guns out, the pair were firing quick shots as The Shadow swung to meet them. They expected him to dive away, to become a helpless target when they found their aim. Instead, he gave them bullets with a precision that promptly ended their thrust.

With each crack of The Shadow's rifle, a thug floundered in the air, came down a writhing chunk of sprawled humanity, thinking no longer of battle. Neither of those doubled fighters tried to pick up the revolver that he had dropped.

The men in the hangar heard the rifle shots but could not see what happened. They were yanking revolvers of their own, raising a wild shout as they headed for The Shadow. He was up the passage again, firing the rifle as they came; but this time, his shots clipped only one adversary. The rest were scattering quickly, to find cover about the big plane.

As he completed his hurried fire, The Shadow made a fast retreat. His rifle was empty; he needed cover of his own. One gunman, scenting the dilemma, came loping through the passage. The Shadow sidestepped before the fellow's revolver spurted, then met the crook with a clubbed stroke of the rifle just as the man began to shoot.

Staggered, that foeman reeled away. Flinging the rifle aside, The Shadow reached the central room. Picking a strategic corner, he unlimbered the reserve rifle, ready for the next attack. He was baiting the crooks from the hangar, hoping that they would try to ferret him out.

Yet, all the while, The Shadow had his eye on the passage that led below. He would have to reach it later, to release Geraldine. He was depending upon the stewardess to take care of matters herself, by way of start, for she had a gun of her own. One shot, however, from that gun would have brought The Shadow straight to her aid.

THEY were here, the mob from the hangar, howling as they sought their prey, swinging their guns in every direction. The Shadow met them with a sudden fire that sent the whole crew to scattered cover, so rapidly that he could scarcely tell which of the scramblers had been wounded.

Amid the puny bursts of answering revolvers, The Shadow tossed away the second rifle. From now on, it would be a close-quarters fight, quick sallies with his automatic—a reserve weapon he pulled from his aviator's jumper—as the prevailing weapon. He wouldn't have to worry about reloading. There would be plenty of unfired revolvers to be picked up as he went along.

With one quick sideward dive, The Shadow met a rising foeman point-blank, beat the crook to the shot. Hurtling the sagging foeman, he used the fellow as a bulwark, while he aimed for another. Coolly, he was scooping up the dropped revolver with his free hand, when, amid the scattered fire of bewildered enemies, he heard the rise of a new tumult.

Men were coming from everywhere except the lone passage where Mildred stood guard over two sullen prisoners. They were the distant outpost guard, heading in from the various corridors. At the same moment, a cluster of men piled up from the lower passage. With them was Geraldine, her arms pinned behind her. The blonde was struggling furiously to get at the gun that she carried.

Crooks didn't know that she had a weapon; they simply thought that she was trying to break away. Geraldine had waited until they dragged her from the cell, and then had found it was too late. The hands that pinned her, to prevent her escape, were so many that she couldn't even draw the gun.

At least, Geraldine was keeping her captors fully occupied. The Shadow let that group rush across toward the hangar. He saw Geraldine stumble, come up half stunned. No longer struggling, she was dragged along limply. Her captors weren't stopping to fight. The only way to overtake them and rescue her would be to blast a path through the other crooks who had flooded the big meeting place.

The Shadow proceeded to that herculean task. In appearance, he still was Allard; but in action, he was The Shadow. A combination that worked surprisingly to his advantage, in this dim-lit battleground. Gunmen didn't expect the shifts from Allard that they would have from The Shadow.

When the lone fighter stopped, he looked like a fixed statue, the sort of target that any marksman could pick off with a slow aim. Then, with a whirl, he would be gone, while surprised crooks were firing too late. Out of each twist, he would abruptly halt again. Invariably, his shots would drop the one marksman who had the best chance of getting him.

Sometimes he swooped, to come up with a fresh revolver. It was startling, the way he plucked those weapons in haphazard fashion; juggled them squarely to his trigger finger, and fired straight to a living target while his hand was still on the move.

Wounded crooks weren't heeding the howls of their pals to stick around and help. They were crawling, staggering in the direction of the hangar, anxious to join the men who were hacking away the remnants of the canvas and preparing to board the plane.

AGAINST overwhelming odds, The Shadow had paved the way to conquest. Victory seemed in his grasp, despite the fact that he had been forced to meet criminals in united combat. It had been skill, not luck, that had served him in the struggle. When the first fluke came, it worked against The Shadow, not for him.

He had snatched a fresh revolver from the floor beside a wall; probably the last of those captured weapons that he should have required. His hand had made its flip; the muzzle was swung toward a wild-eyed foeman who was taking hasty aim. Then, almost with his trigger tug, The Shadow went into a sudden dive.

The revolver was empty; he seemed to feel it as the hammer hit. Instead of a shot from The Shadow's gun, one came from the foeman's weapon. Something stung The Shadow's gun arm, jolted it high up. The revolver spun flashing in the dim light, as his dive became a sprawl.

There were gleeful howls from crooks, but they were very few. All but a mere three or four had been silenced, or had fled. The remaining thugs fired ardently, but their shots were as few in number as themselves, for they had almost emptied their guns.

In fact, the man who had clipped The Shadow had done it with a final bullet, and he was the only one close enough to add more damage. Rolling across the floor, regardless of his burning shoulder, The Shadow was followed—not overtaken—by the pinging slugs that ricocheted from the rocky ground.

With a long lunge, he clamped his good hand on a revolver that lay in his path; came suddenly up on his elbow and began to pull the gun trigger. Luck balanced; the revolver was a loaded one. Attackers, their own guns exhausted, took to frantic flight.

Half groggy, The Shadow didn't clip them as they ran; but his shots were close enough to spur the fight. The battlefield was his; he was still determined to overtake the fugitives and prevent their getaway in the plane. But a new situation intervened to delay him.

During The Shadow's flounder, Mildred's prisoners had decided to jump her gun. The girl had been startled by their sudden rush, but had proven equal to it. With a backward step, Mildred fired; then stopped in blank amazement at the thing that happened.

One of the huskies sank without a gulp. From a snarling, threatening human beast, he had been transformed into an inert mass. The other crook dropped back against the wall; he, too, was changed. His hands were no longer reaching claws; they were flabby. His raucous voice had softened to a pitiful plea; he was begging Mildred not to shoot.

Her eyes upon the crumpled form in front of her, Mildred scarcely heard the other man's whine. Her hand sank, carried downward by the weight of the automatic. Though the silent man before her would willingly have killed her, Mildred was stunned by her deed of self-defense.

Her head whirled; the world seemed blank, except for that sprawled shape upon the passage floor. She didn't realize her own bewilderment; but there was someone who suddenly recognized it—the other crook.

His whine chopped short. With a howl of ugly joy, he sprang upon Mildred and flung her across the passage. The gun bounced from her hand, landed in darkness. The noise it made was the clue to its location. Diving for the gun, the crook grabbed it, swung about to shove the weapon directly between Mildred's dazed eyes.

HE must have relished the thought of murder, that crook, for he was deliberate, in a tantalizing way, when he fingered the gun trigger. Perhaps he wanted Mildred to realize what was due; to have the girl beg for mercy that he would never give.

Whatever his thoughts, they were so intent that he had forgotten the battle in the cavern; had taken it for granted that the rolling figure of Kent Allard had stilled after a final writhe.

The Shadow had heard Mildred's shot. One arm dangling, he was approaching the passage, sacrificing speed for stealth. He was banking wholly upon the killer's deliberation, until he came within reaching distance of the would-be murderer.

Then, his good hand thrust before him, The Shadow drove. His fingers clamped a gun wrist, his weight sent the crook across the passage. The gun spoke, but not in Mildred's direction. The bullet was lost against the passage wall.

Roused by the shot, Mildred saw two flaying figures. She realized that though the advantage was Allard's, he was wounded; striving with one hand to out-wrench his foeman's two. The gun disappeared suddenly between the grapplers; Mildred heard it speak a muffled blast and added a scream that was a horrified echo.

She saw the two figures coil to the floor, like the man that she had dropped. Then, after a moment that seemed interminable, Allard's shoulders moved. Coming weakly to his knees, he shook aside dead arms that clutched him. The crook's form flopped heavily, to settle as still as the stones that formed its resting place.

Weakly, The Shadow pointed with the gun he had wrested, and Mildred understood. He was still intent upon pursuit through the passage to the hangar. But he could scarcely rise when Mildred tried to help him. When he finally stood, wavering from her supporting grasp, they both heard sounds that told them chase was useless.

From the hangar came an echoing roar, that faded as the transport plane taxied out to the landing field. Then came the more distant rumble of the take-off; finally, the purr that trailed to nothingness, signifying that the plane had taken the air.

Manned by a skeleton crew, carrying a quota of crippled crooks, with Geraldine along as a lone prisoner, the ship was off on the long flight to its unknown Eastern base.

Though he had outbattled the horde that served Silver Skull, The Shadow had found his efforts nullified. He had rescued Mildred, but Geraldine had been captured. Among the crooks who strewed the underground lair, none was alive to blab the trail.

Still, the campaign was not ruined. There would be future ways to meet and frustrate Silver Skull and the mobsmen who served him.

The Shadow knew!

CHAPTER XVI
THE SECRET SEARCH

THOUGH The Shadow's battle had not brought him the desired result, he had certainly banished all opposition from the desert air base. That fact was a fortunate one, for during the next few hours, the intrepid fighter could not have rallied to another fray.

His wound, though not a serious one, had brought considerable loss of blood before Mildred stanched it. The Shadow found himself far weaker than he expected.

It was Mildred who kept vigil while they waited for new arrivals, hoping that the newcomers would be friends responding to the wireless call.

The little wireless room served as the temporary refuge. There, Allard lay stretched upon a rickety army cot, while Mildred kept guard at the door. Most of the wait was spent in silence, but at intervals, the girl heard Allard's tired tone advising her on certain important matters.

Mildred was to say nothing of their previous acquaintance; nor was she to remember that Geraldine had accompanied Allard here. Her own story, too, was to be a hazy one. She could mention Sleed and Thelma; give brief recollections of another base somewhere in the East.

But she was to know nothing whatever concerning Silver Skull and the plane which had flown over to give the warning. As for the supposition that such men as her uncle and John Lenville were still alive, no one was to know that it had even occurred to Mildred Wilbin and Kent Allard.

The safety of those supposed victims might depend upon such pretended ignorance. Mildred understood that from Allard's tone, and reasoned the rest for herself. Who Silver Skull might be, she couldn't guess; but it was obvious that he would try to reconstruct his schemes, if he saw the opportunity.

Vital to those schemes was the fact that dead men lived. If chance for further plotting should be ended, Silver Skull would no longer have need for those prisoners. He would snuff out their lives, and turn to other fields of crime.

Aloud, Mildred repeated the story that she intended to tell, until she had it perfect. She was still repeating it to herself when she saw the bobbing of lights entering the central cavern, heard the shouts of approaching voices. Fearful for the moment, Mildred looked to Allard for encouragement and saw him give a tired nod.

The Shadow had recognized that these must be rescuers; and he was right. With an answering cry of her own, Mildred went out to meet them. Soon, she was telling her well-rehearsed story to a group of eager listeners.

AMONG the rescuers was Norwood Parridge. Searching for the lost *Traveler*, he had picked up Allard's SOS and had headed here from the mountains. That call had carried no signature; when Parridge learned that Allard had sent it, he hurried to the side of his wounded friend. Propped on the cot, The Shadow weakly gave his version of what had happened.

Flying alone, so he said, he had chanced to observe the desert landing field. He had finished his solo flight on the sands a few miles away, and had come here to investigate. Finding Mildred unwatched, he had released her; had sent the wireless call. Then came the battle—for which The Shadow, as Allard, took but modest credit.

Some of the crooks, he claimed, had mistakenly supposed that he led a band of invaders. Hoping to square themselves with the law, they had turned against the rest. Outnumbered, the mutineers had been eliminated; but the victors, their own ranks considerably thinned, had taken to flight in a plane.

As always, The Shadow was covering his real identity of Kent Allard; and he knew that his tale would have weight, even with Silver Skull. The crooks who had fled would themselves believe the version of the fight that Allard was making public. In the gloom of the hazy cavern, they had taken bullets from so many directions that they must have found the one-foe theory incredible, when they discussed it.

Allard's lips were holding back a weary smile, as they spoke that blunt story. Deep in The Shadow's brain was the important realization that Silver Skull believed him to be dead, which put the 'certifying mark' upon the yarn. For only The Shadow could have put up the single-handed battle that Allard so carefully disclaimed.

It was Parridge who insisted upon taking his friend Allard back to civilization. Mildred was anxious to go along in the same plane, but Allard's eyes told her no. They had a few moments when they spoke alone, when Allard gave her brief instructions. The substance was that Mildred should find her chance and disappear again, this time to join certain persons who would keep her safe from Silver Skull.

DURING the long night, Parridge's plane winged eastward. Upon reaching New York City, Kent Allard was taken to a hospital. Later, at his own insistence, he was removed to the quiet hotel suite where the Xinca servants waited like a pair of faithful watchdogs. Once in that seclusion, Kent Allard defied all orders that the hospital physicians had given.

He became The Shadow.

Not that he garbed himself in cloak of black, to set out upon immediate foray. He was still too weak, and such a venture was unnecessary, for the present. Also, his arm must heal. But he busied himself with many tasks; calls to Burbank; experiments with radio apparatus; long study of newspaper accounts; the tracing of lines upon large-scale maps.

A wide search was underway for the missing plane that had carried the gunmen from the desert. Though nearly nothing was known of Silver Skull, with even his real name undisclosed, it was taken for granted that some mastermind had created the desert air base, to prey upon passing skyliners.

Who was the master crook? Why had he dealt in murder? Where was his Eastern base, which a thousand planes were trying to locate without success?

These were questions to which only The Shadow knew the answer and the last-named had become the most important.

At the desk where The Shadow sat with one arm bundled in a sling was a compact apparatus with a tiny light that changed as he adjusted it. Through this direction finder, he had picked up, here in New York, automatic radio impulses from the apparatus he had put in the crooks' transport plane—a piece of luck upon which he had not reckoned.

Luck, however, which was unnecessary. For by this time, The Shadow's agents were posted at several spots outside of New York City, seeking that same beam. Only two findings were needed, and The Shadow already had three others reported through Burbank. He was using his own, however, to make the final check.

His elbow steadying a long metal ruler, The Shadow drew lines upon a map. Converging from the various points where the beam had been picked up, the lines arrived at a focal spot. Shifting to a large-scale map, The Shadow changed that dot into a circle.

Somewhere in that area, limited to a few miles in radius, lay the Eastern base used by Silver Skull. It was well north of New York City, not far off the main air route to Montreal, a fact significant in itself; for it meant that Silver Skull could intercept planes bound to Canada, as well as those that flew to the Pacific coast.

Contrasted to that fact was one that presented a real riddle.

From reports that lay upon Allard's desk, it appeared that many planes had scoured that very terrain, while going from one area to another. They had eliminated the very district where the base must lie, because it showed no possible landing fields. In that circle, and miles around it, were stretches of unbroken woodland, partly the result of reforestation projects.

Reaching for the telephone, The Shadow made a call to Burbank. His instructions were for certain agents to cover that area again, by air. Since planes had frequently flown over it, they would excite no suspicion, particularly because The Shadow's plan called only for passing visits.

WORK ended for that day, The Shadow rested. It was very late the next afternoon when a package was delivered at his hotel. The flat bundle contained a sheaf of aerial photographs, all recently developed. Their backs were marked with cryptic numbers that enabled The Shadow to place them in a definite order.

His injured arm no longer numb, The Shadow used both hands to arrange the pictures, until they completely covered the table. His keen eye promptly detected differences remarkably conspicuous. From the straight lips of Kent Allard came a tone of satisfied mirth: the whispered laugh of The Shadow.

Again, The Shadow made a telephone call; but it was not to Burbank. Instead, he called the apartment where Norwood Parridge lived when in New York. Using Allard's tone, The Shadow asked for the millionaire aviator and learned that Parridge had just arrived. Soon, the millionaire was on the wire, but his voice lacked enthusiasm.

"Hello, Allard," said Parridge. "It's good to hear from you. I've just come back from another hunt, and it's the same story: No luck!"

"Perhaps you've been looking in the wrong place," remarked The Shadow. "Or you may not have noticed the right place often enough."

"Do you mean"—Parridge had caught new interest from Allard's tone—"that somebody has found something?"

"Precisely that," replied The Shadow. "I'll be around in half an hour, to show you the evidence."

The call concluded, The Shadow placed photographs and maps in a large envelope. From a desk drawer, he produced an automatic and tucked it beneath his coat. Then, in the imperturbable style of Allard, he strolled to the door, which a prompt Xinca servant opened as soon as he approached.

Darkness was settling as Allard appeared upon the street, bound upon this visit that was known only to himself and Parridge. Yet, with all the secrecy that he had preserved, The Shadow was prepared to meet the unexpected. For his mission, in itself, had an importance that made it dangerous.

During his coming conference with Parridge, The Shadow intended to decide the fate of Silver Skull!

CHAPTER XVII
THE MAN WHO HEARD

PARRIDGE'S apartment was a small one, but lavishly furnished. Though already familiar with the place, The Shadow gave it a careful scrutiny as soon as he was admitted by Parridge's stocky, well-groomed manservant, whose name was Jeffrey.

Informed by his master that Allard was to arrive, Jeffrey promptly led the visitor through a short hallway, past the bedrooms, to a little living room at the rear of the apartment. Though originally planned as a bedroom, Parridge used the rear room for a living room because it afforded an outlook toward Central Park.

Attired in a dressing gown, Parridge received Allard with a handshake that seemed to lack its usual strength. He looked tired, his face more haggard than ever, and his shoulders showed a marked forward sag. He had been at the controls all day, he explained, and for once, his interest in aviation had waned.

"Whoever this mastermind is," declared Parridge, "he's no hare. He's a fox; and we've been hopping plenty of hurdles trying to find him! But he's got a hole in the ground, better even than the place you uncovered out on the desert."

Instead of a reply, Parridge saw Allard's lips smile confidence. Noting the envelope that his visitor carried, Parridge became intently curious. Then he caught a motion for silence.

"Everything is all right," assured Parridge. "Jeffrey can be trusted. He has been with me for years."

The Shadow opened the envelope. First, he brought out maps. He indicated one that bore a penciled cross.

"Whoever the fox is," began The Shadow, in Allard's short-clipped style, "is something that does not matter. What we need to know is where to find him. This cross shows the place."

While Parridge was staring at the map, The Shadow called his attention to another one, of larger scale. It showed a circle in which were tiny dots that indicated buildings.

"This place," Parridge heard Allard say, "appears to be a hunting lodge surrounded by large grounds. Probably a private game preserve, fenced off so no one can enter."

Parridge looked perplexed.

"It's all woods," he objected. "There's no landing place anywhere near it."

"The ground is level" was Allard's reminder. "And from this older map"—he pointed to another sheet—"the place was once a small racetrack."

As proof, The Shadow produced a photograph. Parridge saw exactly what he meant. The ground did have a level look; but that did not cover Parridge's objection. Young trees were frequent all through the clearing that Allard traced with his pencil.

"You're wrong, Allard," declared Parridge. "No one could possibly make a landing there. Not even you could—"

"Agreed," came the interruption. "No landing could have been made at the time this photograph over—"was at three-thirty yesterday afternoon. But things were a trifle better, Parridge, just before sunset."

He showed a picture taken after six o'clock. Parridge saw his finger point from one photo to the other. The haggard man hesitated, his lips moving as he stared. Then:

"Some of the trees have moved!" he exclaimed. "They are back toward the fringes of the larger woods!"

"And after dark," added The Shadow, "they must have moved back entirely. Look at these other photographs, Parridge. They show how the trees crept out again."

THE first of the present day's photographs had been taken just after dawn. The space was half cleared; the trees, as The Shadow said, could have been coming outward. Other photos, taken at later hours, showed them farther advanced. The final one, snapped at noon, showed a tree-filled area.

The Shadow came to his conclusion:

"Those trees are obviously mounted on tractor treads, or broad rollers. At night, they can be drawn back to make a landing field. Probably the task was such a long one that the workers started early, yesterday. Similarly, they waited until too near dawn to push the trees back in place, this morning.

"Of course, they stopped when planes flew over. They had enough trees in place to make a landing look impossible. But they did not reckon with the aerial camera. Since I couldn't make a hunt myself, I had photographers do it for me."

"That was smart work, Allard," declared Parridge. Then, staring at the photographs: "But how did you happen to pick this place?"

"I had cameramen everywhere," returned The Shadow, quietly. "These were but a few of the many thousand photographs that I examined."

Parridge accepted the explanation, which was well, as The Shadow did not care to mention the matter of the direction finders that he had used. That would have indicated too much previous planning on the part of Kent Allard.

It befitted Allard to be stolid, of single purpose, rather than versatile in method. His boldness, too, should be a stubborn sort. He should base his plans upon the proposition that what had once been accomplished could be done again. Therefore, the next suggestion was the very sort that Parridge expected.

"The landing field will be clear again tonight," decided The Shadow, bluntly. "If I take off at midnight, I can be there by three o'clock."

"To make a landing?" exclaimed Parridge. "In that nest of crooks?"

"Like I did before. With excellent results! If I can depend upon you to follow, bringing reinforcements—"

"You can. How soon will you need them?"

The Shadow pondered, then set half past three as the proper time. Parridge inquired why he was delaying the start until midnight, which was some few hours away.

"Because of the moon," explained The Shadow. "It doesn't set until nearly three o'clock. I don't want to be seen from the ground. Besides, you will need time to collect the right people to accompany you. I'm leaving that to you, Parridge."

The compliment pleased Parridge. He expressed concern, however, regarding Allard's landing. With the ground dark, Allard would not be able to tell if the trees had been drawn back. It was a big risk, Parridge thought; but it brought a smile from The Shadow.

"I'll know how the ground lies when I get near to it," he predicted, confidently. "I'll fly across the clearing first, and come back into the wind. I've shaken my landing gear right out of treetops before. Don't worry about that, Parridge."

NO more assurance was needed. Parridge straightened his shoulders, his weariness gone. His face had brightened with a look of anticipation toward the part that he was to play in the coming venture. Then came a sudden twitch of his features, ending in a painful tightness of his lips, a narrowing of his eyelids.

Parridge, on one side of the table, was looking straight across it over Allard's shoulder, to a mirror on the far wall. The glass reflected a doorway that led to the front bedroom. That door was a trifle open; from it gleamed the object that had turned Parridge rigid.

The Shadow's eyes took a side glance. They also saw the revolver muzzle. The hand that held it was out of sight; but it was steady. For, although the gun moved, it did not waver. An invisible marksman was merely deciding upon which target he should choose first: Allard or Parridge.

Through The Shadow's brain flashed instant thoughts, as he tried to fit this new crisis into the well-patterned schemes of Silver Skull. He had the answer, a singular one, almost before he had finished his mental question. He knew why that gun was there; exactly what it intended.

To meet the dilemma, he would have to drop the stolid way of Allard, to show the quickness of The Shadow. This would be different from the gloomy cavern in the desert. In full light, Allard's transformation would be recognized. Silver Skull would learn that The Shadow had not died while posing as Lamont Cranston. Disclosed, coming plans would never carry.

All that momentarily restrained The Shadow was the motion of the gun. He wanted the hidden killer to concentrate upon one person. That act would mark the instant for The Shadow's counterthrust. It was well that The Shadow waited as he did, for during that tense time space, matters took a curious twist. One that suddenly made it unnecessary for The Shadow to reveal himself.

The gun swung finally toward Parridge. Noting the motion in the mirror, Parridge mistook the reversed reflection and thought that it had moved the other way. Thinking that he was not covered, Parridge acted on his own before The Shadow's zero moment arrived.

Lunging his shoulders forward, Parridge grabbed a desk lamp. With a wide fling of his arm, he hurled it toward the connecting door. His heave was so earnest that he followed with it, sprawling half across the floor.

The gun was talking as the lamp crashed; but with the lamp's impact against the doorway, its lights were extinguished, plunging the room into blackness, except against the windows. No figures could be seen against that background; for, with darkness, The Shadow had copied Parridge's dive to the floor.

Parridge was unhurt. The glare of the flying lamp had made the marksman shift. From the floor, Parridge was opening fire with a gun of his own, while The Shadow—still as Kent Allard—chimed in with his automatic. Between shots, they could hear a scramble through the other room.

As Parridge sprang in pursuit, The Shadow doubled out through the hallway, where he could intercept the fleeing man. As he reached the lighted hall, he was met by a driving figure coming toward him. Seeing Allard, the other fired; but his shots were wide. With one quick sidestep back into the living room, The Shadow inserted the shot that counted.

The man came stumbling into a grapple; for a moment, he and The Shadow were locked. Then The Shadow had flung the man aside and was back into the living room, as shots burst from the front hall. It was the wounded man who received those bullets. A few moments later, Parridge arrived, a smoking gun in his hand.

Panting, he stooped to look at the man that he had finished with those final shots. Gazing up toward Allard, Parridge showed an expression of dismayed amazement.

"It's Jeffrey!" he exclaimed. "It was he who overheard us! Faithful old Jeffrey—"

From somewhere, The Shadow caught a sound that Parridge did not hear, the soft scrape of a lowering window. Someone was making a stealthy exit from the apartment. It wasn't Jeffrey who had made the murder threat, though the servant had certainly shown a killer's instinct later.

Shakily, Parridge poured himself a drink from a handy decanter.

"We both fired in self-defense," he was saying. "We can explain that, Allard. But we can't drop our plans for tonight. We've got to go through with them, to justify ourselves."

THE SHADOW was stooping beside Jeffrey's body. He had noted a bulge in the man's vest pocket. The Shadow's fingers dipped in quick probe; his hand gave a slight juggle, and formed a loose fist. Joining Parridge, he considered what the millionaire had said, and finally gave agreement.

Together, they left the apartment and took their separate ways. With a few hours remaining until midnight, The Shadow first rode back to his hotel. In the cab he opened his fist, saw the object that had come from Jeffrey's pocket. It was a tiny silver skull.

That satisfied The Shadow regarding Jeffrey's actions. Parridge's servants, like many other persons who posed as honest people, was a crook in the service of Silver Skull. Perhaps if Parridge hadn't been so hasty with his gun, shooting recklessly along the hall, Jeffrey would still be alive, and therefore of some use.

As it stood, Jeffrey had taken what was due him. He didn't matter any longer. What did concern The Shadow was the identity of the man who had managed to duck out while Parridge was getting his trails mixed.

The Shadow settled that with a low-toned laugh. He had already formed an opinion regarding the fellow's identity, and decided to keep it.

What mattered most was The Shadow's coming expedition. It was a venture that could still work as he had planned it. For The Shadow, thanks to Parridge's intervention, had managed to keep his own identity hidden.

He was still Kent Allard; and that was vitally important. Because The Shadow was certain that by this time, Silver Skull had learned what Kent Allard intended to do tonight. Oddly, The Shadow's plans called for exactly that.

For Silver Skull, in planning a reception for Kent Allard, would not reckon with the measures that The Shadow had designed for Silver Skull!

CHAPTER XVIII
THE NIGHT FLIGHT

IT was three o'clock. Darkness lay thick and hushed about the hidden landing field that The Shadow had traced, despite the wiles of Silver

Skull. Sham trees had been rolled back into the woods, where vaulted spaces sheltered them beneath huge overhanging boughs.

Men were crouched in the blackened clearing, beside a plane that waited like a grounded bird of prey. Those hours allowed by The Shadow had proven useful to Silver Skull. This was his plane, ready for another deed of piracy; the men about the silent ship were his ground crew.

The moon was gone, but the sky showed twinkling starlight. Barely visible, the tops of the higher trees were bending in a wind, pointing northward like a wavering compass needle. Those treetops served as a wind indicator, telling that Allard's plane would be coming from the south.

For Silver Skull had learned the plan in its entirety—how Allard first intended to cross the landing field, then head back into the wind. All that the master crook and his crew awaited was the drone of an approaching plane.

It came, a slow hum that rode ahead of the wavering wind. Eyes strained skyward, hoping to spot the approaching ship. It was difficult against the blackness, until the twinkle of lights appeared like little colored stars shifting from the firmament.

There were surprised mutters among the ground crew; then grunts of understanding mingled with satisfied oaths.

The lights, of course, were Allard's most sensible measure. He was taking it for granted that there might be watchers in the clearing. Such watchers would be suspicious of any ship that soared without lights. He was hoping that he would be mistaken for an ordinary pilot, passing across this forest region.

Once beyond the field, he would extinguish those lights and glide back to a landing. The slowness of his plane was proof that it was suited to such a feat. But there was a danger, other than that of landing, to anyone who flew a lazy crate in vicinities where Silver Skull lurked.

Kent Allard would have no worries regarding a proper landing, once Silver Skull was in the air. The air pirate had a way of picking landing spots for all planes that he tackled.

The lights were almost overhead. No chance of Allard hearing other sounds, with the drone of his own motor in his ears. Silver Skull gave the order for contact; before those lights had passed the landing field, his trim pursuit plane was spurting to its takeoff.

The scattering ground crew glimpsed the craft as it met the breeze above the treetops. Then it was gone into the blackness of the higher air, twisting like a skillful bird, to take up the trail of Allard's lights.

WITHOUT a glimmer of its own, the speedy plane knifed upward. Silver Skull was anxious to down Allard's plane as far as possible from the landing field, for it wouldn't do to have wreckage found too close to the hidden headquarters. That was why he didn't push his speedy ship until he saw the lights begin to turn.

Five miles had been covered. Enough to satisfy the murderous pilot who wore the silver headgear. He veered to bring himself in Allard's path; then, as he saw the lights climbing upward and toward him, he gave his plane the gun.

That wasn't all. Silver Skull focused a searchlight alongside his machine gun, pressed the switch, to send a brilliant path ahead. That flood of light outlined the climbing plane, gave Silver Skull a slanted glimpse of Allard's black hawk emblem painted on the side.

The machine gun began its drill. In the vivid path that Silver Skull was following, the other plane bulked like a big unwieldy box kite. It seemed that a crash was coming, when those two planes met; but Silver Skull knew there wouldn't be one. He was riddling Allard's craft to shreds.

Lights vanished from the crippled ship. There was a puff of flame from the fuselage. A wing drooped; the plane did a topple in midair. It was wallowing downward, spinning like a lopsided top, trailing smoke behind it, when Silver Skull rode through the space where it had been.

Banking sharply, Silver Skull kept his searchlight glued on the fluttering wreckage, as it strewed itself among the trees. He played the searchlight wider, as he circled the spot where the crash had come. He was looking to see if Allard had bailed out. If so, Silver Skull would have another target, and an easy one: a helpless man dangling from a sinking parachute.

No sign of Allard near the treetops. Silver Skull circled the searchlight higher, slower, finally adjusting it to the exact speed of the banking plane. Swinging ahead of him, the cleaving path cut high above the horizon. Then came the sight that riveted Silver Skull.

It wasn't a parachute. It was something that seemed unbelievable: an object that might have dropped from one of the distant stars. The thing was a giant propeller, as Silver Skull first viewed it; nothing else.

It seemed to be coming straight toward him, as though it had a mammoth plane behind it. As Silver Skull grabbed for the machine gun, the whirling thing tilted, to take a horizontal position. Then, beneath it, the searchlight showed the sleek shape of a streamlined jet-black body.

The ship was a wingless autogiro! Its only support were those mammoth revolving blades that Silver Skull had first supposed to be a gigantic propeller!

With that discovery, Silver Skull guessed everything. He knew why Allard's crate had flown so slowly over the landing field. It hadn't been a plane at all, that hulk with the telltale lights. It had been nothing but a flimsy oversized glider, painted with Allard's insignia. A glider towed by the invisible giro up ahead!

The motor of the autogiro had provided the sound effects for the decoy. Silver Skull had taken the bait. He had gone after the glider and had riddled it; a small tank of gasoline stowed in the glider had provided the explosion. When the decoy had dropped, it had carried its towline with it.

Meanwhile, high above, unseen by Silver Skull, the autogiro had completed a long, lazy loop. In its turn, it had become the thing of prey, using Silver Skull's searchlight as its objective. Its own course timed by a skilled pilot, the autogiro had intercepted the pursuit plane, to give real battle.

Its pilot was The Shadow.

THAT fact drilled home to Silver Skull, as he tried to straighten his plane. The thought gripped him that he should have disposed of Kent Allard, not Lamont Cranston. But that regret did not help his present situation. From below the giro's spinning blades, straight through its actual propeller, Silver Skull could see the spurting jabs of a machine gun outside a small cabin.

There was no time for new maneuvers. Viciously, Silver Skull answered the attack. Chattering guns outroared the motors, as the air duel reached its height. Bullets smashed the searchlight close by Silver Skull. From then on, the only targets were the spurting guns themselves.

Whatever the advantage of the pursuit plane over large craft, it had none in this battle. Its speed, could Silver Skull have used it, would have enabled him to flee; but that was all.

The thing that he was trying to bring to earth had no vulnerable wings. Its whirling blades never quivered as bullets tore through them. The tiny body of the autogiro was a target that he might eventually have found; but, meanwhile, his own plane was a better mark for The Shadow's fire.

One machine gun ended its rattle with a cough. That gun belonged to Silver Skull. His plane took a steeper bank, slid sideward, downward, toward those same trees where a fake plane had landed a dozen minutes before.

From the autogiro, The Shadow saw a quiver of the trees as a dull-gray mass encountered them. Then came a spurt of short-lived flame, that faded beneath the blanketing blackness. The flash was caused by the small supply of fuel that remained in the pursuit plane's well-drilled tank.

The crash had marked the end of Silver Skull— a deed that The Shadow had postponed until this timely hour. For the death of Silver Skull meant more than the deserved vengeance due a murderer.

That death was to be The Shadow's passport to the dead crook's own headquarters!

Well did The Shadow know that the men at the landing field were ready for surprise attacks, either by air or land. They had been, at least, until Silver Skull had taken off, intent upon finishing Kent Allard, the troublemaker who had come back for more.

Right now, however, the ground crew would be expecting Silver Skull. If they heard a plane, they would suppose it to be his. But The Shadow doubted that they would even hear the next ship that arrived!

He lifted the autogiro into a steep climb, and guided it back toward the landing field. A mile up in the air, The Shadow cut off the motor. The ship went into a steep-pitched drop, rapid at first, then slower, steadier. Big spinning blades were working with the silence of a parachute, while The Shadow studied the darkness below.

Sharp eyes detected a thinness in that inky ground: a rounded space free from thick-boughed trees. That vacancy became The Shadow's goal. Unseen against the silent sky, the autogiro continued its sure descent.

Servers of Silver Skull were waiting there to greet their master's return. But *they* would receive the greeting, not Silver Skull.

A greeting from The Shadow!

CHAPTER XIX
STRANGE ALLIES

THE autogiro settled with a silent *plop*, close to the center of the landing field. A full minute passed while The Shadow waited, in case any sounds came from the ground crew. That minute produced nothing but silence.

As The Shadow had expected, the crew was waiting in the woods, on the path that led to the tree-shrouded headquarters. They were watching for Silver Skull to flash a signal that would denote his return.

Carefully, The Shadow descended from his ship. He was cloaked in black, the attire that suited his return to life. Tonight, the followers of Silver Skull would know that they faced The Shadow. But that discovery, according to The Shadow's plans, would not come until he had reached the heart of their headquarters.

There, The Shadow was sure that he would find the prisoners whose lives Silver Skull had so carefully preserved. If opportunity afforded, The Shadow would first release the captives, then spring his surprise upon the crooks who guarded them.

That much depended upon The Shadow alone. But he was counting upon others, once battle began. He had sent instructions to his agents, giving them three o'clock as the zero hour. At this minute, they were closing in upon the fence that surrounded the game preserve. Given a signal, they would rally to The Shadow's aid.

Once on the ground, The Shadow used his flashlight; but its blinks were the sort that distant observers could not see. He held the torch cupped in his hand, close against his cloak; its rays were directed squarely upon the ground. The light flickered, while The Shadow advanced a dozen paces; then it suddenly went off.

In the darkness, The Shadow had caught a stir: the approach of stealthy figures. While his left hand pocketed the light, his right was whipping out an automatic. The move was quick but The Shadow cut it short. It was better, for the moment, to stand stock-still.

From out of the darkness, two guns had poked into The Shadow's ribs, one from each side.

The sensation was not new to The Shadow. He had felt gun muzzles before, and knew what they meant. Persons who were quick on the trigger didn't bother to announce themselves by gun thrusts. Whoever these challengers were, they would not fire without provocation. They had something to say, and The Shadow was willing to hear it.

"Hello, Silver Skull!" came a whisper, close to The Shadow's ear. "So you had a happy landing, didn't you? Found the joint in the middle of the dark. Pretty classy, I'll say!"

"It sure was!" The voice was a woman's, speaking in The Shadow's other ear. "But maybe you wouldn't have been so smart, if you'd known we were waiting for you!"

There wasn't any question about those voices. One belonged to Dr. George Sleed, the other to Thelma Royce.

"You ducked me once tonight," growled Sleed, "but I'm just as glad you did. I was out to get you for a double crosser, and I missed. But I heard enough to figure what came next; and when I spilled the dope to Thelma, she had a better idea."

"That's right," voiced Thelma. "I talked sense into Doc, I told him maybe you thought he was dead, but the rest of the mob didn't. That silver skull he carries for a watch fob was just as good as gold! It got him past the guys that are watching at the gate; and I came through with him."

THE SHADOW kept his silence. His only response, if it could be called one, was a nervous squirm that pleased his captors. They pressed their guns tighter; and Sleed growled a threat that they would shoot.

That stopped The Shadow's squirming. But it didn't give away what he had done. In his uneasy shift, he had nudged his elbows backward, working them in between his ribs and the gun muzzles.

"What we want is dough," announced Sleed, "and plenty of it! All you've got to do is climb into that crate of yours and take us along with you. Yell for your ground crew and tell them you're going back to town. Brag about what you did to Allard, if you want; only, remember that we'll be nudging you with these rods—"

Sleed was interrupted by a fling of The Shadow's elbow. The guns weren't nudging any longer. They were wide, and The Shadow was bounding forward in the darkness, invisible to the pair who had held him trapped a moment before.

One long leap, then a drop to one hand. Spinning about, The Shadow made a quick dive in the reverse direction. His balked captors almost brushed him as they dashed past, shooting as they took up the imaginary chase.

Flashlights blinked from the woods. Their glow caught Sleed and Thelma. Forgetting Silver Skull, the pair opened fire on the ground crew—with remarkable results. Flashlights began to drop like ducks on the rack of a shooting gallery.

Another gun had joined in the fire: the .45 in The Shadow's steady fist. He was clipping off those lights; clearing the path for the pair who had held him covered only a few seconds before. Since stealth was no longer possible, The Shadow was opening the way for the two crooks who had mistaken him for Silver Skull!

He could have chosen no better allies in that situation. Neither Sleed nor Thelma knew that Silver Skull was dead; and they had a score to settle with the master crook. Thinking that Silver Skull had headed for the hunting lodge, they wouldn't stop until they reached there.

A block of light showed suddenly at the end of the wooded pathway. It was the door of the hunting lodge, flung open by startled guards inside. Sleed and Thelma thought that Silver Skull had gained that refuge, and began to fire at men who bobbed into the light.

Guns answered. For the first time, the invading pair lost courage. Then they were spurred ahead by shots that came from behind them; shots that they thought were supplied by rallied members of the ground crew.

Actually, those shots were The Shadow's. He was aiming for the door, to clear it. Seeing men sprawl, Sleed and Thelma thought that their own puny fire had accomplished it. They drove into the hunting lodge, to find one huge room where men were scattering for cover.

Most of them were taking to smaller rooms that served as living quarters for the mob; but one man, coming down a stairway that overhung from a wall, decided to return above. He had a gun; he aimed as he retreated. Sleed saw him and beat the fellow to the shot.

Sight of a figure rolling down the stairway made the other crooks dive deeper into cover, while Sleed and Thelma began to poke their heads through doorways looking for Silver Skull. How long they would survive such heedless tactics was a question that did not concern The Shadow when he arrived. Once inside the lodge, he saw something that interested him more.

Above the side stairway was a passage that led to bunk rooms. The Shadow could see the glint of steel in the gloomy lights. Those bunk room doors were barred; they were the cells where Silver Skull had placed his prisoners.

The man that Sleed had shot was a guard who watched the upper corridor. This was The Shadow's chance to reach the captives and protect them until reserves arrived. Aid would come soon, for The Shadow had planned a gunshot as a signal; and by this time, his agents had heard that token oft repeated.

HALFWAY up the stairs, The Shadow heard a cry behind him. It came from the guard that Sleed had dropped. The crippled crook had come to life; forgetful of other feuds, he was raising a hoarse shout as he tried to aim his gun.

Sleed scarcely heard the cry; but Thelma did. She turned, sprang back into a little room; voicing the startling news:

"The Shadow!"

Criminals needed no other battle cry. They were united on that instant. They sprang from the rooms, to see Sleed shooting for the balcony above the stairs, where a cloaked shape was weaving toward the corridor. Along with Sleed's wild shots came fierce tongues of flame stabbing down from that balcony. Those quick-knifed jabs proved the truth of Thelma's shout.

Sleed crumpled; the suddenness of his fall showed the power of The Shadow's gunfire. Crooks opened a barrage against the fading shape in black, to be answered by shots that wilted them. Seeing some sprawl, the rest would have given up the battle, if Thelma had not rallied them. She had noted the sudden finish of The Shadow's quick fire.

"Rush him!" bawled Thelma. "He's out of slugs! Get him, before he loads those gats again!"

A half dozen mobbies reached the stairs, shooting as they drove upward. Wheeling back into the passage, The Shadow made ready for a surge. His only chance was to club his way through the arriving thugs, using his big automatics as bludgeons.

A chance that he had taken in other battles, but one that might prove suicide on this occasion. The only outlet was that stairway; and if he reached it, The Shadow would be a point-blank target for Thelma, waiting below. She was as skillful with the trigger as any member of the driving mob; something that The Shadow knew from previous experience.

Then, almost on the verge of the thrust that seemed sure death, The Shadow was gripped by a staying hand that seemed to come from blackness beside him. He turned, and with that motion, flung his empty guns aside.

Beside that plucking hand was its mate—a welcome hand that held a fresh automatic, offering the loaded gun to the fighter who so badly needed it!

With one swoop, The Shadow took the weapon and wheeled toward the head of the stairway. His laugh rang out in sinister, taunting challenge to the crooks who sought his doom!

CHAPTER XX
CRIME REVEALED

THOSE hands from the dark were Geraldine's; the gun was the one that she had received from Allard at the beginning of their expedition on the desert. After her capture, the blond stewardess had realized the futility of battle, and had concentrated upon smuggling the weapon wherever she was taken.

Her hope had been to find a future use for it; and she could not have picked a better moment. Realizing that The Shadow was battling off crooks, she had supplied him with the needed weapon.

Continuing the sweep with which he took the gun, The Shadow drove straight for the stairway. Through the bars of the cell door, Geraldine saw him meet the arriving crooks, who halted perceptibly when they heard The Shadow's startling laugh.

His gun hand thrust ahead of him, The Shadow slanted into the throng, providing the opening fire as he struck. Those shots put his foemen into utter rout. Revolvers popped, but they were gripped by staggering crooks who had received the unexpected fire before they could take aim.

Reeling backward, two gunmen trapped a pair of pals against the balcony rail. The weight of four bodies splintered the wooden posts. As the rail went, two crooks pitched from sight to the floor below, leaving their wounded comrades on the balcony edge.

There were two others still to be considered. They were on the steps, only a few below the top. They fired as they saw the cluster break; but they shot at blankness, not at The Shadow. He had dropped low, along with the slumping crooks. His gun jabbed twice again, almost from the level of the topmost step.

Independently, the gunmen on the stairway wavered; each took a backward topple. They were bounding crazily to the foot of the stairs, where Thelma was waiting with her gun. Sight of the pitching bodies made the nurse spring away before she started to aim up the stairway.

Thelma was too late. Her eyes saw the balcony before her gun could point. She met The Shadow's burning gaze, a looming muzzle just below. The smoke that curled from the automatic's mouth denoted its hunger for more prey; and Thelma knew that she was eligible.

Her lips twitched in a ruddy writhe, but the snarl that came from them was almost soundless. Numbly opening her hand, Thelma let her revolver drop.

The Shadow greeted that submission with a mocking laugh; one that made Thelma realize her folly. The Shadow could not have kept her covered, for there were others that he had to meet. The two men who had fallen from the balcony were on their hands and knees, trying to regain their dropped guns.

WITH Thelma no longer armed, The Shadow stopped their efforts with a warning hiss. They squatted, with their arms lifted, to gaze sourly toward the balcony. From the top step, The Shadow kept his .45 wangling back and forth between the crooks and Thelma, so that none had a chance to make a move.

Each moment, though, was reviving the squatting thugs. Their sidelong glances told that they were itching for a chance to grab their guns and dive beneath the balcony. Their opportunity seemed at hand, when The Shadow let his eyes roam beyond Thelma, toward the open door of the lodge.

Crooks dived. In a flash, The Shadow was half across the balcony edge, to cover them before they had their guns. Thelma, no longer covered, made a scramble for her own revolver. A hand clamped her arm, flung her half about, to the bottom of the stairs. Shouts stopped the crooks below the balcony before The Shadow had to use his gun.

A trio of picked fighters, agents of The Shadow, had arrived through the open door. It was Harry Vincent who had whipped Thelma away from the gun she wanted. The other two agents were upon the crooks below the balcony, taking over for The Shadow.

Then Harry was gone, to aid in the easy roundup; and Thelma was looking into a gun muzzle held by another hand. She saw brown eyes beneath a flurry of brown hair. She heard the icy tone that came from lips above a determined chin.

"You look very pale, Miss Royce," gibed Mildred Wilbin. "Just relax, and follow my advice. If you don't, I may have to give you a few pills. Ones that you wouldn't like!"

Thelma wasn't anxious to test the effects of Mildred's bullets. Quivering, she arose to her feet and let Mildred march her past the stairway, to be huddled with the other prisoners. Once there, Thelma gave a fearful gaze up toward the balcony. The Shadow was out of sight; but the fact didn't solace Thelma, for Mildred and The Shadow's agents were in complete control.

There was a muffled gunshot from the corridor above. With that one bullet, The Shadow smashed the lock of Geraldine's cell. He brought the blonde to the stairs, pointed her to the outer door. The Shadow gave a signal to his agents, then followed Geraldine outdoors.

They reached the autogiro, and listened there to distant sounds. Men were blundering through the woods, and The Shadow recognized who they must be. The time had come for his own departure. Helping Geraldine into the autogiro, The Shadow started the motor.

With a sudden roar, the big blades whirled; the ship jerked forward, taking off with a sharpness that left Geraldine breathless. Climbing straight for the darkness high above the trees, the autogiro had begun another of its mystery flights.

BACK in the lodge, Harry and Mildred were smashing locks of cell doors. Among the prisoners that they released was Herbert Wilbin, hugely joyful to find his niece awaiting him. The others, grateful for their release, were introducing themselves as Carter Curry, Roy Breck and John Lenville.

Filing down the stairway, the rescued prisoners were met by arrivals from outside. A man with a sheriff's badge stared goggle-eyed at the sprawled thugs who strewed the place. Sternness showed on his beefy face, as he demanded explanations.

Facts came, leaving the sheriff and his deputies bewildered. They'd heard all about the recent air disasters, and the murderer's airport in the Western desert. They knew that a hunt had been going on, its purpose to uncover a similar Eastern base.

Mildred Wilbin told them who she was, then introduced The Shadow's agents as friends who had helped her seek her uncle. No further details were necessary; for the fact that Herbert Wilbin and other supposed victims were alive, was something that dwarfed everything else.

At last, the sheriff found voice to quiz the prisoners. They received his questions in sullen silence, which did not seem to annoy him.

"We'll find out who the big-shot was," he predicted. "There was a crack-up about five miles from here, and people reported it. Some fellow with a searchlight, who couldn't land his plane. We were looking for the wreck, when we heard the shooting here.

"I'll bet it was the fellow behind the racket, trying to find his way here. Come along"—he gestured to Wilbin and the other rescued men—"and we'll see if they've found that plane. And bring her, too"—he pointed to Thelma—"because maybe she'll talk when we've got her alone."

Soon, cars were rolling along wheel ruts through the woods, to a spot where searchers had located the crashed plane. On foot, the group reached the wreckage. In the glare of flashlights lay a shattered human form; beside it, an aviator's helmet that glinted with a silvery hue.

Herbert Wilbin nodded solemnly, as he scanned the haggard, deep-lined face of Norwood Parridge.

"He was the man who visited me," said Wilbin, "the night when Fortner turned traitor. Only Parridge could have left the token that served as order for my capture."

Gurry and Breck knew Parridge, too. So did John Lenville. He provided another comment.

"Parridge sold me his shares in Federated Airways," declared Lenville. "I had them with me when I was trapped at Zurman's office. So Parridge got them back again, along with my half million, leaving no one the wiser."

The sheriff turned to Thelma. This time, he did not have to question her.

"Yeah, Parridge was the big-shot," said Thelma. "The guy that called himself Silver Skull. Take a look"—she pointed to the ruined plane—"and you'll see the skull right there. It was the picture that Parridge put on every plane he flew.

"Nervy, wasn't it? But he got away with it easy enough. Because the only people who called him Silver Skull were those that worked with him. We never talked about Silver Skull to anybody that wasn't in the know."

ELSEWHERE, far from that lighted circle, another voice was reviewing the deeds of Silver Skull. It was the calm tone of Lamont Cranston, a guise to which The Shadow had returned. The Shadow was talking to Geraldine in the tiny cabin of the autogiro.

"Then Parridge trapped me," he explained, "thanks to a letter that he forced Lenville to sign. I suspected the trap; still, I fell into it. Once there, I knew definitely that Norwood Parridge was the brain behind the crimes.

"He openly revealed the fact, by talking from a life-sized silver skull. I was familiar with the insignia of many private pilots, Parridge's among them. I knew, too, that Parridge felt certain that I would never leave that trap; otherwise, he would not have revealed himself.

"Also, Parridge's plane was so fast that he could follow a transport West, shoot it down, and get back East the next day."

Geraldine nodded. She was understanding facts that The Shadow had revealed only in part, during their former journey together. She understood, at last, why he had preferred to play a waiting game. Knowing the true identity of Silver Skull, The Shadow had spun a web of his own, to trap the master murderer.

"I had Allard visit Parridge tonight," continued The Shadow, "to spring the final move. While Allard was there, someone tried to kill Parridge. Curiously, Parridge thought it was his own servant, Jeffrey, a crook like himself.

"Actually, Jeffrey was trying to help Parridge; for Jeffrey, too, was mistaken. Hearing shots, he thought that Allard had fired them. So he attacked Allard, only to be shot down by Parridge. That is the way with crooks: they trust no one, when they are in a hurry."

"But, who"—Geraldine halted, puzzled—"who was it that *did* try to murder Parridge?"

"My old friend Sleed" was Cranston's reply. "He missed fire, and managed to escape. That's why he showed up, later, at the hunting lodge. He had heard enough to learn where it was."

"Odd, that Parridge didn't suspect that it was Sleed."

"Not at all! Because Parridge thought that Sleed was dead. Don't forget that Sleed had been told to take my place as a passenger on the *Traveler*."

It was all clear to Geraldine, at last. There were other questions, though, that intrigued her as much as the fate that had overtaken Silver Skull.

"What about Kent Allard?" she asked. "Does he know all these facts?"

"Kent Allard"—Cranston's tone carried a chuckle—"is an aviator, and a very daring one. A man, too, who will undertake any difficult task. But if you told Allard that I was The Shadow, I am certain that he would never believe you."

That settled the Allard question once and for all, so far as Geraldine was concerned. She didn't catch the subtle touch behind the statement that Kent Allard was The Shadow, and Lamont Cranston as well!

Moreover, Geraldine had shifted to another question—one that she regarded as more important than any that she had put before.

"Will you tell me, Mr. Cranston," she asked, "just where this present flight of ours is going to end?"

"Somewhere near the Rockies," replied The Shadow, "where we can take another freight train."

"Back to where we were?"

"Or near there. So we can stumble, weary and ragged, into some mountain cabin, to tell how we survived the crash."

Geraldine smiled. She'd forgotten that she and Cranston would have to explain their return to life. But she hadn't forgotten that day when they had trekked across the mountain slopes; a day, that to her present recollection, had been much too short.

She didn't have to tell The Shadow that she was glad they were returning to the Rockies.

The Shadow knew.

THE END

FROM PULP PAGE TO SILVER SCREEN
THE SERIAL THAT ALMOST GOT IT RIGHT *by Ed Hulse*

Hollywood has never gotten The Shadow quite right. Its periodic attempts to bring the Master of Darkness to movie audiences have produced surprisingly inconsistent results, largely because filmmakers—unsure whether to concentrate on radio or pulp incarnations of the character—usually opted to take a hybrid approach that did justice to neither. Columbia's 1940 serial version has much to recommend it and in proper hands might have been the definitive film adaptation of The Shadow.

Harry Cohn's Columbia Pictures Corporation was a late player in the serial game, coming to bat in 1937 after various independent producers had left the field for good. With only Universal and Republic as competition, the studio initially outsourced chapter-play production to the father-son team of Louis and Adrian Weiss. Their three serials for Columbia—*Jungle Menace*, *The Mysterious Pilot* and *The Secret of Treasure Island*—were undistinguished efforts and Cohn summarily dismissed them, assigning producer Jack Fier to make *The Great Adventures of Wild Bill Hickok*, originally intended to be the fourth Weiss/Columbia serial of the 1937-38 season.

Fier determined the only effective way to seize serial market share was to bring Columbia's chapter-play production in house and on a grander scale than originally contemplated. The four 1938-39 efforts—led by *The Spider's Web*, an action-packed adaptation of Popular Publications' violent pulp hero—enjoyed considerable box-office success but failed to return the expected profit margin because production costs were so high. While the average Republic and Universal serial cost $150,000 to $175,000, Fier spent over $200,000 on each Columbia serial. Since rentals averaged only five dollars per chapter, the extra expenditures significantly cut into profits.

The lavishly appointed Fier-produced chapter plays were successful in building Columbia's client base for future serials. Having done this, the studio retrenched by once again outsourcing production, this time to Larry Darmour, who for some years had been supplying Columbia with short subjects and "B"-grade Westerns on an independent basis. Cohn and Fier determined that serial production quality was secondary to promotional value: It would be just as easy to sell each chapter play based on the presence of a marketable star or a popular character adapted from another medium.

It fell to Jack Fier to select properties with appeal to the generally youthful audience that patronized serials. This meant securing screen rights to pulp, comics and radio properties. With Darmour hired to produce four chapter plays per "season" (a movie "season" began sometime after Labor Day and extended through Spring to the beginning of Summer, which typically saw a reduction in theatergoing), Fier began by licensing Milton Caniff's *Terry and the Pirates*. Then, he chose Edgar Wallace's celebrated mystery novel *The Green Archer*—turned into a wildly successful 1925 Pathé serial—as a yarn that could be remade and promoted not only to thrill-hungry adolescents but also to adults who might have seen, or at least heard of, the original adaptation.

But Fier reserved the important season opening slot for his most prominent acquisition: *The Shadow*. Following negotiations with Street & Smith, Columbia on May 26th, 1939 licensed for a reported $7,500 the right to produce one motion picture, specifically a serial, based on the popular character. Surviving documents indicate that S & S vp/general manager Henry W. "Bill" Ralston and licensing director William de Grouchy exercised great care in crafting the agreement, insisting that the chapter play maintain fidelity to the pulp Shadow. The deal permitted Columbia to adapt episodes of the radio show as well as novels from the magazine. In a July 19th letter to the publishing company, Columbia vice president B. B. Kahane informed Street & Smith that the studio had decided to use as source material *The Green Hoods*, *Silver Skull*, and *The Lone Tiger*, along with a single radio script, "Prelude to Terror" (which follows beginning on page 116).

Apparently, Fier at first intended to produce the Shadow serial in-house. Brief news items published

> "... I'd have to say that more people know me from *The Shadow* than anything else I've done." —VICTOR JORY

in movie industry trade papers during early Summer reported that the female lead would be taken by Lorna Gray and that Norman Deming and D. Ross Lederman would direct in tandem. As all were under contract to Columbia, these accounts lend credence to the supposition that the chapter play was initially slated for a more extravagant production. But when Darmour was contracted to supply serials for Columbia, the property was assigned to him.

Writers Joseph F. Poland and Ned Dandy, who had collaborated on the previous two Fier-produced serials, teamed with accomplished scripter Joseph O'Donnell to come up with a script containing 15 episodes of thrills that could be realized cinematically on short money. They were assisted by Charles R. Condon and John Thomas Neville. Reportedly, Darmour's Columbia serials were budgeted at $100,000—less than half what Fier had been spending. *The Spider's Web*'s huge cast and *Overland with Kit Carson*'s costly location jaunts were things of the past; speed and economy were the new watchwords of Columbia's serial unit. Sound-stage scenes could be shot at Larry Darmour's studio on Santa Monica Boulevard in Hollywood. Exterior scenes could be filmed in Burbank at what was called the Columbia Ranch, or on the nearby Warner Brothers backlot. The screenwriters kept cost limitations very much in mind as they concocted the scenario, and by mid-July a first draft had already been completed.

Of course, helming production of action-packed, highly melodramatic serials required a master's touch, so at Fier's suggestion Darmour hired James W. Horne, who had co-directed *The Spider's Web* and *Flying G-Men*. Although Horne was known for his comedies, including most of the best shorts and features starring Laurel & Hardy, he'd also directed numerous chapter plays in the silent era, among them *Bull's Eye* (1917) and *Hands Up!* (1918), which had made top box-office stars of their respective leads, Eddie Polo and Ruth Roland.

The casting process yielded mixed results, although Darmour scored a coup by landing highly regarded major studio player Victor Jory for *The Shadow*. Actually, Darmour didn't make the deal himself. Canadian-born Jory had been working for Columbia off and on since 1934, and enjoyed a good relationship with the notoriously irascible Harry Cohn. Even though the darkly handsome, vaguely sinister-looking actor had played leads, he found steadier work in character parts and in 1939 was considered one of Hollywood's top heavies. His film roles that year already included well-regarded turns in *Dodge City* and *Gone with the Wind*. "My agent told me he'd made a two-picture deal for me at Columbia," Jory told me in a 1980 interview. "Harry Cohn threw me into [the serial]. He said, 'Vic, you're going to be The Shadow.' It was as simple as that.

"I've been in a lot of good films and worked with many of the best stars, writers and directors in the business. But, you know, I'd have to say that more people know me from *The Shadow* than anything else I've done. I still get fan mail mentioning it. Here [at the Charlotte Western Film Fair] I've probably had a dozen people come up to me and ask me to do the laugh. It's the damnedest thing."

The serial's storyline combined elements of both pulp magazine and radio show, although it leaned toward the former. The chief addition from The Shadow's airwave adventures was Margot Lane, a radio creation who wouldn't be featured in the pulp until 1941. The Shadow's "friend and companion" was played by blonde, brassy Veda Ann Borg, a former Warner Brothers starlet most frequently seen as a gangster's moll or a wisecracking showgirl. Borg had lost her berth at Warners following a serious car accident in which she suffered serious facial injuries after being thrown through the windshield, and agreed to do *The Shadow* while waiting for another round of plastic surgery. Since she still bore facial scars, Veda had to be lit and photographed carefully, so she received few close-ups. A talented actress, Borg was nonetheless ill-suited to play the glamorous, sophisticated Margot depicted in the radio series.

Rounding out the starring trio was Roger Moore, cast as The Shadow's chief aide, Harry Vincent. (Moore was in fact Joe Young, the older brother of minor movie star and future Marcus Welby of TV fame, Robert Young.) Also seen as familiar figures from the pulp magazine were veteran character actors Frank LaRue playing Commissioner Weston and Edward Peil, Sr., as Inspector Cardona.

Principal photography began in the fall of 1939 and proceeded at a rapid clip. "We did 15 episodes in 30 days," Jory recalled. "Less, actually, because we didn't shoot on Sundays. It was hard work—early mornings, late nights, a lot of rushing around." The Fier-produced serials, by contrast, had consumed six to eight weeks of shooting time.

Horne impressed upon his actors the need for speed and didn't waste any time on the niceties of staging scenes. "He instructed us very quickly," Jory remembered. "No real direction in terms of the performances, except that we had to take everything 'big' [with exaggerated reactions]. He'd sketch the where and how of a scene, and he'd give us the basic attitude of it, but mostly it was a question of hitting the marks and delivering the lines on cue. We did damn few retakes, and only then if there had been a problem with camera or sound. On serials you didn't get multiple takes to experiment with different line readings."

While shooting *The Shadow*, Horne introduced another time-saving innovation to shave hours off the schedule. In those days, fight scenes were always shot twice—once in a "master" shot that took in the whole set and covered the mêlée from beginning to end, then with a series of shorter, closer shots that sometimes showed the principals throwing punches, rather than their stunt doubles. These "insert" shots would be cut into the masters to quicken the scene's pace and further the illusion that the actors were doing their own fighting.

George DeNormand, an experienced stuntman who doubled Victor Jory in *The Shadow*, explained to me in 1973 that Horne came up with a way to avoid the time-consuming process of relighting the set for close-ups and refitting it with duplicates of props that were damaged or destroyed in the first take. "Instead of shooting the scene twice," said DeNormand, "[Horne] got actors who could do their own fights and used them as the heavies. Then he set up two cameras, side by side. One camera took the master shot from a fixed position. The other was tricked out with a special lens that would give you a closer view. The second operator was told to follow me around the set [by swiveling the camera]. This way, the director could chop up the second unit footage to get those quick, close cuts he needed to edit into the master shot, without having to set everything up a second time. There was never a worry I'd be recognized in the closer view because I was wearing the hat and the cape and a little strip mask that covered the bottom half of my face."

Cinematographer James S. Brown, Jr., and his assistants "undercranked" the fight scenes to speed up the action, making the brawls seem more furious but also giving them a Keystone Kops aspect that latter-day viewers find ridiculous.

The Shadow entered national release on January 5, 1940, several months later than the typical season opener. Street & Smith promoted the film extensively, mentioning it several times in the "Highlights on The Shadow" column and some of the company's other pulps. The chapter play's theatrical playoff period coincided with a general effort to exploit the character; 1940 saw the marketing of numerous licensed products and multimedia spin-offs. Street & Smith launched a Shadow comic book on January 21, 1940, and a newspaper strip syndicated by the Ledger Syndicate followed shortly thereafter. Fans could buy Shadow hats, masks, cloaks, board games, makeup kits, gun-and-holster sets and other paraphernalia tangentially connected to the Master of Darkness.

Serial fans who huddled in darkened theaters all across the country learned in Chapter One, "The Doomed City," that the economic life of an unnamed metropolis was threatened by a well-organized criminal body headed by the mysterious Black Tiger, whose mad ambition was to acquire "supreme financial power." To this end he waged a systematic campaign of terrorization and destruction—blowing up factories, crashing trains and planes, extorting money from fear-paralyzed tycoons.

The city's captains of industry prevailed upon "noted scientist and criminologist" Lamont Cranston

The Shadow, as doubled by stuntman George DeNormand (inset)

to help combat the Tiger and his minions. Unbeknownst to them, Cranston had created two separate identities to further his fight against crime: Lin Chang, a shifty Chinese merchant with underworld ties, and The Shadow, a mystery man whose hat, cloak, and sinister laugh were trademarks instantly recognizable to evildoers everywhere.

The Black Tiger's identity was a closely guarded secret even to his own men, because he possessed the power of invisibility and transmitted instructions to the gang through a wood-mounted tiger head outfitted with glowing eyes and radio speaker. But as the serial progressed it became apparent that he was one of the industrialists who met regularly with Cranston and Commissioner Weston at the Cobalt Club.

Week after week, The Shadow fought the Black Tiger to a standstill, nearly losing his life at the close of each episode only to escape miraculously at the beginning of the next. The chapter-ending perils lacked ingenuity: an inordinate number of chapters found a ceiling collapsing on a fallen and unconscious Shadow—who groggily disengaged himself from the wreckage and staggered away the following week.

Truth be told, *The Shadow* didn't follow the pulp or radio show as closely as it did *The Spider's Web*. The similarities are marked: *The Shadow*'s Lamont Cranston, like *Web*'s Richard Wentworth, is identified as a scientific criminologist rather than as the wealthy dilettante and world traveler he is in Walter Gibson's novels. The Lin Chang identity corresponds with no character in the Shadow saga but performs the same function as Wentworth's Blinky McQuade character. Likewise, the serial's Harry Vincent doesn't act independently as in the pulp yarns; he stays close to The Shadow in the manner of Wentworth's aides Jackson and Ram Singh.

Moreover, *The Shadow* utilizes the same plot as *The Spider's Web*. Both serials feature a deranged mastermind who employs an army of henchmen to terrorize industrial leaders in a bid for economic control of a major city. Both show the police powerless to stem the tide of terror resulting from heedless destruction of life and property, concentrated on modes of transportation and newly invented devices.

The writers didn't entirely ignore the Shadow of pulp and radio. The serial is littered with bits and pieces of the licensed material. For example, the master villain's name and a courtroom scene in Chapter One are clearly inspired by *The Lone Tiger*. The opening installment's climax, in which exploding light bulbs are set off by a sudden surge of current, is adapted from "Prelude to Terror." A Chapter Two sequence, in which a disguised Shadow enters the Black Tiger's lair by donning one of the full-face masks worn by the villain's henchmen during meetings with their leader, was obviously inspired by a similar scene in *The Green Hoods*.

Victor Jory

The serial's writers mined several plot nuggets from *Silver Skull*. For example, a scene in Chapter IX finds The Shadow trapped in an underground chamber and taunted by the mystery villain, speaking through a life-sized mechanical skull outfitted with a radio speaker. While making his speech Silver Skull fills the room with gas—which, ignited by sparks, causes an explosion that brings the roof crashing down on The Shadow. Poland, Dandy, and O'Donnell got *two* cliffhanger endings out of that single Gibson-devised incident. Other *Silver Skull* elements employed in T*he Shadow* include the systematic kidnapping of wealthy men and the repeated destruction of airplanes by mysterious means.

Aside from Margot's presence and the exploding light bulbs, the serial took little from the *Shadow* radio show. Darmour and company made a reasonable if ultimately slipshod effort to ensure that followers of the pulp Shadow would recognize their hero on screen. But there were several inconsistencies. Harry Vincent shuttles The Shadow to and from most of his confrontations with the Black Tiger's men. Sometimes, however, he is shown driving a taxicab and wearing a hack's cap. This suggests that the pulp Shadow's usual driver, cabbie Moe Shrevnitz, might originally have been included in the script, only to have his character combined with Vincent's for cost-cutting purposes. Also, The Shadow is rarely seen with his trademark automatics; more often than not he uses .38-caliber revolvers.

Some of these inconsistencies are puzzling

> "Everybody knew that laugh, even people who didn't listen to the radio show every Sunday afternoon.... So I practiced that chuckle until I felt I had it right. You wanted it to give the kids goosebumps; that was the idea." —VICTOR JORY

because Street & Smith had specifically requested changes to the first-draft script forwarded to them by Columbia. A July 21st letter from the studio's F. L. Weber to Bill Ralston acknowledged receipt of a Street & Smith memo expressing concerns about some of the scenario's deviations from Shadow lore. After expressing gratitude for cooperation extended to the serial's scriptwriters by Walter Gibson and *Shadow Magazine* editor John Nanovic, Weber assured Ralston that numerous minor but significant corrections would be made based on their input. "The Shadow's guns will definitely be two .45 automatics, as they requested," wrote the Columbia executive. That promise went unfulfilled.

Weber also addressed the fact that Harry Vincent was occasionally seen driving a cab in usurpation of Moe Shrevnitz's function in the novels: "As regards Harry Vincent, we are not using the character of Moe Shrevnitz. We will place a line in the first episode stating that Harry is filling in for Shrevnitz, due to his illness." Another note stated: "As regards Burbank, we are changing this character, so it will be Richards playing the role of the manservant." Both characters were regulars in the pulps, but neither turned up in the Columbia chapter play, suggesting that cost-conscious Darmour had second thoughts about including them after script revisions had been made. Other changes requested by Street & Smith included altering the screenwriters' Metropolitan Club to the Cobalt Club and making Cranston an independent research scientist with his own lab, rather than an employee of industrialist Stanford Marshall.

Nonetheless, The Shadow fared better in his only serial than many characters adapted from other media. Spy Smasher got a twin brother, while Captain America received a new civilian identity. Blackhawk lost two of his subordinates, and Captain Marvel lost his superpowers in the final chapter of *his* serial.

Victor Jory deserves much of the credit for the serial's effectiveness. His Saturnine features closely remeble those described by Gibson. He projects confidence and authority in the role, and it's easy to appreciate his approximation of The Shadow's trademark laugh. "Oh, I *had* to get that right," Jory recalled in 1980. "Everybody knew that laugh, even people who didn't listen to the radio show every Sunday afternoon. It was a thing, you know, kind of like a catch phrase. 'The Shadow knows' was a popular saying. Comedians on the radio joked about it. So I practiced that chuckle until I felt I had it right. You wanted it to give the kids goosebumps; that was the idea."

James W. Horne's deliberately arch directorial style makes it difficult for some of today's viewers to appreciate *The Shadow*. The combination of overacting, undercranking, and what film historian William K. Everson called "moments of truly lunatic comedy involving the villains" irritates serial buffs used to the more serious chapter plays of other studios. But Everson, in his introduction to Alan G. Barbour's 1970 history of serials, *Days of Thrills and Adventure*, probably got it right: "[Horne] was too good a director, too much a past master of great silent and sound comedy, not to know precisely what he was doing.... Playing them for comedy didn't make them better, but it did keep them lively, distinctive, and different."

Actually, of the ten Columbia chapter plays James Horne made for producer Larry Darmour, *The Shadow* contains the fewest cringeworthy moments of campy humor. It surely could have been more faithful to the source material, but ultimately *The Shadow* has a lot more going for it than the character's other big screen incarnations.

It still remains to be seen whether Hollywood will ever produce a Shadow movie that does full justice to the pulp magazine version of the character as developed by Walter B. Gibson so long ago. For several years now it's been rumored that another feature film was being developed. Perhaps there's a future director out there, reading the Sanctum Books reprints and envisioning a faithful Shadow screen story as I write these words. Until such time as one appears, though, I'll stick with Victor Jory and *his* Shadow—the one that almost got it right.

Ed Hulse is the editor-publisher of Blood 'n' Thunder, *the leading journal for fans of adventure, mystery and melodrama in American popular culture of the early 20th century. A noted film historian who has been writing about vintage motion pictures for more than 30 years, he is the author of* The Films of Betty Grable, The Blood 'n' Thunder Guide to Collecting Pulps *and most recently* Distressed Damsels and Masked Marauders, *a history of silent-era serials. For more about* Blood 'n' Thunder *and Ed Hulse's books, visit www.muraniapress.com.* •

Victor Jory and Ed Hulse in 1980

THE SHADOW
"Prelude to Terror"
as broadcast January 29, 1939 over MBS

	(MUSIC: GLOOMS OF FATE … FADE UNDER)
SHADOW:	Who knows what evil lurks in the hearts of men … THE SHADOW knows! (LAUGHS)
BARCLAY:	Your local Blue Coal dealer presents THE SHADOW. These half hour dramatizations are designed to forcibly demonstrate to old and young alike that crime does not pay …
	(MUSIC UP … FADE)
ANNR:	THE SHADOW, mysterious character who aids those in distress and helps the forces of law and order, is in reality Lamont Cranston, wealthy young man about town. Cranston's friend and companion, the lovely Margot Lane, is the only person who knows to whom the unseen voice belongs, the only the true identity of that master of other people's minds … THE SHADOW … Today's story—"Prelude to Terror."
MUSIC:	(MUSIC UP … OUT WITH …)
	(WIND OFF … KNOCKING ON DOOR)
BAKER:	Come in!
	(DOOR OPEN)
BAKER:	Oh, it's you, Cooper!
COOPER:	(FADE IN) Yes, Professor Baker. I thought you'd like this cup of hot tea, sir. (SOUND OF TEA CUP)
BAKER:	Oh, yes, thanks. Helps to keep me awake. I have a lot of work to do tonight.
COOPER:	Shall I pour it, sir?
BAKER:	Yes, please. Isn't this your night off, Cooper?
COOPER:	Yes, sir. I passed the house on my way home. Saw your lights on—I know how you enjoy a late cup of tea.
BAKER:	Very considerate of you, Cooper—very. But it's late. You must get your rest.
	(DOORBELL WELL OFF)
BAKER:	The doorbell! I wonder who that could be at this hour of the night!
COOPER:	Shall I answer it, sir?
BAKER:	Yes, Cooper. I'll take care of the tea.
	(DOOR OPENS AND CLOSES … DOORBELL LITTLE LOUDER THROUGH COOPER'S RAPID FOOTSTEPS DESCENDING STAIRS)
	(PAUSE … DOORBELL CONTINUES)
COOPER:	(MUMBLING TO HIMSELF) All right, all right!
	(HEAVY DOOR OPEN … WIND UP)
COOPER:	Heeney!—(ALARM)
	(PAUSE)
COOPER:	What're you doing here?
HEENEY:	(HUSHED) Cut the gab. Close the door.
	(HEAVY DOOR CLOSE … WIND DOWN)
COOPER:	I know, Brayden sent you.
HEENEY:	Where's old man Baker?

COOPER:	Upstairs … in his study.
HEENEY:	(TURNING AWAY) Okay.
COOPER:	Wait! I won't let you do this—I won't let you hurt him!
HEENEY:	(SLIGHTLY OFF) You keep your mouth shut unless you want to go back and finish out that prison term you ran out on.
	(FOOTSTEPS GOING UPSTAIRS SQUEAKY)
COOPER:	Leave Professor Baker alone—please!
	(FOOTSTEPS CONTINUE)
COOPER:	I'm not going to be in on this. (FADE OFF) I'm getting out.
	(HEAVY DOOR OPEN AND CLOSE … FOOTSTEPS SLOWLY CLIMBING LONG FLIGHT OF STAIRS, SQUEAKY … FOOTSTEPS STOP)
	(DOOR OPEN)
BAKER:	Well? Who was the late call—Oh, I thought it was Cooper. What do you—
	(TWO SHOTS)
BAKER:	(GROANS) (BODY FALLS)
	(MUSIC TO BRIDGE … OMINOUS)
	(FADE IN MUMBLE VOICES AND OUT … HOLLOW ROOM—SLIGHT ECHO—WIND OFF … FOOTSTEPS ON STONE)
DRAISE:	Gee, you're sure jumpy tonight, Brayden. What are you walkin' up and down like that for? Somethin' on your mind?
BRAYDEN:	Yeah. Big things. Things you'd never understand. I wonder what's keepin' Heeney. He should've been here half an hour ago.
MORGAN:	You think he might have muffed things, boss?
DRAISE:	I hope not.
	(POUNDING ON HEAVY DOOR … OFF)
DRAISE:	There he is now.
BRAYDEN:	Open up.
DRAISE:	(MOVING OFF) Okay, boss.
	(BAR OFF DOOR)
	(HEAVY DOOR OPEN … WIND UP … OFF)
	(VOICES MUMBLE IN BACKGROUND)
DRAISE:	(OFF) We was just talkin' about you.
	(HEAVY DOOR CLOSES … OFF)
BRAYDEN:	Well, Heeney, what happened? Have any trouble?
HEENEY:	(FADING ON) Not much. I just put two slugs into the old guy. Professor Baker, he's dead. The rest was easy.
BRAYDEN:	What about Cooper?
HEENEY:	He was scared stiff. He lit out.
BRAYDEN:	You let him get away?
HEENEY:	Yeah. You don't have to worry about that guy. He's too scared to talk.
BRAYDEN:	You should've put the silencer on him anyway.
HEENEY:	You're the boss, Brayden. What do you want me to do?
BRAYDEN:	Take no chances. Dig Cooper up and close his trap for keeps.
HEENEY:	Okay, boss. I'll take care of him.
BRAYDEN:	Did you get the stuff I sent you after?

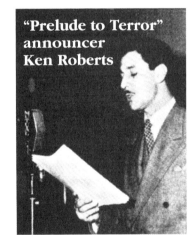

"Prelude to Terror" announcer Ken Roberts

HEENEY:	I sure did.
BRAYDEN:	Good. Let me have it.
HEENEY:	Yeah, I got it right inside here. Here you are, boss. (SOUND OF BOTTLE) The old Professor had it right where you said.
BRAYDEN:	Yes, yes, this is it all right.
DRAISE:	What is it, Brayden? Looks like an empty bottle to me.
BRAYDEN:	It's a colorless, odorless gas—the most powerful explosive in existence—enough to blow up this whole city. This is all there is in the world.
MORGAN:	Yeah! What're you goin' to do with it?
BRAYDEN:	You'll find out. (CALLS) Hey, Egenstahl!
EGENSTAHL:	(OFF … MOVING ON … SLIGHT ACCENT) Yes, boss. (ON) What's on your mind?
BRAYDEN:	You used to be a chemist, right?
EGENSTAHL:	Still am. The best outside the law.
BRAYDEN:	I want you to take this gas out of this little bottle and seal it in that crate of light bulbs I got last night. Think you can do it?
EGENSTAHL:	I guess so. How much gas to a bulb?
BRAYDEN:	Wait—I'll help you. (CALLING OUT) Morgan, Draise—ALL of you. Come here!
	(MUMBLE OF VOICES MOVING ON)
DRAISE:	What's up, Brayden?
BRAYDEN:	Plenty. When we get these explosive light bulbs fixed up, I want you to go out and plant them in light sockets all over the city. In stores, houses, public buildings.
MORGAN:	But what's the big idea, Brayden?
BRAYDEN:	I'm going to plunge the city into total darkness for one night.
MORGAN:	Total darkness?
DRAISE:	How you goin' to make 'em douse their lights?
BRAYDEN:	We get those bulbs planted before noon tomorrow. When it gets dark, they'll turn on lights, and some of these places'll be blown to bits. The next night they won't dare turn on a light.
MORGAN:	But where do we come in? What does that get us?
BRAYDEN:	What does it get us? You sap, don't you see? When the city blacks out, we move in and take over.
DRAISE:	Wow!
BRAYDEN:	I've drawn up a chart showing exactly where the explosive bulbs're to be planted.
HEENEY:	You ain't missed a trick.
BRAYDEN:	This is a big job. We'll need plenty of help for the clean up. Round up every dip, rod-man, gangster—any crook you know. Have them here in the old mill tomorrow night.
	(AD LIB: "Right, boss. Leave that to us." ETC. … "Don't worry, boss, it's as good as done.")
BRAYDEN:	Okay, okay. (PROJECT) Soon's everything's set, we'll move in under cover of darkness.
EGENSTAHL:	(SLIGHT CHUCKLE) The poor cops—they will be helpless, eh?
BRAYDEN:	We'll rob, steal, pillage to our heart's content! We'll take everything that's not nailed down.
MORGAN:	Boy! What a stunt!
HEENEY:	It's a crook's paradise.
DRAISE:	Greatest idea I've ever heard!
BRAYDEN:	It's the greatest idea in the history of crime. I'm going to create a reign of terror like this country has never known!

	(MUSIC TO BRIDGE—OUT)
	(FADE IN DEPARTMENT STORE VERY LIGHT … AND OFF)
CLERK:	(FADE ON) Something for a youngster, you say, madam?
WOMAN:	Yes. I don't exactly know what I want.
CLERK:	Boy or girl?
WOMAN:	A girl. I'm her grandmother.
CLERK:	Is that so? I have a little girl, too. How old is your granddaughter?
WOMAN:	She's just four months old.
CLERK:	Oh, then you must see our modern nursery—the infant things are all in there. (FADE) Come right this way.
	(STORE SOUNDS UP FOR A MOMENT)
	(FADE ON AND OFF—WOMAN CLERK … "Well, perhaps your wife would like something in a suede handbag.")
CLERK:	Step right in.
WOMAN:	Thank you.
CLERK:	Rather dark, isn't it? I'll put on more light. The switch … oh, here we are.
	(CLICK OF LIGHT SWITCH … TERRIFIC EXPLOSION IMMEDIATELY FADE)
	(PEOPLE SCREAMING) (SLOWLY CRUMBLING PILLAR)
1st VOICE:	Watch out! That pillar!
	(PAUSE)
2nd GIRL:	It's coming down!
	(CRASH OF LARGE PILLAR) (PAUSE)
GIRL:	Tom! Tom! Where are you?
	(PAUSE)
3rd VOICE:	Get out! The walls are crumbling!
	(PAUSE)
4th VOICE:	My leg! I can't move!
	(SOUND OF CRUMBLING WALLS)
VOICES:	(SCREAMING—SHOUTING—FADE)
5th VOICE:	(EFFORT) Somebody give me a hand! There's a child buried under here!
	(EXPLOSION… FADE UNDER MUSIC)
	(MUSIC—ACTION—HOLD TO BACK)
	(FIRE SIRENS—AMBULANCE BELLS)
1st MAN:	It's Gullin's Department Store!
2nd MAN:	The whole front's blown out!
3rd MAN:	This is terrible—Awful!
POLICEMAN:	Get back there! Keep away!
	(AMBULANCE BELL OFF)
DOCTOR:	(OFF) Lend a hand here, men! We can't handle the wounded!
1st MAN:	Look, there's a girl in that window up there!
WOMAN:	She's going to jump!
3rd MAN:	(SHOUTING) Don't, don't! Wait!
	(CROWD SCREAMS IN UNISON)

Professor Baker was voiced by former radio Sherlock Holmes Richard Gordon (pictured with script editor Edith Meiser).

(MUSIC UP AND OUT WITH SOUND OF TROLLEY CAR BELL)
(CLANGING OF OLD-FASHIONED TROLLEY CAR ... BELL ... TROLLEY COMING TO STOP)

CONDUCTOR: (CALLING OUT) All out! Castle Street car barns. Last stop!

VOICES: (MUMBLE QUIETLY)

OLD MAN: (FADE ON) But, conductor, I'm going all the way to Henshaw Terrace.

CONDUCTOR: There'll be another car right behind, mister. You folks can sit in the waiting room right here.

VOICES: (MUMBLING AS THEY GET OFF CAR) This is it, I guess.
(DOOR OF WAITING ROOM OPEN)
(SLIDE DOOR)

PASSENGER: It's pretty dark in this waiting room. How about some lights?

2nd PASS: There's a switch right behind you.

PASSENGER: Oh, yes. I'll turn it on.
(CLICK OF SWITCH ... TERRIFIC EXPLOSION ... SCREAMS FADING OFF ... HOLD FOR LONG TIME) (MUSIC UP AND DOWN AND OUT)

BROPHY: (FILTER) Anything else, Commissioner Weston?

WESTON: Yes. Detail as many men as you can spare to the Castle Street car barns and swear in every able-bodied volunteer you can find as a special deputy. I'll broadcast an appeal to all doctors and nurses in this entire territory to report there at once. Stay right on the job, Brophy. Phone me again in ten minutes.

BROPHY: Okay, Commissioner Weston. Good-bye.
(PHONE RECEIVER DOWN ... DOOR OPEN ... OFF)

OFFICER: (OFF) Lamont Cranston to see you, Commissioner.

WESTON: Cranston? Well, you tell him for me ....
(DOOR CLOSES)

CRANSTON: (FADING IN) Hello, Commissioner Weston! Why don't you tell me yourself?

WESTON: I'm busy, Cranston. What do you want?

CRANSTON: I came to see if there's anything I can do to help in this horrible catastrophe.

WESTON: If you can swing a pick, drag a hose or carry a stretcher, there's plenty for you to do.

CRANSTON: I've already done my bit in that direction. For the moment, I'm interested in the reason for these awful crimes.

WESTON: Now wait a minute, Cranston. I've got more on my mind than just sitting here and satisfying your curiosity.

CRANSTON: This is not just curiosity, Commissioner. I've got a theory.

WESTON: So has everybody else. I've got no time for crackpot theories.

CRANSTON: You certainly are flattering, Commissioner.

WESTON: Well, I'm not running a school for amateur detectives.

CRANSTON: No, I'd never suspect you of pedagogic inclinations, Commissioner. But tell me, do you know how the explosions occurred last night?

WESTON: No, I don't. All I know is that the two places went up when the lights went on.

CRANSTON: Then I'm sure I can help you.

WESTON: If you have any evidence—any facts—I'm willing to listen. *But I don't want to hear any more theories!*

CRANSTON: All right, Commissioner. Calm yourself, I'll explain.

WESTON: (SHOUTING) I am calm!

CRANSTON: Of course you are. Now, my theory is this—
WESTON: What!
CRANSTON: All right. Let's put it this way. My "hunch" is this ....
WESTON: Go ahead. Get it off your chest and let me get back to work.
CRANSTON: You want to clear up this mystery of these explosions, don't you, Commissioner?
WESTON: That, Cranston, would seem to be the general idea.
CRANSTON: Then you must first find out who killed Professor Baker.
WESTON: Are you trying to tell me that there's a connection between the death of Baker and these explosions?
CRANSTON: I'm not just *trying*. I'm *telling* you. There is—definitely.
WESTON: Very interesting. What makes you so sure about it?
CRANSTON: I happen to know that Professor Baker was experimenting with an explosive such as might have been used in these two blasts.
WESTON: Where does your theory go from there?
CRANSTON: Professor Baker was killed for possession of that explosive. Find his killers, and you've found the men responsible for the other crimes.
WESTON: But where's the motive? What reason could they have for blowing up those places and killing all those people?
CRANSTON: That I don't know.
WESTON: There you are—in a blind alley. You have a theory and nothing to support it. Run along, Cranston. My nerves won't stand any more of this nonsense.
CRANSTON: (DESPERATELY) You must listen to me, Commissioner. You've *got* to.
(PHONE BELL ... RECEIVER UP)
WESTON: I've got to. We'll see whether .... Hello!
BRAYDEN: (FILTER) Hello, Commissioner Weston?
WESTON: Yes. Who is this?
BRAYDEN: Never mind that. I got some dope for you.
WESTON: What do you mean?
BRAYDEN: Those two explosions last night were bad, eh? Well, that's only a little sample of what's comin' tonight.
WESTON: What? What did you say?
BRAYDEN: You heard me. You're goin' to have a worse mess on your hands if you don't carry out my orders.
WESTON: Orders?
BRAYDEN: I want this city in total darkness tonight.
WESTON: Total darkness?
BRAYDEN: If there's an electric light, auto headlamp, or even a flashlight turned on, you're gonna get a bouquet of explosions worse than yesterday's.
WESTON: You must be stark mad! You'll never get away with this.
BRAYDEN: Try me and see. Either the lights go *out* or the city goes *up*.
(SLIGHT CLICK)
WESTON: Hello! ... Hello! ... Hello!

Bill Johnstone and Agnes Moorehead

122 PRELUDE TO TERROR

Dwight Weist doubled as Commissioner Weston and Egenstahl.

    (JIGGLING OF HOOK)
    (RECEIVER SLAMMED DOWN)

WESTON: (SHAKEN) Cranston! Did you hear that?

CRANSTON: Yes, I did.

WESTON: What're we going to do? It'll be dark in a few hours.

CRANSTON: Commissioner! That man must be stopped somehow. If he's not, this city will be the scene of indescribable horror tonight. We've got to stop him!

    (MUSIC UP … HOLD THROUGH) (HUSHED)

1st NEWSBOY: Extra! Extra! Explosive light bulbs threaten more blasts—(FADE) Mystery voice warns Commissioner Weston! Extra!

    (MUSIC UP)

2nd NEWSBOY: Explosive electric lamps spread through city! Read all about it! Extra … (FADE) … Extry …

    (MUSIC UP … OUT)
    (HUSHED VOICES)

1st MAN: Say, this is terrible! We won't have any light.

2nd MAN: How are we going to see in the dark?

3rd MAN: I don't know, but I'm not turning on any lights in my place tonight.

4th MAN: Me neither! I don't want my family blown up.

5th MAN: What're we going to do?

6th MAN: (WAILING) Can't they stop this! Can't anything be done about it? I'm going out of my mind … (FADE) … out of my mind, I tell you.

    (MUSIC UP)

VOICE: (FILTER …) Emergency! Calling Doctor Marson! … Dr. Marson! … (FADE) Emergency calling … Dr. Marson!

    (PAUSE)

CHILD: (MOANING ON MIKE)

WOMAN: Oh, Dr. Marson, do something. Please save my little bambina.

DOCTOR: I'll do all I can, Mrs. Vinetti. Your child is very sick.

WOMAN: (WEEPING) Oh, my little bambina—my little bambina … (CONTINUES CRIES OFF)

NURSE: What are we going to do, Doctor?

DOCTOR: The child won't last an hour if we don't operate at once.

NURSE: But we can't do that. We don't dare turn on the lights.

DOCTOR: We've got to do something.

NURSE: Couldn't we operate by candlelight?

DOCTOR: That's impossible. The operation is too delicate.

WOMAN: Oh, please, Doctor. Help my baby.

DOCTOR: Nurse!

NURSE: Yes, Doctor?

DOCTOR: I'm going to operate.

NURSE: But the lights, Doctor?

DOCTOR:	I can't stand here and see this child die. We've got to take the chance. Turn on the lights.
NURSE:	But ... all right, Doctor. (FADE) I'll turn them on.
	(CLICK OF SWITCH ... DEAFENING EXPLOSION) (HOLD FOR FEW SECONDS) (BOARD FADE) (PHONE BELL ... SOUND OF RECEIVER)
MAYOR:	Hello!
SHADOW:	(ON PHONE) Mayor Hamilton?
MAYOR:	Yes. Who is this speaking?
SHADOW:	This is The Shadow.
MAYOR:	The Shadow? ... Oh, yes. What can I do for you?
SHADOW:	Mr. Mayor, the hospital has just been blown up.
MAYOR:	What? The hospital? Good heavens, that can't be possible!
SHADOW:	It's true, Mr. Mayor.
MAYOR:	I can hardly believe it. What hellish fiend can be responsible for this?
SHADOW:	Mr. Mayor, you've got to act at once. You must make any other explosions tonight impossible.
MAYOR:	Of course. But how can I do that?
SHADOW:	Order the city power plant to cut the main switch.
MAYOR:	The main switch!
SHADOW:	It's the only way. You can't depend on all the people keeping their lights out.
MAYOR:	But cutting the main power switch will tie up everything in the city.
SHADOW:	It's that, Mr. Mayor, or death, destruction and panic.
MAYOR:	Very well. I'll order the power cut at once.
	(MUSIC AND INTO FOOTSTEPS ...)
	(MANY FOOTSTEPS)
1st MAN:	(HUSHED) Gosh! It *sure* is dark.
2nd MAN:	I can't see where I'm walking.
1st MAN :	Does it matter? — I'm lost. We're all lost. Oops!
	(SOUND OF BUMPING)
2nd MAN:	Sorry, Lady. (FADE) I didn't see you.
FRED:	(FADE ON) Hold that lantern higher, Bill. We don't want to walk off the viaduct.
BILL:	Okay, Fred. Boy, am I glad I found this old wagon lamp! It's a swell idea.
	(SHOT WELL OFF ... GLASS SHATTERING ON)
FRED:	Yeah. It's a swell target.
BILL:	Shot right out of my hand.
FRED:	When that gang said the city'd have to black out, they meant black out!
	(MUSIC UP)
	(FADE IN AIRPLANE FROM INSIDE CABIN)
CO-PILOT:	Joe, we can't keep flying around here all night. Our gas is running out. We've got to set her down someplace.
PILOT:	I can't understand it. I couldn't possibly've missed the city.
CO-PILOT:	We've cruised around for twenty minutes now, and I haven't seen a single light.
PILOT:	We'll just have to keep going while the *gas holds out*.
CO-PILOT:	Then what?
PILOT:	Then we start praying, brother.
	(MUSIC ... MOTOR OUT ... MUSIC OUT)

CRANSTON: Well, Margot, the main switch is turned off. No lights, no power … nothing but bewilderment … uncertainty.

MARGOT: Oh, this is awful, Lamont. What are people going to do?

CRANSTON: I'm afraid this is all a lead to something worse. A prelude to a greater terror.

MARGOT: Lamont, you must do something.

CRANSTON: I've racked my brain for a solution—some faint clue. I'm stuck. I don't know what to do.

MARGOT: But we just can't sit and wait for some new terror to strike, Lamont.

CRANSTON: (THINKING) There must be … some loose thread … that might unravel this whole vicious pattern. (SUDDENLY) Margot!

MARGOT: Yes, Lamont?

CRANSTON: I've got an idea.

MARGOT: Yes?

CRANSTON: Professor Baker's hired man—Cooper. The police released him. They said he proved he was not in the house the night the professor was killed.

MARGOT: Yes?

CRANSTON: It's just struck me. The killer's fingerprints were on the handle of the door to the old man's study. But there were none on the knob of the street door. Don't you see it, Margot? Somebody opened the door for the killer.

MARGOT: Cooper!

CRANSTON: Perhaps.

MARGOT: But, Lamont—

CRANSTON: Come on, Margot. We've got to find Cooper. The Shadow has got to talk to that man. He may be the thread I've hoped for.

(MUSIC UP … DOWN AND OUT)

MRS. KELLY: (FADE ON) That's the last candle I have in the house, Mr. Cooper. They're very scarce now. But at least you'll be able to finish your packing.

COOPER: Thanks, Mrs. Kelly.

MRS. KELLY: (SIGH) Oh, my now … I'm sorry to see you go. But I don't blame anybody for gettin' out of this cursed city.

COOPER: Yes, sure and now if you don't mind I've got a lot of packing to do. Good night, Mrs. Kelly.

MRS. KELLY: Huh, if that's the way you feel. Good-bye and good riddance to *you* … (FADE) … Mr. Cooper.

(DOOR CLOSE OFF …)

SHADOW: (LAUGHS) What's your hurry, Cooper?

COOPER: Who's that?

SHADOW: What are you running away from?

COOPER: Me, why—say, who—where are you? I can't see you.

SHADOW: I'm The Shadow, Cooper!

COOPER: The Shadow!

SHADOW: You know of me, don't you? Now listen, Cooper. I've got to talk fast and so do you.

COOPER: I've got nothing to talk about.

SHADOW: Cooper, you share responsibility for the death and destruction in this city.

Bill Johnstone as The Shadow

COOPER:	No. That's a lie. (FADE OFF SLIGHTLY) I had nothing to do with it!
SHADOW:	You know the man who killed Professor Baker. You've got to tell me who he is.
COOPER:	I can't … (FADE BACK ON) I can't!
SHADOW:	You must. You alone can release the city from the grip of terror that man has placed it in.
COOPER:	I don't know anything about it, I tell you.
SHADOW:	You're lying, Cooper. I know you opened the door for the killer.
COOPER:	I wouldn't hurt the old man.
SHADOW:	You were with him just before he died.
COOPER:	But I had nothing to do with his death. Honest, I didn't.
SHADOW:	If you want to save yourself and clear your conscience, you've got to talk.
	(PAUSE)
COOPER:	All right, I want to get it off my mind. I'll talk … I'll talk … (GASP)
	(DOOR OPEN OFF)
COOPER:	(GASP) Heeney! What do you want?
HEENEY:	Just deliverin' a little message from the boss, Cooper. (FADE) Here it is.
	(TWO SHOTS … DOOR SLAMMED)
COOPER:	(GROANS)
SHADOW:	Cooper? … Speak to me, Cooper!
COOPER:	(MUTTERS INDISTINCTLY)
SHADOW:	Your throat! Talk, Cooper. The fate of this city rests with you.
COOPER:	(GURGLES INDISTINCTLY)
SHADOW:	I can't understand you … for Heaven's sake, man, you've got to tell me—Look, Cooper, I'll put my ear close to your lips. Try to whisper … try ….
COOPER:	(WHISPERS CLOSE ON MIKE)
SHADOW:	Yes … yes … I understood that; His name, Cooper … His name! … Please … (WHISPER) What? … Try again … (WHISPER) … Where? … Where?
	(VOICES IN HALL OFF)
	(DOOR OPEN)
	(VOICES UP)
SHADOW:	Quick, Cooper!—Quick!
MRS. KELLY:	(SLIGHTLY OFF … FADING ON) What happened? We heard shooting.
1st BOARDER:	Look! It's Mr. Cooper. He's been shot! (AD LIB)
2nd BOARDER:	Somebody get a doctor, quick!
MRS. KELLY:	No— (AD LIB OUT) No use for a doctor now. (PAUSE) He's dead, but it's not good riddance, Mr. Cooper … not good riddance … (SOB)
	(MUSIC … OMINOUS … UP AND OUT WITH—) (FADING)
	(FADE IN MANY VOICES … LOUD LAUGHTER, ETC.)
BRAYDEN:	Hey, Egenstahl! Bring me that chart.
EGENSTAHL:	(SLIGHTLY OFF) Yes, boss. (ON) Here you are.
	(RUSTLE OF PAPER)
BRAYDEN:	Have you checked off every place where we planted bulbs?
EGENSTAHL:	Every one—They're all marked in red.
1st CROOK:	What're we waitin' for, Brayden?
OTHERS:	Yeah! Let's go! Etc.

BRAYDEN: I'm waitin' for the boys to come back from the city and give me the low down on how things stand.

1st CROOK: Say, Brayden, how come we got lights here with the city power plant turned off?

BRAYDEN: I've been plannin' this job for over a year. So I put in my own power plant.

(AD LIBS UP SLIGHTLY—OFF)

2nd CROOK: Smart, I'll say.

3rd CROOK: But how did you manage the explosions?

BRAYDEN: See this bulb? (SOUND OF THIN GLASS) Well, it was one of these that blew up the Gullin's Department Store and ….

(AD LIBS UP)

VOICES: (EXCITED REACTION)

BRAYDEN: All right. Don't worry! You're all safe. This won't go off—unless it's put in a light socket and the switch is thrown.

1st CROOK: Just the same, I'd feel better if you didn't wave it around like that.

(GENERAL LAUGHTER … BROAD FADE OUT)
(FADE IN AUTOMOBILE ENGINE ON MIKE … HOLD THROUGH)

CRANSTON: Margot, pull right over here—off the road.

(CAR COMES TO A STOP)

MARGOT: There we are, Lamont!

CRANSTON: Good. You stay here in the car. Take this gun. You'll be perfectly safe. Just keep out of sight.

(CAR DOOR OPEN)

MARGOT: But where are *you* going, Lamont?

(DOOR CLOSE)

CRANSTON: There's an old mill someplace along here. If I understood Cooper correctly, I'll find the man I'm looking for in there.

MARGOT: You're not going in alone?

CRANSTON: I've got to. I phoned Commissioner Weston, as The Shadow, and asked him to send some men.

MARGOT: Then why not wait for them?

CRANSTON: Time's at a premium; there isn't a moment to lose. (FADE) The Shadow's got to work and work fast.

(MUSIC … MOOD … OUT INTO VOICES)

BRAYDEN: (MOVING ON) Quiet … quiet … well, boys? What did you find out in the city?

DRAISE: Boss, you hit a bull's eye. The city's as dark as a landlord's look.

MORGAN: Yeah, it's all set for us, boss.

BRAYDEN: Good! (CALLING OUT) All right, boys. We got the green light! Time to go!

(AD LIBS UP SLIGHTLY OFF)

1st CROOK: Boy, this'll be sweet pickin'! Nothin' to it!

BRAYDEN: Morgan, you take six men, and go to the Macy Street Bank. You know what to do. Draise!

DRAISE: Right, boss.

BRAYDEN: You take twenty men and clean out the hotel. Go through the rooms. Don't leave anything you can carry. You, Egenstahl—the post office. Five men can handle that.

EGENSTAHL: I'm all set.

BRAYDEN: The rest of you got your spots. Work fast. If anyone crosses you, use your guns—let 'em have it.

1st CROOK: I'm shootin' and askin' after.

2nd CROOK: Funny, but dead men ain't never got much to say.
BRAYDEN: All right! Cut the gab and let's go!
(PLEASED EXCITED AD LIBS … STOP SUDDENLY WITH …)
SHADOW: (LAUGHS)
DRAISE: What was that? Am I hearin' things?
SHADOW (LAUGHS)
DRAISE: Did anybody hear that laugh? (AD LIBS UP SLIGHTLY)
2nd CROOK: I did.
3rd CROOK: So did I.
SHADOW: (LAUGHS) Quite a nice little thing you've cooked up, Brayden. But here's where another ingredient is added to your unholy brew.
BRAYDEN: Say, what is this?
SHADOW: Brayden.
BRAYDEN: Well, you're not scarin' me…. You're not stoppin' me either.
SHADOW: I wouldn't be too sure about that, Brayden.
BRAYDEN: (CALLING OUT) Men! This guy's right here in the room with us. He's got some trick so we can't see him. But that don't mean we can't get him! Draise, stand by that door. (SHUFFLE OF FEET) Keep your back against it, and don't let anybody or anything open it. Morgan, pick up that machine gun and spray the other end of the room … where that voice came from.
(CLICKING OF LIGHT SWITCH)
(GENERAL PANDEMONIUM)
1st CROOK: Somebody's doused the lights!
2nd CROOK: I'm gettin' out-a here!
(SQUEAK OF BULB BEING SCREWED INTO SOCKET CLOSE TO MIKE)
BRAYDEN: (CALLING OUT) Don't be afraid, men. Take it easy! Somebody switch on that light!
SHADOW (LAUGH) You don't dare turn on that light.
BRAYDEN: Wait a minute … what're you talkin' about, Shadow?
SHADOW: When I turned out the light, I put one of the explosive bulbs into the light socket. Now, Mr. Brayden, do you want to turn on the light?
BRAYDEN: You're bluffin', Shadow.
SHADOW: All you have to do to prove that point is to throw on the light switch.
(AUTOMOBILES HEARD OFF … DRIVE UP … STOP OUTSIDE)
DRAISE: Hey! What's that?
MORGAN: (OFF) A lot-a cars drivin' up outside.
SHADOW: It's the police, gentlemen.
(AD LIBS OFF)
BRAYDEN: They'll never take me alive.
SHADOW: Alive or dead, Brayden, you've got to be taken.
(HUSHED, FRIGHTENED AD LIBS)
WESTON: (OFF) You men in there! Come on out, or we're coming in after you!
SHADOW: You might as well do as Commissioner Weston commands. Walk out the door with your hands in the air.
BRAYDEN: There's nobody walkin' out of this place! I know *I'm* chair bait. I'll die anyway. But there's one thing I'm gonna do first. I'm gonna take you along with me, Mr. Shadow!

PRELUDE TO TERROR

       (AD LIBS UP)
1st CROOK: Keep your hands off that switch, Brayden!
BRAYDEN: Out of my way!
       (AD LIB: "DON'T LET HIM GET TO THAT SWITCH! STOP HIM!" ... ETC.)
BRAYDEN: Keep your hands off me ... Here's calling your bluff, Shadow!
       (CLICK OF SWITCH ... TERRIFIC EXPLOSION ... HOLD FOR SEVERAL SECONDS)
       (BOARD FADE)
       (EXCITED VOICES OF POLICEMEN WELL OFF)
CAPTAIN: (OFF) Look out, Commissioner! There may be another explosion. Get back!
MARGOT: (SOBBING ON MIKE) Lamont! Oh, Lamont!
WESTON: (OFF) Anyone alive in there, Captain?
CAPTAIN: (OFF) Not a single one, Commissioner.
MARGOT: (SOBS CONVULSIVELY ON MIKE)
SHADOW: (ON MIKE) It's all right, Margot! I'm safe!
MARGOT: (OVERJOYED) Oh, Lamont, thank Heaven! I thought you'd been killed in that explosion.
SHADOW: It was close, Margot. But I got out when they were trying to keep Brayden away from the light switch. You go back to the car now, Margot. I'll be with you in a minute. (CALLING OUT) Commissioner Weston! Commissioner Weston!
WESTON: (OFF) Hello! Is that The Shadow?
SHADOW: Yes, Commissioner.
WESTON: (MOVING SLIGHTLY ON) Well, we're in a fine jam now. They're all dead. Now, how're we going to find out where the other explosive bulbs are planted?
SHADOW: It's all right, Commissioner. I got Brayden's chart, showing the locations of the explosives.
WESTON: Where is it?
SHADOW: You'll find it on the front seat of your car.
WESTON: Then the city is safe!
SHADOW: Yes, Commissioner.
WESTON: Good! (CALLING OUT) All right, men, get in your cars. We've got to gather up those lamps right away ... and my gratitude, Shadow, for a job well done!
       (MUSIC SNEAK IN—HOLD BEHIND)
SHADOW: (CLOSE ON MIKE) Come, Margot. We're going home. The Shadow's work is done for tonight. This reign of terror is ended.
MARGOT: Thanks to you, Lamont.
SHADOW: It was bound to end this way, Margot. The plots and plans of criminals are devices of their own destruction. Law and life know no compromise with the evildoer.
       (MUSIC UP TO FINISH)
ANNR: Today's adventure is based on a story copyrighted by THE SHADOW magazine. All the characters and all the places named are fictitious. Any similarity to persons living or dead is purely coincidental. THE SHADOW magazine is now on sale at your local newsstand.
       (MUSIC: GLOOMS OF FATE ... UP AND UNDER)
SHADOW: The weed of crime bears bitter fruit. Crime does not pay—The Shadow *knows*. (LAUGH)
ANNR: Next week, same time—same station—Blue Coal, America's finest anthracite, will again present another thrilling adventure of THE SHADOW. Be sure to listen. And be sure to burn Blue Coal. The solid fuel for solid comfort.
       (MUSIC) (APPLAUSE TO FILL)
ANNR: This is Mutual. •